D0501980

América's
Dream

América's
Dream

Esmeralda Santiago

HarperCollins*Publishers*

AMÉRICA'S DREAM. Copyright © 1996 by Esmeralda Santiago. All rights reserved. Printed in the United States of America. No part of this book may be used or reproduced in any manner whatsoever without written permission except in the case of brief quotations embodied in critical articles and reviews. For information address HarperCollins Publishers, Inc., 10 East 53rd Street, New York, NY 10022.

HarperCollins books may be purchased for educational, business, or sales promotional use. For information please write: Special Markets Department, HarperCollins Publishers, Inc., 10 East 53rd Street, New York, NY 10022.

FIRST EDITION

Designed by Nina Gaskin

Library of Congress Cataloging-in-Publication Data

América's dream / Esmeralda Santiago. —1st ed.
        p.   cm.
      ISBN 0–06–017279–7
      1. Puerto Rican women—New York (State)—Westchester County—Fiction.
      2. Women domestics—New York (State)—Westchester County—Fiction.
      3. Mothers and daughters—Puerto Rico—Fiction. 4. Women—Puerto Rico—
      Fiction. I. Title.
      PS3569.A5452A44   1996
      813'.54—dc20   95-25706

96 97 98 99 00 ❖/RRD 10 9 8 7 6 5 4 3 2 1

Hija fuiste, madre serás
según hiciste, así te harán.

❧

You were a daughter, mother you will be
as you did, so will be done to you.

Acknowledgments

While this is a work of fiction, it takes place in Vieques, which is real. La Casa del Francés exists, in better condition than described here, and with a different history. I am indebted to Irving and Helen Greenblatt for their hospitality and generosity in allowing a fictional América Gonzalez to work in their lovely hotel.

Muchísimas gracias to my friend and agent, Molly Friedrich, for her guidance and encouragement, and to my editor, Peternelle van Arsdale, for taking a chance on me and on *América's Dream*.

Gracias to Judith Azaña, and to all the empleadas who provided stories and insights.

And finally, dear Frank, Lucas, and Ila, thank you for being there for me. Your support means everything.

The Problem with Rosalinda

〰〰〰〰〰〰〰〰〰〰〰〰〰〰〰〰〰〰〰〰〰〰〰〰〰〰〰

I t's her life, and she's in the middle of it. On her knees, scrubbing behind a toilet at the only hotel on the island. She hums a bolero, a love song filled with longing. She's always humming, sometimes a ballad, sometimes a lilting cha-cha-chá. Often, she sings out loud. Most of the time she's not even aware of the pleasing music that comes from her and is surprised when tourists tell her how charming it is that she sings as she works.

The tiles are unevenly laid behind the toilet, and she catches a nail on the corner of one and tears it to the quick. "Ay!" Still on her knees, she moves to the sink and runs cold water over her middle finger. The bright pink crescent of her nail hangs by the cuticle. She bites it off, drawing salty blood.

"¡América!"

The scream bounces against the concrete walls of La Casa del Francés. América scrambles up, finger still in mouth, and leans out of the bathroom window. Her mother runs back and forth along the path at the side of the hotel, peering up at the second floor.

"What is it?"

"Ay, nena, get down here!" Ester wails and collapses into a squat, hands over her face.

"What is it, Mami? What's the matter?" From above, Ester is a circle of color on the path, the full skirt of her flowered housedress a ring around narrow shoulders, brown arms, and pink curlers on copper hair. She rocks from side to side, sobs with the gusto of a spoiled child. For an instant América considers a shortcut through the window. Seeing her mother from above, small and vulnerable, sets her heart racing, and a lump forms in her throat that threatens to choke her. "I'm coming, Mami!" she yells, and she runs through the guest room, down the stairs, around the courtyard, out the double doors of the front verandah, past the gardenia bushes, through the gate to the side garden, and down the path, where Ester still squats, still wails as if the world were coming to an end.

Sleepy guests lean out of their windows or step onto porches, concerned expressions clouding their vacation faces. Don Irving, the owner of the hotel, runs heavily from the back of the building, reaching Ester at the same time as América.

"Whasgononere?" he bellows in English. "What's all the screaming about?"

"Ay don no!" América kneels next to Ester. "Mami, please! What's the matter?"

"¡Ay, mi'ja!" Ester is hyperventilating and can't get the words out. América's breathing quickens, and a whirling pressure builds around her head.

"Please, Mami, what is it? What's happened?"

Ester shakes her head, sprinkling the air with tears. She presses both hands against her chest, as if to control its rising and falling. She gulps air and, in a halting voice that rises to a final wail, gives América the news. "¡Rosalinda se escapó!"

At first she doesn't quite understand what Ester means by Rosalinda has escaped. Her fourteen-year-old daughter is not a prisoner. But the words echo in her head, and the meaning becomes clear. América covers her face, squeezes her fingers deep into her flesh, and sobs. "Ay, no, Mami, don't say such a thing!"

Ester, who has gained some composure now that the problem is no longer hers, wraps her arms around América and rubs her shoulders, her tears mingling with those of her daughter. "She went with that boy, Taino."

América stares at Ester, tries to make sense of what she's heard. But the words and images are distorted, go by too quickly, like a movie in fast-forward. And at the end there's a pause, a soft-focus portrait of her daughter, Rosalinda, and pimpled Taino with his innocent brown eyes. She shakes her head, trying to erase the picture.

"What the hell's going on here?" Don Irving stands over them, blowing great gusts of cigar-scented breath. Behind him, Nilda, the laundress, Feto, the cook, and Tomás, the gardener, run up from different directions. They surround América and Ester, and the men help them stand.

"Ees my dohter," says América, avoiding Don Irving's eyes. "She in trubel."

"Rosalinda ran away with her boyfriend," Nilda interprets, and América cringes with shame.

"Oh, fahcrysakes!" Don Irving spits into the oregano patch. "Geddadehere, c'mon." He steers the sobbing América and Ester out of earshot of his guests, to the back of the building, where he leaves Feto and Tomás to escort them to the path behind the stables. Don Irving walks back to the front garden, mumbling. "Every day it's something else. A damn soap opera. Jesus Christ!" He waves at the curious tourists at the windows and porches. "It's okay, everything's fine. Relax."

Supported by Feto and Tomás, América and Ester go in the opposite direction. The tourists stare long after they have all disappeared behind the outdoor bar.

América and Ester shuffle home through the path at the rear of La Casa del Francés. Nilda accompanies them, rubbing the shoulders of one, then the other.

"Calm yourselves. If you don't control your nerves, you won't be able to help the child," Nilda reminds them. Her voice vibrates with the joy of a busybody who has stumbled into the middle of the action.

"You can go back, Nilda," América suggests between sniffles. "We can manage on our own."

But Nilda is not so easily dissuaded. América is not like other women. She's not willing to talk about her life, to commiserate with other women about how tough it is. She goes around humming and singing like she's the happiest person in the world, even though everyone knows different. No, Nilda will not leave her side. It's not every day she can plunge into América Gonzalez's reserve.

"I'll just get you home and make sure you're all right," she insists.

América doesn't have the energy to argue. Her head feels stuffed with cotton. She wants to clear it, to enter into her own brain and figure out what to do. But it's as if she were facing a door she doesn't want to open.

Their house is a ten-minute walk from the back gate of La Casa. América walks this path five days a week, once in the early morning and again when her job is done in the late afternoon. It is so familiar, she's sure she can get home blindfolded if necessary and won't stumble or step into a ditch or crash against a mango tree or a telephone pole.

But today she's on the path at a time when she should be mopping the tile floor of one of the guest rooms. Her uniform seems out of place at midmorning, on the way home. The sun is too bright for her to be out on the street. Curious neighbors come to their porches or stop watering their plants to stare, mocking her. She doesn't look at them, but she knows they're watching. She feels Nilda, bloated with consequence, between her and Ester, guiding them home, smiling kindly at one, then the other, mumbling worn sayings as if words, and not her legs, impelled her forward.

On the other side of Nilda, Ester whimpers like a hurt puppy. Fifteen years ago it was Ester who had to be found and told that América had run away with her boyfriend. They've never talked about that day, and América wonders where Ester was, what she was doing when told that her only child had run away with the handsome young man who had recently come to the barriada to lay pipes for a sewer system.

Thinking about Correa, América's skin pimples into goose bumps. What will he do when he hears that Rosalinda has run away? She envisions his handsome face redden with anger, his green eyes disappear under thick eyebrows, his nostrils flare over his well-tended mustache. She raises her arms as if to ward off a blow or perhaps to cover her eyes from the sun, and Nilda strokes her shoulders and leads her through the gate Ester left open.

The thirty feet to the front steps are a fragrant gauntlet of roses, and as usual when she goes past them, América sneezes.

"¡Salúd!" Nilda wishes her, and she steers them up the walk, dodging the invading rose branches, whose spines catch in her clothes and hair. At the top of the steps she looks resentfully at the distance separating her from the sidewalk.

"Here we are," she announces cheerfully, pushing the door open, making herself at home in their house as if she were a frequent visitor. "Have a seat, I'll get you something to drink." She pulls out chairs for them. América and Ester flop dumbly at opposite ends of the dining table and stare at the tile floor. In the kitchen, Nilda opens and closes more cabinets than seems necessary to find a glass. "Here, this will help you feel better." She places a tumbler of water over ice in front of each. América drinks in long, thirsty gulps. Ester eyes her drink suspiciously.

The cool water revives América. As she rises, the chair legs scrape angrily against the tiles, making Nilda grimace and cover her ears. Ester emerges from her silence with the attitude of someone who has been rudely awakened from a restful nap.

"Some people should mind their own business," she says, lurching past Nilda into the kitchen, where she dumps her ice water down the sink.

Nilda's obsequious smile is replaced by a resentful tightening of the lips. "I'm just trying to help." She sulks, but Ester ignores her.

América gently guides Nilda by the elbow to the door. "Don't take it personally. You know how she is." She opens the door and stands aside to let Nilda pass. "Thank you for your kindness, but you'd better get back to the hotel, or Don Irving will fire us both."

"Yes, I should go," Nilda agrees reluctantly. "I'll drop by later to see if there's anything I can do."

América smiles thinly. "Don't worry about us, we'll be all right." She pulls herself up straighter, stands solid at the threshold looking down at Nilda.

"Well, all right, take care." From inside the house, Ester snorts in disdain.

América all but pushes Nilda out and closes the door behind her.

América leans her back against the door and breathes a sigh of relief. On her right is Rosalinda's room, its walls papered with posters of rock and roll and salsa singers. She enters it stealthily, as if afraid to wake up a sleeper. Rosalinda has taken most of her clothes, her boom box and CDs, the gold jewelry Correa has given her over the years, and the stuffed blue pelican Taino won for her at the midway in last year's patron-saint feast days. There is no letter telling them where she has gone, but it's clear she's left with no intention of coming back. She's taken the Cindy Crawford wall calendar on which she charts her menstrual cycle.

América sits on the edge of her daughter's bed, neatly made as if she hasn't slept in it. The dressing table has been stripped of mousses and gels, pimple creams and hairbrushes, blow-dryer, colognes. How long was she packing, América wonders, impressed with how well her daughter must have planned her escape to be able to take so much. She's probably been taking things out of the house for days, and no one has noticed. Ester, whose room is on the other side of the wall from Rosalinda's, sleeps soundly, especially when she's been drinking. Her snores are loud and hearty, and Rosalinda could have left in the middle of the night and no one would have heard a thing.

América stands up, smoothes the edge of the bed, as if to erase all trace that she's been there.

"I made breakfast for her, as usual," Ester says when América comes back to the kitchen, "but when I went to get her, she wasn't there." In the compost pail she has dumped Rosalinda's Rice Krispies with sliced banana.

América dries the dish Ester has been washing. "Was Taino here yesterday while I was working?"

"He was here a couple of hours. They sat out on the porch doing their schoolwork. I made them sandwiches." Ester takes the dish from América's hands, puts it away, goes to the refrigerator for a beer.

"It's too early for that, Mami," América warns.

"Don't tell me what to do," Ester snaps. She pulls out a frosty Budweiser and goes into her room.

América stares at the closed door, stained with grease, the knob hanging uselessly from the lock. The muted hiss of a beer can opening feels as if air were being let out of her.

She splashes water from the kitchen tap on her face, dries it on her apron. It smells like ammonia. She leans over the yellow porcelain sink, fingertips massaging her temples. She's exhausted. It's an exhaustion she feels at times like this, when the whole world seems to have collapsed beneath her feet, leaving her at the bottom of a hole with sides so steep she can't climb out. It's the exhaustion of having attempted and failed so many times to crawl out that she's just going to sit on the bottom and see what happens next. But she only gives up for as long as it takes tears to roll down her cheeks and plunk into the dirty dishwater, one two three.

She crosses the house to her own room in the back, switches on the overhead light as she enters. A neatly made bed takes up most of the space. There is a phone on her bedside table, but service was disconnected long ago because she couldn't afford to pay the bills.

When Correa built this room out of a back terrace, he left space in the concrete wall for a window but never put one in. The rectangle where a window should be is covered with plywood. América leaned a mirror against it and keeps her cosmetics and hair preparations on the unfinished sill. At night she sleeps with her door ajar and a fan on for air. Correa didn't put in a closet either, so her clothes hang from nails in the concrete walls or are folded inside two mismatched dressers.

América changes out of the nylon uniform Don Irving

makes them wear. It's green, with a little white apron, also nylon ("so you can wash it easily"). In the humid days of summer the uniform feels like a sausage casing, tight and sticky. She hangs it up against the wall, in its usual place near the door. On days she doesn't work she sees it every time she goes out of her room.

She puts on a flowered dress cinched at the waist with a wide belt. Ester appears at the door of her room.

"Es muy llamativo," Ester says, "too festive for the occasion."

"What do you want me to do, dress in mourning?" She slips her feet into a pair of low-heeled sandals.

"At least show some respect."

"Like the respect she's shown me?"

"She's a kid. She's supposed to be disrespectful."

"Since when are you an expert on teenagers?"

Ester harrumphs. She turns a stiff back on América, retreats out of the kitchen door to the rear garden.

América adjusts the bodice of her dress, runs her hands over her breasts, down to her waist, cinches the belt a little tighter. She's not about to dress in black so the whole vecindario will know how she feels. Let their tongues wag if they want to talk about her. And besides, Ester knows what Correa does if she leaves the house looking unkempt.

The soft crackplink of pigeon-pea pods being dropped into a metal bowl counterpoints the shuffle of Ester's slippered feet on grass.

América powders her face and hurriedly applies blusher and lipstick. She takes one last look in the mirror, fixes a stray curl by her left eye, and rummages in her dresser for the appropriate purse to carry with her sandals. She puts her things into a shiny black one that Correa gave her three Christmases ago.

"I'm going," she calls out the kitchen window at Ester, whose arms reach delicately among the curving branches, seeking out the plumpest pods. Ester looks toward the window, pouts in her direction, then continues her rhythmic chore as if the interruption had been a pause in a subtle dance.

América dodges the rose branches arcing over the cement walk, sneezes, closes the gate behind her, pats down her hair one more time, and walks the half block down Calle Pinos toward the children's park. A dog looks up from his spot under a tamarind tree, yawns listlessly, then settles back, a paw over his eyes. She crosses the street in front of the Asambleas de Dios Church where Reverend Nuñez, his tie askew under the open collar of his white shirt, prunes a hibiscus bush that has encroached on the parking space for the church's van. He nods in her direction, and she nods back, quickening her pace as she turns left onto Calle Lirios. A rusting car rattles past. Its driver eyes her, slows down, sticks his head out the window to stare at her and to comment under his breath that he'd like to eat her. She responds that in her current state he'd die of indigestion, and turns left onto Almendros.

She has to find Correa before someone else tells him Rosalinda has run away from home with a boy. It's his duty to find them, to bring them back from wherever they're hiding. But she doesn't know what will happen after that. Taino has probably told Rosalinda he's going to marry her, but at fourteen she's too young to get married. It's probably illegal for her to be having sex. The thought of Rosalinda entangled with Taino enrages her. How dare he take advantage of them! She trusted him, believed that the serious, hardworking boy would be a good influence on her spirited daughter. She had forgotten that Taino was like other boys, after the same thing all men are.

Her rage increases with every step, and by the time she exits the alley leading to the main road, she's seething. If Rosalinda were to appear in front of her right now, she'd be sorry she ever set eyes on Taino. Both of them taking her for a pendeja, sneaking behind her back for who knows how long, while she slaves her life away scrubbing toilets and mopping floors. She assumed Rosalinda was smart enough not to repeat her mistake. Doesn't she see how my life has turned out, América asks herself, and has to fight the tears that threaten to ruin what composure she's been able to manage.

Up the road, a girl walks a baby. From the back she resembles Rosalinda. Same shoulder-length hair gelled into a lion's mane around her face. Same tight denim shorts worn with heavy boots. She wears a denim jacket like the one Correa gave Rosalinda for her birthday, with gold braiding around the arm-holes, the back lined with pink lace. She turns onto an alley leading to Calle Lirios. América follows her, but the girl feels someone behind her and speeds up. She looks over her shoulder fearfully. It's a schoolmate of Rosalinda's. She starts when she sees América, smiles guardedly, wraps the jacket around her bony shoulders, picks up the little boy, and goes into her yard. América follows her to the gate.

"Carmencita!" she calls as the girl reaches the house.

Carmencita sets her brother on the porch, takes her jacket off and throws it inside, then comes timidly up to América.

"Mande."

"Have you seen Rosalinda this morning?"

"No."

"How about last night? Did you see her last night?"

"I saw her day before yesterday when she . . ." Carmencita looks away, "If you want the jacket back, my mother said you'd have to return me the money."

"What money?"

"She sold it to me. I saved up for it. I know it's worth more than ten dollars, but that's what she asked." Carmencita's eyes fill with tears. From inside the house, the baby screeches, and Carmencita runs to see after him.

América waits a few minutes, but the girl doesn't return. A neighbor comes out of the house next door to water her plants. "¡Buenos dias!" she calls out. América returns the greeting but doesn't stop to chat. It's clear that for the next few weeks she'll be seeing her daughter's clothes on the girls and women of the barriada.

She retraces her steps toward the guardhouse outside Sun Bay, where Correa will be sitting in his pressed uniform checking IDs. She walks briskly down the asphalt road, stepping into the weeds whenever a vehicle passes. Several times she's offered rides by neighbors, who look at her curiously, doubtless wondering why she's not at work. But she refuses them, not wanting to talk to anyone about her daughter's whereabouts.

Her mouth feels dry. She stops at La Tienda Verde and takes a Coke from the refrigerator. Pepita dusts cans of tuna fish and boxes of unsweetened cereal flakes that only the Yanquis who rent houses in the village buy.

"How are things going?" Pepita asks brightly, moving behind the counter to take América's money. Pepita is always cheerful, which América attributes to the fact that she's never been married and doesn't have children.

"Okéi," América answers, popping the can open, avoiding Pepita's gaze. She takes a long draught of the cold soda. It makes her hiccup.

"Not working today?" Pepita asks, making change for América's dollar.

"No, hic, I'm hic . . ." She stops, covers her mouth, takes a deep breath, and holds it for a count of ten. When she lets the air out, a rumbling burp relieves the hiccups. "¡Ay, sorry! Soda always does that to me."

Pepita laughs. "That's why I never drink it. I prefer water."

"Thank you." América steps out of the shaded coolness of the store and looks down the road, which already ripples with vapor. She finishes as much of the soda as she can, spills the rest against a tree, and throws the can into the bushes. She crosses to the shady side of the road, past the ruins of the Central. A hurricane fence encrusted with weeds circles the property of what was once a complex of buildings for processing sugarcane. Beyond it, the road curves toward the sea. Thick-branched flamboyants and almendros lend intermittent shade, cool the air where butterflies flit among wildflowers.

Correa sits inside the guardhouse at the entrance to Sun Bay. Near him, a radio is tuned to a salsa station, and he drums the counter and sings along with Willie Colón while he waits for something to do. His job is to sign in and out anyone who comes in or leaves the public beach and parking area. This time of year there are mostly Jeeps rented by Yanquis who want to drive to the naval-base beaches hidden in the jungle at the end of rutted roads accessible only by all-terrain vehicles or horse-back. They always come to this one first, however, its long crescent dotted with palm trees reminiscent of the advertisements that lured them to the Caribbean in the first place.

An orange Isuzu passes her, driven by an Americano with skin pale as clam meat. A young woman sits in the passenger seat. She's wearing a bikini top and shorts. In the backseat, three children jostle to be first to see the ocean. In their wake América smells the oily scent of sunscreen. They stop at the guardhouse as she nears it.

Although he sees América, Correa doesn't acknowledge her. He turns down the radio, walks to the driver, clipboard in hand. The tourists are always surprised that the guard has to see ID even at the public beach and has to write down their names, addresses, and license numbers. Once she asked Correa why he has to write so much information on the sheets attached to a clipboard. "It's in case something happens on the beach, we know who was there."

It seems stupid to América, since the road and parking area are not the only ways to get to the beach. You can walk to it from other beaches, from the town, and, on horseback, from the wild vegetation surrounding it. She thinks the tourism office goes through all the trouble of taking down people's information to make tourists feel safe.

She stands in the shade of the guardhouse, her profile to him, looking toward the sea. Correa eyes her, lingering on the curve of her buttocks. He talks in English to the people in the Isuzu. "Jur licenss plis."

The man hands him his license, and Correa writes down the information, points to the woman and the kids with his clip-board. "Deir neims too, plis."

The man looks quizzically at him, but the woman has studied a little Spanish and decides to use it. "Yo soy Ginnie," she responds, enunciating every syllable as if she were in class, "y estos son nuestros niños, Peter, Suzy, y Lily." Correa smiles at her approvingly, like a teacher with his best pupil.

"Muchas gracias." He writes everything down.

"Is there a charge for parking?" the husband wants to know.

"If you want to pay . . ." Correa grins, and the woman pulls out two folded dollar bills from her pocket and hands them to him. The tourists think if they tip the guard, he'll keep an eye on their cars.

"Gracias, señora," Correa says, waving them into the parking area, looking at the woman as if she were his type, which she isn't.

América blushes, as the woman in the car ought to. Surely he caught a glimpse of her tetas, barely covered by the bikini top. Even though the guards have been trained not to look at the Americanas the way they look at the native women ("Look them in the eyes, not anywhere else," the trainer told them), some of them can get away with it. And some of the turistas encourage it.

Correa waves the family through, touching the brim of his hat in the lady's direction. "Have a good time," he says to them. The children wave at him.

People love Correa. He's good-looking, charming, with a smile that makes women melt and children trust him. He takes care of himself, and it shows in his bodybuilder's shape, the neatness of his close-cropped hair, the fastidious crescent of his well-clipped nails. He's the kind of man women love to see sweat. The moisture on his skin highlights the taut arm muscles, the powerful thighs, the graceful curve between his buttocks and upper back.

He steps into the guardhouse, puts the clipboard ledger on the shelf, stuffs the two dollars into his pocket, and joins América in the shade.

"What's new?" he asks, casual, ignoring the fact that she has never come after him when they should both be working.

"Your daughter has run away with that mocoso who works at the supermarket." She doesn't waste words. Like her mother, she's never learned the art of dissimulation.

She senses his reaction before he voices it, takes a few steps away from him but feels him looming over her.

"How the hell could you let a thing like that happen?" He steps closer, fists clenched.

She's been standing tall up to now, but his words discourage her. She resists the urge to cry. Her tears excite him, sometimes making him angry, other times so tender she believes him when he says he loves her, that he will take care of her.

"I didn't let it happen. It just did. When Mami went into her room this morning, she discovered Rosalinda was gone." Her voice is tight, as if sobs were strangling her from the inside. She pulls a tissue out of her handbag and blows her nose. "I didn't look in on her before I left for work because she went to bed so late. She must have gone in the middle of the night." She feels his attention shift, the tension that surrounds him press away from her.

"I'll kill that hijo de la gran puta." Correa stomps toward his custom-fitted Jeep, as tough and macho as he is.

"Wait! Correa, where are you going? We don't even know where they went!" América runs after him, reaches his side just before he jumps in, fumbling for his keys. She pulls on his sleeve, like a child seeking an elder's attention. His slap sends her sprawling onto the gravel of the road.

"Even if they're at the edge of hell, I'll find him. That son of a bitch! How dare that fucker mess with my daughter!" He starts the vehicle with a screech of grinding gears, leans out the open side, raises his finger in warning. "You go home and wait for me." His tone of voice, his eyes, convey a menace that makes her shiver. She drops her gaze, and he speeds off, spraying gravel and dirt in a broad circle. When she's sure he's gone, she pushes herself up, brushes dirt and grass from her clothes, picks out tiny sharp pebbles from her burning palms. A car drives up to the guardhouse, and the driver leans out, staring after the speeding vehicle with the uniformed attendant at the wheel, at América on the other side of the empty guardhouse, tear-stained and rumpled.

"Are you all right?" he asks, and América wipes her nose with the back of her hand and waves him through.

She picks up her handbag, which landed near the guardhouse when she fell, brushes the sand off it, and walks to the road.

"¡Idiota!" she sobs under her breath, aware that she doesn't know if she means the tourist, herself, or Correa. To the left, the road curves toward Esperanza. Across from where she stands, a cow munches noisily on some grass in a fenced meadow. A cow that has been there as long as she can remember. It can't be the same cow she saw when she was growing up less than a mile from here. But it looks like the same cow, white with black splotches on her rump. She chews placidly, watery eyes fixed on América, slobber dripping from her leathery lips. Her udder is long and skinny, gray at the tips. A big black fly lands on her left hip, and the cow slaps it with her tail, without breaking the rhythm of her chewing.

América tugs her dress down at the hips, runs her fingers through her hair, and heads not toward Esperanza, but away from it, toward Destino.

The Man She Could Have Had

It's all uphill from Esperanza to Destino. The flatlands on the southern shore of the island rise gently but consistently toward low mountains speckled with flat-roofed houses. Once these lowlands were a sea of sugarcane, which elegant señores oversaw atop sprightly Paso Fino horses. But when the U.S. Navy appropriated two-thirds of the island for its maneuvers, the great sugar haciendas disappeared and the tall stacks that dotted the island were bulldozed out of the way. This is history, and América doesn't think about it as she walks the slope of the narrow road, sweating in the stretches between shady patches. Several times she stops and studies the road in front of her, trying to gauge how much farther she has to walk. It is a short view, as the road curves sharply right or left. On the few open stretches there is no shade. Visible heat bounces off the blacktop until she feels as if she were slowly roasting, her clothes like wrappers to keep the juices in.

A público passes in the opposite direction, and the driver waves at her. It is an air-conditioned van for twelve passengers, full of tourists gawking at the lush vegetation and doubtless at the brightly dressed woman walking along the road. She tries to ignore their rude stares, the feeling that to them she represents the charm of the tropics: a colorfully dressed woman walking along a sunlit road, her shadow stretching behind her as if she were dragging her history.

After the last of the many curves, she arrives at the open road leading up a steep hill beyond the gates of Camp Garcia, the naval base. Cars and trucks are parked helter-skelter outside the gates. There's a line of battered Isuzus and Mitsubishi four-wheel-drive vehicles waiting to gain admission into the hidden beaches owned by the U.S. Navy.

She's breathing hard. Even though she works on her feet all day long, up and down the stairs, around the interior courtyard and wraparound porches of La Casa del Francés, she's not used to this much exercise under the hot sun. Her feet, encased in pretty but uncomfortable sandals, feel large and heavy. Her shoulder-length hair, which she keeps up during the day, has slipped out of its pins, and her usually well tended curls droop around her neck in sticky wisps that she keeps peeling off and pinning as she walks.

I should have worn sneakers and shorts, América thinks. But I wasn't thinking. What am I doing here anyway? Correa said to wait for him. But I can't just stand by and let him do it all. She's my daughter too. I should have thought of that before I went to see him. What good is he anyway? A hothead, is what he is. He's just going to make a scene everywhere he goes and then nothing. Rosalinda is not stupid. She's not on the island, that's for sure. Everyone here knows her and Taino. I'm sure his mother would be out looking for them if she knew he'd run away with Rosalinda. Her with her airs of la gran señora.

The image of Yamila Valentín Saavedra in her hilltop house makes América feel hotter. It's not that she doesn't wish Yamila well. It's that Yamila, who has come up in the world, acts as if she's always lived in the hills where the Yanquis build their vacation homes. If I'd had the good fortune to marry a rich man, América assures herself, I wouldn't have become as uppity as she has. It's not in my nature. But Yamila has always been that way. Always acting superior to everyone else. Now that she lives in the hills with the Yanquis, you can't even look at her.

América climbs the steep hill flanked on either side by the gated mansions of El Destino. The houses here are built on a monte with a view of Phosphorescent Bay and, beyond it, the turquoise Caribbean Sea. Each house in this neighborhood has a four-wheel-drive vehicle in its marquesina, the lawns are neatly trimmed, and potted plants sway from hooks on the shaded decks. The community was devastated by Hurricane Hugo. Within a year of the hurricane, however, the lots were owned by Yanquis who have built cement-and-glass mansions dangling from precipitous slopes, adorned with elaborate wrought-iron rejas at the windows, doors, and marquesina gates. Rejas that seem to be decorative but are meant to protect the part-time residents from the vandalism and robbery they fear is imminent the minute they turn their cars in the opposite direction.

América stops to catch her breath before stepping in front of Yamila Valentín's house. A prissy dog runs out of a rear door and growls at her feet on the other side of the gate as América bangs on the lock.

"Yamila Valentín Saavedra, come out and talk to me!" She feels the eyes of Yamila's neighbors on her back. A doctor lives on this street, so does the American accountant who handles Don Irving's finances. América has been in this neighborhood many times, cleaning the houses of the doctor and the accountant, the retired navy colonel, the developer who has built almost every new house on the island since the hurricane, the Italian count who comes every winter and stays three months.

"Yamila Valentín Saavedra!" she calls again, and this time a gate scrapes shrilly against cement, and the ratlike dog runs toward the door at the far end of the marquesina, from which Yamila Valentín Saavedra emerges wrapped in a white bathrobe, wet hair flat against her skull and down the nape of her neck.

"Who's calling me?"

"It's América Gonzalez."

A look of distaste crosses Yamila's face, and her pretty features harden into a mask of imperturbable dignity. "I was in the shower," she says icily, and she wraps the robe tighter around herself. She comes closer to the gate but makes no move to open it. The dog resumes its screechy barking, and Yamila picks it up and holds it against her chest, where it growls and shows its tiny teeth at América.

"Have you seen my daughter?"

"Why should I know your daughter's whereabouts?" She arches her thin eyebrows, kisses the top of her dog's head.

"Because your son sweet-talked her into running away with him."

Yamila's mouth flies open, her eyes water, and the mask of impassivity breaks into a look of shock, disbelief, then rage. "My son! With your daughter!" She drops the dog and runs inside the house through the same door she'd come out. América hears her yelling at someone inside, and a lot of shuffling and opening and closing of doors, and then Yamila comes out again, her face contorted into a grimace that América can't interpret.

"That little slut! What has she done to my son?" Yamila throws herself at the gate, attempting to reach América through the iron bars. But América jumps back, dropping her purse, its contents spilling and rolling in every direction.

"Your son seduced my daughter! She's a child, just fourteen. How dare you call her a slut!" América reaches through and grabs Yamila's wet hair, but Yamila's long, well-manicured nails scratch at her with the ferocity of a tiger.

"She's a slut and you're a slut and so is your mother, you bitch!"

An elderly woman emerges from inside the house and tries to pull Yamila away from América, but she's too old and weak. Screaming obscenities, América and Yamila claw and punch from opposite sides of the gate, their fists connecting more often against the curved wrought iron than against each other. Neighbors run out of their neat houses and stand on their porches or lean out of their windows, but no one comes to stop them. A woman holds a phone to her ear and narrates what's happening to someone on the other end.

Forceful arms wrap around América's waist and drag her away from Yamila's claws. She kicks back at the man, losing a shoe in the struggle. He presses his left forearm around her neck and with his right pushes her in front of him, up against a car parked across the street. He squeezes his arm tight around her throat, until she can hardly breathe, and leans his whole weight against her. The struggle has excited him, and América feels his erection pressing against her buttocks.

"I knew you'd come here, you stupid bitch. Settle down, you're making a fool of yourself!" Correa snarls into her ear.

"Let me go! You ass-kisser, always kissing up to these rich bitches!"

"Settle down and shut your dirty mouth, or I'll shut it for you!" He turns her over to face him and slaps her hard, once on the right, once on the left, drawing blood where her teeth cut her bottom lip. She tries to kick his groin but misses. Across the street, Yamila screeches abuse at them both, while the old lady mumbles ineffectually at her side.

Correa lifts a struggling América into his Jeep, slams her against the passenger seat, fastens her seat belt as if it will hold her in place. "You stay here," he warns, backing away. He picks up her lipstick and wallet, hairbrush and compact from the slanted curb in front of Yamila's marquesina, all the time keeping an eye on América.

She sits in the passenger seat staring daggers into him. Rummaging through the glove compartment, she comes up with a crumpled tissue to wipe her bloody lip.

"Great macho you are, getting your kicks from hitting women," she says loud enough to hear herself but not so loud that he does. Her dress is torn at the collar, and a splotch of blood has fallen on the only white spot in the flower print of the bodice. She tugs here and there, pulls her skirt down, unpins her hair, runs her fingers through it, then pins it up again. In the fight with Yamila she lost a couple more nails. Her arms are scratched, and her lip hurts. She can feel it swelling inside her mouth.

Correa climbs in, carrying her purse and her shoe. He throws them at her feet and roars off down the street. Behind them, Yamila still screams, proving to anyone who didn't know it that her upbringing was neither as genteel nor proper as she would have them believe.

"They left in the early ferry," Correa says, as if continuing a conversation that had been interrupted. "I figured that's what they'd do."

América tries hard to ignore him. She sits on the farthest edge of her seat, hands crossed atop her handbag, eyes trained on the familiar scenery whizzing by. Fifteen years ago she and Correa had run off on the 7:00 A.M. ferry to Fajardo. She had been a virgin when she left with Correa, but she can't be sure that her daughter is.

"I'm going over in the afternoon ferry," Correa continues. "They're kids. They can't get too far."

She and Correa had hidden out in his aunt's house. They returned to Vieques after a month, to live in a shack he'd inherited from another aunt. The day they arrived, Ester came to see them, carrying all of América's things in pillowcases. She dropped them in the middle of the floor. "You made your bed, now lie in it." Then she left. Eight months later, when América was seven months pregnant and Correa had begun an affair with another woman, América wrapped up her things in the same pillowcases and moved in with her mother in the house she had grown up in, where eight weeks later Rosalinda was born.

"What do we do if she's pregnant?" América asks, her voice calm, even to herself.

Correa slaps the steering wheel. "I'll make him marry her."

"She's fourteen, Correa. People don't get married at fourteen."

"What are you suggesting then?" He looks at her with real curiosity, as if he has no idea what she's going to say.

"I'm not suggesting anything. She's fourteen, that's all I'm saying. She's too young to get married."

"Son of a bitch! It's illegal to do it with a girl that young. I'll kill that son of a bitch."

América hummphs. Men are so stupid! Doesn't even occur to him that she was that young when he took her off the island.

And there has never been any talk of them marrying, not before, not after Rosalinda was born.

"You're my woman," he said to her. "We don't need a paper to prove it." He'd gone on to prove it to the whole island, however, in other ways. She examines her face in the side mirror. Her cheeks are puffy, her lower lip swollen. Correa's woman stares back.

They pull up in front of América's house. Correa waits for her to climb down from the passenger seat. "Stay home and don't get into trouble," he warns. "I'll take care of everything."

He waits until she's gone into her house, then roars away as if he can't wait to get out of there.

Ester has made a thick asopao, but América isn't hungry. She changes out of her torn clothes and takes a shower. Her arms, neck, and shoulders are etched with deep red scratches that sting when she soaps. The first tears she sheds are of pain. But the ones that follow come from a deeper place than the surface scratches on her skin. She beats her fists against the tiles and sobs until it seems her insides rip.

The look of disdain in Yamila's eyes is hard to erase. Yamila, who as a girl went around with her nose in the air, like she was better than anyone else in the barriada, then married a Nuyorrican who can't even speak Spanish, a civilian consultant to the U.S. Navy who built her a house high on a hill, looking down on everyone else. América has cleaned her house too, has done her laundry, and once walked in on her by accident and saw her shaving her pubic hair. A week later Yamila fired her and has had it in for América ever since.

She raises her face to the stream from the shower and lets the water mingle with her tears, fill her mouth, enter her ears, trickle down her neck, between her breasts, over her belly.

"What are you doing in there?" Ester bangs on the door, her speech slurred.

"Go away, I'm taking a shower!"

"I have to pee!"

She stumbles out of the shower, grabs a towel, wraps herself in it, and leaves the bathroom. Ester stares at her as she goes by. América can barely see where she's going, her eyes so swollen they can hold no more tears.

"I told the boy's family that if he runs away, there's nothing we can do. These are family matters, understand?"

Officer Odilio Pagán sits at the kitchen table, eyeing Ester's frosty beer. América puts a tall glass of lemonade in front of him. "But she's underage. There must be a law—"

"Of course there are laws, but these things are better handled privately." He gulps the drink down, avoids her gaze. "There was no coercion involved. They're mixed-up kids who think they're grown up." He sets the glass down delicately, as if afraid to break it. "Of course, it's something else if you or Correa start making trouble." He looks at the scratches on her arms, at her puffy cheeks.

"That woman has a mouth on her," América says, turning away from him.

"I bet you can keep up with her."

"I don't let anyone insult me, if that's what you mean." She sniffs.

"You can get arrested for assaulting a person, especially in their own home."

She faces him again. "But some people's sons can't get arrested for raping someone else's daughter."

"Who said anything about rape?"

"When a girl is fourteen years old, it's rape."

"América, you've been listening in on too many conversations at La Casa."

"The people who stay there are well educated. They know what's going on. Doctors stay there, and lawyers."

"And they're on vacation. And the last thing they want to do is bother with the problems of a maid." He stands up. "Where did Correa go after he dropped you home?"

"How should I know?"

"I can find out if he was on the ferry."

"Good for you."

He stands so close to her his lemon-scented breath fans her bangs. "You don't get it, do you? I'm trying to help you. If he does something stupid, we'll all be sorry."

"Correa is all talk, nothing else." América bites out. "If he finds them, he'll give them a lecture and bring them home." She feels the lump on the inside of her lip with her tongue. "Besides, Correa thinks the sun rises and sets on Rosalinda. He wouldn't do anything to make her hate him."

"Did he do this?" Pagan asks, touching her lip with his index finger.

She moves her face away, and he backs off.

"He took the afternoon ferry to Fajardo," Ester grumbles from her end of the table. América glares at her.

"Do you have any family there?"

"No," América responds, aware that Pagán is just doing his job as investigator. Everyone knows she has no family in Fajardo. Everyone knows that's where Correa comes from.

"I have a sister in New York," Ester mumbles out of nowhere. "Haven't seen her in years."

Pagán and América stare at her for a second, then exchange a look that might make them both smile under other circumstances. América is the first to recover.

"Rosalinda sold her clothes, probably her jewelry and boom box, too."

Pagán seems startled that they're not still talking about Ester's long-lost sister. He blinks uncontrollably for some seconds, as if mentally searching for what it is he's supposed to be doing. "The boy took two hundred dollars out of his savings account yesterday," he says finally. "Didn't know there was that much money in bagging groceries, did you?"

"Who knows what else he's been bagging."

Pagán doesn't smile. He's an investigator again, on official business. "I'd better get going," he says briskly, moving to the door. América walks him out.

It's early evening. The street is empty, but from inside the houses, televisions drone competing programs and commercials, drowning out the sounds of insects hiding in the grass. In a few minutes the church across the street will begin its nightly services, broadcast to the neighborhood over speakers placed near the front and side doors of the church. The air is scented with roses.

On the porch, Odilio Pagán puts his hand on América's shoulder, squeezes it gently. "Don't worry," he says softly, "everything will be all right." She turns her face away from his gaze. He dodges the gauntlet of spiny roses to his patrol car, opens the door, looks at her longingly, then steps in and drives off.

She could have had this man with the black eyes, the slight paunch, the stubby, delicate hands. As children, they played together in this very neighborhood, before it got built up, when every house was set back behind broad yards, surrounded by mango, breadfruit, and avocado trees. Before urbanization. They didn't have running water then, or electricity. The road was a dusty path in winter and a treacherous, muddy trail when it rained.

Correa had come to the barriada with the contractors improving the roads, stringing electric wires from tall poles, digging up ditches to lay pipes for running water and sewers. Correa was a man, Odilio Pagán a boy, and América a girl who hadn't seen much. La conquista, the seduction, didn't take long. She ran off with Correa, and even though eight months later she returned to her mother's house, she is still Correa's woman. He lives on the other side of the island, has other women, has, in fact, a legal wife and kids in Fajardo. But he always comes back to América, under the pretext of seeing his daughter. And when he does, he stays in her bed. And if any other man dares get too friendly, he beats her up. In the fifteen years Correa has been in her life, no other men have dared enter it, for fear he will kill her.

A Fuerza de Puños

It rains all night, but she doesn't realize it until the next morning, when she comes out of her windowless room and the air feels moist and new. The house is dark, but through the slats of the front windows a frail gray light seeps in like mist. América sets the coffeemaker on brew, slips two slices of white bread into the toaster, goes to the bathroom to wash her face and mouth. The swelling on her lip has gone down, but her eyes still feel heavy, and the scratches on her arms and shoulders rub painfully against her nightclothes. When she returns to the kitchen, the coffee is ready, the toast crisp. She brings her cup and toast smeared with grape jelly into her room, switches on the light, changes into her uniform in between bites and sips. She doesn't put on makeup, avoids the mirror. The radio is tuned to a station that plays salsa, and she hums the familiar rhythms absently as if her mind were empty and her heart light. Ester pads in, her greñas sticking out in every direction because last night she didn't set her hair in curlers.

"You going to work?"

"Sí."

"Have you no respect? Your daughter is missing, and you're going around like nothing's happened."

"What am I supposed to do? Sit around all day waiting for them to show up?"

"What will people say, with you running all over town . . ."

"I'm not all over town, I'm at work. And I don't care what they say."

"You say that—"

"Since when are you so worried about the neighbors' opinion?"

Ester sniffs and retreats to the kitchen, pours herself some coffee. América brushes her hair into a ponytail held with a barrette in the shape of a colorful fish. She folds her white apron and stuffs it into her pocket, puts on white sneakers with short socks. Her movements are quick and determined, with the authority of years of practice. Ester appears at the door again.

"When you left I ran all over town looking for you."

América looks up. Ester stares into the fragrant liquid in the brown-and-yellow mug she holds in her hands, the fingers laced around one another as if to draw warmth. Her face, still creased from sleep, has the softness of a child's, but the deep diagonal lines from her nose to the corners of her mouth, the crow's-feet scratched around her eyes, the furrows etched between the eyebrows are those of someone who has lived hard in her forty-five years. América turns her gaze from her mother's face, walks past her to the front of the house.

"Mami, you didn't have a man to help you. Rosalinda has a father."

"Bah!" Ester responds, and scuffs back through the kitchen into her room.

América stands at the door, waiting. The moment is so fleeting, it's gone before she knows it was there, and unmourned, it passes. It is their dance, a brief coming together in which they follow the same rhythm, hear the same music, perform the same steps. But each time, the dance gets shorter, and they exit in opposite directions, into the wings, to gather strength for the next combination.

América steps into the cool early-morning moisture. Rainwater drips from the broad leaves of a breadfruit tree at the side of the house. The branches of the rosebushes curve down heavily. Red, yellow, and orange petals are strewn over the front walk, and it seems a pity to tread on them in her grooved sneakers.

The street is shiny wet, the gutters fast-flowing rivulets, the potholes clear puddles that reflect gray sky. In the dark recesses of foliage, invisible tree frogs sing happily. Her sneakers squeak wetly against the pavement, and as she enters the path at the rear of La Casa, they sink into a squishy, sandy mud that's not slippery but splats against her legs as she walks. A slight breeze shakes more moisture from the leaves of mango and avocado trees as she passes, drops on her like holy water on a pilgrim. Fog rises from the green hollows where vines have engulfed an abandoned car and the skeletal remains of a house long unin-habited. Beyond them is a mound that sprouted from the ground seemingly overnight a couple of years ago, its steep sides like an infant volcano consumed by thick vegetation. América quickens her step as she passes it.

When she arrives at the back door of La Casa, the house pul-sates with the even breath of sleeping bodies in the rooms around the central courtyard. The flower garden shimmers, the ornate cement balustrades around its perimeter like midget sol-diers watching over the warblers caged in the center, covered with a sheet so that they will not wake up too early and rouse the guests. Shallow puddles of rain collect in the walkways around the courtyard. Above, a square sky brightens from steel gray to the color of a dove's breast, purple gray, soft. And rain-water drips into every hole and crevice, a sibilant gossip of reproaches and complaints.

She's the first one at work. As she enters the house, she takes her apron from her pocket and ties it snugly around her waist. From the supply room behind the kitchen she fetches a mop and begins to dry off the walkway puddles so that guests will not slip on their way to the back porch where breakfast will be served. She swishes the mop in clockwise circles, backing away from the area she has dried. Her mop erases the faint tracks of toads who claim these halls once the lights have been turned out, after the last guest has stumbled by exhausted from too much relaxation or too much drink, wanting only to collapse on the crisp sun-dried sheets.

She likes these early mornings. The sharp, sweaty smell of sleeping bodies. The rustling of the sheets as people awaken. The creaking box springs. The mumbled good mornings, the slap of bare feet against tiled floors. Toilets are flushed. Showers run. Glasses clink against porcelain sinks, the narrow glass shelf beneath the mirrors. A few electric razors buzz behind the louvered doors of some guest rooms, doors that look so charming but afford no privacy. She can hear, as she mops the halls, everything that goes on in each room she passes. The huffing and puffing of couples making hurried love, the groans as some turn over or try to get up, creaking knees, morning farts, bumps against unfamiliar furniture in dim rooms.

She finishes wiping down the ground floor, squeezes the mop in a pail, then climbs up to the second story, where she repeats the ritual, backing away from the spot she has dried, around the square of light and air, the tops of the ficus tree under which the birdcage stands. Light streams in, moist sun that makes her sweat inside her nylon uniform.

Downstairs, Feto rattles pots, runs water. He wheels the squeaky breakfast cart, topped with a coffee urn, mugs, and spoons, onto the back porch. Within minutes the passageway fills with the scent of brewing coffee, and the tourists emerge from behind their doors. One by one, as if the aroma were drawing them out, they leave their rooms, some with hair still wet after a shower, some stopping to check that the buttons on their shirts and zippers on their pants are secured. From rooms 9 and 12 children burst into the hallways, followed by parents shushing them not to run, not to yell, not to wake up the other guests. Behind door number 7 someone snores, then whistles, then snores again. From room 1, reserved for disabled guests, a man emerges pushing a walker in front of him, followed by a woman who walks step by laborious step beside him, every so often touching his elbow as if to steady him or, perhaps, herself.

What does América think about as these people emerge from

their rooms dressed in bright vacation clothes? She thinks the women are too skinny and the men too pale, even the Puerto Rican tourists. She thinks people with enough money to stay in a hotel must have many other luxuries in their lives. Fancy cars, probably, lots of clothes, jewels.

She knows more about them than they will ever know about her. She knows whether they flail in their sleep, or whether they sleep quietly on one side or the other. Whether the tropical night is so cool they have to use blankets, or whether they sleep exposed to the foul sereno. She knows the brand of toothpaste they use, whether they have dentures. She knows if the women have their periods. She knows if the men wear jockey or boxer underwear, and what size. She notices how they look right past and pretend not to see her. She feels herself there, solid as always, but they look through her, as if she were a part of the strange landscape into which they have run away from their everyday lives. Those who do see her, smile guardedly, then slide their gaze away quickly, ashamed, it seems, to have noticed her.

She cleans each room clockwise once she makes the beds and picks up the dirty towels. She dusts, sweeps, and mops the guest room, then disinfects the shower, sink, and toilet. She scrubs the floor after a guest checks out but only mops it down if the same people are staying for a few days.

She checks that there's enough toilet paper, empties the trash, tidies the bedside tables.

"Izevrydinalride?" América nearly jumps out of her skin at the unexpected voice. Don Irving stands at the door of room 9.

"Excuse?"

"I didn't expect you to come today."

She doesn't know how to respond, whether he's being kind or critical. "Is busy day."

"Yes, well." Don Irving sticks his cigar back in his mouth. "I have to change the lightbulbs in that bathroom." He goes in, and she hears him puttering as she dusts. Tomás usually does things like change lightbulbs and fix what's broken in the rooms. When Don Irving leaves, closing the door behind him, América breathes a sigh of relief.

Room 9 has a sleeping porch walled with shutters, so that it's really two rooms. Usually, it's rented to couples with children, because there's enough space in the porch for a bed and a crib. This time there are toys scattered around, and a couple of mangy-looking stuffed animals on the small bed and in the crib. In the bathroom there are three baby bottles with nipples. The garbage can is stuffed with dirty diapers.

From the clothes, she can tell they're boys, one of them under three perhaps. Overalls and sneakers with cartoon characters are neatly folded on top of the dresser. So many clothes! A stack of Huggies for toddlers, a few clean diapers on the bedside table. A box of wipes.

She dusts, noting how much this couple has brought. They must have needed a separate suitcase for all the toys, books, puzzles, and plastic figures of muscular manlike creatures with loincloths and green skin. On the bedside table closest to the sleeping porch, the mother has left a pair of earrings in the shape of bananas, and a purple suede headband with the rounded tips worn to the plastic. On the husband's side, a pair of glasses with severe black frames, a thick paperback book with a gavel pictured on the cover.

They read a lot, the tourists who come to La Casa del Francés. They always bring fat books with them, the women's with lace and flowers or beautiful girls entwined with brawny men, the titles in cursive writing. The men's books are austere, usually no more than the title and the author in block letters, with few colors, no gilded edges or ornate designs. Sometimes they bring magazines, and she's noticed that they too seem designated male or female. On one of them, the cover was nothing but a white background with a large dollar sign in red. The women's magazines have pictures of movie stars, or teenage girls with pouty lips and smooth skin where there should be a cleavage. When the guests throw them out, América saves them and brings them home to study the fashions, the picture-perfect din ners, the tips for making rooms over. In one, they changed the look of a room by draping sheets on the walls, the windows, the furniture. To América, it looked like a house abandoned, protected from dust, ghostly and unwelcoming.

"Buzzzz . . . You're an airplane. . . . Buzzzz. . . . rat tat tat tah . . ." The door flies open and a man carrying a toddler comes in. "Oh, I'm sorry!"

"Is okéi," she says. "I finish later—"

"No, no, that's all right. You can keep working. We just came to change a stinky." He drops the child on the bed, tickles him with one hand, while with the other he reaches for a clean diaper in the box next to the bed. "You're a stinker, yes, you are, a stinker . . ." The little boy is delighted with his father's silliness, and giggles.

"I'm a stinker . . . stinker . . ."

América watches as the father deftly slips a clean diaper under the dirty one, wipes his son's bottom with a wet tissue from a plastic box, blows air on the child's belly before fastening the tapes.

"There you go!" He pulls the child up, slings him over his shoulder. "All done!" he says and pats his padded bottom. "See you later," he says to América, and they leave the room.

All the while he was changing the baby, América had to restrain herself from offering to do it for him. His movements were confident, as if he had done it many times, but she couldn't help herself. She wanted to change that baby's diaper.

If Rosalinda is pregnant, there will be a baby in the house. América has no doubt that her daughter will be home before a baby is born. Yamila and Roy are not about to sacrifice their son for Rosalinda's sake. What mother would do that to a sixteen-year-old boy? If Rosalinda was stupid enough to get pregnant, she'll have to take responsibility for what happens next. As Ester said, "You've made your bed, now lie in it."

A dull ache forms in América's chest. She didn't learn from Ester's mistake, why should she expect Rosalinda to have learned from hers? Maybe it's a family curse. Just as Ester left her mother with a man who promised her God knows what, América left, at the same age, with Correa, whose promises she doesn't remember. Perhaps there were none. Maybe, when you're fourteen, no promises are necessary, just the insistent need to be with a man in a way you can't be with your mother or your friends. Maybe, when you're fourteen, you're not running toward something, you're running away from it. Maybe all girls go through this phase, but only some act on it. América doesn't know. América has no idea what she's done to make Rosalinda do what she's done. Or what Ester did that made her run off with Correa, come back to the island, and remain his woman all these years, in spite of the fact that he has betrayed her again and again.

Is it my fault? she asks herself, but she can't answer. She's tried to be a good mother to Rosalinda. She's told her straight out that she hopes Rosalinda will not repeat her mistakes, that she should get an education and make something of herself. Rosalinda always seemed to understand, to share América's dreams for her, to have dreams of her own. América shakes her head, as if trying to unfasten a clue to her daughter's escape. I've brought her up the best I could, she assures herself. I did everything to make sure she'd have a better life than mine. What happened?

"Boys are easier to bring up than girls," Nilda declares in between mouthfuls of yellow rice with ham. "They're not as moody, and they're up front about what's bothering them. Girls are deceptive that way."

América eats her lunch under a mango tree behind the kitchen, sitting at a picnic table set up for the help's meals and coffee breaks.

"I don't know about that," says Feto, father of six daughters. "It's all a gamble. Some kids are easy, others aren't. It has nothing to do with their sex."

They chew thoughtfully, considering Feto's statement. Since they sat down to lunch, the conversation has circled around sons and daughters, their merits and drawbacks, but no one has come straight out and asked América what's happening with Rosalinda.

"One good thing about daughters," says Tomás, who lives with his in a small house surrounded by lush gardens, "they never leave you."

Everyone looks at América.

"Or if they do," amends Nilda, "they always come back." Everyone nods.

"Buen provecho," América says, getting up to carry her half-finished lunch to the kitchen. As she's scraping the leftovers into the compost bowl, Nilda comes up the back steps.

"We didn't mean to offend you when we were talking," Nilda apologizes.

"No offense taken," she responds crisply.

"There are only so many things we can talk about when we've known each other so long."

"Don't worry about it." She knows that they all think she's conceited and uppity. That when she comes to work with bruises on her face and arms, she deserves it. That Correa has to control her with his fists because otherwise she would be too proud.

She's heard the men talk about how a man has to show his woman, from the very first, who wears the pants in the house. Especially nowadays, when women think they can run the world. Even Feto, father of six daughters, says a man has to teach women the way he likes things, and if the only way she can learn is "a fuerza de puños," well, then, his fists should be the teacher. Tomás says he doesn't believe in hitting women with his fists. An open hand, he says, is as effective. "A man who hits a woman with his fists," he says, "is taking advantage."

América doesn't talk much at lunchtime. Anything she says can get back to Correa, who plays dominoes with these men. And often Correa is part of their conversations. He eats lunch at La Casa three or four times a week and sits with the men on their end of the table while she and Nilda huddle at their end pretending not to hear them.

América gets her pail and rags from the supply room and goes back inside. She's almost done with the rooms in the main house and has brought down the laundry for Nilda to wash and hang out to dry. It's Friday, a busy day for check-ins. Most of the tourists from New York leave early, either on the 7:00 A.M. ferry to Fajardo or on one of the flights to the international airport in San Juan. There's a short lull right before and right after lunch between the checkouts and those coming in, but it picks up again before dinner.

Most tourists arrive looking tired but eager. If they've never been to La Casa del Francés, they're impressed by the colonial architecture, the broad verandah that circles the house, the colorful mosaic floors, hammocks strung outside the first-floor rooms, wicker chairs and loveseats with the woody smell of rattan, wrought-iron tables with colorful cloths and vases full of fragrant blossoms.

When they enter the house itself, they're amazed to discover the central courtyard with flower beds, ficus trees, colorful birds singing inside a giant cage. Don Irving greets his guests on the back porch, seated on a rattan chair with peacock back. He's always dressed in white, looks like something out of a movie, large, white-haired, with a white mustache, a straw sombrero shading hazel eyes under severe white brows. To América, he looks like Anthony Quinn, the Mexican actor, and in the ten years she's worked for him, she keeps expecting him to speak Spanish when he opens his mouth, but he never does.

When she comes down to return her supplies, Don Irving is in the kitchen boiling water at the ancient six-burner stove, left over from the days when the hotel was the most luxurious house on the island, home to the owners of thousands of acres of sugarcane planted in long rows stretching toward the sea.

"How're you doing," he says.

"Okéi," she answers, rinsing out her pail at the low sink in the supply room.

"Any word from your daughter?"

It all sounds like one long word she's never heard: eniwoidfromerdora. "Excuse?"

"Yerdora. Eniwoidfromeryet?"

"I'm sorry," she responds, burning with embarrassment. "I no understand."

"Never mind." Don Irving pours steaming water over the teabag at the bottom of the large mug he always carries with him, from which he sips all day long. He ambles back into the house.

América has worked for Don Irving since he bought the decaying plantation house and converted it into a hotel. She and Ester were the first maids to work at the place, and she's picked up some English listening to him and his guests. He has never learned Spanish and speaks as if it didn't matter, as if it were the person he's talking to who has to make sense of what he's saying. When she first began working for him, América lost much sleep over the conversations they had, which consisted of him talking nonstop and her bobbing her head up and down or interjecting "okéi" every now and then so as not to seem stupid.

Ester, who has much less patience than América, would answer him in Spanish, and they talked to each other in their own languages, América not sure if either knew what the other was saying. They became lovers, and for a while Ester lived with him in the casita he built for himself at the back of the property, in a glade surrounded by a pabona hedge. But she left him after a couple of months, claiming she'd lived without men for so long, she couldn't live with them anymore. They still get together from time to time, always in his casita because Ester won't share her own bed with anyone.

Because Ester and Don Irving are lovers América has a more familiar relationship with him than the other employees do. He's come to their house for dinner, has even had a few conversations with Correa about the way he treats América. It didn't change Correa much, but América has always been grateful to him for trying.

The other employees resent the fact that Don Irving favors América and overlooks Ester's failings as a maid. She works at the hotel two days a week, and the other five, América does the work of two, scrubbing the bathrooms Ester didn't, dusting the corners she overlooked, placing extra toilet paper in the bathrooms so that there will be enough over the two days Ester takes care of them and forgets to check.

She finishes all the rooms, humming a bolero or a salsa tune, seemingly lighthearted. The tourists at La Casa del Francés who bother to notice her are greeted with a bright smile and sly chocolate eyes that seem to dance beneath thick black lashes.

"Everyone on this island is so friendly," they say to one another, then forget her the minute they step into the bright tropical sun, the afternoon buzzing with hummingbirds sucking life out of the hearts of flowers.

Correa's Gifts

One week passes. Someone steals Correa's radio from the guardhouse at Sun Bay Beach. It rains, and the lined forms with the tourists' names and addresses written in Correa's block letters soften in the moisture, then curl in the sun.

When her turn comes, Ester refuses to go to work because of what people might say about Rosalinda, and she spends her days in the garden, a can of beer at her side. She cooks dinner, then slumps on her easy chair watching television and sipping beer. América works both of their shifts at La Casa.

On the eighth day, Correa calls her at work and says he's found the kids.

"Don't worry, I've taken care of everything," he says. A Mexican corrido is playing full blast in the background.

"Is she pregnant?" América asks.

"I don't think so," he says, as if it occurred to him to ask.

"Can I talk to her?"

"She's not here," Correa answers. "She's with my aunt."

"Why?"

"I have to do some things while I'm here. I'll bring her back this weekend." América knows the "things" he has to do probably involve his wife and three kids in Fajardo.

"Where's the boy?"

"His father took him to New York. We all thought it was better this way."

"Así son las cosas," she sighs.

"What was that?"

"Nothing. When will you be here?"

"I told you. This weekend."

"All right. Tell Rosalinda I love her."

He hangs up, and she's not sure if he's heard her last instructions.

The weekend comes and goes with no sign of Correa or Rosalinda. Officer Odilio Pagán stops by to tell América that Roy and Yamila Saavedra will not press charges of assault against her.

"Am I supposed to be grateful?"

"You know very well they could have made it ugly for you. The whole neighborhood saw you jump on her and bang her head against the rejas."

"Did they also hear what she called me? ¿Y que me mentó la madre?"

"You were both angry—"

"That's no reason to be cursing people out. I went there to talk to her mother to mother."

"That's not what I heard."

They talk on her porch. From inside the house, lugubrious organ music announces the beginning of Ester's favorite show, a drama about a woman (blond) who is blinded by her rival (brunette) to eliminate her from competition for the affections of a rich and handsome landowner.

A neighbor goes by with a heavy bag of groceries in each hand. She stops halfway down the block, puts the bags down, takes a deep breath, rubs her hands against her hips, adjusts the grip on the shopping bags, and continues down the street, her sandals clapping against her heels.

"I'd better get going," Odilio Pagán suggests. América is not in the mood to talk. He crosses to his patrol car, seeks her eyes for a despedida, but she's lost somewhere else, he doesn't know where. He drives off down the street, flashing his lights at nothing in particular.

Across the street from América's house, the faithful enter the Iglesia Asambleas de Dios. Shrill electronic feedback announces the beginning of services. The familiar voice of Reverend Nuñez reverberates through the neighborhood. "Probando. Uno, dos, tres. ¿Se oye?" A chorus of yeses is heard through the microphone into the street. "Bienvenidos, hermanas y hermanos," Reverend Nuñez begins, and in a few minutes his melodic nasal voice is heard detailing God's goodness and Jesus' sacrifice.

América sits on her porch and listens. She's been attending his services from her front porch for four years now, rocking back and forth on the chair Correa gave her six Christmases ago. "Regalo de Santa Clós," he said, a proud smile on his face, his large even teeth shining as if he were a toothpaste commercial.

"I don't need any more furniture in the house," América told him, so he put it out on the porch, where it has remained, the shiny finish peeling off in spots where rain and sun in equal measure have soaked it. When the congregation begins to sing, América hums along to the familiar hymns, rocking back and forth, her bare feet touching and leaving the cold cement floor in rhythm to the promise of everlasting happiness.

On Tuesday Rosalinda steps from Correa's Jeep as if she were about to tread on quicksand instead of hard cement. América waits for her inside, not wanting to make a scene one way or the other, aware that neighbors are peeking to see what happens when Rosalinda is returned home. Correa tells her to wait for him while he gets her pack from the backseat. She stands with her back to the house, arms wrapped around the stuffed blue pelican Taino gave her. She seems taller to América, her hips more rounded, her back broader. She's wearing her hair away from her face in a French braid studded with white and yellow beads. From the back she looks womanly, but when she turns around and follows Correa up the walk to the porch steps, her face is that of a little girl in spite of all the makeup, the bright red lips, the lined eyes cast down as if she were embarrassed or afraid or both. América steps back to let them by. Behind her, Ester rushes forward, her arms toward Rosalinda.

"Don't ask me anything!" Rosalinda says, and she runs into

her room, slamming the door against them. Ester follows her, knocks softly.

"Let me in, nena. I want to hug you," she calls. There is no sound from Rosalinda's room.

"Well," says Correa, dropping Rosalinda's backpack at América's feet, "here we are." He goes to the refrigerator for a beer.

"Mami, leave her alone." América tugs Ester away from the shut door.

"She shouldn't act like that. We didn't do anything to her." Ester returns to the door and shakes the knob. "Come on out, Rosalinda." There's a thud as something strikes the inside of the door. Ester backs away.

"Mami, why don't you make us supper," América suggests, pulling Ester away from the door again, trying to maintain her composure, to control the rage that's threatening to erupt, to make her break the door down, to take her daughter by the hair and shake some respect into her.

Ester reluctantly moves to the kitchen. "She shouldn't be like that. You're letting her get away with it."

"Leave her alone, Mami," América says loud enough for Rosalinda to hear on her side of the door. She steps closer and yells into the crack between door and jamb. "Rosalinda, we're going to leave you alone, but we have to talk about this later." There's no response. "Did you hear me?" No sound.

"She didn't want to come back here," Correa says, pouring his beer into a frosted glass. "I had to convince her."

"Did she think Taino would take her with him to New York?" América responds, moving to the table, pulling a chair out, settling into it as if a great weight were pushing her down, down, down past the seat, into the ground, below it.

"She didn't want to be here," he says, looking at her as if she should know the reason. His green eyes are his best feature. Almond-shaped, hooded just enough to make a woman wonder what he's thinking. "I told her she had to come back and discuss the situation with you."

She wonders what he's really saying. Something tells her "the situation" is not the same for him as it is for her. Correa sits on the sofa facing her, leans against the corner, his legs open as if to display what's between them. She turns her gaze away.

"How come Odilio Pagán's been here twice in one week?" he asks casually, as if the answer didn't matter.

Her chest tightens. "The first time he came to tell me Yamila Valentín Saavedra reported me to the police." She feels his eyes on her, looking for a twitch, any movement that might betray a lie. She watches Ester in the kitchen, who looks at her out of the corner of her eye, guiltily, as if what América is saying carries some hidden meaning that Correa shouldn't catch. "The second time he came to tell me she wouldn't press charges. I guess that must have been part of the deal to let Taino go." She looks at him defiantly, but he simply returns her look, sips his beer, his eyes on hers, then drops his gaze to her bosom, to the deep crevice between her breasts. In spite of herself, she blushes.

Rosalinda cracks her door open. "Mami," she calls from the other side, her voice breaking in the same way as when she has hurt herself, or when she's afraid of thunder, or when she's confused. América runs to her daughter's door but doesn't open it, stands in front of it, waiting for Rosalinda to let her in.

When she's inside, Rosalinda shuts it, then throws herself in her mother's arms, presses her body against América as if trying to fuse into her.

"I'm sorry, Mami, I'm so sorry," Rosalinda cries into her mother's bosom, and América holds her close, crying into her hair that it's all right, it's okay, everything will be all right. They rock against each other, against the door, their tears mingling as if from one pair of eyes, one body.

Rosalinda holds on to América as if afraid her mother will leave her in the darkened room decorated with posters of half-naked singers and actors, their hair disheveled, their eyes wild. One male star offers himself, hips thrust forward aggressively, his thumbs pulling the waistband of his pants so low it doesn't take much imagination to imagine what comes next. The women display their breasts and buttocks in barely there tops and shorts crisscrossed with gold and silver chains.

América sighs deeply. "Ay, Rosalinda, what were you thinking?"

The child tenses in her arms, withdraws from her bosom as swiftly as she had thrown herself into it. She turns her back on América and plops on the bed, buries her face in the pillow.

"Leave me alone!"

"But nena, I'm trying to understand."

"You don't understand anything! Leave me alone."

"Rosalinda, don't yell at me like that. I'm your mother."

"You don't care about me. You're just worried about what people will say."

"I don't give a shit about other people. I'm trying to talk to you."

"Well, there's nothing to talk about. I don't want to talk about it. Now will you leave me alone, please?"

"No, I won't leave you alone! You can't run away with your boyfriend and expect me to forget about it. You owe me an explanation."

"I don't owe you anything!"

She can't stop her hand once it begins its arc toward her daughter's face, once it slaps her full in the mouth, the sound flat against her daughter's echoing scream. After the first slap, Rosalinda covers her face, climbs onto her bed, cowers in the corner as América climbs up after her, punches her against the corner where the wall and bed meet.

Ester comes running, followed by Correa, who separates them, holds América's hands down against her belly, drags, almost carries her out of the room, into her own bedroom, where he pushes her onto her bed, then backs out, closing the door behind him, leaving her there in darkness, facedown, sobbing with rage, beating her fists against the pillows, the mattress, the stuffed cat propped against the headboard. She scissors her legs as if swimming toward a distant shore. When she raises her head, there is nothing but blackness ahead. Her hands still smart from the blows to her daughter's face. She laces them behind her head and presses her face into the mattress, suffocates herself in her own hot breath. She's ashamed for herself, ashamed for Rosalinda, ashamed for all of them.

She lies in bed for a long time; she might have even fallen asleep, she's not sure. The room is stifling. The television is on in the living room, the house smells like fried chicken. She rises in the dark, stumbles to the door, switches on the light. The sudden brightness makes her eyes water, and she has to rub away the swelling, the gritty texture of salty tears on skin. She brushes her hair, blows her nose, tugs her wrinkled clothes around her body, smoothing the skirt at the hips, stretching the top so that it doesn't pull across her breasts. She turns out the light before opening the door.

Correa is lying on the couch, watching television. He looks up when she comes out, evaluates her as if she were new in town. Then he turns his attention back to whatever he's watching. She goes to the kitchen, and Ester comes out of her room, eyes clouded with liquor and some unmentionable pain that, try as she might, doesn't go away.

"There's rice and beans. I'll fry you up a drumstick if you like."

"That's all right. This is fine." América serves herself white rice, tops it with a ladleful of kidney beans.

"At least let me heat it for you." Ester tries to take the plate from América's hand.

"It's all right. I'll eat it like this."

"It's going to make you sick."

"I'm fine, Mami. Leave me alone."

Ester backs up, lets América go by, waits until she sits at the table.

"Do you want something to drink?"

"Is there any coffee?"

"I'll make some." She goes back to the kitchen, and América hears her puttering around.

She chews slowly and deliberately, as if each morsel contains some precious nutrient that must be savored, rolled around the tongue several times before swallowing or it will not have its curative effects. She stares straight ahead, her back to the kitchen. To her left, across the room, Correa is stretched out on the couch he bought, his couch, he reminds them if they ask him to move. She looks at the glass-fronted cupboard on the opposite wall, at the vajilla Correa gave her for her twenty-fifth birthday, fifty-two pieces of matching cups and saucers, plates and bowls, a covered soup urn. She only uses it on special occasions, because it's too delicate for every day.

Ester sets the steaming cup of black coffee in front of her. She brings another cup, creamed and sweetened, to Correa, who sits up, takes it, his eyes on the television, sips from it, not once acknowledging the hand that made and served it. Ester returns to the kitchen and comes back with a can of beer in one hand and a cup of coffee in the other. She sits across from América, blocking her view of the beautiful vajilla in the cupboard, and lights a cigarette, eyes on her daughter. América avoids looking at her. Of the fifty-two-piece vajilla, only a cup and saucer have broken. It happened one Three Kings' Day when Correa hired a group of musicians to serenade her. She foolishly took out her best to serve them coffee and sweet rice with coconut. The man who played the cuatro accidentally dropped both cup and saucer filled with fresh coffee on the tile floor. There were many apologies. She saved the pieces with the intention of putting them together with Krazy Glue, but the pieces never fit.

"Did Rosalinda eat anything?" she asks Ester.

"No, she didn't want to eat." Ester looks at her resentfully. She sips her beer, sets it down on the table, drags on her cigarette, sets it down on the ashtray, sips her coffee. "Do you want me to fry you up a leg?"

"No, I'm fine."

"You shouldn't eat cold food like that. It'll give you gas."

América gets up, scraping the chair against the tiles. She takes her plate to the sink, washes it, and sets it to dry on the rack. It looks like Correa will be spending the night. She dries her hands on the dishcloth hanging from the refrigerator handle, returns to the table to finish her coffee, her eyes on the incomplete vajilla, a gift from Correa.

Later, she lies in bed face up in the dark, dressed in a cotton nightgown she made herself. It's pale blue, with thin ribbons around the neckline and on the cap sleeves. It makes her feel like a princess. Its hem is a ruffle of lace, with tiny bows at intervals. It took a lot of work to tie those tiny bows, to then stitch them in one by one along the frilled hem.

The fan is on, but the door is closed, so it's hot air that flutters her clothes hanging against the walls like ghosts.

When Correa opens the door, a square of light crosses from one end of the room to the other, broken in the middle when he steps in and gently, quietly, closes the door behind him. She hears him take his clothes off, fold them in the dark, drop them on the chair next to the dresser. He's a cat. Doesn't need light to see. She tenses when his weight dips the edge of the bed, creaking the bedsprings. He lies quietly next to her, as if not to wake her. She waits until his hand finds hers, squeezes it. Her breath quickens, but she tries to control it, to not let him hear. He drags her hand across the sheet, up his right hip, onto the soft warm hair on his pubis. He leaves her hand there, crawls his own hand up to her breasts.

She rubs her fingers in the down, grabs his penis, massages it hard and upright. Correa moans, turns over, rolls up her princess nightgown until it's around her neck, but doesn't pull it off. He separates her legs with his, kisses her breasts, licks her nipples like a kitten lapping milk, then dives inside her. The first plunge always hurts, always feels as if he were tearing her insides. But she settles into the rhythm of his thrusting, rocking movements, and soon the bed is rattling. He kisses her mouth. His mustache tickles her lips, his lips press on hers, his tongue insinuates itself between her teeth. And she returns his kiss.

He kisses her neck, runs his fingers through her hair, squeezes her breasts against his chest. He kisses her cheeks, her forehead, rocks on her from side to side as if he were a ship and she a turbulent sea. Her eyes open to the darkness in the windowless room, and she lets herself go, catches his rhythm with her hips, bucks upward to bring him closer. She rubs his broad shoulders in tight circles, kisses his neck, his jaw, his temple, presses her legs together, squeezes his balls with her thighs. In the moment when her insides seem to catch on fire, she loves him, believes he loves her, receives the promises he mumbles into her ear as, with a forceful jab, he thrusts himself even deeper, then tenses and collapses, lies on top of her, his breath fanning her hair, tickling her ears.

Krazy Glue

~~~
❧❧❧❧❧❧❧❧❧❧❧❧❧❧❧❧❧❧❧❧❧❧❧❧❧❧❧❧❧
~~~

"Mami, you have to get up." América shakes Ester gently.
"Hhmm? What?" Ester moans, flails her hands as if she were dancing. She opens her eyes slowly, startles when she sees América leaning over her. "What happened?"

"You have to go to work, Mami," América whispers, and Ester lifts her head, pushes herself up on her elbows.

"It's not Tuesday, is it?"

"No, it's Wednesday. I have to stay home today, so you have to go."

Ester collapses on the bed again and rolls over. "All right." Within seconds she's fast asleep.

"Mami, you have to get up now. Come on." She jiggles Ester, who swats her with open palms as she would a bothersome fly. "I'm not going to stop until you get up."

Ester rolls over and gradually pushes herself to a sitting position with América's help. "¡Ay! Every bone in my body hurts." She fumbles in the dark for the light switch. "You should have told me last night. I would have gone to bed earlier." América draws open the curtains. Dim light creeps into the room. "It's still dark out!" Ester complains.

"It's cloudy, it will clear up before you get there." América looks around the room. "Where is your uniform?"

Ester points to a dresser under the window. She shuffles to the bathroom, the familiar hacking cough of her mornings punctuating every step.

Ester's room is crammed with relics. One wall is papered with family photographs. She calls this her wall of memories. The rest of the room is lined with shelves laden with figurines. In a corner, an ancient table holds the altar to Saint Lazarus, her patron saint, a votive candle at his feet, its phantasmal light flickering yellow red yellow.

The drawers are full of clothes Ester hasn't worn in years. Blouses and skirts that have gone out of style. Cotton brassieres that no longer fit. Dresses with the ruffles and flounces of a woman not afraid to flirt. In the bottom drawer, the green nylon uniform is folded on top of the dress Ester wore as the maid of honor at her sister's wedding a month before she ran away from home. América pulls the uniform out, presses at the wrinkles with her palms, and lays it at the foot of the bed, then goes to make breakfast.

"Just coffee," Ester says in between coughs as she goes by, "too early to eat."

América pours Ester a cup of coffee with heated milk and sugar. With the first sip, Ester's cough dissipates, and after the third or fourth gulp, it's almost completely gone. "My medicine," Ester calls her first cup of coffee. She moans and groans with every step, sighs loud enough for América to hear, takes her time undoing her curlers, combing out her hair, painting in her eyebrows and a black line around her eyes. In the kitchen América registers the muted protests but pretends she doesn't hear them. She puts her slices of bread in the toaster and leans against the counter sipping her black coffee, her thoughts racing ahead to the hour when Rosalinda wakes up. She's not sure what she will say to her. At least, she'll remind her she has to go to school.

Ester emerges from her room a different woman. Hair combed and sprayed, face made up, one could even call her beautiful, life's creases an adornment that highlight deep-set eyes, a fleshy mouth, a high brow. The uniform fits tight across her hips and buttocks, the apron tied around a waist smaller than América's. "You look great," América says.

Ester smiles, twirls in front of her. "Not bad for an old lady."

"Forty-five is not old, Mami."

"I was old when I was born," she responds.

América can't help herself. "If you'd take better care of your-self—"

"Stop with the sermon. I'm going."

She leaves the house but stops on the sidewalk in front to light a cigarette, her cough returning briefly after the first puff. She punches her chest to loosen the phlegm, spits into the gutter, and walks on, trailed by a curl of smoke.

Correa shambles out of the bedroom scratching his head. While he's taking a shower and shaving, América cooks up eggs and toast, fresh coffee. As she's serving, he comes up behind her, wraps his arms around her waist, kisses her hair.

"Deja eso," she mumbles, ducking out of his grasp.

He grabs her arm, pulls her, kisses her wetly on the lips. "You missed me, didn't you?" he whispers into her face. She turns away, steps out of his embrace.

"Your breakfast is getting cold." She carries the plate to the table, where she has already set up a mat, fork, knife, spoon. He watches her walk, smiles to himself, follows her. She brings him coffee, toast with butter. When she's close again, he grabs the waistband of her jeans.

"Stop that!" She tries to loosen his grip.

"Sit with me," he says, pulling her down on his lap.

"You can't eat with me sitting here."

"On the chair, then. Don't run away like you always do."

He lets her go, keeps his hand in her waistband until she sits next to him. She pulls the chair back so that she can't see his face, just the back of his neck, the fraying collar of his shirt, the dark crevice between his skull and ear. I hate you, she drills into his brain. He has big hands, wide and solid. He pushes the scrambled eggs onto the fork with a piece of toast, turns his head to look at her.

"Cat got your tongue?" he asks.

She tsks, shifts her gaze to the window. He burps delicately and goes on eating. The wall clock above the door tick tocks in between silence. América picks a loose thread from the fly of her jeans. Correa chews, and his ears move back and forth as if he were doing it on purpose. A rooster sings outside somewhere. The cup clinks against the saucer when he sets it down. A car drives by, spewing acrid fumes. Correa sneezes. "¡Salúd!" she says without thinking, claps her hands on her thighs, starts to get up. "I have things to do."

He turns and looks at her as if deciding whether to let her go, picks up the empty cup, hands it to her. "Bring me more coffee." She takes it, walks slowly, in case he changes his mind, her eyes focused on the coffeemaker in the kitchen, a gift from Correa last Christmas. Her hands trembling, she pours hot coffee, and a few drops fall on the tender space between her thumb and index finger. It burns, drips toward her wrist, but she barely feels it.

He goes home to change into his uniform. He has missed a week and a half at work. She wonders how he gets away with it, taking off whenever he feels like it, coming back as if nothing.

She opens all the windows and doors. Rosalinda's is still closed, and the couple of times América stands in front of it, she hears no sound. She tries the knob. It's locked. She sways around the living room humming a bolero, dusting everything in sight, spraying glass cleaner and furniture polish, wiping down each surface with long, even strokes. She puts the chairs on top of the table, rolls up the area rug in the living room and drags it out to the porch. She sweeps the room, mops it down, polishes it. Rosalinda's door is locked; no movement comes from the room. No sound.

She lifts figurines from the shelves next to the television, washes and dries each one, replaces them in new configurations. The shepherd playing the flute to a dancing lady now faces a gaggle of geese, the dancing lady flirts with a mother duck leading her ducklings. She takes down the curtains in the living room, kitchen, and from the sliding door that leads to the backyard. She sets them to wash in the machine, then deals with her room, leaving the door open so she can see when Rosalinda crosses to the bathroom.

She strips the bed, puts on fresh sheets, moves all her cosmetics from the windowsill, dusts and polishes the wood, wipes down each can, bottle, and jar with a cloth dipped in rubbing alcohol, places each with its companion products; hair spray with gel and mousse, cold cream with witch hazel and liquid face soap, tweezers with nail files, orange sticks, and emery boards. Rosalinda's door squeaks. América is sitting on the edge of her bed relacing a sneaker so the ends will be even when her daughter walks by to the bathroom without looking at her.

"I just made you some breakfast," she calls from the kitchen when Rosalinda comes out.

"I'm not hungry."

América puts a plate of scrambled eggs and ham on the table, a cup of steaming café con leche, toast. "Come and eat something. You didn't have dinner last night." But Rosalinda has gone into her room and locked the door. América knocks gently. "Nena, your eggs will get cold."

Rosalinda opens the door but doesn't come out. "I said I'm not hungry. I don't want anything right now."

"I already made it."

Rosalinda peers suspiciously past her mother at the table set with a place mat, her breakfast served on the good vajilla. América follows her look. "I was washing everything out," she chuckles, "and thought, might as well use it."

Rosalinda steps around her to the table, sits, picks at the food. When did she get this sullen? América doesn't remember this look on her daughter's face, this world-weary, nothing-can-please-me air. It must be new. Or maybe it's that she's not wearing makeup, and her features even out, so that every expression plays across her face, without the distraction of highlights or shadows.

"I thought we might talk a bit . . . "

Rosalinda slams her fork on the table, gets up, but América, faster than she is, blocks her path.

"I don't want to talk about it! I told you that."

América holds her by the shoulders, squeezes them so that Rosalinda won't shake loose. "It's not going away because you don't want to talk about it. I have some things to say, and you have to listen."

Tears stream down Rosalinda's face. "I don't have to listen, I don't." She covers her ears, closes her eyes as if that would make América disappear. She squirms, trying to release América's grip.

"I'll let you go if you sit down and talk to me." She doesn't want to sound angry, is in fact trying hard to stay calm, controlled, to not lose her temper the way she did last night. She relaxes her grip on Rosalinda's shoulder, and the girl pulls herself away, slumps on the chair in front of her half-eaten eggs and toast. She hides her face in her hands and sobs.

América's chest tenses, as if a strap were tied around her ribs, tightening with each breath. Tears sting her eyes, but she blinks them back. Gingerly, as if she might break, she touches Rosalinda's shoulder, and the child pulls it away but then relents, lets América caress her shoulders, her hair. Lets her embrace her, at first grudgingly, but then gratefully, as if it were this she'd been seeking all along. América helps Rosalinda stand up, leads her to the couch, where they sit next to each other, Rosalinda's face pressed against her mother's chest. América lets her cry, lets her own tears fall quietly, as if not to contaminate Rosalinda's misery.

"I don't know why you're all making such a big deal about it," Rosalinda whimpers to her mother. "I'm not the first one around here to run away at fourteen."

"You're being disrespectful," América warns.

"But it's true, Mami," she says.

América takes a deep breath, trying to control the rage that boils inside her, threatens to spill out and burn both of them. "It's true, but that doesn't mean it's right."

Rosalinda considers this for a moment, looking at the shiny, polished furniture her father has bought, at the figurines Ester collects.

"Taino and I love each other."

"Are you pregnant?"

Rosalinda shifts her gaze.

"Because if you're pregnant," América continues, "we should do something about it."

Rosalinda's eyes widen, stare at América as if she's lost her mind. "Do you mean . . ." She buries her face in her hands. "Oh, my God, Mami, how can you even think such a thing!"

América is not sure if Rosalinda means a pregnancy or an abortion. She blushes. If she were pregnant, she'd never consider an abortion, but then, she has been smart enough to use contraception for the past thirteen years.

"Did he . . . protect you?"

Rosalinda stands up. "I can't talk to you!" she screams, and runs into her room, slamming the door.

"Rosalinda, this is important!" She hears the plop on the bed, the screaming sobs. She bangs on the door. "Do you think it'll go away? I have news for you. It doesn't!"

Rosalinda screams even louder, bangs on her bed. "Leave me alone. I want you to leave me alone."

"Well, it's not going to happen. As long as I'm your mother, I'm a part of your life. So get used to it."

Rosalinda opens the door just enough for América to see her face distorted into an angry grimace. "No, I don't have to get used to it. Papi said he'd take me away from here if I want to go. I hate you. I can't stand to be around you anymore."

América freezes. Rosalinda's door slams again. Correa has never threatened to take her daughter away. Through all the years of arguments, the beatings, the jealousies, the you can't do this and you can't do that, he's never once threatened to take Rosalinda away from her.

She clears Rosalinda's abandoned breakfast. Correa has three children in Fajardo with a woman he married because her father threatened him with a gun if he didn't. He supports them with his meager pay and with whatever extra money he earns doing odd jobs for the mansion owners. He's never contributed much toward Rosalinda's support, except for the gifts he gives her on special occasions, trinkets and clothes he picks out when he visits Puerto Rico. He gives Rosalinda spending money every so often, but that's it. América has paid for everything else, for her school uniforms and everyday clothes, her schoolbooks, the birthday presents for her friends, the Christmas presents for her teachers. She has paid the doctors when Rosalinda was sick, the dentist when she had a tooth out, the surgeon when she got appendicitis. Correa claims Rosalinda is his favorite child, the first child he ever fathered, the fruit of his and América's love. He puts it just like that, "the fruit of our love." But he's never taken responsibility for her upbringing, has left the parenting up to América because "She's a girl and you're a girl, and girls need their mothers." What business does he now have offering to take her away?

He must see a chance to be a hero, América thinks. Now that Rosalinda is so rebellious, Correa must see it as his opportunity to gain stature in his daughter's eyes. That must be it. Big macho father, saving his little girl from her mean mother. Son of a bitch! She slams the plate from the beautiful vajilla on the tile floor. It shatters into a million bits, too many to be put together again with Krazy Glue.

It's Not Forever

By the time Ester comes home from work, there is nothing left to clean. Even the porch steps have been scrubbed and polished, the spiders routed from their corners along the eaves. A potful of bone soup with plantain dumplings simmers on the stove.

"I missed my novela," Ester whines when she comes in, as if missing one episode of her favorite afternoon soap opera made a difference.

She grabs a beer on her way to change clothes. Doesn't even notice América's somber expression. When she comes out in a pair of shorts and T-shirt with no bra, she plops in front of the television and surfs channels until she finds the one she wants. América, sitting on Correa's couch, doesn't move from her place until a woman appears on the screen, her mascaraed eyes dripping with tears that a mustached man is kissing away with great tenderness. Ester sighs. América gets up and leaves the room, sits on the porch rocking back and forth, waiting for Correa.

He brings a loaf of fresh bread and his dirty clothes stuffed inside a duffel bag. He tries to kiss her when he comes in, but she ducks, takes his clothes, and goes to the kitchen to serve supper. As soon as she sees him, Ester turns off the television and burrows into her room, acknowledging his role as master of the house, even though the house belongs to her. Correa stretches out on his couch, flips to his channel, and waits for América to call him to the table.

"Aren't we eating together?" he asks when she sets only one place.

"Rosalinda hasn't been out of her room since this morning," she answers.

His face darkens. "Set the table for all of us," he snarls in her direction as he strides to his daughter's door and bangs on it. "Rosalinda, come out of there and have supper with us."

"I'm not hungry!"

"I don't care if you're hungry or not. Come out and sit with your mother and me."

A lot of shuffling and sniffling. "I'll be right there."

Correa looks at América triumphantly. She gives him a dirty look, sets the table, calls Ester. "Are you eating with us, Mami?"

"No, I'll eat later."

Rosalinda has made up her red and swollen eyes, has blushed her cheeks, has brushed her hair into a loose ponytail. Correa stares at her with a severe expression as she scuffs her way to the table, taking her sweet time about it. Correa points to the place next to him, so that she's sitting between him and América, trapped against the glass-fronted cupboard.

América serves the soup in the tureen from the vajilla, and Correa looks at her quizzically. She ladles soup into their bowls, giving him the bone with the most meat.

"Where's the bread?"

"It's warming in the oven."

Rosalinda stares into her soup. América sets the crusty bread in the middle of the table. Correa rips up a chunk, passes it to América, then another to Rosalinda, who ignores it. "Take it!" he growls, and she does, setting it on her plate. He puts a piece in his mouth and watches his daughter as he chews, as if considering what to do or say next. She doesn't budge. Her eyes cast on the pattern the noodles make at the bottom of her bowl, Rosalinda is as imperturbable as a cemí. Correa studies her for a minute, tries to meet América's eyes, shakes his head. América avoids his gaze, sips her soup delicately. The only sound is Correa's chewing, his restless body making the chair creak and groan with every twitch. He takes a few spoonfuls of soup, looks at the two females in front of him, one as still as a stone, the other avoiding his gaze at all costs. He slams his hand down, pushes his chair sprawling behind him.

"Maldito sea," he bellows, "a man can get indigestion eating with you two!" América freezes, Rosalinda looks up fearfully but doesn't move. Correa studies them for a moment, considering their alarmed expressions. He shakes his head as if refusing to listen to some internal voice, then strides out of the house, climbs into his Jeep, and is gone.

América and Rosalinda exchange a look of relief. The girl picks up her spoon, fills it with the steaming broth, and blows on it quietly, as if she were whispering a secret only the spoon can hear. América resumes her eating. Ester shuffles in chuckling, a bowl and spoon in her hand.

"You really know how to push his buttons," she laughs in between spoonfuls. "It's remarkable how well you both do that."

América and Rosalinda look at each other. For the first time in days, América sees the tiniest smile flicker across her daughter's face.

The next morning, when América comes out to make breakfast, Rosalinda is in her school uniform, sitting at the table, reading a thick history book as if she were posing for a picture.

"I already made the coffee," she says.

América goes to wash up. She hates it when Ester or Rosalinda or Correa disrupt her morning routine. She likes to make the coffee. Ester makes it too strong and Rosalinda too weak. She likes having the house to herself while she dresses, sips her coffee, and eats her toast as she does her hair and applies makeup. It is her quiet time, and it throws her off when her day begins with conversation or a variation from her morning dance between bedroom, kitchen, and bathroom.

"I should probably send a note for your teachers," she offers on her way back.

Rosalinda winces. "I think the whole island knows why I was gone."

"Let me know if they need one."

She goes into her room to dress. It's a good sign that Rosalinda is going back to school without being told. América was not looking forward to another battle with her today. But her stomach churns and her face flushes when she imagines Rosalinda facing her schoolmates, some of them wearing her clothes and jewelry. Some of them will avoid her, will whisper behind their hands at the girls next to them, all the while looking slyly in Rosalinda's direction. They will make comments about Taino, will ask about him in front of her, will drop his name in conversation when she can hear it. The teachers will try to be kind, will pretend nothing has happened because, when a girl runs away with her boyfriend, it's a family matter, not the school's. Rosalinda will be estranged from everyone she knows, will be a subject for gossip, will be teased, ostracized. América imagines her standing alone in the school yard, surrounded by a horde of snickering teenage girls, boys making lewd gestures, teachers looking the other way. América's whole body shakes. She comes out of her room, nervously wrapping a scrunchy around her ponytail.

"Do you want me to come to school with you?" América asks, her voice quivering. Rosalinda stares at her as if she were crazy.

"No!"

"But nena—"

"They will laugh at me if I show up with my mother."

They will laugh at them both. América remembers how her friends avoided her after she came back with Correa, how women pulled their daughters' hands, looked in the other direction if they saw her coming, her belly a symbol of all that could go wrong with their daughters. A fourteen-year-old girl who should be in her school uniform, pregnant! She heard them talk about her and Ester. They called Ester a descuidada because she couldn't prevent her daughter from running away with a man.

They said all the women in her family were loose. That there had never been, in their memory, a husband in that family of hers, only babies, girls bringing up girls, never any boys, never any men. She heard all this after her metida de pata. It's only after you make a mistake that people point to its inevitability.

"You're being very brave," she says to Rosalinda, and she looks up from her book.

"What?"

"Going back to school. Going on with your life. It takes a lot of courage to do that."

"What choice do I have?"

"Rosalinda, I'm giving you a compliment, not trying to start a fight."

"But it's one of those left-handed compliments, like you mean something else."

"I didn't mean anything other than what I said. It's not going to be easy for you to go back to school today."

"Well, you can't go with me."

"That's not why I'm saying it!" She can't check the exasperation in her voice. "Look, if you need me, you know where I'll be."

"Yeah, I know where you'll be." Rosalinda turns the page of her book, as if she'd been reading all this time instead of staring at her mother wishing she'd disappear.

América walks to La Casa del Francés. She feels like crying and slaps her side, as if to bring her attention elsewhere but inside her head, where words and looks and memories lurk like worms in compost, hidden in the darkness until one little scratch sends them squirming to the surface.

When she returns home from work that afternoon, Correa and Rosalinda are sitting on his couch side by side, talking. As she comes in, they fall silent, not bothering to disguise that they're doing it on her account. As usual when Correa is around, Ester is nowhere to be seen. América crosses to change clothes, and Rosalinda disappears into her room. Correa follows América into the bedroom. He throws himself face up on her bed, head on the stuffed animal leaning against the headboard.

"Don't squish my cat," she says, pulling it from under him.

"You love that cat more than you love me," he teases her, with a hint of resentment.

She fluffs it up, props it on her dresser.

"What were you and Rosalinda talking about when I came in?"

He sighs, looks at the ceiling. "She wants to go live with Tía Estrella and Prima Fefa."

"In Fajardo?"

"That's where they live."

"Well, she can't." She makes it sound as if Correa has no say in the matter.

"I told her you'd never agree to it."

"That's not what she said to me."

He sits up, leans on one elbow. "It's probably good for her to get away from here for a while."

"Since when do you know what's good for her and what isn't?"

"I'm her father."

She has many responses to that statement, all of them starting with *what kind of a father . . .* , but restrains herself. When Correa is this calm, this controlled, he's waiting for any little thing she might say or do that will make him explode, that will make it her fault if she ends up bruised and swollen.

"This is her home. She should stay with us. We can keep an eye on her."

"That's just it. She says you don't trust her now, and that you and Ester are always spying to see what she's up to. She wants to be where people are not always reminding her of what she and Taino did."

A white-hot fury races up her spine to the top of her head, setting her on fire. She can't breathe, is suffocated by a savage sorrow that gnaws at her from deep inside her womb. She turns away from him, grabs the bedpost as if it will ground her, will keep her from being consumed into ashes. There is nothing she can say or do that will keep this from happening. The elopement with Taino is the event around which everything in Rosalinda's life will now turn, for which there are no right answers, no right feelings, no right course. It is the anger that makes her cry, the knowledge that she's lost her daughter, the certainty that Correa will take her away even if América doesn't give her permission to go. He will show América quién manda, even in her house. If she resists, he will bruise and batter her. He will call her names and make Rosalinda hate her more than she does now. Her helplessness is enraging. América doesn't want to give in, can't give in one more time to Correa. But her fear of his hard fists tempers her fury, and she leans into the bedpost, sobbing, wishing she had been born a man and could fight him and have a chance at winning.

Correa tries to touch her, one of those times when her tears makes him tender. She shakes him off, grunts at him, pushes ineffectually against him, all the time shielding her face from his kiss or his fist, whichever comes.

"It's not forever, América." He tries to reassure her with a lie. "Just let her have some time away from here. She'll be back in a couple of months."

She wails from the depths of herself, as if the pain she's feeling is not just the pain of losing her daughter. As if she were crying for herself, for the day she was lost to her mother, and for the day Ester was lost to hers, and for all those women in her family going back countless generations, daughters who run away from their mothers as soon as their breasts grow and the heat between their legs becomes insupportable. Mothers who look at their daughters with resentment, seeing in them their own betrayal as if it were avoidable, as if a nameless, faceless prick dangling between hairy legs were not waiting around the darkest corners of each of their lives.

América cries and Correa stands impotent by her, unable to comfort or nourish her, hulking over her like an insult. He's silenced by her grief, a sorrow he can never know, nor tries to understand, nor can.

Distant Thunder

She wakes up at ten minutes to three in the morning, sweating and gasping for air. She's alone in her windowless room but doesn't remember going to bed. She stumbles in the dark to the door and opens it, gulps fresh air into her lungs. Her heart is racing, and she leans against the doorjamb, eyes closed, listening to the pounding in her ears. When it has diminished and her heart regains its normal rhythm, she walks to the back door, slides it open, and barefoot, steps onto the wet grass. Her nightgown captures the cool night air, flutters around her knees as if kissing them. She fluffs her hair, pulls it up, then lets it cascade around her shoulders. A soothing breeze dries off the sweat at the back of her neck, behind her ears.

The air is fragrant with Ester's herbs, which are planted along narrow paths or on raised beds lined with logs and rocks. Pigeon-pea bushes grow along the fence. Two lemon trees reach their spiny branches into the neighbor's yard. Every bush, plant, and vine is edible, or useful in treating burns, headache, or stomach upset.

At the far end of the garden, chickens cluck softly inside their coop, questioning who's walking around this time of night. Four houses away, Nilda's dog barks a warning, then settles, satisfied that no one is invading his territory. América sits on a rusty wrought-iron bench that once stood under a mango tree. The tree was felled by Hurricane Hugo, and when its remains were taken away, Ester put the bench next to the cut-off trunk as if expecting it to sprout branches and take the place of its bro-ken-down parent.

"What are you doing out here?" Ester's voice is a hoarse whisper.

América jumps in her seat. "Ay, Mami, you scared me!"

"How do you think I felt when I heard someone walking around?"

"It never occurred to me. You always sleep so soundly."

"Not tonight," she says resentfully.

"It was so hot in my room," América apologizes.

"You'll get sick, out in el sereno without a robe . . . and you're barefoot!"

América pulls her damp feet up on the bench and sits with her arms wrapped around her knees. Ester rummages in the pockets of her robe and comes up with a crumpled box of ciga-rettes and a lighter.

"Another couple of days and it will be full," she observes, pointing at the moon with her cigarette.

It's a clear night. The dark blue sky is sequined with diamond sparklers. From time to time the sky flashes red, a dull thud is heard, and the ground trembles. Somewhere off the eastern shore of the island, the Navy is using the beaches for target practice.

"What time did Correa leave?" América asks.

"He left early. Didn't even have supper."

"Did Rosalinda eat?"

"She wouldn't come out of her room. I left a plate of rice and beans in front of her door and told her it was there. She opened it just wide enough to get the food." Ester chuckles.

América smiles, shakes her head. "Was I like this when I was her age?" she asks.

"You had just turned fourteen when you . . ." Ester draws an invisible image on the ground with the toe of her slipper. "You were never as rude as Rosalinda is," she concludes, taking a long drag from her cigarette.

América is silenced by guilt. She tries to remember herself at fourteen. She was not deliberately trying to hurt her mother when she ran home from school, tore off her uniform, changed into shorts and a T-shirt, put on makeup, brushed her hair, then sat on the porch with a schoolbook. She was not thinking of Ester when she pretended to do her homework and waited to be noticed by Correa, whose job it was to guide the bulldozer that dug the trench for the sewer pipes in front of the house.

América sighs. I was so willing to be seduced, she remembers with amazement. As willing, I suppose, as Rosalinda. She's so used to anger when she thinks of her daughter that it surprises her when she's filled with pity. She looks at Ester, who is absently blowing smoke rings toward the moon. She too was fourteen once, let a man seduce her, returned to this very house when América's father abandoned them. Did Ester, when América ran away fourteen years later, stand in el sereno in the middle of the night with her mother, Inés, wondering what to do about her?

"Rosalinda wants to live with Correa's aunt in Fajardo." América says, a catch in her voice.

"Are you letting her?" Ester's tone says she certainly wouldn't allow such a thing.

"I don't have a choice. Correa already gave his permission." She hates herself for sounding so defensive, so childlike.

Ester compresses her lips. "Ese hombre," she starts, as if calling him "that man" explains everything about him.

"His aunt is a good woman," América interrupts, not giving Ester a chance to say more about Correa. "She's old, though. I don't know if she can handle a teenager. Rosalinda will run all over her." Like she runs over us, she thinks but doesn't say.

"You're not going to let him take her, just like that?" Ester's voice drips with contempt for América's weakness.

América hugs her knees tighter to her chest, drops her eyes to a dark corner of the fragrant garden, feels more than hears the bomb exploding on the distant beach, the trembling of the ground beneath her.

"I don't know what else to do," she says in a voice so soft she's sure Ester hasn't heard. She looks at her mother, who has gone back to blowing smoke rings at the moon with a calm that América finds eerie because of its contrast to her own inner turmoil.

"Why don't you send her to Paulina?"

"To New York?" Ester could as easily have suggested she send Rosalinda to China, and América would have responded with the same astonishment, the same trembling fear of the distance between Vieques and anywhere else in the world farther than Puerto Rico, which seems far away enough.

"At least she would be with our family."

A family whose smiling faces adorn Ester's wall of memories in a chronological sequence of photographic greeting cards with "Merry Christmas from the Ortiz Family" printed at the bottom. Ester's sister, Paulina, moved to New York a week after her wedding. She writes, sends clothes, gifts, sometimes even money. The whole family visits Vieques on infrequent vacations. They all speak Spanish with an accent and sometimes use English words that they make into Spanish by adding an o or an a. Paulina used the word liqueo to tell Ester the faucet had a leak.

"Rosalinda doesn't speak English," América says as if that were the only consideration, and Ester doesn't respond. In the silence, América hears herself say the real reason why she won't consider sending Rosalinda to New York. "Correa will never let her go."

Ester takes one final drag from her cigarette, drops and steps on the stub. She grinds it into the dirt fiercely, until América thinks she's made a hole deep enough to bury much more than a cigarette stub.

"He doesn't have to know," Ester says quietly, as if testing the sound of her own voice. América drops her feet onto the damp ground, seeks her mother's eyes. But Ester has turned away, and América is faced with the grotesque shape created by the pink foam rollers on Ester's head.

"Mami, he's her father. I can't send her away without telling him." She tries to leave all emotion out of her voice, so that it doesn't sound like an excuse, so that she doesn't have to hear Ester's contempt again. But Ester is silent. "And who knows what he would do to me," she adds, unable to hide the tremor in her voice. Ester still doesn't say a word. She stares at the almost full moon as if it held the answer. She's so still and silent that América thinks she's fallen asleep on her feet.

Finally, Ester takes a deep breath through her mouth, as if she were still smoking. "You should go with her," she says.

"Are you crazy? What am I going to do in New York?" América's hands shake, and her body breaks out in a fine sweat, like dew on a blossom.

"The same thing you do here. Irving knows people."

"What does he have to do with this? Have you been talking to him about me?"

Ester looks guiltily away. "He asks, I answer. Sometimes he makes suggestions." She rummages again in her robe, pulls out the crumpled box of cigarettes, lights one with unsteady hands. "Correa doesn't have to know where you are. No one will tell him."

But América is so focused on an image of Ester and Don Irving drinking, smoking, and discussing her and Correa that she hasn't heard. She stands up close to her mother, anger replacing fear.

"My life is none of your business," she hisses, "and I wish you'd stay out of it."

Ester won't look at her. She turns on her heel and walks back into the house saying something América doesn't hear.

América stares after her mother's slender figure, the lit cigarette a punctuation against the shadows of the garden. Fights with her are unsatisfying, because they usually end with Ester walking away, mumbling to herself. Having stoked her anger in preparation for a quarrel, América is left smoldering to think of different ways of saying the same thing: It's my life, stay out of it.

But even as she mutters that Ester is no great example of how one should lead one's life, even as she discounts the message because the messenger is unreliable, América feels the weight of Ester's concern. My life is not really mine, she tells herself. Correa rules every action I take, whether he's around or not. Is that any way to live?

She can't answer the question. It is the only life she's known. The first fourteen years of her life centered around Ester and her demands as a mother. The second half of her life has been shadowed by Correa. Is that any way to live, she asks herself again but is afraid to answer. The question hangs in the fragrant air of her mother's garden, punctuated by the flashing red sky, the thumps of bombs finding their target, the yielding earth quaking beneath her feet.

"I'm taking you out tonight," Correa announces the next evening.

"Why?"

"I can't take my woman out if I want to?" He smiles as if he were teasing, which América knows he's not.

"I have to work tomorrow."

"I know, but I want to go out, and I want you with me. Come on, don't make me beg." He catches a stray curl from her hair and twirls it around his finger. "Go get pretty for me."

This is the Correa she loves. The man with the soft touch, who speaks softly, who finds beauty in a curl along her neck. When he's like this, she's again the fourteen-year-old girl willing to be seduced.

She's already showered and changed out of her uniform, has eaten dinner, has argued with Rosalinda to come out of her room to eat something and lost. She was looking forward to a quiet evening to make up for the past couple of nights.

"I don't want to stay out late," she tells Correa as she goes into her room to change. In the kitchen, Ester bangs a lid hard on a pot.

She chooses a dress she's worn only a few times. It's green, with a contrasting print scarf that pins to the back of the collar and comes around to a low-cut V in front, where she ties it into a bow held with a brooch. She pins up and sprays her hair, applies makeup, and dabs on White Shoulders cologne. The preparations put her in a good mood. She enjoys making herself pretty, selecting and putting on the few nice pieces of jewelry she owns. The cloud of perfume in which she walks feels real, like a tulle cloak. When she comes out, Correa is sitting stiffly on the edge of the couch so as not to wrinkle his freshly pressed pants and shirt. He stands up, whistles his appreciation, wraps his arm around her waist, kisses her cheek. América smiles shyly, avoiding Ester's sullen looks from the kitchen.

Correa knocks on Rosalinda's door.

"Rosalinda, come out and look at your mother." His voice bounces against the concrete walls, so that Rosalinda would have to be dead not to hear it.

"Leave her alone," América says, afraid that, given Rosalinda's shifting moods, the evening will end in another argument. Now that she has made the effort to forget her problems for a night, she wants to forget them, not face them on the way out. But Rosalinda's door opens, and she actually walks into the room and eyes her mother admiringly, as if the past few days had never happened. "You look nice," she offers, and backs into her room again, so that América believes that she and Correa planned this moment to soften her up for something else. The thought dampens the joy she was beginning to feel.

"All right, baby," Correa whispers into América's ear, "let's go."

He steers her with a light touch on her lower back, opens the gate, lets her go ahead, places himself, gentlemanlike, on the curb side of the sidewalk. Once on the street, she brushes her suspicions of Correa's motives aside and lets herself savor the soft evening air, her pretty clothes, the sense of going somewhere other than work or home.

It's Saturday night. Down the street, couples stroll hand in hand toward the beach, which is two blocks away. From squat cinderblock buildings, passionate ministers and their congregations broadcast salvation through tinny loudspeakers. On the street, nonbelievers gamble with their souls and head towards El Malecón, where drinking, dancing, and sex on the beach are commonplace.

As América and Correa join the groups heading toward the

beach, they greet neighbors and acquaintances. She's proud of what a handsome couple they make. Many of the women greeting her so amicably would gladly exchange places with her. And she knows that many of the men escorting their wives and girlfriends would pursue her if she weren't already taken. She smiles her guarded smiles, lets Correa hold her tighter around the waist when they reach the main road.

Almost every bar on the beach is playing loud music. At Bananas, the tourists accompany their hamburgers and french fries with frosty piña coladas. A group of teenagers grunt and growl at a video arcade in back of the restaurant, while their parents eye the locals parading up and down the boardwalk. Across the street, at the Fisherman's Cooperative, the music is traditional Puerto Rican salsa. The narrow dance floor being full, the dancers have taken to the street, where they perform intricate arm combinations without missing a step or losing the rhythm. América's feet itch to dance. She presses closer to Correa.

"It's too crowded here," he says and pulls her along toward El Quenepo. He likes to check out the action before committing, so they walk up the road, stopping here and there for a few minutes, looking to see who's around and what kind of music is playing.

Even though she knows better, it seems as if the whole town is out on the narrow road, eating, drinking, dancing. The tourists seem delighted with all the activity, as if Saturday night in Esperanza were a show put on exclusively for their enjoyment. They watch the dancers twirl and come together in complicated routines that appear rehearsed, and clap appreciatively at the more flamboyant couples. A tourist wearing baggy pants and a sleeveless shirt videotapes Maribel Martinez being led by her husband, Carlos. She's quite pregnant, but it doesn't seem to bother her. She's light on her feet, and graceful as a palm frond. When they dance close, she wraps her arms around Carlos's neck, and he places his hands on the sides of her belly and rubs tenderly.

Around the corner from the dive shop, musicians are setting

up instruments at PeeWee's Pub. In the meanwhile, huge speakers vibrate with merengues.

"We'll go there when the live music starts," Correa tells América and guides her across the street, to La Copa de Oro, where another stereo plays a different merengue full blast. The place is small, crowded with tables spilling into an open-air dance floor. At a corner table, a group of people wave them over, and Correa leads América in that direction. On either side of them people smile and say hello, until América feels like a visiting dignitary.

"Buenas noches, compadre," one of the men greets Correa, with a handshake and a pat on the shoulder. The other men rise and shake his hand, nod at América, who shakes hands with the women at the table. Chairs are found for them, and Correa and América sit side by side, his arm over the back of her chair. The music is so loud that conversation is impossible, so América and the women compliment one another's clothes and jewelry with gestures and glances. As soon as the waitress takes their orders, everyone at the table pairs up and joins the dancers.

It is a merengue about a man whose wife went to New York and now that she's back, she won't do his laundry, won't cook his meals, and won't have sex with him unless he speaks to her in English. "Ay, pero ay no spik," the singer tells his wife, who responds, "Geev eet tú mí, beybee."

Correa is a good dancer, loose-limbed and creative. He holds her firmly enough so she knows who's leading, but not so tight that she has no room to turn. He looks at her while they dance, which she finds incredibly romantic, as if they were the only two people in the place. A half smile on his lips, he guides her between other couples, from one end of the dance floor to the other, his hips marking the rhythm against hers, separating only slightly as he folds her in and out of his arms in complex turns. The heat of his body against hers is exciting, and her eyes glisten with happiness and desire. She feels eyes on them, the envious glances of women whose partners are neither as good-looking nor as agile as Correa, the

veiled admiration of men who glance at her sinuous hips form-
ing a figure-eight against his. She returns her gaze to his eyes,
shadowed in the dim light.

"Who were you looking at?" he whispers in her ear, and
even though the music is deafening, she hears him.

"No one," she replies, tensing in spite of herself.

She feels the distance between them grow, even though he
hasn't let go of her, even though they dance as if the exchange
hadn't taken place.

Correa has slapped her in public if he thinks she's flirting, so
she narrows her gaze to him, to the Brut-scented space he occu-
pies. It is a small space, even though he's a big man.

They stay at La Copa de Oro for a few numbers, then walk
across the street, to the live band at PeeWee's Pub. He orders
rum and Cokes for himself, plain iced Cokes for her, because he
doesn't like her to drink liquor.

The place is so crowded that it's difficult to dance, so they
listen to the band for a while, then return to the boardwalk. His
step is heavier than it was at the beginning of the evening,
when his head was unclouded by rum. But the sea air seems to
restore him. He jokes with passersby, greets his friends' women
with exaggerated courtesy and respect, as if to demonstrate how
a woman should be treated. América hangs back as he glad-
hands everyone like a politician on election day. She's a gray
and sober shadow at his side. The joy and freedom she felt at the
start of the evening has dimmed with his scrutiny of everyone
she talks to, looks at, or comments upon. She avoids eye contact
with men, even those she knows well, like Feto and Tomás, who
are also out on the boardwalk.

"I'm tired," she tells him in a quiet moment. "Let's go
home."

"It's not even midnight yet," he says, looking at his watch.
He pulls her closer, kisses her hair. "What's the matter, aren't
you having fun?"

She pulls away from him. "I have to work tomorrow."

"Don't worry," he says, "I won't keep you up all night." He
slaps her rear smartly.

As they turn a corner to check out the action at Eddy's, they meet Odilio Pagán on his way out. Correa pulls América closer, a move not lost on Pagán, who veils his dislike of Correa behind a cordial greeting.

"How is Rosalinda doing?" he asks, looking at América.

"Everyone's fine," answers Correa before América opens her mouth.

"Good," responds Pagán with a terse smile.

They part in opposite directions, wishing one another a good evening, but as soon as Pagán turns the corner, Correa makes América face him.

"I don't want him coming around the house when I'm not there," he warns.

"It's not like he comes around all the time," she responds, sullenly, forgetting for an instant that Correa doesn't like her to talk back. She feels the slap before she sees his hand, has barely enough time to realize she's let down her guard before another slap crosses her face from the opposite direction.

"Don't you talk back to me," he snarls. "You listen. I don't want that maricón coming around the house anymore."

She nods silently, holding her face in her hands as if to create a barrier between it and his fingers.

"Are you all right?" he asks, pulling her hands away, kissing them, kissing the red and painful cheeks. "You know I love you, don't you?" he mutters, holding her close. "Don't you?" he insists. She doesn't respond. He draws her to the shadows beyond Eddy's, where the couples coming in and out of the bar can't see them. "I wanted this to be a nice night for you, América. I didn't want to fight." He sounds truly contrite, even though he hasn't asked her to forgive him. She feels herself softening. "Sometimes," he says, "I forget myself. But that's because I love you so much." It's the same as always, not quite an apology, but an excuse. "And I know you love me, don't you, baby?" he asks, but she doesn't respond. "Don't you?" he insists, and she has to nod, because she's afraid of what he will do if she doesn't. He kisses her on the lips, rubs himself against her, guides her hands to the bulge between his legs. "See what you do to me?" he asks, and she nods. "Come on," he whispers hoarsely, "let's go home."

She lets him guide her, his arm tight around her waist. Every so often he stops her in the dark shadows of a breadfruit or mango tree to kiss and fondle her. And she lets him, and tries to remember when her responses to his caresses were not defensive but a demonstration of the love she knows she once felt.

The next day, when América returns from work, Rosalinda is secluded in her room. América wonders what she does in there for hours at a time. Certainly not homework. Rosalinda has never been that dedicated a student.

Ester has gone to spend the night with Don Irving. Without the constant drone of the television, the only sounds are the hens clucking in the backyard and the steady hum of the refrigerator.

Rosalinda's door opens. América looks up from the hem she's been stitching.

"Mami, I'd like to talk to you." Rosalinda stands before her mother, hands clasped behind her back, as childlike and vulnerable as América would like to believe she is. "I don't want to fight with you anymore," she says softly, so that América's heart fills.

"Okéi." she sets down her sewing basket, is about to push up and embrace her daughter.

"I want to live in Fajardo with Tía Estrella and Prima Fefa."

That again, América thinks, but she bites her lips so that she won't say it. She settles back on the couch. "Why?" she asks and immediately knows it's the wrong question because her daughter's face hardens.

"It's not that I don't love you," Rosalinda concedes, as if she's rehearsed it. "It's just that, I don't feel right in school. Everyone's calling me names and stuff—"

"Everyone who?"

Rosalinda winces. "Kids . . . in school." She hedges, looking down.

"Just ignore them," América says. She resumes her hemming, tries to brush from her mind an image of herself at fourteen, pregnant, hiding behind a tree until two schoolmates went past.

"I knew you'd say that," Rosalinda whines, and América looks up. "I can't ignore them, Mami. They write me nasty notes, and they turn their backs on me when I try to talk to them."

"All of them, or just the uppity ones?"

"What difference does it make who it is?"

"Would you please lower your voice?" América asks, even-toned, trying to maintain her own composure. Rosalinda starts back to her room but thinks better of it and slumps on a chair.

"I wish you could understand," she sniffles.

"I'd like to," América says, "but it's hard for me to understand how leaving your home and family is necessary. Running away from your problems doesn't make them go away," she concludes as if ending the discussion.

"I'm not 'running away from my problems,'" Rosalinda says, mimicking her mother's tone of voice. "I want to start over, and I can't do it here."

Why not, América wants to ask but knows the effect that will have. "You haven't given it a chance," she says. "I want to help you, but you haven't let me talk to you." She can't hide the tears in her voice. "I'm your mother. We should go through this together." She tries to go to her daughter, to hug her, but Rosalinda pushes her away as if she were infected.

"This is not your problem, Mami. It's mine," she says with a vehemence that stuns América.

"No, mi'ja, no. It's ours, you're not alone in this." Again América tries to embrace her daughter, who steps back. Rosalinda's expression is angry, but América doesn't know what she has done to deserve such fury. "You won't even let me touch you," she whimpers, reaching for her once more. But Rosalinda stands firm, a fourteen-year-old child who looks like a woman, who thinks herself a woman because she's had a man. América drops her arms to her side, hardens her stance, swallows her tears. "You think it's so easy," she warns, but Rosalinda doesn't hear the rest of what she's about to say. She's run back to her room and slammed the door shut.

Five Days a Month

For as long as La Casa del Francés has been standing, a member of América's family has been mopping its floors, making its beds, washing its walls. The first owner, the Frenchman whose name is lost to memory, designed the house while still a bachelor, appointing it with the finest details that the time and his wallet could afford. He lived in a rotting wood shack while his casa was raised by the peons inherited with the hacienda from a relative he'd never met. When it was finished, he returned home with the intention of buying furniture and finding a wife, both of which he could now afford due to his shrewd management of the acres of sugarcane planted in long rows stretching in every direction from the hill where his stone casa stood.

He envisioned his bride floating through the airy rooms, tending flowers in the central courtyard without having to mingle with the dark natives whose work made his fortune possible. He found a wife and filled her head with stories of the mysterious land where they would make their life, the jungle at the edges of the fields, the turquoise ocean at whose foot lay a town he had named himself, Esperanza, town of hope. For their wedding trip they toured France and Italy, buying furnishings, linens, delicate china, all shipped to the house he had built as a monument to his good luck and careful administration in the New World.

Madame brought Marguerite, her sixteen-year-old maid, the fatherless daughter of her mother's maid. The long journey across the Atlantic was plagued by storms and rough seas even on sunny days. When Madame arrived at her beautiful home, she was pregnant and suffering from fever. After a prolonged delirium in which she thought she was home in Vichy, she died, taking the heir with her, leaving Marguerite stranded in a new land where she couldn't even speak the language. The Frenchman grieved for many weeks, but soon discovered gentle Marguerite, who shared his sorrow and loneliness. They had a daughter, Dominique, who was never legitimized by her father, who couldn't bring himself to admit he had fallen for his dead wife's maid. When he died, the hacienda passed to a Venezuelan who visited the casa in the summers. Marguerite was retired to a cabin at the edge of the property, within walking distance of the house, where she was housekeeper to the new owners. Over the years, La Casa changed hands many times, and each time, one of Marguerite's descendants, a woman with a child and no husband, appeared at the back door claiming to be the housekeeper. No one ever questioned her right to clean its hallways, tend the courtyard, dust its rooms, scrub its tubs, polish its tiles. Don Irving is the latest in a long history of foreigners to own the house that is still referred to as La Casa del Francés, The Frenchman's House. América is the daughter of the great-great-great-granddaughter of the resourceful Marguerite.

She thinks about this history as she polishes the tiles the women in her family have polished for more than a hundred years. América had hoped that Rosalinda would break from her history, that she would educate herself, marry above her station, like Yamila Valentín, and live in a house where she would employ maids, not be one.

She shakes her head. I'm not ashamed of being a maid. It's housework, women's work, nothing to be ashamed of.

She's never known anything else, has never wanted to learn to type or work computers, like so many of the girls in the town are doing. She's not embarrassed to say she likes taking care of a house, enjoys all the little tasks that are sabotaged the minute a human enters a room she has worked hard to put in order. That's what I like about housework, she often says; there's always something to do.

She dreams of someday having her own house, like the ones in the magazines the turistas leave in the garbage cans, with carpeting and drapes, wallpaper and formal furniture. A house in which the living room is as big as the house she now lives in, and candles are set on the dining room table in ornate candelabra like Liberace used to put on his piano.

She had a tape of Liberace at his piano, but it broke, and then she couldn't find another. He appeared on television every once in a while, and that was the only time she sat in front of it, enthralled by the music, tunes which she remembered accompanying the cartoons she watched as a child.

It doesn't seem so long ago I was watching cartoons on television. And here I am, a grown woman with a daughter who thinks she's grown up. Ay, how it hurts to be a mother!

América doesn't often escape into flights of feeling sorry for herself, but she has her period, and she can't help it. For twenty-five days a month she takes a white pill, and for the next five the little plastic bubbles contain a blue one. The day the birth control pills change color, her whole personality does, too, from white to blue for five days. She's sure something in the pill makes her depressed, but the doctor at the family-planning clinic says she's imagining it.

"Then I must have been imagining I'm depressed five days a month for thirteen years," she told the last doctor she talked to, and he laughed and patted her on the shoulder and wrote her another prescription—for the same thing.

But something happens those five days. All the hurts and anger, the fears and frustrations accumulate, to be released five days a month in fits of crying and a hypersensitivity to the smallest irritations. Correa knows not to come around when América has her period. Ester cooks soups and rice with milk, which América eats with an abstracted expression, as if she were watching an internal travelogue. On the sixth day, when she starts a new box of white pills, she's back to herself, humming and singing.

The guests in room 8 are horny. They have left two condoms on the floor near the bed, all snotty and slimy. She picks them up with a paper towel, rolls the whole thing into a ball. "¡No les da vergüenza!" she mumbles as she dumps the mess into the trash can. That's one thing she has never understood about Yanquis. They do things like leave their used condoms on the floor, or bloody sanitary pads, unwrapped, in the trash cans. But they throw a fit if there's hair in the shower drain, or if the toilet is not disinfected. They don't mind exposing other people to their germs, but they don't want to be exposed to anybody else's.

In her irritated, critical mood, she notices things that she usually overlooks, like the wet towels on the bed, the toothpaste smears on the bathroom sink and mirror. When on vacation, people leave their clothes all over the place, as if knowing this is only a temporary situation, they don't want to hang anything up or store it away in a drawer. Worst of all are the people who decide they don't like the arrangement of the furniture in the rooms. More often than she'd like, América has come into a room to find the mattress on the floor. She knows the beds in La Casa are lumpy, but the least people could do is put things back.

It might be different if Don Irving bothered to make the rooms nicer. Some have no screens in the windows, and every so often a shriek is heard from a guest who has come face to face with a bright green lagartijo parading across the headboard. None of the linens match. If a sheet or blanket is torn or too faded for use, Don Irving simply goes to the market in Isabel Segunda, Vieques's largest town, and buys whatever fits. It irritates América that the pillowcases don't match the sheets, and that the towels are all different sizes and colors and don't match the facecloths. The furniture is nothing to look at, odd pieces Don Irving has found who knows where and places wherever there is a need. Ester says that when she was a child, there were still magnificent Colonial-style furnishings in the house, but they were taken away by the last owner.

América leans against the wall, takes a few breaths. She's so tired! The five days of the month in which she allows herself to feel depressed are also the five days in which she feels her exhaustion, the aches and pains caused by hours of lifting, scrubbing, mopping, polishing, bending, and straightening up numerous times as she picks up the clutter tourists leave behind.

She has one last room to finish before she goes home. Number 9 has to be readied for new guests. Tomás has taken out the crib and put in another cot, which América makes up with tight corners that will hold a child should he be in the habit of falling out of bed. Last year, a little girl hurt her head on the tile floor, and since then América wraps the blankets around so that, once a child crawls under them, he or she is swaddled against the mattress. Better that than a concussion.

She straightens up, places her hands on her waist, and bends backwards to let out the kinks. The motion makes her momentarily dizzy. She sits for a minute, something she rarely does in a guest room, and holds her head in her hands until the feeling passes. Then she takes her pail and mop, cleaning supplies and rags, out to the supply closet downstairs, where she stores everything in its place so that tomorrow, when Ester comes to work, she can find everything she needs.

Every step away from La Casa toward her own home is like walking in a swamp. Her feet feel heavy and seem to resist the motion of her stiff knees. This is what a fly must feel like on flypaper, she thinks, and smiles at her own cleverness. As she exits the back gate of La Casa, she's in the middle of a group of children playing tag. They whirl around her, throw off her balance so that she stretches out her arms to steady herself, like a tightrope walker. They laugh at this movement, and once again she smiles, and they think she's smiling at them. Their cheerful voices fade as they run away from her, through an alley between two houses. She follows them with her eyes, recalling her own childhood in these streets. She played tag, she laughed, she got dirty. But it seems like such a long time ago! When, she asks herself, was the last time I laughed? It takes her a while to remember. It was at the movies, with Correa. "Don't laugh so loud," he whispered in her ear after a particularly funny scene, and the rest of the movie lost its humor.

Ay, she sighs as she opens the gate and contemplates the tunnel of spiny rose branches leading to her front door. She takes a deep breath before thrusting herself through the invading branches, avoiding the bigger thorns, careful not to bruise the enormous blossoms that sway as if intoxicated by their own perfume.

"Mami," América says as she comes in, "you have to do something about those roses."

"What's wrong with them?" Ester asks, rousing from her seat in front of the television.

"They attack everyone who comes in."

"All right," she says, "I'll trim them."

At another time of the month, Ester would have argued with América about the fate of the roses. But not during América's blue days. It's as if, during those five days of the month, mother and daughter change personalities. Ester, irritable and set in her ways, becomes as compliant as América, who takes on her mother's prickliness.

Ester serves them fish broth with corn dumplings.

"Rosalinda ate when she came home from school," Ester informs, as if to prevent América from needless worry.

América looks in the direction of Rosalinda's door. "What's she doing in there?"

"Redecorating," Ester guesses. "She's taken out three bags of garbage in the last couple of hours."

América nods. "I'm going to bed," she says, stacking her dirty dishes in the sink.

On her way to her room, América stops in front of Rosalinda's door, listens to the muted activity inside but doesn't knock.

She burrows into her room with single-minded purposefulness, like a bear going into hibernation. She falls asleep instantly, even though it's not yet dark. Sometime later, she hears Correa's voice just outside her door. But she doesn't wake up enough to make out what he's saying.

She sleeps fitfully the rest of the night, wakes up several times in the middle of unpleasant dreams. In one she's trapped in a room full of mirrors. In another, she's on an open raft hurtling toward foamy rapids, afraid to jump out and afraid to stay on. In a third, she's searching for needles in Ester's garden and the rosebushes attack her. After the last one, she decides not to sleep anymore. She showers, makes coffee, then sits at the dining table going through her magazines until Ester comes out of her room to get ready for work.

"What day is it?" she asks hopefully when she sees América awake, and is disappointed when América confirms it is indeed Tuesday and she has to go to La Casa.

Once Ester is gone, América knocks on Rosalinda's door.

"Time to get ready for school," she calls, in as gay a manner as she can muster. A few minutes later Rosalinda comes out of her room, but she's not dressed in her uniform. "Why aren't you ready?" América asks, and Rosalinda screws up her face.

"Didn't Papi tell you? He's coming to get me later."

América's heart drops. "No," she says, "he didn't say anything to me."

"We're taking the afternoon ferry," Rosalinda says with fear in her voice.

"When were you going to tell me?" América asks, her hands on her hips.

"We talked about this, Mami!"

"Did we? All I remember is I tried to talk to you and you slammed the door in my face. I'm surprised it's still on its hinges."

"And I remember telling you I need to go away for a while, and you gave me a lecture."

They stand face-to-face, Rosalinda almost as tall as her mother, so that she doesn't have to look up to her.

For an instant, América doesn't know what to do. Whatever

I do now, she realizes, will be remembered the rest of our lives. She's relieved when Rosalinda is the first to speak.

"Please, Mami, let me go. I promise I won't do anything to make you ashamed. Please let me go, Mami."

América wraps her daughter in her arms and holds on to her tightly, as if by doing so she will ensure that Rosalinda will never even think of leaving her. Dry-eyed, she feels her daughter's sobs rip into the deepest part of herself, the part that bore this child, that carried her for nine months, that binds them woman to woman. She hugs her fiercely, embracing all that she was, is, and will be. This child, this woman, her child, a woman. She lets her go, wipes the tears from Rosalinda's cheeks, kisses her streaked face the way she did when Rosalinda hurt herself and needed to be reassured that the hurt would heal. And the same soothing rhyme she used to sing to Rosalinda enters her brain, and she sings it softly as she caresses her daughter's hair away from her face. "Sana, sana, colita de rana, si no sana hoy se sana mañana." Rosalinda listens to her mother, not with the delighted trust of the child who knows only Mami can make it better, but with the certain knowledge that Mami often makes it worse.

América waits on the porch for Correa to arrive. The ferry leaves at three, so for them to make it, Correa has to pick up Rosalinda no later than two-thirty. She made no promises to Rosalinda, didn't agree to let her go, has no intention of letting Correa take her away. I've never stood up to him, she tells herself, but this I will not allow. He will not take my daughter from me. Even if he kills me, he won't take her. She rocks back and forth, steeling herself for the moment Correa enters the path strewn with rose petals.

He forgot, she thinks, that today I don't work. He planned to take her when I wasn't here, so that I wouldn't know she was gone until I came home. Rosalinda was hoping to sneak out of here the same way she snuck out with Taino.

She stews in her fury, creating scenarios for Correa and

Rosalinda that would make her laugh at her foolishness if she stopped to think how unlikely they are. She's had the same work schedule for years. Correa is not likely to forget her whereabouts at any given moment. Rosalinda keeps América's and Ester's schedules, with phone numbers for La Casa and Don Irving's private line, pinned to her wall, and another copy in her school assignments book. It's impossible that both of them would forget that América doesn't work on Tuesday and Wednesday. If América stopped to think, she would wonder why Correa chose the one day both he and Rosalinda knew for sure she'd be home.

When his Jeep rounds the corner, she loses some of her determination. He parks it in front of the house, nods in her direction when he sees her sitting on the porch. The frown that crinkles his forehead further erodes her confidence. She should have waited for him inside.

In the time it takes him to walk around the vehicle and open the gate, América's emotions run from fear to anger to resentment to fear again. He pays no attention to the thorny branches grazing him as he comes up the walk. His graceful, loose-hipped gait does not alter its rhythm for any obstacle. Even the three porch steps seem designed to help rather than impede his progress toward her.

"What's so interesting out here?" he asks looking around the empty sidewalk, at his Jeep shimmering in the midday sun, the heat-wilted vegetation in the garden and across the street.

She goes into the house without a word. He follows. Rosalinda's door creaks open, and she peeks out, a question on her face.

"Stay there," América orders. The door closes instantly.

"What's the matter with you?" Correa demands, his eyes lively, going from América to Rosalinda's door to América again.

"I think you know." América winces when she hears how weak her voice sounds, how much less confident than it did when she played out possible scenarios in her mind. She's glad her back is to him and he can't see her frightened eyes.

She hears him take a deep breath, as if he were trying to figure out what to say next. "América." He pronounces her name softly, a sigh, as if he were tired. "You know this is the right thing to do for now. She needs a break from all this."

She whirls to face him. "When did you become an expert on what Rosalinda needs?"

"América," he says, tight-lipped, "deja eso."

"Leave it?" Anger replaces fear. Fifteen years of reading Correa's moods, his body language, the tone of his voice, of anticipating how he will behave next, fly out the window on the wings of her fury at having to give in to him one more time. Fifteen years of negotiating with herself just how far she will go to prevent a beating disappear the instant she hears him asking her to leave it alone as if "it" were a trivial thing, as if "it" didn't include every other moment in those fifteen years in which she has "left it alone." "No," she screams, "I won't leave it alone. I won't." And she lunges at him, beats her fists into his chest, scratches his smooth-shaved cheeks with her nails, screams at the top of her lungs, "No! No! No! No!"

Correa's surprise lasts less than a blink of his green eyes. His muscular arms tense, his hands reach hers after only two or three scratches have reddened stripes on his skin. He pulls her off him with one hard push and, with the other hand, catches her before she falls against the shelves with the dancing lady and the shepherd playing the flute. Once she's upright, scratching at him still, he looks at her for an instant, then slaps her twice before her own hands cover her face. A punch to her stomach takes her breath away. She doubles over on the floor, where he kicks her, first with the right foot, then with the left.

"You stupid, stupid bitch!" he snarls so softly he might be calling her baby, baby.

She lies on the floor, blind with tears, her hands not knowing where to go, where to cover her soft flesh from his hard boot. But he doesn't kick her anymore. He stands over her, watching her squirm, while Rosalinda tugs at his sleeve.

"Stop it, Papi, stop!" she screeches. He pushes her away as he would a buzzing fly, and she crashes through the open door of her room, sprawls on the floor and cowers.

"Get up," he orders América. She pushes up painfully. He offers his hand to help her, but she slaps it away, and he kicks her again. "Get up!" he yells. Blindly, she throws herself at him, knocks him off his feet. He falls on top of her, cursing. She kicks up at him, but he's too heavy for her to have much effect other than to make him madder. His breath is quick and hot. He pins her down on the floor and hits her, picks up her head by the hair, slams it against the tiles. Rosalinda is on top of them now, screaming, pulling at her father, her carefully applied makeup a grotesque mask of streaks and splotches. Rosalinda's screams pierce through América. Correa's growls are savage, animallike. She keeps punching him, kicking him, not knowing if her strikes connect, but getting satisfaction from the effort. Rosalinda and Correa yell and tear at each other. She feels them struggling, hears their screams echo dully, as if rather than being pinned to the floor by a great weight, she were swimming under a vast pool, every sound a mere vibration. But then she doesn't hear anything. She's floating on an icy floe toward a dark island with a flashing red sky and the dull steady drone of distant thunder.

I Could Kill Him

S he's on Rosalinda's bed, lying on her back, a wet cloth on her face. Her head is turned all the way to the right, because if she moves it, a sharp pain by her left ear feels as if her head would explode. Everything hurts. She tries to move her legs, and her hips hurt. She raises her hand to remove the cloth, and her arms and chest hurt. The rising and falling of her breath, now faster than when she woke up, hurts her belly and around her ribs. She opens her eyes. They feel swollen, and even the lids hurt.

Every move she makes is accompanied by an "¡Ay!" followed by another "¡Ay!" followed by more. She manages to get up, to shuffle step by tiny step to the door. In the living room, the television is tuned to Cristina Saralegüi's talk show. The topic, América learns as she staggers to the bathroom, is men who are in love with transsexuals awaiting their operation. Are these men, Cristina asks the audience, homosexual if they make love with a man, even if that man wants to be a woman? América doesn't care.

Just as she reaches the bathroom door, Ester flies out of it, eager, it seems, to find out what Cristina's guests have to say for themselves about their situation.

"Why are you out of bed?" she asks América. "I'll bring you whatever you need."

"Shower," América mumbles, moving past her, withholding her moans so that Ester doesn't know just much pain she's in. It hurts more when she can't say "¡Ay!" with every step.

She usually avoids the mirror after Correa's beatings, but this time she looks. She has a black eye. She takes off her clothes and finds bruises on her abdomen, her hips, her upper arms. Her bra has cut deep welts into the swollen skin around her back and on the shoulders. There is an enormous lump just behind her left ear. Lifting her leg to get into the shower brings more pain in a new place, in the tailbone, right between her buttocks. She runs the water as hot as she can and soaps herself slowly. She's startled when she sees blood and then remembers she has her period. "¡Ay!" she moans, as if this were a new wound.

She comes out of the bathroom wrapped in three towels. One around her waist, another covering her breasts, and the third draped over her head like a veil because the throbbing lump makes it impossible to wrap it turban-style. Ester has served a fish soup thick with grated plantain.

"I have to get dressed first," América mutters as she goes past, and Ester looks at her resentfully, as if letting the food sit more than a minute after it's served were an insult.

América dresses in clothes that will hide the bruises. She chooses a loose housedress with sleeves to the elbows and a high-enough neckline that the black-and-blue marks on her chest won't show. The black eye she can't do anything about. And she can't comb her hair because of the lump, so she lets it dangle over her shoulders, the moisture soaking into the collar of her dress.

Sitting is painful. There are bruises on her buttocks. But she lowers herself without complaints, avoiding Ester's eyes across the table.

"I made you a poultice for that eye," Ester says, her lips stretched in a straight line, so that the wrinkles around her mouth look like faintly drawn lines.

Her neck hurts when she looks down at the bowl of soup.

Her shoulders ache when she moves the spoon from front to back of the bowl, when she lifts out a bay leaf and sets it aside. It hurts to open her mouth. It hurts to swallow. It hurts when the warm food slides down her throat, into her stomach. It hurts to look at her mother.

"He took her anyway," Ester says, and América nods her heavy head, which makes her spine ache from neck to tailbone.

"But she knows I didn't let her go," she says, her tongue thick, each syllable a deliberate effort that hurts.

The next day it's Ester's turn to work. América stays in bed as long as she can. The sharp pains of yesterday are dull aches today, relieved with aspirin and Ester's compresses and ointments. She can't stay in bed for too long because she's not used to it. It makes her feel worse to lie there with nothing but her thoughts. She gets up and does some chores, avoiding sudden movements and too much bending, the radio tuned to the salsa station. If she fills her head with music, if she sings along, she's able to forget everything else, even some of the pain.

She doesn't remember how she ended up in Rosalinda's room once she passed out. She enters it as if looking for clues. The walls are stripped of all the posters. Square brown blotches of adhesive stain the cement walls where Rosalinda's fantasies were born. América remembers lying in this room when she was a teenager, staring at the posters she had ripped out of magazines or purchased at the carnival concession stands during the patron-saint feast days. When Ester was a teenager in this house, she too, had ripped out pages from magazines, had tacked up pictures of movie stars with intense dark eyes and thick bigotes.

Rosalinda left some things. A couple of stretched-out bras in the dresser. A broken comb, three pennies. Her school uniform hangs forsaken on a wire hanger in her closet. But nothing else to remind América of her daughter. It's as if she wanted to erase herself from here, as if she wanted no one to know that this was her room, this her house. América sits on the edge of the bed as she did the day Rosalinda ran away with Taino. What was I feeling that day, she asks herself. Did I have any idea it would come to this? Should I have acted differently? She remembers her anger at Rosalinda for being so stupid, for gambling with her future when she has two examples at home of all that can go wrong for a girl who doesn't think further than the empty promises of a good-looking man. What else should I have done, she wonders. But try as she might, she can't figure it out.

She pushes off the bed with effort, turns her back on Rosalinda's room as if an answer were there but she doesn't want to know it. She slams the door after herself, surprised at the satisfaction it gives her, at the feeling that the hollow noise is a punctuation to a story she didn't know she was telling herself. It's her life, she mutters, pulling herself up to her full height, and I can't live it for her.

She misses two days of work. The black eye looks particularly nasty, and it's hard to comb her hair because of the hard lump behind her ear. Ester complains about having to work four days in a row but goes anyway.

On Saturday América gets up early, feels well enough to send Ester back to bed when she comes out of her room coughing and wheezing. She walks to La Casa, dreading the day ahead.

The other employees notice her bruises, can guess who gave them to her. She avoids them, doesn't even eat lunch so that she will not have to sit with them and face their scrutiny, the pity in Nilda's eyes, the triumph in Tomas's and Feto's.

She reddens with shame when Don Irving sees her black eye and glides his gaze away, as if he too were embarrassed. A few guests notice the black-and-blue bruise, and she imagines some of them must be wondering how she got it, but no one asks, and if they did, she would lie.

Humming to herself, she tidies the small and large messes left behind by strangers whose life she can only guess about, who don't think of her unless they run out of toilet paper or if there aren't enough towels in the room.

On Sunday Correa appears carrying a box of Fannie Farmer chocolates and a cordless telephone. After every beating, he shows up a few days later with a gift in place of an apology. The size and expense of the gift is usually in proportion to the severity of the beating. Electronics typically mean he knows he's really hurt her, but chocolates always mean she deserved it.

América turns her face when he tries to kiss her as if their last meeting had been nothing to think about or remember. He expects her to be cold the first time after a beating. But if she's too distant, he accuses her of provoking him into another fit of anger, something he insists he wants to avoid.

"I bought this for you at the PX," he says, as he does each time he brings her a gift. Correa is not a soldier, a veteran, or an employee of the U.S. Armed Forces. But somehow, Correa can shop at the Navy PX. She imagines him there, walking up and down the aisles, evaluating each item. A coffee brewer for a split lip. A toaster oven for a black eye. A rocking chair for a broken rib that kept her out of work for a week.

"We don't have telephone service," América mutters, as she puts the box on a shelf in the kitchen.

"You should have it connected," he says, taking a beer out of the refrigerator, "in case Rosalinda needs anything."

She looks at him archly. He returns the look with a frown, a warning that whatever she was about to say she should keep to herself, or else. América is glad Ester is at Don Irving's today. If she were here, she'd be grunting sarcastically in the background, directing scornful looks at her. As it is, she's disgusted with herself.

Have I lost all self-respect, she asks herself as she silently prepares his dinner. She wonders, as she rinses the rice, what would happen if she put rat poison in it. Would it change the flavor? She looks under the sink but finds no poison there. There's bleach. But bleach has a distinctive odor that she doesn't think will disappear if cooked. Besides, she suspects, he'd have to eat a lot of Clorox-laced rice for it to have any effect. She wonders if any of Ester's herbs and spices are poisonous. But she imagines if they were, Ester would have used them on Correa by now. How many times, she asks herself as she slices a plantain, would I have to stab him before he bleeds to death? She shakes her head, imagining the bloody mess and how hard it would be to clean up. Maybe I can hire a hit man to shoot him, like that woman in the United States who was having an affair with her minister. She laughs at herself for thinking such a thing could be arranged in Vieques, where everyone knows everyone else. She serves dinner. Maybe while he's sleeping I can bash his head in with a bat. Or I can set the bed on fire. I can set the whole room on fire, and he would suffocate in that windowless room he built for me. The thought of Correa gasping for air, his body in flames, sends shivers up and down her spine. He eats the food she's prepared with undisguised relish, commenting every now and then on how fluffy the rice is, how well spiced the beans, how crispy the fried plantains. But América doesn't hear him. I could push him off the Esperanza dock, she thinks. I could lace his coffee with sleeping pills. I could fix the brakes on his Jeep.

No Balls

América, canayhafawoidwidyu?" She wishes Don Irving would take the cigar out of his mouth when speaking. It would make it easier to understand what he's saying.

"Excuse?"

"Kemir."

"Yes?"

"Kenyubeibisitunayt?"

"Excuse?"

He takes the cigar out, wipes his mouth with the back of his hand. "María is sick. A guest needs a baby-sitter."

"Ah, sí, baby-sit!"

"Kenyuduit?"

"This night?"

Exasperated. "Yes, tonight."

"Okéi."

"Six-thirty."

"Okéi."

"All right." Don Irving trudges away, chewing on his cigar.

From time to time, guests at La Casa require the services of a baby-sitter while they have a night out. María, Feto's oldest daughter, is usually called in, because she speaks English and her sweet disposition is reassuring to the parents. But every so often

América will baby-sit if María is not available. She gets paid by the hour and often a tip as well. While almost her entire salary is spent on necessities, her baby-sitting money she spends on herself, on a beauty-parlor permanent or cosmetics.

After work, she goes home to change and eat dinner. She puts a box of crayons and a coloring book in a straw bag. She also packs scissors with blunt tips, a few pieces of construction paper, glue, thread, and scraps of fabric from her sewing. Most of the Americanitos she's baby-sat are not used to nights without television. None of the rooms at La Casa have a TV, and it takes the children a few days to adjust. Even though the parents are warned, and most of them bring toys for their kids, América likes to come prepared, just in case.

"Hi! I'm Karen Leverett," says the young woman who opens the door when she knocks. "And this is Meghan."

América smiles at the three-year-old girl in Mrs. Leverett's arms, who hides her face in her mother's neck. A young man is tying a little boy's shoelace.

"This is Kyle," says Mrs. Leverett, her free hand tousling the seven-year-old boy's hair, "and my husband, Charlie."

América bends over to shake Kyle's hand. "Hello."

"Hi." He smiles, returning the gesture. Mr. Leverett nods in her direction.

"Meghan, say hello to América, okay?" Mrs. Leverett pries the little girl's face up. "Here she is. Say hello."

"Hello," Meghan says, then buries her face in her mother's neck again. Mrs. Leverett sends her husband an exasperated look.

"Okay, Meghan," says her father, trying to free her from her mother's arms. "We're going out, and this nice lady will stay with you." The girl wraps her arms and legs tighter around her mother.

"No!"

Mr. Leverett looks at América apologetically. "She's a little shy." He goes to the night table and stuffs his wallet, eyeglasses, and keys into his pants pockets. "Karen, we'll lose our reservation if we don't leave soon." The tone is not lost on América. Mr. Leverett is not a patient man.

"I have crayons," América offers. She strokes the child's hair. "We color." Meghan doesn't budge. Mrs. Leverett's pretty dress is getting wrinkled from Meghan's grip.

"Come on, Meghan, don't be such a baby," Kyle says, tugging at his sister's leg.

América takes Kyle by the hand. "Okéi, Kyle, you and me, we color."

She takes the boy's hand and leads him to the table on the other side of the room.

"Meghan, Mommy and Daddy have to go now, and you and Kyle will play with América, okay? Isn't that a pretty name, América?"

"America is where we live," she mumbles into Mrs. Leverett's neck.

Mrs. Leverett blushes. "No silly, that's America, our country! She is América. It's a proper name here."

"I know a boy named Jesus," Kyle says, as he rummages through América's straw bag, "just like at church."

"You're intelligent boy." América strokes his head. Kyle beams. From the corner of her eye she notices that Meghan is watching to see what Kyle takes out of her bag. She positions herself so that the girl can't see and has to pull away from her mother's shoulder.

"Look at what América brought," Mrs. Leverett says. "Would you like to see?" Meghan shakes her head but cranes her neck trying to look past América.

"Karen, Irving said it takes ten minutes to get there." Mr. Leverett is at the door, his hand on the handle, his right shoe tapping a flat rhythm on the tiles.

"All right, Meghan, you go with América now, okay? Daddy is in a hurry."

"I don't want you to go!" Meghan wraps her legs and arms around her mother again, tighter, and sobs disconsolately.

América comes to her, massages her back gently. "Come on,

baby, come with América." When she hears a child crying like this, it makes América want to cry, and her voice takes on a querulous tone that Meghan finds intriguing. "I take good care you. Come with me." Mrs. Leverett pushes a struggling Meghan toward América, who disentangles her from her mother and holds her tight. Meghan screams, fights América, shoves her trying to get to her mother. But Mr. Leverett has grabbed his wife's elbow and ushered her out.

"You kids behave, now," he calls as he closes the door.

América's throat feels tight. She feels both for the child crying in her arms and for the mother who didn't kiss her goodbye. She saw Mrs. Leverett's expression as Meghan was wrested from her. It was a mixture of relief and fear, as though she's glad América intervened but doesn't really want to go with her husband. Meghan's tears have affected Kyle, who leans against América, sniffling, as if his courage was only good in front of his father and mother and disintegrates when they're gone. She holds both children close and comforts them, sings to them "La Malagueña," which is not a lullaby, but she figures they don't speak Spanish, so the sense of the words doesn't matter.

When the children have quieted, she guides them to the table. "We make pictures," she tells them. The children look at each other as if they don't understand, so América takes a crayon and draws a stick man with wavy hair. She puts a blank piece of paper in front of each, spills the crayons in the middle of the table. "Now you," she says. They are as pleased with themselves as she is when they figure out what she wants them to do. "Okéi," she tells them, "you good kids."

When the Leveretts return, the children are tucked in bed, fast asleep. On each of the Leveretts' pillows there is a drawing.

"Oh, this is beautiful!" Mrs. Leverett exclaims, picking up her drawing.

Mr. Leverett studies his drawing as if seeking meaning in the doodles his son has scrawled across the paper. "Very nice," he concludes, then places it on the bedside table.

"You have good time?" América asks, enunciating every word.

"It was lovely," Mrs. Leverett answers.

"The food was great," Mr. Leverett agrees. He takes some folded bills from his shirt pocket and hands them to her. "Thank you very much."

"Thank you." She picks up her bag and prepares to leave.

"See you tomorrow," Mrs. Leverett says, and América thinks she's asking her to baby-sit again, but then realizes she means just what she's saying.

"Good night," she wishes them on her way out.

When she comes downstairs, Correa is waiting for her by the back door.

"Ay, Dios santo, you almost gave me a heart attack!"

"Need a lift?" He smiles like a matinee idol. He smells like aftershave and rum.

"How long have you been here?"

He guides her in the dark toward his Jeep. "I was at the Bohío," pointing to La Casa's outdoor bar under a mango tree. "Ester said you were baby-sitting. Was it for the couple who just came in?"

"Yes." She climbs into the passenger seat, her whole body tensing against the inevitable interrogation.

"Who are they?"

"Mr. and Mrs. Leverett, from New York."

"Hmm. He should have given you a ride home."

"He offered, but I told him I was all right." She's glad it's dark and he can't see her blushing at the lie.

"He should have insisted."

"He did. But I insisted too." Once a guest at La Casa drove her home after baby-sitting, and Correa beat her up for getting into a car with a stranger.

"You should have called me to come pick you up then."

She winds herself tighter within herself, hardening into a ball, tensing every muscle from the inside out. "Thank you for coming to get me." She steadies her voice as calm as his, with no hint of a challenge, no tears, no fear.

"Hmm," he responds as he pulls up in front of her house.

She goes in, and he follows her, carrying a case of beer from the backseat. Ester is already asleep but has left a light on over the stove. América gets ready for bed, puts on a pretty nightgown, loosens her hair. If she can distract him from his jealous thoughts, he might not beat her tonight. But she can't be too aggressive, or he will beat her up for acting like a slut.

She comes out of the bedroom as he puts beer in the refrigerator and stands by the sink, sipping water as if she had a great thirst. In the window glass over the sink she can see him look at her as he's about to grab a beer. Her nightgown is sheer, a babydoll that ends just below her hips. His reflexes are a little slow. He stands in front of the open refrigerator door, watching her, she watching his reflection, his face a study of indecision. She hums a bolero softly, leans over the sink to rinse out the glass, and as she does, pushes her buttocks ever so slightly in his direction. He smiles, rubs the back of his hand across his lips, and closes the refrigerator door.

"Boonus dees, América."

"Buenos dias, Kyle." A couple of days later, Mr. Leverett and the children are by the pool when América goes by with a load of sheets for the wash. "You remember very good," she tells Kyle.

To his father he says, "I can also say boonus tardus, that means good afternoon."

"Excellent!" Mr. Leverett beams at his son, smiles at América. "You've been teaching them Spanish?"

"Little words," she says. "You remember too, Meghan?" The girl smiles at América through the thumb in her mouth, shakes her head shyly. América pats her shoulder. "Where Mami?"

"She's resting," Meghan says through her thumb. Her father pulls it out of her mouth impatiently.

"Meghan, it's rude to talk to people with your mouth full."

The little girl clams up, sucks on her thumb again.

"Okéi," América says. "Adios," she says to Kyle.

"Uhdeeos!" he responds with a grin.

She really likes the boy, his openness, his intelligence, his eagerness to please. Unlike so many of the Americanitos who stay at La Casa and are wary of strangers, he seems to get along with everyone.

Later in the afternoon, as she's leaving, the Leveretts are returning from the beach, sand stuck to their arms and legs, the backs of their necks. Mr. Leverett is slightly sunburned.

"Hi!" Mrs. Leverett sings out. Kyle jumps out of the Jeep and runs toward América, lugging a plastic beach bucket.

"Look, I found about a million seashells!" His sister follows him with her own bucket full.

"Me, too. A million!"

They display the many shells in shades of pale pink and ivory, some burgundy striped, others with mustard-colored streaks. "They beautiful!" América exclaims, picking one from Meghan's bucket and examining it. "So pretty."

"Look at mine! In this one you can hear the ocean!" He holds a conch shell to América's ear, and she winces. She's always imagined an animal will come out of one of those shells and pinch her ear. "Ooh! Thank you." She pulls it away.

"We'd better get going," Mr. Leverett says. "Do you want to cool off in the pool?" he asks his son.

"Sure!"

They walk up the path lined with flowering hibiscus.

"I'll be there in a minute," Mrs. Leverett calls after him, turning to América. "We were wondering if you could baby-sit again tomorrow night."

"Yes. Same time?"

"A little earlier, six maybe."

"Okéi."

"And if you wouldn't mind having dinner with the kids. Irving doesn't start serving until then, and last time we had to rush—"

"No problem," she says, hugging Meghan to her side. "You stay with América, no cry?" Meghan sticks her salty, sandy thumb in her mouth and looks doubtfully at her. América pulls her closer and kisses the top of her head. "You good girl."

"See you tomorrow, then," Mrs. Leverett says, grabbing Meghan's shell bucket. "Let's go swim with the boys, okay?"

América watches them go toward the pool. Mrs. Leverett is fashion-model pretty, and young. América guesses she must be in her early thirties. Her wide, deep blue eyes and short golden hair make her look childlike, but the hardness about the mouth is that of a woman, and the eyes, after the first look, are not innocent so much as wary. It's a look América has seen many times. American women cultivate a girllike body, hair that never grays, unlined faces. But their life experience is something that can't be erased. You can see their age in the curl of the lips and the knowing looks. In the set of their shoulders. In the hands, which, although manicured and soft, are webbed with wrinkles.

Correa says he can't understand how American men can make love with those "bags of bones." América agrees that women should be soft and round, not sharp and angular. Her own body is full at the hips and buttocks, ample in the breasts, with enough flesh to cushion the bones, but not so much that it jiggles. Well, some parts jiggle, but only if she makes them. She's proud of her sinuous walk, which she developed after much practice before she met Correa, in the innocent afternoons of her early adolescence. She registers men's admiring glances when she passes, listens for the mumbled piropos or soft whistles for confirmation that she looks good, that all the trouble she takes in the morning dressing, brushing her hair, putting on makeup is worth getting up a half hour earlier.

"A woman should smell good and look good," the men she knows have said many times, and she agrees, and has taught this to her daughter. Rosalinda spends most of her allowance on cosmetics and perfumes. Like Ester and América, she's particular about her clothes, spends a great deal of time selecting what shoes to wear with what dress or pants.

Every time Rosalinda enters her thoughts, América feels an invisible fist land between her breasts. It sets her heart racing, and tears threaten. It is then that she sets her jaw against her skull, as if she were biting something hard that requires a great deal of force to break in two.

On the second night she baby-sits Kyle and Meghan, América takes them on a walk around the grounds of La Casa before they go in to have dinner. They pick flowers from the gardenia and hibiscus bushes, which they put in a glass on their mother's bedside table. They climb the mango tree near the picnic table and visit the shed where the laundry gets done. They sit on the high stools of the Bohío, and the bartender gives them each a Coke and a bowl full of popcorn. They visit the ramshackle stables where Don Irving keeps five Paso Fino horses for guests who want to ride along the beach. Felipe, the groom, is brushing Silvestre, the oldest horse in the stable. He lets the children pet the horse, gives them a handful of oats, and after much giggling and coaxing, they let Silvestre eat out of their hands, laughing at the sensation of his thick lips against their palms.

"It tickles," screeches Meghan, pulling her hand away, dropping most of the oats in the dirt.

"Can we ride him?" asks Kyle.

Felipe lifts him onto Silvestre's broad back.

"Be careful no fall off," América calls out as Felipe leads the horse around.

"Me too, me too," says Meghan.

"You too baby go horsy," América tells her, but Meghan insists.

"It's an old horse," Felipe reassures her, "she'll be all right."

He hoists Meghan up behind her brother, wraps her little hands around his waist, and leads the horse in a tight circle, while the children laugh and squeal in delight.

América is a little nervous, but she trusts Felipe. What she doesn't trust is the horse. She's never been fond of horses. Their big eyes seem to her to look resentfully at humans, and she thinks they're waiting for the opportunity to buck and drop their riders, stomp on them with their broad hooves.

"Ya no más, you get off," she calls out, and the children

protest, but América comes over and helps lift them off the animal. "The horsy tired," she explains to them.

"Can we do it again tomorrow?" Kyle asks, and Meghan joins him. "Can we?"

"We ask your mami y papi."

"They won't mind," Kyle says, and she promises to ask their parents and thanks Felipe as she takes the children away.

At dinner she orders tostones. After much urging, the children taste them and say they like the crispy plantain rounds. They even try them the way she eats them, with a drip of olive oil and garlic. Afterward, they go back to their room, and she helps them glue some of their shells onto a piece of driftwood. She talks to them in her broken English, and they delight in correcting her pronunciation. When tired or bored, they become cranky, and Kyle lords it over his sister, who cries in frustration.

"You be nice little sister," América warns, but Kyle loves to torture her. "If you no be nice, I no take you see horsy tomorrow."

"Daddy will take us, then."

"No, he won't," Meghan warns, "'cause I'm gonna tell."

"Tattletale! Tattletale!"

Meghan throws a crayon at him, and he throws it back, and América is beside herself trying to figure out how to keep them from hurting each other. If they were her children, he'd get a good spanking and a talking-to for abusing his sister, who's much younger and weaker. But they're not her kids, and so she finds ways of distracting them until they're too tired to protest when it's time for bed. She tucks each of them in, sings "La Malagueña," and kisses them good night, smelling the garlic on their breath.

She tidies the room for the second time today, puts away toys, folds clothes, straightens books on shelves. This room is as familiar to her as her own, and she moves around it as if it were and these her children sleeping peacefully on the screened porch.

After the Leveretts return from their evening out, she walks home, a small flashlight in her hand. She will turn it on only when she comes to the dark stretch where two trees on opposite sides of the path block the light of the moon. She's not afraid of the dark but wouldn't like to stumble and hurt herself. The moon is so bright it illuminates the familiar stretch, creating long shadows blacker than the ones the sun makes. The air is silver gray, cool, filled with the night sounds of invisible creatures that hop and dart and fly as she walks, as if making way for her, as if she were a queen, and they, the toads, the snakes, the owls, her subjects. The only ones to touch her are the mosquitoes, who, finding a soft spot, prick her and suck her blood before she realizes she has to swat them.

The next afternoon, once she's done with her work and is ready to go home, América finds Mr. and Mrs. Leverett and the children by the pool.

"I promise take kids see horsies," she explains to Mrs. Leverett.

"Can we go, Mom?" Kyle asks, and his sister hops around her mother crying, "Horses! Horses!"

Mrs. Leverett looks uncertainly toward her husband, who's swimming laps. "We went earlier, and they were all gone."

"Silvestre is there," América tells her.

"Okay, let's go then," she says, throwing a T-shirt over her swimsuit.

América leads the way with Kyle, and Meghan and Mrs. Leverett follow on the path behind the outdoor bar. Felipe is walking Pirulí, a reddish horse that confirms all of América's worst fears. She's a spirited filly, her gait proud and aggressive. She rears her head and neighs for what seems to be no reason at all. They watch Felipe take her around a couple of times, then lead her into her stall, where, it seems, she doesn't want to go. He has to persuade her, to the amusement of the children and to América and Mrs. Leverett's worried expressions.

"You no like horses?" América asks, and Mrs. Leverett smiles.

"I grew up in a horsy town, but I never got into it."

Felipe brings Silvestre out. América turns to Mrs. Leverett.

"Can they go on horsy?"

"Please, Mom!" the children plead in unison.

"Be real careful and hold on, okay?" she instructs as Felipe lifts one, then the other.

"He very gentle horse. Old horse." América reassures. Mrs. Leverett's worried expression doesn't change.

Because of her fear of horses, América insisted that Rosalinda learn to ride when she was quite young, so that her daughter wouldn't be paralyzed by the same fear. It occurs to her now that perhaps Rosalinda is too brave, too careless about consequences. América stares into the dirt at her feet.

Mrs. Leverett has been talking, and she hasn't heard her. ". . . vacation. But I suppose to you it doesn't feel like that, since you live here."

América looks up, hoping that no answer is required to whatever Mrs. Leverett was saying. As they pass, the children wave, and they wave back.

"How long have you worked for Irving?" Mrs. Leverett asks.

"Ten years. Since he came."

"Did you grow up nearby?"

"I live here all my life."

"You haven't lived anywhere else?"

América looks at her, waves at the children, looks at her again. "I left once, for one month, but I came back."

"It's such a beautiful island."

"Yes."

"Too bad about the Navy base."

América doesn't know how to respond, so she sighs.

"Are you married?"

"No." She says the word as if she had just bit into the bitter skin of an unripe purple mombin, but Mrs. Leverett doesn't seem to notice.

Felipe lifts the children off the horse. They come running to their mother, their faces ecstatic.

"Can we have a horse, Mom?"

"Yes, Mom, can we?"

América and Mrs. Leverett chuckle. The children tug at their mother's T-shirt, begging her to get them a horse. She looks at

América as if they were accomplices in some scheme. "We'll talk about it, okay?" she says to the kids, smiling mysteriously.

América says good-bye, going in one direction as they go in the other, wondering about Americans' habits of asking personal questions when they barely know you.

Correa is stretched out on the couch. "Where've you been?"

"I promised the kids I baby-sit that I'd take them to see the horses."

"What's with you and those Yanquis?"

"Nothing's with me. I baby-sit their kids, that's all."

She goes to change. In the kitchen, Ester is making something that smells so rich and spicy, her stomach churns with hunger. She wishes she were as good a cook as Ester, who has a flair for mixing condiments and making even the humblest ingredients taste spectacular. It is her one gift she's proudest of, the one people use to describe her. Oh, yes, Ester, she's a great cook. She can make stones taste like butter.

Because she's such a great cook, Ester is popular with the neighbors, who are willing to overlook her perpetual ill humor, attributed to her love of beer. Whenever there's a wedding or a birthday party, Ester is invited, and her gift is always a caldero full of the best arroz con gandules anyone has ever had, or a Pyrex dish full of the creamiest flan, or if it's someone she really likes or someone who has paid for them, a couple of hundred pasteles. "I could have been a cook in the best hotels in San Juan," she's fond of saying, but she never explains why that didn't happen.

There is no pattern to Correa's visits. He shows up when he feels like it. The fact that he has come around so many times in the past few weeks América attributes to "el problema con Rosalinda." At other times when he has come almost every night, it signals he's jealous, his presence a message to América and her alleged suitor about who she belongs to. But América doesn't think that's why he's here again tonight. One thing about Correa, he doesn't keep her guessing. He comes right out with an accusation, usually just before he hits her in the face if he's drunk, or in her abdomen and back if he isn't.

She thinks maybe the problem with Rosalinda has changed Correa, that he's now ready to be the man she always wished he would be. He hasn't hit her in two weeks, since the day he took Rosalinda away. She notes the days he comes and lies with her like any other man with his wife, makes no demands for sex, asks before he pulls up her nightgown and fondles her breasts. Of course, were she to say no, it might be different. But she doesn't want to think about that. She has stopped thinking of ways to kill him. Has listened when he brings news of Rosalinda because he has a working phone and she doesn't. His easiness with her, his verbal caresses are like a pledge. In the hopeful act of lovemaking, she believes he's a changed man and for a moment forgets the swollen lips and bruises of days past, the blackened eyes, the tender scalp where he has pulled her hair.

How sweet a child feels on your lap, her head on your bosom, her soft hair newly washed, damp, so fine it tickles your chin as you press your head closer to kiss her. How lovely the weight of a child against your breast, her little body coiled against your belly as you rock her back and forth, singing a lullaby. Her little heart beating so fast, her breath coming in slower and slower as she falls asleep, her thumb in her tiny mouth, the pupils shadows behind finely veined eyelids.

América holds Meghan, sings softly to her while across the room her brother sleeps, his breath parting the fur of the teddy bear he hugs. América could hold on to Meghan for hours, but sleep has made her heavy, and so she carries her to bed, tucks her in, pulls the sheet up around her neck, tightens the edges so that she won't fall out. She watches her sleep, the sucking motion of her cheeks, her index finger hooked on her nose, the eyes fluttering as if she were watching a movie. She then fixes the blankets around Kyle, who pulls his teddy bear closer to his chest, mumbling something she can't quite catch.

It is the Leveretts' last night in Vieques, and she's staying with the children while they enjoy the last hours of their vacation. She's never spent so much time with a guest's children, and she knows that these two have won a place in her memory, unlike the countless others who have passed through this room. She's sat with them four of their ten nights at La Casa, has taken walks with them after her shift, has stopped in the middle of mopping a hallway or making a bed to admire a seashell or the long seed pod called bellota, or a butterfly captured in a jar. Their innocence, their chatter, the way they listen to her, patiently trying to understand what she's saying, have changed the rhythm of her days. And Meghan's sweetness has awakened a longing she has suppressed for years, the desire to have another child, to hold a baby in her arms, to suckle an infant at her breast, to feel the warmth of a being she has carried in her belly.

How often she dreamed of a house full of children, girls and boys running in and out of a neat home with curtains fluttering in the breeze, gardens flowering in a million colors, birds singing sweetly in the shade. There was a husband in her dreams, a man not unlike Correa, tall and dark, muscular, with a lovely voice and thick black hair. They would stand on the porch of their sweet-smelling home, arms around each other's waists, watching their children play under a mango tree. And they would be filled with love for each other, for what they had brought forth, for a future shiny with promise.

She shakes her head, chides herself for having such old-fashioned dreams when women nowadays want to be scientists and leaders of nations. But I never wanted that, she argues with herself. All I ever wanted was a home and a family, with a mother and a father and children. She sits on the armchair, picks up one of the magazines Mrs. Leverett brought with her. It's mostly fashions, skinny women with big faces and extraordinary outfits. She wonders if people in the United States really dress like that.

Someone is coming up the stairs, across the hall. It's too early for the Leveretts, but maybe they're tired, or didn't like the restaurant they went to or the loud music in the bars on the boardwalk. The door opens.

"There you are." Correa's eyes are shiny with the unmistakable luster of too much liquor and suspicion. He stands just inside the door, listing a little to one side, licking his lips as if preparing for a feast.

It is the old Correa, the one she fears, not the one of her domestic dream. His expression softens her knees to jelly, hollows the inside of her chest. Her head drones with a million voices, replays of countless accusations over the years. There are no men on the island of Vieques whom Correa has not cited as someone she's cheating with. Neither the longtime residents nor the casual visitors are immune from his suspicions, and América searches her mind for the last time she had contact with a man, asks herself who she has talked to, who she has even looked at in the recent past that would qualify as a candidate for Correa's jealousy.

She looks toward the porch, and he follows her gaze and stumbles toward the sleeping children. She stands behind him as if afraid of what he will find in the little cots. He smiles, softening enough to make her feel that maybe this time he'll just leave.

"Their mami and papi are having a good time at Eddie's," he says. "You should see those gringos dance!" He laughs, and it seems to her as if thunder has struck, so loud does it sound. She's certain the children have awakened, but as he passes by her and throws himself on the armchair, she sees they are still asleep.

"You can't stay here," she says. She stands between him and the porch, on the shadowed edge of the light from the lamp by the armchair.

He picks up the magazine she set down, flips through the pages, chuckles. "Look at how these women dress. Hangers with clothes on, that's what they look like." He throws the magazine across the room, picks up a stuffed animal on the shelf behind him, a lion with a silly grin. He turns it over, legs up.

"They never give them balls," he says, and growls at it, then growls at her, pushing the stuffed lion in her direction in a manner that might be considered playful if she weren't so scared.

She jumps back, and he laughs, growls, stands up, grabs her, tickles her with the toy.

She tries to free herself, but he holds her with one arm and, with the other, rubs the animal across her shoulders, follows it with a gentle growl and a soft bite with his lips. She pushes him, but he holds her, pretends to be a lion, growls, purrs, pokes her with clawed fingers, bites with his teeth now, her shoulder, her neck, her arms. "Correa, stop!"

She looks behind her, at the porch where the children sleep. Kyle turns over, holds his teddy bear closer. Meghan sucks on her thumb. Correa shoves her onto the bed, climbs on top of her, scratches her with clawed fingers, bites her thighs, her belly, her breasts. She resists him, tries to get his attention. "No, Correa. We'll wake up the kids." He rubs his erection against her legs, bites her lips, purrs into her ears, rolls her shirt up to her neck. She forces him away with more strength this time, and his face changes from playful to serious, and he weighs himself on her, fumbles for the zipper of her jeans, oblivious to anything she might say or do.

She can't fight him. His breath comes in hot, rum-scented blasts, and still he bites her cheeks, her neck, her breasts, and bares her lower body. She wants to scream, but she imagines the scared faces of the children, who have nothing to do with this. She guides his head so that he will bite her where no one will see, below her shirt collar, on her chest, her shoulders, and he does. Bites into her and plunges his penis as if she were a hole, just a warm hole the right size and texture. She'd bite him back but doesn't want him to think she's enjoying this, is in any way participating in what he calls his pleasure, the taking of América whenever and however he wants her. Her thoughts are on the other side of the screen, on the sleeping porch where two innocents sleep, she hopes, oblivious to what's happening not ten feet away. She prays as Correa rides her. Prays to Jesus protector of children, that He keep their eyes shut and their ears deaf to everything but the coquí singing outside the window, its shrill song more like a scream than a melody.

When he's done, he rolls over, ready to sleep. She has to coax him, pull him up, convince him this is not his room, his bed. He looks about as if he has amnesia, not recognizing his surroundings, not quite understanding what she says to him.

"You have to go, Correa," she begs, helping him pull up his pants, tucking his shirt in for him. "I'll get fired." Childlike, he lets her turn him this way and that as she straightens his clothes, her own body naked from the waist down. He walks like a drunk bear, his weight settling on one foot, then the next. The cool air from the courtyard revives him, though, and at the door he lifts his finger at her. "I'll wait for you downstairs." He's not done with her. What she's just been through was a mere distraction. She closes the door as he moves down the hall, brushing his hair with his hand, while with the other he holds on to the wall as if the floor were waves.

She washes up, dries herself with toilet tissue so as not to soil the Leveretts' towels. In the mirror, she examines the bite marks on her chest and breasts, her belly, her upper arms. Her face is swollen. She splashes cool water on it, brushes her hair, straightens her clothes. She places one of Mrs. Leverett's scarves over the lampshade, to darken the room, soften the light, create shadows that will hide her bruises and deny the outrage committed on their bed, in their room, not ten feet from where their children sleep.

There's a Phone Call
for You

The day the Leveretts leave she cleans their room, which feels different than it ever has before. Each corner has a significance it never had. The little cot where Meghan slept seems emptier. Kyle's fingerprints on the bathroom mirror appear deliberately placed, a secret message for her to decode.

It's inexplicable, she puzzles, how fond I am of those children, how, in a few short days, they filled a place in my heart that I didn't know was empty. Maybe, she tells herself, I'm just looking for a replacement for Rosalinda. But the theory sounds suspiciously like the ones Cristina Saralegüi propounds to distraught mothers on her talk show.

Just before they leave, Mr. and Mrs. Leverett and the children find her in one of the rooms.

"We wanted to say good-bye."

América has to fight back tears. The children hug and kiss her. Mr. Leverett shakes her hand.

"You really made our vacation a vacation." He hands her an envelope. Guests usually leave a tip for her on top of a dresser. Getting it handed to her is confusing. She's not sure if she should look inside or if that would be rude. There's some writing on the front of it, block letters with all their names in a row. "We wrote our address and phone number," Mr. Leverett explains. "If you're ever in New York, call us."

Mrs. Leverett embraces her warmly, and as they leave, América is jealous of their togetherness, their ability to move in and out of her life with such ease, with no thought to what they might have meant to her. She imagines that the minute they get on the plane to New York, she will be just another of their vacation memories. But she wishes to be remembered specifically, not as one of the smiling faces tourists encounter on their way to the beach or in a restaurant or quietly pushing a cleaning cart down a hall.

With the money she earned from the Leveretts, including the twenty-five dollars they gave her in the envelope, América is able to afford reinstalling telephone service. The first person she calls is Rosalinda. Their conversation consists of silence more than speech, as each word on either side is evaluated by the other for hidden meanings and innuendoes.

"How's school?"

"It's okay."

"Are the nuns nice?"

"They're okay."

"Have you made any friends?"

"Why do you want to know?"

"Well, it's a new town and everything . . . "

"I met some girls."

"Do you like Tía Estrella and Prima Fefa?"

"They're okay." Silence. Silence. Silence. "Why do you ask so many questions?"

"How else will I find out how you're doing?"

"I'm fine!"

"I want to make sure—"

"If I need anything, I'll call."

"Will you come back for a visit, the long weekend maybe?"

"I have exams."

"Maybe I'll come out and see you."

"If you want to."

"All right then, take care of yourself."

"Okay."

"Bye."

"Bye." América hangs up, feels like throwing the phone across the bedroom the minute she does. It is this rage in her that Rosalinda must sense, this anger that dealing with Rosalinda generates within her, which evolves into a painful, vacant longing to hold her close.

Every mother she knows talks about her children this way, a mixture of love and displeasure coloring the words, a sense of defeat lurking beneath the surface but never emerging fully, as if hope keeps squelching it down. She imagines she was a disappointment to Ester and concludes that it's a mother's fate to be continually disappointed by her children.

Maybe I expect too much, she considers, then shakes her head. I only expected her to do the opposite of what I did. That's not so hard. She sees what getting pregnant at fourteen has meant. América turns over on her bed, punches her pillow a couple of times before settling her head.

But there's hope. She's in school, trying to get her life together. So what if she had sex? The fiery rage that bubbles beneath her skin explodes, and she beats on the pillow, her fists tight, again and again, beats the pillow until it's flat in places, lumpy in others. She throws it across the room, cries quietly, her hands pressed against her belly.

If Rosalinda were a boy, she would be calling him a man. If Rosalinda were a boy and were having sex at fourteen, there would be sly looks and jokes, and pride that his "equipment" works. If Rosalinda were a boy, América would forgive him, because that's what men are, sexual creatures with a direct link from brain to balls.

It is expected that boys will be men, but girls are never supposed to be women. Girls are supposed to go directly from girlhood to married motherhood with no stops in between, to have more self-control, to not allow passion to rule their actions, to be able to say no and mean it. When a boy has sex, it elevates him in the eyes of other people. When a girl has sex, she falls.

That was my mistake. I fell and never rose above it. América gets up, picks up her pillow, fluffs it up, sets it on her bed, and lies down again, on her side, hugging the pillow around her head. No, I fell and let Correa keep me down. The thought startles her, forces her eyes open to the dark. I let him. I let him because he's a man. No other reason. He's not smarter than me. He's bigger, and stronger, and he frightens me. But I'm smarter. She shuts her eyes tight, and bright balls of light explode inside her head. Some kind of smart I am, letting Correa control my life. Real smart!

She sits up. Outside her door, one of Ester's soap opera stars is screaming hysterically. The screams trail off, and a male announcer tells viewers that new, improved Tide with Bleach outcleans all others.

We're stupid! All women are stupid! We've let ourselves believe that men are better than we are. And we've told our sons that, and we've told our daughters.

She undoes her ponytail, pulling off the scrunchy in one tug. ¡Ay, Dios mío! I'm going crazy. I sound like those feminists that tell every woman to have an abortion and every man to clean house. She shakes her head to loosen her hair, lets it brush her shoulders. If it were only that easy! She ties her hair up again, into a knot atop her head. Pagán is probably right. I have been listening in on too many conversations at La Casa!

"Dersafoncolferye."

"Excuse?" She's changing the tablecloths on the verandah when Don Irving finds her.

He takes the cigar out of his mouth. "A phone call, in the office."

"For me?" It can only be bad news. The last time she was unexpectedly called at work was when Rosalinda keeled over in school after lunch and had to be rushed to the hospital to get her appendix removed. Running from the front of the hotel, through the courtyard, down the back steps, around the pool to the office, she imagines all sorts of scenarios involving Rosalinda in an emergency room in Fajardo. When she finally comes into the office from where Don Irving manages La Casa, she's out of breath, her heart is racing, and she's almost in tears.

"¿Haló?"

"Hi, América?" It's a familiar voice, speaking English.

"Sí."

"Itskarnlevret."

"Excuse?"

"Karen Leverett, remember, with the children, Meghan and Kyle?"

"Ay, Mrs. Leverett! How are you?" She drops onto the chair by the counter where the tourists sign their credit card bills.

"You sound out of breath."

"I run." She takes in air, lets it out slowly.

"Oh, I'm sorry, I didn't mean—"

"I'm okéi now. How the children?"

"They're good, everyone's fine here. How are you?"

"Fine too." There's only one reason why Mrs. Leverett is calling her. "You're coming back?"

"Oh, no, no," she giggles, "it's only been a week. I wish we could vacation that often."

She giggles again, but América doesn't know why because she hasn't understood everything she's said. "Yes," she responds.

"América, Charlie and I have been talking—"

"Excuse, Mrs. Leverett?"

"Yes?"

"Can you talk little more slow?" América blushes. She must think I'm stupid, she tells herself, and holds the phone closer to her ear. "Sorry, I no understand inglis too good on phone."

"Oh, sure, I'm sorry, of course. Anyway, Charlie, Mr. Leverett, and I were talking, and we talked to Irving. You know he has a very high opinion of you."

Mr. Leverett. Talking. Irving. You. A response is expected. "Uhmm."

"And we, well, the children really like you. And our housekeeper, she was from Ireland and she had to go back. And we have to hire someone. And, well, Irving says you could use a change. So, we were wondering if you would ever consider leaving La Casa and coming to work for us here."

Children like you. Housekeeper. Island. Higher someone. Irving. Leave La Casa. Work here. "I'm sorry . . ." She's dizzy with the effort to understand.

"You don't have to answer now. You can think about it and call me, collect. You have the number, don't you?"

"Number?"

"Our telephone number. If you lost it, Irving has it."

"Ah, yes, your number. I have at home."

"Great! Can you call me on Tuesday if you think you might be interested? If you are, we can talk in more detail."

"Call Tuesday."

"In the evening is best. After eight o'clock."

"Tuesday, eight o'clock."

"Talk to you then. The children send their love."

"Okéi."

She sets the phone down. In her left hand she still holds the rag she was using to wipe down each table before replacing the clean tablecloths. She thinks she knows what Mrs. Leverett asked but is not sure. Leave La Casa and go to New York? It can't be.

Don Irving walks in, sits on the office chair behind a desk usually occupied by his bookkeeper, who's out sick.

"Whadyathink?" His hazel eyes twinkle, as if he's heard a very funny joke and is still laughing.

"You talk to her?"

"She wanted to know if you would come work for her, in New York."

"In New York?"

"In her house, as her housekeeper, and, you know, baby-sitter."

"You say yes?"

He laughs, and the glint in his eye makes him look younger. "I have nothing to do with that! I told her it might be good for you to do something different." He leans toward her, lowers his voice confidentially. "It might be good for you to get away from here. You know what I mean." He looks vaguely out the window.

She follows his gaze, half expecting to see Correa standing under the mango tree. But he's never where she expects him to be.

"In New York is cold?"

"That's why they all come here." Don Irving chuckles.

"I don't know."

"If it doesn't work out," he leans toward her again, "you'll always have a place here."

It makes her nervous to have him so close, so fatherlike. "I think about."

He leans back, punctuates the end of the conversation with a slap on the knees. "You do that," he says, and turns toward the ledger on the desk in front of him.

"Thank you," she says, but he doesn't seem to hear her.

She returns to the verandah, troubled as much by the phone call as by Don Irving's interference. She suspects Ester's influence. Didn't Ester suggest to América that she leave Vieques? Didn't Ester tell her Don Irving could help her find a job? Maybe the Leveretts are Don Irving's friends. Maybe he called them and asked them to come to Vieques. Maybe the day he asked América to baby-sit for them María was not sick at all. Maybe Don Irving asked the Leveretts to convince her to go to New York with them. But why would Don Irving do such a thing? He likes her and Ester, but she doesn't believe he would concoct such an elaborate scheme.

Correa will never let me go. He won't let me leave Vieques to work interna, in someone else's home. As it is, he's always snooping around La Casa, suspicious of every man whose bed I have to make, whose clothes I have to pick up from wherever he dropped them after a night on the town.

New York. It's so far away. América has never been anywhere but Fajardo, and she only stayed there a month, hiding out in the same house where Rosalinda now lives with Correa's aunt and cousin. She didn't think much of it. It was a big town, noisier and more congested than Vieques.

Some of her neighbors who have gone to New York talk

about how hard life is over there, about apartments infested with roaches and mice, about drive-by shootings and drug deals on their doorsteps. The ones who've had success in New York come back with a stick up their ass. Paulina's daughter Carmen, who's a few months older than América, is like that, always criticizing Puerto Ricans, talking about how things would be better if the island were a state.

No, she couldn't live in New York. The tourists who come in the winter gather around the portable radio in the Bohío to listen to the news, and they whoop and holler when the weather is announced and there are snowstorms in New York and they're in Vieques. She's seen stories on television of long lines of cars stuck on wide highways covered with snow, and trucks jackknifed across roads packed with ice and people holding on to one another as they try to hop slushy puddles with the wind blowing hard as a hurricane, their heavy clothes making them look like bears with scarves. When tourists from New York show up here, they're pale and sickly-looking, and it takes them a while to look healthy, once the sun touches their cheeks and they can move freely because they're not wrapped up in all that clothing they must wear all the time. No, I couldn't live like that.

Correa will never let it happen. Even if she swore it was for a few weeks, to try it, he'd not allow it. Once, when Paulina was visiting and offered to take her back for a couple of weeks he said she couldn't go anywhere without him. If he couldn't go, she couldn't go. And he couldn't go, so she didn't.

He says that Puerto Rican women who go to New York come back behaving like Americanas, and he doesn't like Americanas. "Our Portorras," he says, "the old-fashioned ones I'm talking about, know how to treat a man, they know the meaning of the word *respect*. Our women," he tells his friends, "are well trained."

She winces at the memories of Correa's training, the punches and slaps, the kicks, the rapes. It is rape, she tells herself, if I don't want to do it. She shakes her head. ¡Ay, Dios mío! It's too much to think about! She hits her temple with the palm of her hand, as if to chase away the thoughts.

She's finished with the tables on the verandah, has dusted the railings, swept and mopped the tile floor, chased spiders from the corners. She brings the dirty tablecloths to Nilda in the laundry shed.

"Are you okay?" Nilda asks.

The question startles América, and she peeks in the little mirror over the sink, where her reflection looks back, a deep furrow between her eyebrows, her lips pursed tight as a dog's asshole. "I'm fine," she says, rubbing the expression away.

"You looked mad."

"No, I'm not angry. Just a little tired. See you tomorrow."

She feels Nilda's eyes on her. Busybody! Always meddling in other people's affairs. If I go to New York, I won't tell anyone. I'll not show up for work one day, and a week later they'll get a postcard with a picture of a tall building or something. No one has to know my business. It's my life.

She stops in the middle of the path, where the two trees on opposite sides form a canopy over pebbly dirt. No one has to know. She shakes her head, walks on. A snake crosses in front of her, slow and sinuous, unconcerned. She freezes, stares as it esses its way across the sandy portion of the path, leaving a faint trace of its shape, subtle but unmistakable. She jumps over where the snake crossed, so as not to disturb its signature. She walks fast away from it, wondering if it's bad luck or good luck or no luck at all when a snake crosses your path.

"You're really considering it, aren't you?" Ester and América face each other over dinner, rice with cuttlefish, fried sweet plantains on the side.

"I guess."

Ester chews for a minute, gesticulates with her fork. "What about Rosalinda? Would you take her with you?"

"It's probably better if I send for her once I'm settled."

"Are those people going to want your daughter in their house?"

It occurs to América that Mrs. Leverett hasn't asked her if she has children. Maybe she doesn't care. Or maybe Don Irving told her about Rosalinda. "Maybe I can rent a place for us both near where I work."

Ester takes another forkful, chews quietly, looks down at her plate, picks out the tiny gray tentacles, distributes them so that each forkful will have a piece of meat on it. América watches her, waiting for the inevitable question, knowing it's lurking in the back of Ester's mind but she's afraid to articulate it, or, perhaps, is waiting for América to say something.

"If you want to come too," América says, "you can."

Ester looks up, eyes watery, whether from liquor or emotion, América can't tell. "Nah. I don't like cities," she says, as if she's traveled extensively.

"But you might like to visit. You haven't seen Paulina in years."

"Bah!" Ester waves her fork as if it were a magic wand and all the things she doesn't like will disappear with the right move. "What about Correa?" It's a threat, not a statement, as if Ester were testing her resolve.

"He doesn't have to know where I am," América says, eyes twinkling, repeating her mother's words of a few weeks ago.

Ester smiles mischievously. There is still a bit of child in her, América notes. There is still spirit.

"I'm not going to tell him," she says with a chuckle. "Just don't tell me where you're going, in case he . . ." she stuffs a forkful in her mouth as if to shut herself up.

"He wouldn't dare hurt you, Mami. He's never tried, has he?"

Ester shakes her head. "He threatens."

"We'll tell Odilio to keep an eye out. This is your house. If he tries anything, you can have him arrested."

She wonders where these words are coming from. Arrest Correa? Five times Officer Odilio Pagán has shown up at her house when Correa is beating her, because the neighbors have complained about her screams. Five times Rosalinda has stood on the porch screeching at her father to stop hurting her mother. Five times Odilio Pagán has wrestled Correa outside, has told him he has to take him to jail. Five times América has run out and told Odilio to leave Correa alone, that he didn't do anything, that the bruises on her face and arms are self-inflicted. "I fell off a chair when I was hanging curtains." "I fell down the steps at La Casa." "We were just arguing. The neighbors should mind their own business." "And you, Rosalinda," América has yelled at her daughter, "get back to your room and stop making trouble for your father."

Five times Odilio Pagán has pulled her aside, has told her she's within her rights to have Correa arrested. Five times she's said no, it was nothing, he's just had too much to drink. "You know how he gets when he drinks." Countless times Odilio Pagán has told her she's a fool to let Correa get away with it. And many more times América has wished she weren't so scared of what Correa would do to her if she pressed charges against him, if she caused him the embarrassment of spending a night in jail.

Ester smiles sadly, all the mischief gone out of her. "Yes, of course. I can have him arrested."

She writes her questions on a piece of notebook paper that she folds and keeps inside her bra. How much will I make a week? How many hours will I work? How many days? Do I get a vacation? Do I have my own room, or do I sleep with the kids? She writes the questions down as they occur to her, not sure if she will ask them, using them to organize her thoughts, to make herself focus on the job, not the opportunity.

Do I have to cook? Do I have to iron? Do I get paid when you go on vacation with your kids? The list grows as the days pass. She finds herself adding other things to the list, what to bring, what to leave home. Whose addresses to take, whose phone numbers. Who she knows in New York other than her Aunt Paulina and her cousins. The paper, folded and carried under her left breast, yellows with sweat, the writing feathers until it looks out of focus, the creases begin to tear at the edges. How much money I have saved. How much I will leave for Mami to pay the electricity and water bills. Rosalinda's address and Tía Estrella's phone number. Rosalinda's dress and shoe size for sending her presents. Ester's dress and shoe size. Their birthdays. The list grows, and pretty soon she has to write in the margins, around the edges, in between items already listed, as if she had forgotten them the first time.

Correa comes three times in one week, and she hides the paper under the mattress, on her side of the bed, deep inside, where there is no possibility that an edge will show, that he will discover she has been hiding something from him. He slaps her around because there are only three of the kind of beer he likes, less than what he drinks in one night. He has sex with her, quick, bitter-scented sex that sends her to shower while he sleeps.

He doesn't come on Tuesday. América calls Karen Leverett collect. "I will come," she says after she's asked as many questions as she feels comfortable asking, and Mrs. Leverett sounds so happy, she's sure she's made the right decision. She strikes off the questions she asked, and adds more things to the list. Mrs. Leverett will send her a ticket. She's to leave two weeks from Sunday. She'll tell Don Irving tomorrow. Ester will work her shift at La Casa, in case things don't work out and América needs to come back. Her stomach churns at the thought. Correa will kill her for betraying him. No matter what happens, she can't come back.

Ester will carry América's packed suitcase to Don Irving's casita behind the pabona hedge, and everyone will think she's moving in with him again. Early in the morning Don Irving will drive América to the airport, and for the first time, América will get on a plane. She'll fly to Fajardo first, visit Rosalinda before she goes to the international airport in San Juan. If Correa comes on Saturday night, it will complicate matters, but, she thinks, she can still get away. He's used to her leaving early on the mornings she works. He won't realize she's gone for at least a day. And by then she'll be in New York. In a new life. Starting over.

Going Blind

Tía Estrella and Prima Fefa live in a concrete house in an urbanización shadowed by an enormous hotel. "It's the biggest hotel on the island," Tía Estrella says. "People come from all over to stay there."

She's nearly blind, her eyes caged behind thick dark lenses that don't seem to help much. Her hair is gray, worn in a careless knot at the nape of the neck. She's stooped like an old woman, but América thinks she's only about ten years older than Ester.

"I was so surprised when you called this morning! I'm glad you came." She leads América, dragging her heavy suitcase, into the neat house barred with wrought-iron rejas painted yellow. "Fefa and Rosalinda are at church, but they'll be back soon."

América leaves the suitcase by the front door, against the wall. Tía Estrella stumbles over her own furniture, pushes the air in front of her on her way to the kitchen. Several times América has to lead her in a different direction from where she's heading, but Tía Estrella seems to need to make these mistakes, like a baby learning to walk.

"It's terrible, you know, my eyesight. The doctors are worried that I'll be blind soon, but I can see a bit more now than a few months ago. I'm healing, you know." América can't imagine what it must have been like, if this is an improvement. She's reminded of children playing pin-the-tail-on-the-donkey, heading with conviction in the exact opposite direction from where they need to go.

"Sit down, sit down." Tía Estrella motions toward the refrigerator. "I'll make us some coffee." She heads for the bathroom door.

"I'll make it," América offers. "You sit down and tell me how Rosalinda is doing."

"Ay, thank you, it's tricky, you know. I'm still not used to it. Going blind, that is." She takes off her glasses and wipes them on the hem of her skirt. Her eyes are larger than América remembers, gray, filmed at the corners with a substance that looks like gelled fog. "Rosalinda is doing well. You would be proud of her. Off to school every morning, bien paradita, and comes home right after." She puts her glasses on again. "She's been such a help, you know. With my problem and Fefa the way she is." Tía Estrella's only child is deaf from birth. "She's become quite good at reading Fefa, wait till you see her."

At Tía Estrella's, coffee is brewed the old-fashioned way, through a flannel filter black with use, well seasoned. América finds things easily because Tía Estrella's kitchen is all shelves, everything displayed where one can see it. No cabinet doors to open and close.

América sets down the cups of steaming coffee and sits near Tía Estrella. "Rosalinda needed a change," she tells her, "and I appreciate all you've done for her."

"Ay, nena, don't worry about it! She's delightful. Such a bright child."

América sips her coffee and wonders if trusting, blind Tía Estrella has mistaken someone else for her surly teenage daughter.

"And how is Fefa?" América asks.

Estrella waves her hand as if to dismiss the question. "Same as always."

From where she sits, América can see the front door, and when it opens, Rosalinda steps in, smiling at someone behind her, holding the door open with great care so that the person can step through. It is Prima Fefa, who is as gray and stooped and wrinkled as her mother. How did these two women grow so old in just fourteen years?

Rosalinda notices the new suitcase against the wall before she realizes who it belongs to. Her eyes open in amazement when she sees América.

"Mami!" She runs to her mother, hugs her with a warmth América hasn't felt from her in months.

She embraces her daughter, breast to breast. Rosalinda is the first to let go. Prima Fefa hurls herself at América, kisses her wetly on the cheek. She gesticulates, tugs her hair, makes an hourglass shape with her hands, kisses her fingertips. Rosalinda interprets.

"She says you look great, Mami, but that she remembers you with darker hair."

"Miss Clairol," América enunciates clearly toward Fefa, and Fefa laughs, a distant guttural sound, like a stifled cough.

"Why don't you show your Mami your room?" Tía Estrella suggests, and Rosalinda panics for a second but then leads her mother to the back of the house.

The room is neat, one wall adorned with Rosalinda's old posters, a little ragged from the trip across the strait. It is the same room Correa and América stayed in, Estrella's sewing room, lined with shelves stacked with bolts of cloth, threads, and supplies. The fabrics are old, with patterns no longer in style. A section of shelving is now laden with Rosalinda's belongings.

"What are you doing here?" The question begins innocently but by the last syllable becomes an accusation as Rosalinda's face darkens with suspicion.

"I wanted to see you. Remember, I told you I might come sometime?"

"But you didn't say anything when you called last week."

"I decided last night." She tries to ignore Rosalinda's fixed look, her effort to read something in América's appearance that is not being said.

"You dyed your hair blond."

"Miss Clairol," América says in the same tone as when Fefa asked, but Rosalinda doesn't laugh. "I needed a change."

"Why the suitcase?"

América sits on the edge of Rosalinda's bed. Pulls her dress over her knees, as if trying to press out the wrinkles. "I'm going away for a while."

"Where?" A whiny near scream. América thinks she hears fear in it.

"To the United States."

Rosalinda's mouth flies open, but no sound comes out. She seems to have been struck by an invisible solid object, her eyes startled, her whole body rigid.

"Your father doesn't know." América has to tell her everything she can now, while Rosalinda can't talk, won't argue. "He mustn't know. I can't take his abuse anymore. If I stay, he'll kill me." She looks at her lap again, pulls the dress further down over her knees, stretches the hem until it's taut.

"Mami! Don't say such a thing." Rosalinda throws herself at her mother, hugs her as if protecting her from a blow.

América lifts Rosalinda's face, seeks her eyes, struggles to maintain her voice even, unafraid. "Do you understand? It's important that he doesn't know where I am, Rosalinda."

"I won't tell him, Mami. I know how he is."

"I'll send you money. I'll call as soon as I can. But I won't give you my address or phone number."

"What if something happens? What if I need to get in touch with you?"

"Don't scare me, Rosalinda. I need you to be a good girl and take care of yourself." She kisses the top of her head. "I'll send for you if you want to live . . ." she lifts Rosalinda's face up again, searches her eyes, "if you want to live with me again."

Rosalinda hugs her closer. "I don't want you to think I stopped loving you, Mami." So sweet, so sweet and tender, like a child again, her little girl.

"I know, baby." They hold each other, without tears, creating heat in the space between their bodies, the breach that separates them. A distance wide enough to hold either one of them or, if each moved halfway, to hold them together. América is the first to let go.

I Wonder If He Knows

‍‍‍

I've never been anywhere, América thinks, but here I am, on an airplane over the ocean on my way to a foreign country where they speak a language I barely comprehend. She adjusts the bouncy pillow the flight attendant gave her, pulls the short blanket up to her chin. I wonder if he knows.

Each hour since she left Vieques has been punctuated by that question. Did someone see Don Irving take her to the airport? She rode in the hotel van, surrounded by tourists, her eyes alert for Correa's Jeep on the road or parked in the airport lot. Don Irving waited with her until she boarded the small plane. People looked at her curiously. But she maintained a serious expression, discouraged conversation, sat with her hands on her lap wondering how such a little plane could fly so steadily over the water. Inside, she was wound tight, rigid with fear.

I have only one chance to run away from Correa. If he catches me, I'll never have another. He'll kill me. Or if he doesn't, he'll beat me until I can't walk, then watch me ever more carefully, until every breath I take will be his.

She's safe in the big airplane taking her to New York. There is no one she knows here. Tourists and Puerto Ricans. Old people wearing bright colors. Families with screeching children. A woman dressed in black, praying a rosary. In the aisles in front of her, businessmen work busily at portable computers, a woman sets her hair in curlers, another paints her fingernails. Several people read. A young man wearing a baseball cap snores quietly. His head bounces up from his chest, wakes him up. He looks around, disoriented, goes back to sleep.

América closes her eyes. She aches, as if, sitting down for the longest time she ever remembers sitting, she's suddenly aware of how tired she is. She hasn't slept well since the day she decided to leave Vieques. She spent the nights Correa didn't come sorting her things, deciding what to take and what to leave behind. She has all her pictures of Rosalinda, from infancy to last year's school picture. Three pairs of jeans and T-shirts. Two dresses, three skirts, three tops. Her sneakers. Two pairs of shoes, one with heels, the other flats. Two pairs of sandals. New bedroom slippers. Five nightgowns, bras, and panties. A sweatshirt with a dancing Minnie Mouse. She's wearing her prettiest dress, turquoise with sequins along the collar and long sleeves. Blue shoes with rhinestones on the heels. And over her shoulders, a gray sweater with silver threads woven in the fabric. She felt a little foolish dressed like that at six o'clock in the morning, but she'll be arriving in New York in the evening, and she didn't know if she'd have a chance to change. Now she wishes she'd packed her dress in a separate bag. It's wrinkled from all the traveling. She could have changed in the airplane bathroom.

The woman setting her hair across the aisle is an experienced traveler. She got on the plane wearing shorts, a T-shirt, and sandals. Over the past couple of hours, she has done her nails, applied makeup, and changed into a leopard-spot jumpsuit with long sleeves and cuffed legs. From the bag in front of her, she's also pulled out a pair of short boots and brown socks. All that's left before they land is to take down her rollers, comb and spray her hair.

Next time I travel, I'll know better, América thinks. She looks out the window at the sky above, the clouds below. There won't be a next time, not as long as Correa lives. She wraps the blanket tighter around herself. I wonder if he knows.

A blast of cold air greets her as she leaves the plane and follows her down the long tunnel to the terminal. There's no one to meet her. People hug and kiss, hold hands as they walk away from the plane. Many more people wait in discreet areas presided over by uniformed attendants behind a counter. A public address system blares incomprehensible directions. Maybe I was supposed to come another day. But the ticket says today.

América follows the travelers to the baggage claim. So many people, dressed in heavy overcoats and boots, hats pulled over their foreheads, gloves stuck in their pockets. She's trembling with cold, her pretty dress with its sequined collar and sleeves is too thin for late February. There is more confusion where the luggage is handled. People jostling to be in front of the snakelike conveyor rattling in sinuous curves from one end of the room to the other. The automatic exit doors open and shut, and each time, cold air sets América's teeth chattering. A Yanqui wearing sweatpants and a flowered shirt smiles at her. She looks away, hoping to spot Mrs. Leverett. People bang into her with their bags, tell her to excuse them as if it didn't matter whether she does or not.

She spots her suitcase and must push through the throng of people to get to it. "Excuse? Is mine. Excuse plis?" People make way for her, then close in her wake. The man in the flowered shirt gets to her bag before she does, helps her lift it off before the conveyor takes it away again.

"Oomph! It's heavy!" he says as he sets it down next to her.

"Thank you." She smiles shyly, and he helps her drag it away from the crowd. "Is okéi. I take now." He makes her nervous.

"Crazy here tonight!" he says, and she nods as if she understands what he's said.

"Did you come off the Puerto Rico flight?" he asks.

América scans the crowd looking for Mrs. Leverett, tugs on her suitcase as if she were going somewhere.

"Did you?" the man insists. A faint trace of alcohol wafts its way to her.

"Sorry. I no speak inglis."

He seems appeased but makes no move to go. "No one's here to meet you?"

"I sorry." She repeats, tugging on her suitcase, her heart racing.

"Over here, América!" Mrs. Leverett waves from across the room.

"¡Gracias a Dios!" With effort, América picks up her suitcase. "Thank you," she mumbles in the man's direction, as she drags it toward Mrs. Leverett. He bows, a gesture she finds offensive, because it seems to mock her.

"Oh, I'm so sorry you had to wait!" Mrs. Leverett embraces her quickly, steps back, looks her up and down critically. "You look so nice!" América feels how overdressed she is, even at night, even in New York. Mrs. Leverett hands her a coat and hat. "Here, you're going to need these. It's bitter out there." She spots América's high-heel shoes with rhinestones. "Those will get ruined. I didn't bring boots."

The coat is bulky, too big for her, and the hat, wool with multicolored stripes, will squish her hair if she puts it on. She stuffs it in a pocket. Mrs. Leverett chatters about the cold, the traffic, something about dinner. "I'm parked across the way. Is this all your luggage?" She tries to help América with it.

"Is okei. I take." América lifts it as if it weighed nothing.

The automatic doors open, and América is paralyzed by a gust of cold air. "¡Ay, Santo Dios!" she exclaims out loud. The suitcase drops on its side next to her, and Mrs. Leverett picks it up.

"Let me help you with this."

"No, no, Mrs. Leverett. Is okéi. I do." But Mrs. Leverett, taller and skinnier than América, is strong. She hefts the suitcase and walks rapidly away. América is mortified. She has come across the ocean to be this woman's helper, and the first thing that happens is she can't even carry her own luggage. What must Mrs. Leverett think!

Her high heels are treacherous on the slippery pavement. Fat snowflakes pelt her face, melt on contact. Her hair, curled and sprayed into shape, is damp. She pulls the hat out of her pocket and sets it lightly on top of her head. But it needs the tension of her skull to stay on, so she has to pull it down, squishing her curls.

"We're right up here," Mrs. Leverett says, leading América across a road congested with cars, buses, vans, limousines.

América can't walk as fast as Mrs. Leverett. Her feet are wet from the slush, her legs, covered only with panty hose, are numb, especially her knees, which feel as if they need to be oiled. The bones of her hands feel brittle, and she stuffs them into the deep pockets of the coat, hunches her shoulders as if protecting her chest from a blow. She's never thought of snow as anything but what tourists avoid by coming to Vieques. But here she is, in the middle of a snowstorm, in a place most of the people she's ever met try to get away from. What have I done, she asks herself, not quite believing that she's come this far, and already she's having second thoughts.

Mrs. Leverett lifts the rear door of a bright red Explorer, struggles a bit with the suitcase but, with América's help, manages to stuff it inside. She dashes around to the driver's side, motions to América to climb in, the door is open, and starts the car. She sits in front of the wheel rubbing her hands together, blowing air on them.

"Let's give it a chance to warm up."

América tries to fasten her seat belt, but her fingers are so stiff she can't do it. Mrs. Leverett reaches over and smartly clasps it for her, as if she were a child.

"Thank you," América says, and notices that whatever she says is visible in spurts of foggy air. Mrs. Leverett chatters as if América can understand her. Home. Traffic. Storm. Children. Charlie. América nods from time to time, catching most of what she says, hoping that what she's missing will eventually be repeated or is not important.

There is a long line of cars ahead of them. They inch their way out of the airport into a congested highway banked with three- and four-story buildings. Snow falls steadily, as if the whole city will be buried in frozen water. She wonders if there are floods when it all melts. Ay, Dios mío, she asks herself again, what have I done? What am I doing here?

As they go over a bridge, traffic eases.

"There's New York," Mrs. Leverett points to her left. Sharp-edged buildings are silhouetted against a dense sky, and dim lights like still fireflies blink a message through the falling snow.

"Beautiful!"

The tall buildings seem to be grouped in one part of the city, to her left, while to the right most of the structures are lower, the lights less bright. The bridge they're on is graceful, but América, aware of being on a slippery surface high over a black river, can't enjoy its beauty. She sighs in relief when they are on solid ground again, albeit lined up before a tollbooth that seems very far away from where they're stopped.

Mrs. Leverett curses under her breath, but América pretends not to hear. She feels bad that Mrs. Leverett is out in this dangerous weather on her account, but she doesn't think it would do any good to apologize, since it's not her fault. Somehow, she still feels guilty.

Mrs. Leverett turns on the radio, scans until she finds a Latin station. "There we go!" A blast of trumpets followed by a sweet tenor voice singing about lost love makes América smile, and Mrs. Leverett grins, as if this were a special gift only for América.

"How far you live from Bronx?" América asks, and Mrs. Leverett turns down the radio to answer.

"About an hour by train. Do you know people there?"

"My aunt and cousins."

"Oh, that's nice," she says, seemingly disappointed at the news.

"I don't see them since many years," América tells her.

"Is it your father's sister, or your mother's?"

"My mother."

"Is she still alive?"

América's heart thumps as if the thought of Ester dying has never occurred to her. "Yes. I live with her."

"Oh, right, Irving told me. You have a daughter too, don't you?"

"She live with her father aunt." Please don't ask any more questions. Please stop.

"She must be very young. How old are you?"

"I thirty in May."

"Oh, nice. We'll sing you happy birthday."

She smiles. Her birthdays have gone unsung by everyone but Correa, who every year takes her out for a lobster dinner followed by dancing at PeeWee's Pub. He always presents her with something special—a gold chain, a dress, a bed when the old one got too lumpy. She wonders what he was planning to give her for her next birthday. A thud of fear bumps inside her chest. Oh, God, I wonder if he knows yet.

". . . your daughter?"

"My daughter?"

"How old is she?"

"Oh, she . . ." It's never been embarrassing to say Rosalinda's age, but now she feels so absurdly young to have a teenage daughter. "She fourteen."

"Wow!" is all Mrs. Leverett can muster. "Fourteen!" As if it were a marker of sorts, a surprise that anyone ever gets to be that age. She takes her eyes off the road for a moment, looks at América as if she were a new specimen of human. She catches herself staring and concentrates on her driving again.

"I made mistake," América apologizes, her whole body burning with shame. "Fifteen too young have babies."

"Yes, that is young." Mrs. Leverett says, and for the rest of the trip they're silent in the dark car, surrounded by more darkness, the windshield wipers tapping a rhythm to the falling snow, out of tune with the salsa music on the radio.

She's going to fire me, América worries. She thought I was more responsible, and now she knows how stupid I can be. She hunkers down inside the coat, no longer against the cold but trying to hide within its confines. I should have told her when we talked on the phone. I should have said something then. Now she has a bad opinion of me, and who knows what her husband will think! Ay, bendito, what's to become of me if she fires me?

It feels like a journey into darkness; each route they take has fewer streetlights until they're on a curvy road with no lights at all. Leafless trees reach out from either side, their roots protruding into the edges of the asphalt sculptured around them as if not to disturb a natural order. The car swerves to the left, to the right, to the left again under Mrs. Leverett's confident hand, as if now that they're getting closer to home, she's no longer worried about the slippery conditions. "Almost there," she says, with a sidelong glance at América, whose hands grip the armrest. "Here we go." She pulls into a driveway that lights up as she approaches, a garage door that opens by itself into a neatly organized room with shelves along the walls. On the far end a door opens, and Mr. Leverett and the children stand on the threshold. Meghan and Kyle are in their pajamas. Mr. Leverett comes down to shake her hand, but the children stay at the door, hopping up and down, waving their hands.

"Hi, América!" "Welcome, América!" "It's snowing!" squeals Meghan as if she has just noticed.

"Go on in. I'll get your things." Mr. Leverett retrieves her suitcase while Mrs. Leverett leads her into the kitchen.

"Here she is, guys!" Mrs. Leverett says to the children.

"Hello, baby," América scoops up Meghan in one arm and with the other hugs Kyle to her side. The children seem startled at her ardor but settle into it as onto a comfortable cushion. "What beautiful house!" América exclaims, and Mr. and Mrs. Leverett beam with pleasure.

"Do you want to see my room?" asks Meghan, and Kyle pipes up that she should see his room too.

"Now, guys," Mr. Leverett interrupts, "América must be tired from her trip, so why don't we let her rest now and show her around tomorrow?"

"Is okéi, I no tired," she tells them, and Mr. Leverett looks annoyed. She sets Meghan down. "But is better tomorrow when not dark," she amends. Mr. Leverett nods in her direction.

"Let's show América her room, okay?" Mrs. Leverett leads the way up a narrow staircase to the second floor. The children troop after them, pointing out the direction of their rooms as they come up. In the hall they turn left down another hall, to a wide door painted white with a brass handle and a lock.

Mrs. Leverett opens the door, turns on a light. The room is over the garage, with low slanted ceilings and dormer windows on two sides. A double bed with a comforter and many pillows is set against the far wall, opposite a sitting area with a couch in front of a television set, a small round table with two chairs and shelves against the wall. The whole room is carpeted, painted pale blue and white, with matching drapes.

"Is beautiful!" América exclaims, and Mrs. Leverett relaxes, a proud look on her face.

"This is the key to your room," she says, taking a leather key purse from the dresser by the door. "The rest are for the house and cars. We'll go over them tomorrow."

Mr. Leverett comes in with her suitcase. "How do you like it?" he asks with a grin.

"Is very nice!" She doesn't have to pretend enthusiasm. The room is the nicest she's ever lived in, bigger than her living room.

"You turn on the TV with this control." Kyle demonstrates.

"This door leads to your closet," Mrs. Leverett continues.

América's head is spinning. Still wearing Mrs. Leverett's heavy coat, she enters the lit walk-in closet with racks on either side and shelves at the far end. The inside of the door is mirrored.

". . . and over here is your bathroom."

An enclosed tub, matching sink and toilet, a small rug on the tile floor. Another huge mirror. Kyle and Meghan follow her into every room, chase each other around her.

"Children, stop that!" Mrs. Leverett says, her back to them, and they stop in their tracks, wait a few seconds, then continue.

"All right, kids," Mr. Leverett says firmly, "let's let América get settled. You'll see her in the morning."

The children look uncertainly at their father, then decide to follow him.

"Good night, América," they repeat dutifully after their mother.

"If you're hungry or thirsty—" Mrs. Leverett suggests.

"I okéi, thank you," América reassures her. "Good night."

They leave, the children chasing each other down the hall, their father yelling at them not to run.

She's relieved when they're gone. She wants to explore the room without them watching her reactions. She doesn't want to seem like a jíbara who has never seen walk-in closets and mirrored doors. She doesn't want them to see her kick her high heels off and dig her frozen toes into the warm carpeting or throw herself on her back on the soft comforter, her head against the fluffy pillows. There's a knock on the door.

América sits up, straightens the bed. "Yes?"

Mrs. Leverett opens the door and stands on the threshold. "I forgot to show you the thermostat." She leans in, fiddles with a dial by the door. "If you're cold, turn the heat up here. Rest well!" She disappears.

América stands by the dial. She's not sure what Mrs. Leverett did, or why, but a soft cackle comes from the baseboard. She touches it and it feels warm. "Oh, okéi," she says to herself. She takes off the coat and opens the closet door, which makes a light go on inside. She drapes the coat over a hanger, then can't decide which side of the closet to hang it in, decides to do it on the right as she goes out. Her suitcase is in the middle of the floor, where Mr. Leverett left it. She tips it over and opens it.

The first thing she pulls out is her white stuffed cat with the blue eyes. She snuggles him against the pillows. There is a telephone on the bedside table, with a dial tone. A clock radio by the bed. She fiddles with the dial but can't get a station. It's only nine o'clock, but it feels later. Days later. She takes her clothes out of her bag, hangs everything up in the closet, where they take up very little space. She's glad she brought her cosmetics and toiletries because on the way to the house she didn't see any stores. Not since they left the city and Mrs. Leverett pointed to a sign that said, WESTCHESTER COUNTY, NEW YORK. Maybe the stores close during a snowstorm, but then there would have been signs or something. She can't imagine having to drive to the city to buy groceries. She takes off her makeup, brushes out her hair, changes into her nightgown. The towels in the bathroom are thick and soft.

The room is eerily quiet. She goes to the window, pulls up the shade. It's so dark outside! Snow drifts past in thick clumps, settling into mysterious white mounds and dips, a huge rectangle, a little house with a peaked roof, and beyond, solid darkness. She shivers. Her cotton nightgown is not warm enough. She turns off the lights, crawls under the comforter, punches the pillows into shape, decides there are too many for comfort and slides them off the side to the floor.

There are stars above. She closes her eyes, opens them, and still sees stars, glowing palely above her. She turns on the bedside lamp. A constellation of plastic stars is stuck to the ceiling. She turns the light off and stares at the stars above the bed, counts them, realizes it's been years since she has lain on her back looking at stars. Heavy on the bed, soft covers around her like clouds, the earth is moving, no, she's moving, going down, down, down into a soft dark place with stars shimmering above, green stars, like his eyes, green. His eyes. He's so angry. He's going to hurt me. Don't, Correa! Stop! She sits up, her arms around her head. It's so quiet, so dark. No one heard her scream. She lies down again. It's so strange and quiet, stars above. So cold. I'm in New York. Not home. He's looking for me. He knows.

Hungry

A hiss by her ear wakes her. A snake? She sits bolt upright. She's in a huge room, with too many windows and sloping ceilings. Pale light stripes the sills around and below drawn shades. América presses her fists into her eyes, rubs them, opens them to a fuzzy view of the same room, same stripes of light around the shaded windows, and the hiss that woke her up. The clock radio is playing static. It is six-thirty in the morning. She chuckles at her foolishness and throws herself back against the pillows, pulls the comforter up to her chin, stares at the stars above, not quite so brilliant now, as if the coming of morning has dimmed them. Her face feels cold, and she pulls the covers over her head and curls up.

Someone bangs on a distant door. Knock knock knock knock. Pause. Knock knock knock knock. "Amé-rica!" She turns over, uncovers her face. The clock radio is still hissing, but the time is now 7:48.

"¡Ay, no!" She throws off the covers and is blasted by cold air.

Knock knock knock knock. "Amé-rica." Mrs. Leverett sounds exasperated.

"Sí, I come. One minute plis." She runs to the door, opens it, hides her nightgowned body behind it. Mrs. Leverett stands in the hall with her hat, coat, boots, and gloves on. América cringes in shame.

"I sorry. I never slip so much."

Mrs. Leverett smiles feebly. "I'm taking the kids to school. I'll be back in fifteen minutes. We can go over the house then."

"Okéi. I get dressed."

Mrs. Leverett walks down the long hall to the stairs without looking back. América shuts the door and leans against it, rubs the cobwebs from her brain. Her first day on the job, and she oversleeps!

She needs to focus on what to do next. Shower. No, it's too cold for that, maybe later. She gives the heater dial another half turn. She washes her face, brushes her teeth, her hair. She dresses hurriedly in the closet, which feels warmer than the room.

She makes her bed, tries to place the extra pillows as artfully as she found them but can't. She opens a shade. The world is white. Snow covers the ground along the driveway, which is cleared. Beyond it, a dirt road. Tall pointy green trees and wide, bare-branched trees surround the house, so that no other dwellings are visible. Clumps of snow soften the landscape. Bright sun makes it seem as if it were warm out, but the bottom of the windowpane is crusted with ice.

As she stands at the window deciding whether to wait downstairs for Mrs. Leverett to return, the red Explorer pulls into the driveway. América draws away from the window guiltily. She reaches the bottom of the stairs just as Mrs. Leverett comes in from the garage.

"Hi!" Mrs. Leverett's cheeks are rosy. When she takes off her hat, fine golden hair swirls around her face, like in a shampoo commercial. América smiles. "Let me take my boots off . . ." Mrs. Leverett goes into a closet under the back stairs, and América has a chance to look around.

The kitchen has an island counter that divides it from the room where the family takes meals. The table is crowded with plates, bowls, cups, a box of cereal, soiled napkins, glasses, and spoons. América begins to clear the table, placing everything on the dividing counter.

"No, don't do that now," Mrs. Leverett calls out. "Let me show you around first."

She's wearing a pair of slippers that make her feet into bear claws. When she sees América looking at them, she blushes prettily. "I know, they're ridiculous, aren't they? But they're warm and comfortable."

Even though she's wearing so many clothes, Mrs. Leverett still seems slender to América. But a look at the crowded breakfast table lets her know that the family certainly has enough to eat. She wishes she'd come down earlier and poured herself some coffee, which, by the looks of the abandoned filter at the bottom of the sink, must be somewhere in the crowded kitchen.

Mrs. Leverett stands by the counter. "As you can see, this is the kitchen." She points her hand at things the way models on television game shows demonstrate what you could win if you answer the question correctly. "We usually take our meals in the family room," as she points to the table and chairs. "Sometimes Charlie watches the news before he leaves," as she points to the television high on the wall. She fetches the remote control from under a napkin on the table and places it on a shelf under the television.

She leads América into a narrow room lined with glass-fronted cabinets filled with china, glasses of various shapes and sizes, serving platters and bowls. On the long stone counters, food-preparation appliances, candleholders, vases. Mrs. Leverett opens and shuts drawers to display serving implements, folded napkins and tablecloths, extra parts for the appliances. One section of the room is reserved for plastic ware, colorful cups and plates that look good enough for everyday service but that Mrs. Leverett says are used only in the summer.

"And this way," she says, sidling past América without looking at her, "is the dining room."

She waits for América to be impressed. The dining room is as large as América's house in Vieques. On one wall there is a huge stone fireplace, and on the opposite side, a massive, elaborately carved sideboard. In between, a long table under two chandeliers. Twelve chairs with upholstered seats are lined up on either side of the table and at the head and foot, and four more of the same type are against the walls, two flanking a long buffet table that matches the sideboard and the other two between the floor-to-ceiling windows that look out onto the neat rows of what América guesses is a garden of some sort, now covered with snow. Underfoot, a huge rug with fancy designs feels thick and soft, and América wonders how long it must take to clean this room after a dinner party.

"We entertain here," Mrs. Leverett says as she walks around the room, "mostly in the fall and winter. In the spring and summer we cook out a lot."

"Okéi." América hopes the longer she's in New York, the easier it will be to understand what people are saying. Mrs. Leverett speaks so fast!

"This is the living room," Mrs. Leverett says as they flow into the next room. It's easily as big as the dining room, with another fireplace in front of which two matching sofas face each other across a coffee table with magazines fanned on its surface, four upholstered chairs with cushions, four more side tables with bowls and china boxes and framed photographs. On one end, a piano, and next to it a music stand.

"You play?" América asks, and Mrs. Leverett shakes her head.

"Charlie can play, and we want the children to learn."

Shelves laden with books and more framed photographs line two of the walls.

"That one's at our wedding reception," Mrs. Leverett explains when she catches América peering at a large photograph of herself and Mr. Leverett smiling, their arms around each other's waists as if in the middle of a dance. "Here's our wedding picture." Mrs. Leverett in a long fitted white gown that accentuates her thinness, a lace veil drooping languidly from a crown of flowers, her hair under it longer and fuller, gypsylike.

"You look beautiful," América says admiringly, and Mrs. Leverett blushes faintly, looks at the picture, straightens it on the shelf. "Ten years ago," she says softly and strokes the photograph, leaving faint fingerprints on the glass.

"Around this way," she says in a louder voice, as if trying to change the subject, "is the den." She crosses a hallway with stairs leading up, and they're in another living room, smaller than the first but still impressive, with a huge black leather sectional and two leather recliners, and a rectangular coffee table made up of a highly polished slab of granite. Its sharp corners are shin height, and América bangs against one as she passes it. Mrs. Leverett doesn't notice América grimace in pain.

One entire wall is lined with electronic equipment, including a large-screen television. In a corner between windows there is a table with a computer and other machines with tiny green and orange lights, stacks of paper and a bulletin board with drawings and messages pinned on it so that there is very little surface for even one more scrap. "That's the kids' computer," Mrs. Leverett says. "Ours are in our offices." She goes out a door, and América follows her, finding herself back in the kitchen.

"Oh!" She exclaims, and Mrs. Leverett laughs.

"Yes, I know it seems confusing, but you'll get used to it."

"Is big house," América says. Mrs. Leverett laughs and points to the back stairs.

"There's more."

América looks up the stairs. Her stomach growls, and she brings her hands to her belly as if trying to calm a wild beast. She hopes Mrs. Leverett didn't hear it, but she's already moving away from América toward a row of appliances under a cabinet next to the enormous stove with eight burners, two ovens, a grill. She imagines that the Leveretts must entertain every night to need a restaurant stove in their kitchen. She wonders if it will be up to her to do all the cooking, serving, and cleaning up after their dinner parties.

"We'll go upstairs later. I've written a list of what needs to be done when, and we should go over it now." Mrs. Leverett finds two cups in the cabinet over the appliances and pours coffee from a thermos. "I made a potful before I left. We go through coffee here like you wouldn't believe!" She hands América a cupful, and the warmth and aroma set her stomach churning again. When was the last time she ate? Last night on the airplane. A chicken breast and broccoli. No wonder.

"Would you like milk in it, or sugar?" Mrs. Leverett asks, taking a container out of the refrigerator.

"No, thank you."

Mrs. Leverett pours cold skim milk in hers and leads América to the family room. She wipes the crumbs off a corner of the table, pulls out a chair for América, sits in the chair across from her. There is a pad with a long list on it.

"If I don't write everything down, I forget to do it." She smiles ruefully. América sips her coffee, which is strong and bitter, as if it has been sitting around too long.

Mrs. Leverett goes through her list, and América listens, although not everything Mrs. Leverett says makes sense. She wishes Mrs. Leverett would leave and let her discover where things are. She can see the house needs a lot of attention. There is much glass, rugs to be vacuumed, furniture to be polished.

"Charlie leaves by quarter to seven every morning," Mrs. Leverett explains, "to catch his train. I have to be out of the house by seven-fifty at the latest. On my way, I drop Kyle and Meghan off at school. She has to be picked up at noon, and Kyle at three-thirty."

As she speaks, Mrs. Leverett checks off items on her list. The dried cereal flakes on the bowls must be calcified by now, and América is anxious to get up and clean. She hates sitting at table with dirty dishes piled up in front of her. Her stomach growls, and she'd like some toast to calm the roiling but is too embarrassed to ask for food. It surprises her that Mrs. Leverett hasn't offered her more than coffee.

"Your days off are Sunday and Monday. I need you here early on Tuesday. Sometimes if we don't have company on Saturday nights, you can go home early." Mrs. Leverett catches herself, "I mean you can take off early if you like." She sips her coffee and studies her list.

There is no home other than the one I left behind. América looks out the window at the cold, white landscape shimmering

under the deceptive bright sun. She sips the last of the bitter coffee.

"Shall I show you the upstairs now?"

Kyle's room is immediately to the right of the back stairs, and on the other side of the front hall is Meghan's room, all frills and flowers and dolls. Each child has a playroom and a private bathroom. Kyle's playroom is lined with shelves filled with plastic creatures, cars, wooden train sets, electronic games, books, and board games. Meghan's room, too, is cluttered with dolls and stuffed animals, blocks, an easel with finger paints, crayons, and markers. The rear of the second floor is taken up by the master bedroom, his and hers dressing rooms and baths. On the third floor are another bath, two guest rooms, and Mr. Leverett and Mrs. Leverett's offices, each one facing the front of the house, each with its own computer, each neat and orderly, as if very little work actually takes place there. By the time they get down to the kitchen again, it's eleven o'clock.

"Oh, my goodness, how time flies. We still have the basement to look at."

A mirrored room filled with exercise equipment and a television high on the wall, a bathroom, a room with a pool table, a bar with its own refrigerator, and another den with leather furniture, another large television set and stereo, framed posters of athletes.

"We call this the sports den," Mrs. Leverett explains.

On a shelf, there's a glass-fronted case with an assortment of knives. América shudders at the seven sharp and shiny edges lined up one next to the other.

"Charlie collects them," Mrs. Leverett explains, matter-of-factly. "He started when he was a boy."

"There are more?"

"He has a few in his office upstairs and some in the city."

It frightens América that a man with as little patience as Charlie Leverett should have sharp objects lying around within easy reach.

"You no afraid kids touch?"

"The case is locked," Mrs. Leverett replies. "Besides, they know not to fool with their father's things."

The knives give América the creeps. She can't imagine finding beauty in an object designed to inflict pain, can't imagine what makes these knives so special other than the fact that they look more deadly and vicious than the one Ester uses for gutting chickens. She checks to ensure the case is really locked. She wouldn't want the wrong hands getting a hold of those knives.

The laundry and dry storage is behind the sports den. "I buy things in bulk," Mrs. Leverett says pointing to enormous boxes of detergent, a shelf filled with sanitary paper and paper towels, plastic cups and cutlery, napkins, industrial-size containers of cleaning supplies, cases of soda, beer, bottled water.

América is exhausted. Not just from the up and down the stairs, in and out of rooms. But from seeing so much in one place.

How will I ever find time to clean this huge house with two kids to look after? She follows Mrs. Leverett from room to room, half listening to her instructions, taking mental inventory of the number of toilets to be scrubbed and disinfected, the sinks crusted with toothpaste and soap scum, the streaked mirrors to be wiped with vinegar solution, the beds with their profusion of pillows, the stacks of towels to be washed, the rugs to be vacuumed.

When they return to the kitchen, Mrs. Leverett opens and closes cabinets, shows América where food is kept, which drawers hold cutlery, which kitchen utensils. She points to a calendar with the children's schedule printed in block letters. Kyle is to make his bed every day, which explains the lopsided corners and casual position of the comforter. Meghan is to help clear the table after meals. They both look at the crowded breakfast table, and Mrs. Leverett smiles and says, "We were in a rush this morning." She runs her fingers through her hair, pushes both hands into the pockets of her jeans.

"Well, I'd better get some work done before I pick up Meghan. Maybe you can start with the kitchen. If there's anything you need, buzz me in my office." She runs up the stairs without a backward glance at América, who stands in the middle of the kitchen wondering where to begin. Her stomach rumbles, and what she'd really like to do is have something to eat, but she can't bring herself to do so until she clears the messy kitchen.

"Okéi, that's where I start," she says to herself.

She picks up and hand washes the dishes, scrubs the sink, wipes down the table, counters, and chairs, sweeps the floor, rinses out the coffeepot, scrapes the burnt crumbs from the bottom of the toaster oven. A song insinuates itself into her brain, and before she knows it, she's humming, within minutes singing to herself as she rubs down the cabinets with a damp cloth. She's so involved in her work that she jumps when Mrs. Leverett appears at the bottom of the stairs, announcing she's going to pick up Meghan from school.

América doesn't eat all day. As soon as Meghan comes home from school, she has to be given lunch, a grilled cheese sandwich and a glass of milk. A couple of hours later, Kyle has to be picked up.

Once the children are home, América can't do much. They want to show their rooms and are disappointed that she's already been there. They argue over whose rooms she should clean first in the morning, over who should play with her first and whether she should crawl down on all fours with them or sit and watch what wonderful things they can make with their blocks or trains or whatever. She strains to understand what they say, and the effort gives her a headache.

"Charlie won't be home for supper," Mrs. Leverett informs everyone. "I'll make us some pasta, okay?"

She cooks spaghetti with vegetables and garlic bread, fills glasses of milk for the children. América sets the table.

"Set a place for yourself, too," Mrs. Leverett reminds her. "You eat with us."

She's uncomfortable sitting at table with them, jumps up each time the children ask for more milk or extra cheese for their pasta.

"Sit down, relax, I'll get it," Mrs. Leverett tells her, but América doesn't want to relax. She wants to impress her with how helpful she can be. She wants to do her job like she thinks it ought to be done, and that includes serving the family their

supper, making sure the children have plenty to eat, that there's enough of everything.

She now knows why the Leverett family is so thin. The flavorless spaghetti, the steamed vegetables, the gritty bread, the skim milk are all diet food. The entire family is on a diet. Unlike other homes with children, this house has no candies, no cookies in the cupboard, no ice cream in the freezer, no butter in the refrigerator. She feels sorry for Meghan and Kyle.

Mrs. Leverett leads the dinner conversation as if she were a schoolteacher, asking Kyle and Meghan about their day, pressing them for information about what they learned in school, whether this or that friend played with them today, whether the teacher was pleased with their work. Even little Meghan has to relate the goings-on in her classroom, and América wonders if this is for her benefit or if Mrs. Leverett interrogates her children like this every night.

She eats the bland spaghetti because she's hungry but wishes it were one of Ester's thick asopaos or her arroz con habichuelas. She pushes the thought aside as quickly as it surfaced, afraid that if she starts missing her old life so quickly, she'll never get used to her new one.

While the family watches television in the den, she cleans up and decides never to eat with them again. She'll prepare her own meals the way she likes them. She's not about to go on a diet that will make her end up looking as pale and wasted as an Americana.

At 9:00 P.M., after the children are bathed and put to bed, she comes into her room for the first time since she left it this morning and collapses on the bed with her shoes on. She stares at the stars above, going over all she has seen and done today.

A whole day has passed, and she has not once thought about Correa or Rosalinda. Does it happen so soon? Does one leave one's old life behind and in less than a day forget everything? She asks herself what she would like to forget, other than the obvious, and can't answer the question. She doesn't want to forget anything or anyone. She just wants not to have to think about them all the time.

Learning Their Ways

The next morning she gets up early and comes down to breakfast before the family wakes up. It's still dim out, but a feeble
sun is beginning to touch the white landscape like a timid lover.

She sits with her coffee and toast with jelly, enjoying the
quiet house, wishing it were a little warmer, wondering what
time Mr. Leverett came home. She remembers hearing the
garage door going up and down in the middle of the night, but
she was too sleepy to raise her head and look at the bedside
clock. His briefcase is at the edge of the table as if he has set it
down for a few moments.

She hears water running upstairs and knows that the adults
in the family, at least, are up. Mrs. Leverett didn't say whether
América is supposed to waken the children, and she's not sure
what they eat for breakfast, so she picks up around the family
room and den while she waits for them.

Mr. Leverett is the first to come down, and he seems surprised and pleased to see her.

"Good morning! How are you today?" he asks as if truly
interested.

"Very good, Mr. Leverett, and you?"

"Charlie."

"Excuse?"

"I'm Charlie at home, Mr. Leverett at the office."

"Ah, *sí,* thank you, Don Charlie."

"No, just plain Charlie."

"Okéi, Charlie." She smiles to herself. He's cheerful and energetic, moves with the confidence of an athlete. But his brusque manner and efficient movements seem studied, as if he has to keep reminding himself he's a grown-up. "Do you like breakfast?"

"No, thanks, I'll get some coffee at the station." He finds his coat in the closet, tugs his necktie into place before grabbing his briefcase and gloves. "Well, have a good day," he says, and doesn't wait for her to wish him the same before he goes out the back door. In a minute she hears the garage door open and his car's ignition catch smartly.

Upstairs there's a lot of running around, and Mrs. Leverett's and the children's voices speaking incomprehensibly fast. The phone rings and is picked up upstairs. América wonders if she should help the children dress, and as she's about to, Mrs. Leverett runs down, the portable phone at her ear, trailed by Kyle and Meghan.

"Okay, guys, have a seat and we'll get you some breakfast, okay? Good morning," she says as she goes past América and starts frantically opening and closing cabinets, pulling out bowls, cereal, a banana from the fruit basket on the counter at the same time as she's conducting a telephone conversation.

"I do, no worry," América says, and Mrs. Leverett nods, and leans against the counter, points at the cereal, then the kids, and turns around to scribble something on a piece of paper.

América brings everything over to the table, fills the bowls, slices the banana over the flakes, pours the watery milk.

"That's too much," Kyle complains.

"Milk good for you," América says softly, so as not to interfere with Mrs. Leverett's phone call. "You grow strong."

"She put too much milk in it, Mom." América is surprised at Kyle's tone, a whine that she's not heard before. Mrs. Leverett looks up from her scribbling.

"Just a minute," she says into the phone, then comes around

to look. "We only use a little bit," she says. "They like the cereal crunchy." She gets on the phone again.

"I'm not eating it." Kyle pushes his bowl away.

Meghan copies him. "Me neither."

Mrs. Leverett looks at América, as if expecting her to say or do something. What América would like to do is teach the kids some respect and make them eat their breakfast.

She smiles obsequiously. "Eat now, tomorrow I put less."

"I don't want it," Kyle says without tasting. "It's soggy."

América picks up a spoonful of flaccid flakes. "Is good, you see?"

Mrs. Leverett puts down the phone, picks up the bowls, dumps their contents down the sink, and refills them. "América is learning how we like things, you shouldn't be rude to her, okay?" she says to the children as she splashes a moistening of milk on their second serving of dry flakes. Without looking at América, she walks to the other side of the kitchen island to pour herself some coffee.

América stands by the table, feeling like she's failed a test. The children sit at their places like a prince and princess, looking from América to their mother as if both of them had let them down. América gets another banana from the fruit bowl.

"How you like, fat or skinny?" she asks, her lips pressed together, the paring knife poised above the banana over Kyle's bowl. He looks at her, his eyes staring into hers as if trying to understand her intentions. She stares back, unsmiling. He shrugs. She cuts half a banana into his bowl, half into his sister's, in deliberate even slices, not too thin, not too thick. The children silently watch her plunge the edge of the knife into the firm, giving fruit. When she finishes, she looks at them, her face set in an expression that challenges complaints. "Eat," she tells them softly, and they spoon the cereal into their mouths, their eyes on her as she moves to the kitchen, where Mrs. Leverett is waiting for the toaster to ding. "You sit, Mrs. Leverett," América says. "I bring." Mrs. Leverett sits across from the children, who are scooping up every last bit of cereal, milk, and banana.

"Call me Karen," she says. "We're not that formal around here."

"Okéi, thank you, Karen." She smiles thinly as she places the toast in front of her. "You like more cereal?" she asks the children, and they shake their heads in unison, like puppets. "Get ready to school," she says, and they slide off their chairs and go.

Karen Leverett looks up from her dry toast. "I shouldn't have yelled at them," she says, "but they have to learn."

América cleans up the children's places wondering what Karen is talking about and whether she understood correctly. The children come back struggling with their coats, and América helps them while Karen looks for her coat and boots.

"Tomorrow," Karen says, "you come with us so that you can learn the route."

"Okéi." América buttons Meghan's coat up to her neck, pulls her hat over her eyes. "We play when you come back." Meghan nods solemnly.

"I have to do some errands while I'm out. I'll be back in a couple of hours." Karen shoos the kids out in front of her, and América stands at the back door seeing them off. When the garage door opens, a blast of cold air chills her. She waves, and shuts the inside door with a shiver.

We have to get used to each other, she tells herself as she clears Karen's place. They're not used to my ways, and I'm not used to theirs. In the sink, the remains of the children's first breakfast look like vomit. She runs water over the mess, pushes the pieces of still shimmery slices of uneaten banana into the disposal. She feels like crying and attributes the sudden urge to the fact that she doesn't like to waste food.

It takes her a week to learn the family's routines and her role in them. Charlie Leverett leaves the house at the same time each morning, because he has to catch a train, and doesn't come back before 7:30 P.M. and sometimes not until long after the family has gone to bed. Karen Leverett is slow to get herself ready in the morning, and the children wait for her to help them get dressed. They all come scrambling down the stairs with ten minutes to spare. After the third morning, América goes upstairs as soon as Charlie leaves, helps Kyle get dressed, helps Meghan, then escorts them down for breakfast. By the time Karen comes down, the children are halfway through their meal.

"You eat good breakfast," América tells them, "you grow big."

Her statements sound to them like commandments. Unlike their mother, she doesn't punctuate every instruction with "okay?" She doesn't expect them to agree with her, she expects them to obey. If they argue, she tells them she doesn't understand what they're saying and repeats her instructions, and they have to do as she says because otherwise, she gets a look on her face like the morning she cut up the banana as if each slice were a warning. "Cold breakfast not good," she tells them, and the next morning, when Karen comes down to the family room, the children are eating a fragrant bowlful of hot oatmeal with honey and drinking a cup of sweetened warm milk, through which América has swirled a stick of cinnamon to give it some taste.

"Oh, that smells yummy," Karen says, and América places a bowlful next to her mug of coffee.

"Is good for you," she says, and Karen Leverett eats it as if she's never had it before.

As she closes the back door on them the fifth day, América sighs with satisfaction. She's learning their ways and is beginning to change them.

Everything in the Leverett household is done by machine. Some of them she's used in the houses tucked into the high hills of Vieques that she cleaned, others she's seen advertised in the circulars folded into the Sunday paper. But the Leveretts seem to have more than their share. There are three machines for getting a cup of coffee. One to grind the beans, and depending on whether she wants cappuccino or regular coffee, two to make it. There are machines for baking bread, making pasta, steaming rice, pressing and browning sandwiches, chopping vegetables, juicing fruit, slicing potatoes. There are two regular ovens, plus a toaster oven and a microwave, an enormous refrigerator in the kitchen, a smaller one in the sports den, a freezer. There are machines for washing and drying dishes and clothes. Machines for sweeping rugs, waxing floors, vacuuming furniture. Machines for brushing teeth, curling hair, shaving legs, rowing, walking, climbing stairs. A pants-pressing machine, a sewing machine, a machine that spits out steam for dewrinkling garments. Charlie has a machine to shine his shoes, and Karen has one that steams her face. There are three computers in the house, a telephone system with intercom and preprogrammed numbers for the children's schools, Karen's and Charlie's office, beepers, and carphone numbers. And there are other machines whose uses she can't identify.

"They must pay a fortune in electric bills each month," she tells Ester when she calls her on Sunday morning. "At least as much a month as we pay in a year."

"All that electricity floating around causes cancer."

"Where did you hear such a thing?"

"There was a special on it—"

"Mami, not everything you see on television is true."

"Why would they lie about a thing like that?" When challenged, Ester's voice takes on the petulant whine of an exasperated child. "They interviewed people who got brain cancer from living under electric wires. And a doctor said it could happen."

"Well, I'm not going to worry about it."

"It's probably only certain types of electricity."

"There's only one type—"

"Why do you always contradict me?"

"I called to tell you I'm all right and not to worry about me, and we end up fighting."

"I'm not fighting. I was trying to tell you something for your own good."

"Thank you, then." She fluffs up the pillows on her bed, curls into a more comfortable position. Neither has mentioned the name that hangs in the silence between speech. The silences that grow the longer they're on the phone, as each avoids saying the name, avoids being the first to bring him into the conversation.

"Did you talk to Rosalinda?" Ester asks.

"No, I'm calling her next. Did you?"

"She was surprised to see you."

"I had a nice talk with her before I left. She might come live here . . . once I get settled." She will not ask about him, will not admit to herself that she has thought about him, has wondered how he has taken her absence.

"Everyone's talking about how you left," Ester says tentatively, as if probing for a reaction before continuing.

"How I left?"

"Not saying good-bye to anyone . . ."

"I said good-bye to the people that mattered."

"They're talking about you."

"Who?"

"They're saying that you ran away with one of the guests— "

"Mami, that's not funny."

"Correa came over to La Casa and threatened Irving." Her words now come in a breathless rush, as if she's been holding on to them for a long time and can't wait to get them out of her system. "I've moved in with him for a while."

"With whom?"

"With Irving, until Correa cools off. I'm here today because you said you'd call. Pagán thought it would be best."

"Pagán? Mami, what is this? Is the whole island involved?"

"You don't know what it's like here."

"I've only been gone a week! I know what it's like there, that's why I'm here."

"He went crazy. Someone told him you were at the airport, and he was banging on my door before I had my first cup of coffee."

"Oh, my God, Mami. Did he hurt you?"

"I was ready, nena, don't worry." Her voice changes to a jovial gurgle. "I grabbed my machete . . ." Laughter rumbles out of her in rolling fits that make her cough. América imagines her, with her pink curlers and rumpled nightdress, waving the rusty machete she uses to weed her garden at an out-of-control Correa. She winces. "I said to him . . ." she's laughing, coughing, laughing, unable to get the words out. In spite of herself, a smile creeps onto América face.

"Get it out, Mami, what did you do?"

"I took that machete, and I waved it around . . . Ay, Dios mío, you should have been there! I said to him, 'Remember Lorena!'" She laughs, coughs, thumps her chest to soothe the cough.

América guffaws. "Oh, my God, you didn't!"

"I did. I told him I'd cut his dick off if he came near me!"

She hasn't laughed this hard in years. Ester, too, is enjoying herself. But América stops, her hands press the receiver so hard she might crush it. "You're lucky he didn't yell back, 'Remember O.J.'"

But Ester doesn't hear her solemn tone, the sudden change in her daughter's voice. "I think he finally realized someone in this house is crazier than he is." She's laughing at her cleverness, her courage. How long must she have fantasized about confronting Correa this way?

"Has he been around since?"

Ester stops, breathes in spurts that might make anyone else light-headed. "Ay, it was so funny. I've never seen a man so scared."

"Has he, Mami? Have you seen him since?"

Ester is serious again but will not cut the story short. "He ran off with his tail between his legs and flew over to Fajardo, must have just missed you at his aunt's. He came back the next day, so drunk he could hardly stand up. That's when he went to La Casa. Irving had him arrested."

A dull ache begins to pound at her temples. "He's in jail?"

"Nah! Spent a night there. Feto said he was back at work yesterday."

"That's not the end of it. He must be planning something."

"He doesn't know where you are. No one here does, not even me."

"Don Irving knows. Ay, this is so embarrassing."

"He said to tell you not to worry. You just take care of yourself."

In spite of herself, she begins to sob. "Everyone's being so nice to me . . ."

"When are you sending money?"

"What?"

"The reason people go to New York is so they can send money home."

América smiles through her tears. "I'll send you a money order as soon as I get paid."

"And don't forget to call Paulina."

"Okéi, Mami. I'll call her today." The silence that follows feels like a hug. "I'll call you next week."

"I'll be here."

"Thank you, Mami."

"Bye, then."

She sets the receiver down reluctantly and lays back against the pillows. Correa is not dealt with so easily. Especially if he suspects she's run off with a man. How could such a rumor get started? She didn't talk to anyone on the van to the airport or on the plane itself. How could anyone, knowing Correa's temper and behavior, be so cruel as to suggest she was traveling accompanied by a man? It makes no sense. But it doesn't matter. For all she knows, the rumors were started by Correa himself, his jealousy, his possessiveness not allowing him to accept the fact that she would ever leave him simply because she wants to. It's not over. She knows him well enough to fear that he will strike back at her somehow, either through Ester or through Rosalinda. There's no doubt in her mind that Correa will not ignore the public humiliation she has caused him. He's biding his time until he can hurt her as much as she has hurt him.

The phone at Tía Estrella's is picked up on the first ring.

"Rosalinda, it's me."

"Ay, Mami, he was here! He's looking for you."

"Calm down, mi'ja, he doesn't know where I am. Are you all right?"

"He was so mad. I've never seen him like that, Mami. He said horrible things, and he yelled at Tía Estrella. He called you names. And he said he'd kill you both, Mami, are you with another man?" Rosalinda is hysterical. Words come out of her in a torrent, punctuated by sobs. América swallows hard against the tightness in her throat.

"Now, listen to me, Rosalinda, listen. Are you listening, mi'ja?"

"I've never seen him so angry. He slapped me . . ." There's an intake of breath, as if the words had slipped out against her will. "He didn't mean to, I was in the way—"

"Don't defend him, Rosalinda. There's no excuse—"

"He loves you so much, Mami, he can't stand to lose you."

Where are these words coming from? Has she, América, ever said anything that would give Rosalinda the impression that the beatings have anything to do with love? Has she herself believed this?

"Rosalinda, he doesn't love me." Why does her voice catch, her lips tremble? "He doesn't love me."

"He says he'll never let you go. He says no other man can have you."

América closes her eyes, as if the darkness it creates were sharper than the windowed room with slanted ceilings in which she lies surrounded by pillows. "Rosalinda, get a hold of yourself. You must listen to me." The child stops whimpering, but her sniffles punctuate América's words. "I'm not with another man. Don't believe those rumors. I don't know where they started, or why, but they're not true. Do you understand?"

"Yes, Mami."

She bites her lips, switches the phone from one hand to the other. "The way your father has treated me . . . it has nothing to do with love. It's hard to explain, but you mustn't think that's the way men show their love." Her chest tightens, makes it hard to breathe. All of a sudden she's cold, her fingers are stiff and her teeth chatter like castanets. "Or that the fact that I let him beat me means that's how women show theirs." What does it mean? What does it mean? What does it mean? She's so cold she has to pull the covers over herself, speaks to her daughter from the darkness under the comforter.

Rosalinda sniffles, mumbles into the receiver. "Uhumm." But she hasn't heard any of it. "He'll change, Mami. If you come back. He says he loves you so much . . . he wants us to be a family again."

"Rosalinda, we've never been a family." In the darkness every word sounds like a confession.

"What do you mean, we're not a family? He hasn't always lived with us, but . . . but . . . but . . ."

América's voice is low, confidential, as if the words were forbidden. "He has a family in Fajardo, Rosalinda, you know that. A wife and kids."

"How come they're a family and we're not? Is it because he's married to the other woman? He had to marry her. He doesn't love her like he loves you, you know that."

"Ay, Rosalinda. You're hurting me."

"He's not a bad man, Mami."

"No, mi'ja, he's not a bad man. He's just . . . He's not a bad man."

Rosalinda is breathless, calling up every argument she can think of. "He was crying. He sat down on Tía Estrella's couch and he cried. He's never done that, Mami."

He was probably drunk, América wants to respond, but then she feels bad for not giving him the benefit of the doubt. He's not a good enough actor to fake tears in front of women who idolize him, and he does get mushy sometimes. At the end of *Terminator II*, when the robot man dropped into the vat of boiling metal, Correa sniffled and had to wipe away a tear. When the lights went on in the theater, he pretended to have dropped something under the seat until he regained his composure.

"Your father is . . . sentimental," América suggests. "Maybe he's realizing how badly he has treated me all these years."

"He does, Mami, and he swears if you come back, he'll change." There's hope in her voice.

"Did he say to tell me that?"

"No, Mami." There's a lie in her denial.

"I'm not coming back." There's an intake of breath at the other end, followed by another fit of weeping. América can't understand how, all of a sudden, Rosalinda wants her back in her life after trying so hard to get away from her.

"It's because of me, isn't it? Because of what I did?"

It's stifling hot under the covers. "This is not about you, Rosalinda, it's about my life."

"But if me and Taino hadn't—"

"What you and Taino did was wrong . . ." A wail, and for a moment América expects the phone to be slammed down. But Rosalinda hangs on, moans into the phone as if she were being tortured. Each sob is like a rope tying América into knots, each word, each breath out of her daughter's mouth winding her tighter and tighter, suffocating her.

"I made a mistake, Mami, can't you understand that? It was a mistake!" She screams into the phone, so that América has to pull it away, hold it in front of her as if expecting a screeching, moaning, sobbing Rosalinda to fly out of it. After a few seconds Rosalinda does hang up, and América is left staring at a silent receiver.

She's curled up on her bed, knees against her belly, watching the telephone as if it will come alive. It hums a dial tone. It's something, I suppose, that Rosalinda admits her mistake with Taino. She hasn't done that before.

América turns over, stretches her legs, wondering at which point of the conversation with her daughter she curled up into herself, so that her right side fell asleep.

I will not cry for her, for him, for anyone. I will not cry. Tears roll from the corners of her eyes to her temples. He loves me. He's always said he loves me. Rosalinda loves me too. So does my mother. But if they love me so much, why do they treat me like they don't? Rosalinda only loves me if I let her have her way. Mami only loves me if I stay out of hers. Correa loves me, I know he does. But I don't want to be loved that much. Not that much.

"If you'd like to make a call, please hang up and try again. If you need help, hang up and dial your operator."

The mechanized voice repeats its message, deliberate, composed, each word pronounced clearly so that there is no misinterpretation. Help, América whispers as she puts the phone on its cradle. Help.

*   *   *

"On Sundays," Karen Leverett said to her last night, "we usually do something as a family. We go for walks or to a museum or a movie."

"Is América coming with us?" Meghan asked her mother.

"If she likes," Karen said rubbing Meghan's head. "Sundays and Mondays are her days off."

"Maybe better I stay," América said.

Karen seemed disappointed. "If you decide to go for a drive, take the Volvo."

Where would I go, América asked herself.

The house is quiet. After her morning of phone calls, América is glad no one is around to see her swollen eyes and unhappy face. She prepares some canned chicken-noodle soup and two pieces of toast and sits in the family room eating and watching icicles melt on the roof overhang. I can't spend every weekend like this, she says out loud, crying in the morning and eating canned soup in the afternoon. A cardinal lands on the edge of the back terrace. It's the first bird she's seen since she's been in New York. Its red feathers seem out of place against the gray stone, the white snowbanks, the dreary green winter foliage. She made a dress that color one year for her birthday, and Correa made her change out of it into something less bright. Red, he said, made her look like a puta. The cardinal pecks at something in the interstices of the flagstone terrace, raises its head as if someone had called it, and flies away, its plumage a fiery streak against the drab landscape.

When América turned seventeen, Correa taught her to drive. He's always loved cars, spends all his money and free time on wrecks that he buys for next to nothing and then fixes until the engine hums and the finish sparkles.

Early on a Sunday morning he took her to the parking lot at Sun Bay Beach and lifted the hood of his car, at that time a gray Monte Carlo. "This," he said, as if he were revealing a marvelous secret, "is the engine." He showed her how to check the oil and fluid levels in the radiator. He demonstrated how to scrape tiny grains of dirt from the battery connections. He pulled a pencil tire gauge from his shirt pocket and showed her how to read the pressure. "The tires," he said, "are the only contact you have with the road. Keep them inflated, and check frequently for wear."

He took her on the narrow roads of Vieques and let her practice. "Step on the gas, and keep your speed constant. You shouldn't let the engine struggle. Don't ride the brakes, you'll wear them out. Wash the car every week, the salt air is bad for the finish."

When she got her license, he let her drive his car for practice and eventually gave it to her when he bought the first of his three Jeeps. But one day he came to the house and América wasn't there. She had driven alone to Isabel Segunda, a twenty-minute ride to the other side of the island. When she returned, her arms laden with a week's groceries, he beat her, saying that he didn't teach her to drive so she could go running all over town. He took the car away and told her he didn't want her driving anymore.

América sits at the wheel of Karen Leverett's silver Volvo station wagon. She reflects that Correa also didn't teach her to drive so that someday she'd be idling in the driveway of a mansion considering what to do with the rest of a cloudy Sunday afternoon in the middle of nowhere.

She takes a left onto the rutted dirt road. She has to slow down to let a group of riders on horseback line up single file so she can pass them. At the bottom of the hill she takes another left, toward the dry cleaners and the gourmet shop where Karen told her she always buys the coffee beans and extra-virgin olive oil she likes.

Across from the gourmet shop there is a small movie theater. Almost all of the rest of the storefronts on the street are real estate offices with photographs of million-dollar houses on the windows. She drives past a strip of stores with a supermarket at one end and a bank at the other. This is not where Karen said she should do the shopping, even though it's the market closest to the house. Beyond it is a flower shop and a veterinarian, and around the corner from it, a twenty-four-hour gas station. She drives past the fenced green meadows where a mother horse and her pony chase each other. Beyond it, at the bottom of the hill, is the high school, with its playing fields, a duck pond, and a clay track. She drives as if she knew where she was going, under the highway overpass, past an arrow signing a tennis and racket club. The two-lane road continues beyond Kyle and Meghan's school, to a crossroads in front of a hospital.

She takes a right onto the main street of Mount Kisco, the nearest town, seven miles from where she lives. She parks at the first space she finds and hops over the slushy puddle onto the cleared sidewalk. She left the house because she was tired of being alone, playing and replaying images induced by this morning's conversations. But she finds herself as alone on a street whose architecture, signage, and cold air are foreign. A storefront sign next to a karate studio advertises OFICINA HISPANA, and this is the first inkling she has that she's not the only Spanish-speaking person in Westchester County, New York. The office is closed, but through the plate glass she can see posters for Peru, Ecuador, and Guatemala.

Farther down, a restaurant with a Spanish name, Casa Miguel. She peeks in its darkened door and sees a long, dark, narrow room decorated with serapes and sequined sombreros, peopled by Yanquis being served by Spanish-looking waiters. A man asks her if he can help her, and she backs away, shaking her head.

Hair salons, a jeweler, empty storefronts with FOR RENT signs. Across from the movie theater there is a pizza restaurant filled with chattering children and harried adults. América hurries past it.

Around the corner there is a small park by a stream, with a statue of Christopher Columbus in a pose that at first looks to her as if he were peeing. But he's actually holding a scroll of some sort. Across the street, a statue of a feathered Indian turns its face away from Columbus.

Couples walk hand in hand, a group of men smoke on a street corner. They look Spanish to her, but as she approaches, they stop talking, so she can't be sure. She's surprised there are no piropos so typical of groups of young men back home. Maybe, she thinks, I'm not dressed up enough. She's wearing her only warm clothes, jeans, her Minnie Mouse sweatshirt, Karen Leverett's boots and heavy coat. Her curls are squashed under the tight blue knit hat. No wonder men don't say anything to women here, she says to herself, studying the bundled people passing her. We're nothing to look at.

So much walking around in the cold makes her hungry, and she follows a garlicky aroma to a Chinese restaurant. The place is full of Spanish-speaking customers.

"Buenas tardes," says the Chinese woman on the other side of the counter.

"Buenas tardes," América replies, smiling with surprise at a Chinese person speaking Spanish. There's an open kitchen behind the counter, at which three men wearing high white hats cook food in large woks over high fires. They nod in her direction.

"El menú," the woman says, pushing a large printed sheet with the menu in Chinese characters and their English translation, which to América looks as foreign as the original Chinese.

"Gracias." She stares uncomprehendingly at the list of dishes, trying to find chow mein, fried rice, and egg rolls, the only Chinese food she's ever eaten. And she's not even sure if it was really Chinese because the owner of the restaurant was a Viequense who had lived in New York for ten years and had never been to China, as far as she knows. The woman behind the counter points to photographs on the walls.

"El menú," she repeats, smiling, only this time she's not quite so friendly, as she realizes that América doesn't know what to order.

A couple walks in, and the woman smiles and greets them in the same way she greeted América. She hands them a menu, and América realizes that maybe the Chinese woman only knows enough Spanish to greet and serve her customers.

"Número cuatro," she says, pointing to the shrimp and lobster dish with a side of fried rice and egg roll.

"Y para beber?"

"Coca-Cola." The woman gives her a receipt, a Coke, and straw, and points to an empty table.

"Yo llamo el número," and she points to the numbers on the piece of paper in América's hand, at the table again, as if América didn't get it the first time.

As she sits, the people at the next table watch her. When she looks their way, the man nods, and the woman appraises her brazenly, a warning in her eyes. América pops open the can and stares out the window, avoiding the gaze of other women in the restaurant who watch her as if she had come in here to seduce their men right out from under their noses. This is my man, the look says, stay away from him. She's had this look on her face. When Correa takes her out, she's possessive if any woman looks at them. It is the same look Correa wears when he's with her, the same look Don Irving had on his face the three months Ester lived with him. And who knows, might be wearing it again now that she's come back.

Is it possible, América wonders, to love someone without possessing them? Is it possible to love and not worry that the next person who comes in the door is going to take your lover away with one glance?

Her number is called, in Spanish, and she picks up her order, and sits at her table alone, surrounded by couples speaking a different Spanish than she's ever heard but Spanish nevertheless. And she'd like to talk to these people in her language, to find out where they're from and whether they're used to this cold climate and whether they live in this town or, like her, are visiting on their day off. But the looks on the women's faces discourage her. She's a woman alone, and that makes her suspect to every other woman there. She eats the delicious Chinese food in silence, avoiding the dark eyes of the other diners, watching the passersby through the window, feeling as lonely as she's ever felt in her life.

When she returns to the house, América tries Estrella's phone number, hoping that Rosalinda will be calm and able to talk to her. She wants to apologize for sounding as if she were going to lecture Rosalinda about Taino. What she was actually about to say was that, even though what Rosalinda did was wrong, it wasn't the reason she decided to leave Correa. I should've done it long ago, she wants to tell her daughter, but I never knew how, or even that I could. But as she's formulating the words, América fumbles, not quite sure how to answer her own questions, afraid that Rosalinda's, which will be more like demands, will be even harder. She's relieved when the phone is busy.

I suppose Rosalinda's running away with Taino had something to do with it, she allows herself. Knowing that I did what I could for her and that it didn't matter anyway. This line of thinking raises her temperature, so she changes into her nightclothes, even though it's only 6:00 P.M. Maybe I shouldn't call her, maybe she's the one who should be calling me, apologizing for hanging up so disrespectfully. Then she remembers Rosalinda doesn't have her phone number.

She dials again. Either Rosalinda is on the phone with her father, or she has taken the phone off the hook to spite her. She thinks it's more likely that Rosalinda and Correa are on the phone talking about her, then decides she's being paranoid. But then she remembers them sitting on the couch back home, talking quietly until she walked in, silencing each other with a conspiratorial look that they didn't even try to hide. Whose side is Rosalinda on?

The garage door opens and drops below her. The Leveretts must be home from their Sunday together. She hears them puttering around and for a moment considers going downstairs to help them prepare dinner or whatever it is they're doing. But it's her day off. She curls deep into her comforter. If it's still busy next time I dial, she tells herself, I'm giving up. She waits fifteen minutes, dials again, slams the phone down after the insistent buzz. Now she's certain Rosalinda has left the phone off the hook. I'm supposed to feel guilty for mentioning Taino. I'm supposed to forget it ever happened. Well, I have news for you. I'm never forgetting it, never. You've made your bed, she tells her daughter across the ocean, now lie in it.

She makes her last call of the day.

"Aunt Paulina? It's your niece, América."

"Ay, nena, what a surprise! Hold on a second." In a louder voice, away from the phone. "Everyone settle down, it's América. ¿Cómo estás, mi'ja?"

"I'm fine, Tía. Did you get my letter?"

"Sí, mi'ja, but you didn't give me an address or a phone number. Are you in New York yet?"

"Yes, I came last week."

"Really?"

"I have a job with a family here.

"Yes, you said that in your letter. Where is their house?"

"The town is called Bedford."

"I don't know where that is. Hold on a second." The receiver rattles as if she's put the phone on a table. Paulina's voice comes through it muffled and distant as she talks to what sounds like several people. América can't quite make out what's being said, but it sounds as if they're trying to determine where she is and whether any of them have ever heard of the town. Paulina picks up the phone again. "Leopoldo knows where it is."

"How is Tío Poldo?"

"Ay, mi'ja, the same as always. We're all the same here, gracias a Dios. And your mother?"

"She's good. She sends her love."

"When is your day off? Can you come visit us?"

"I'm off Sunday and Monday."

"Good, come next week then. The family is here every Sunday, and you can see your cousins."

"That sounds nice."

"Poldo can come get you."

"I think there's a train from here."

"It would be so nice to see you, mi'ja. It's been years."

"Sí, Tía."

"Let me have your number so we can call you. We're sitting down to dinner—"

"I'm sorry, I didn't mean—"

"Don't worry, nena, how would you know? Here, I've got a pen. No, that one doesn't work. Hang on." América hears her rummaging around, then asking if anyone has a pen. Then she asks if there's paper somewhere, and several voices answer, and there's a rustle and then Paulina is on the phone again, but the pen doesn't work and she has to find another, and people are laughing in the background.

On her end, América feels left out. Paulina, three years older than Ester, has been married to the same man for more than thirty years. In her letters and conversations during infrequent visits to Vieques, Paulina boasts about her family. Their Christmas cards are always a picture of Paulina and Leopoldo surrounded by their children. Even as adults, Carmen, Orlando, and Elena have posed for the picture, as if not doing so will jinx the image of family spirit. On her wall of memories, Ester has a progression of her sister's life, from wedding picture to pictures of Paulina and Leopoldo holding Carmen, and three years later, Orlando, Carmen smiling at the baby, and six years after that, Paulina holding Elena, with Orlando and Carmen on either side of her smiling angelically while Leopoldo stands behind her looking as proud as the only rooster in the hen yard. In recent years the family Christmas card has also included a picture of Orlando's wife, Teresa, and their daughter, Eden.

When Paulina finally gets back on the phone with a working pen and a clean piece of paper, América gives her the number, then hangs up with many apologies for having disturbed their family gathering.

She would have liked to have been invited for tomorrow, Monday. She can't bear the thought of another day in Mount Kisco being watched by women holding on to their men.

But even if they had invited her, she would not have dared drive the Leveretts' car to the Bronx. In the week she has been in Westchester, she has heard the Bronx mentioned three times. The first time was when she asked Karen how far it was from her house, and Karen seemed to make a face, but it was dark in the car and maybe América was reading more into it than was there. Then, a couple of days later, she was watching the news as she prepared for bed and they showed a group of skyscrapers in the Bronx that the reporter said had become the home for several thousand Russian families. She was surprised at this, since the only people she ever knew who came from the Bronx were Puerto Rican. None of the guests at La Casa del Francés were ever from the Bronx. But many of her neighbors' relatives, like her aunt, lived in the Bronx, and so she had always come to think of it as an island for Puerto Ricans. The idea of Russians living in the Bronx adds a new dimension, like when she learned that Rubén Blades was Panamanian.

Last night the news from the Bronx was not so good. Someone tried to carjack an off-duty policeman. Both the car-jacker, who was shot, and the policeman, who shot him, had Spanish last names. But the carjacker didn't look Puerto Rican, nor did he look like the Spanish people she saw today in Mount Kisco. She wonders where people who live in the Bronx come from, other than Puerto Rico and Russia.

"Oh, it's like a United Nations here," Paulina tells her later when she calls América back. "We live in an Italian neighbor-hood, and a few blocks down it's mostly Jewish. The Puerto Rican neighborhood is farther down, but we moved from there years ago."

"Are you very far from where I am?"

"Poldo said you're about an hour away. Mi'ja, you're in the middle of nowhere!"

"It's pretty here, though. I like it. It's quiet."

"It's like Vieques, then. You probably wouldn't like the Bronx because it's too lively." She catches herself. "That's not to say that the people here are rowdy. We live in a very nice neigh-borhood of hardworking people."

"If I come next weekend—"

"There are no ifs, mi'ja. You must come."

América smiles. "When I come next weekend, could you take me shopping for warm clothes?"

"Sí, of course. But why spend money? We have coats and sweaters you can have. You know my girls. They must have the latest, so they give what they no longer wear to me. Not that I can fit into them anymore. I'm almost fifty years old, you know."

"You always sent us such nice things."

"Well, I always say there's no sense hanging on to things you no longer need."

"Mami never throws anything out. She still has the dress she wore to your wedding."

"Ay, mi'ja, my sister has always done that. Always squirreling things away. Your grandmother, may she rest in peace, was constantly after her to throw away empty bottles and pencil stubs and things like that. But Ester was always a collector. She even saved your ombligo from when you were born." Paulina laughs, a clear girlish sound that brings a smile to América's lips.

"I know, and Rosalinda's." On her altar, Ester keeps two small covered jars with her and Rosalinda's umbilical stubs floating in a foul yellow liquid. "I don't know why she does that."

"Who knows why people do things. It must be God's way of making us all interesting to each other. Imagine how boring life would be if we were all alike."

Actually, América thinks as she's getting ready for bed, it would be very nice if we were all alike, if we all had the same things and looked the same and didn't have to worry about whether that neighbor is more good-looking or that one has a nicer car. Reverend Nuñez sermonized on this topic, but she can't quite remember his conclusion. Something about we're all the same in God's eyes and the Day of Judgment. She punches her pillows down before turning off the bedside lamp. That's the problem with religion. You can't get a straight answer until you die, by which time the question doesn't matter.

Asopao

Monday morning América waits until Karen's Explorer turns onto the dirt road before she comes out of her room. The kitchen is as messy as the morning she first saw it, with dishes all over the place, an open box of cereal flakes on the counter, bowls, spoons, and cups left where they were last used. América clears the table, washes the dishes, makes herself coffee and toast. Karen told her that on Mondays a baby-sitter picks up Meghan and Kyle from school and watches them until Karen comes home. Although Karen didn't say anything, América thinks she shouldn't be there when the baby-sitter arrives with Meghan. In any case, if she stays in the house much longer, she's going to start cleaning, like she did in the kitchen even though this is supposed to be her day off.

She decides to take the car and explore a bit more. It would be a good idea, América thinks, to drive to the children's school, to make sure she can find her way there on her own. But this is only an excuse. The truth is, América loves to drive.

She loves being in control of a machine as complicated as a car. She loves the purring sound of the engine, the wind whishing through the open window. She loves how she only has a second to look at things before they disappear behind her.

She negotiates the narrow curvy roads with ease. She learned to drive on roads as narrow, as curvy, as crowded on either side with vegetation. She stops several times to look at the fenced meadows where horses munch placidly on tufts of grass. Behind massive gates, she can sometimes glimpse mansions. She's grateful for the houses close to the road, the ones not hidden behind tall hedges or fences. She stops the car and admires them from across the street, imagining herself inside.

In Vieques, the Yanquis' houses are all concrete and glass, exposed to the sun and winds of the island. Here the houses are tucked amid bushes and trees, with drapes to keep intruding eyes from seeing into the family's secrets. She wonders about the people who own these homes, whether their wealth is something they take for granted or whether they get down on their knees to thank God for their good fortune, as Reverend Nuñez suggests to his congregation. In the week she has been with the Leveretts, God hasn't come up once, and América asks herself if rich people need him as much as poor people do.

She drives into Mount Kisco again but this time doesn't get out of the car. Past the statues of Christopher Columbus and the unhappy Indian, she finds herself in a busy strip of businesses. On this road, she remembers, is the supermarket where she is to do the shopping, although she's sure Karen approached it from a different direction. Beyond it is a huge department store called Caldor. She drives into the parking lots, peeks into the windows but doesn't get out, saving the discovery of what's inside for another time.

"It's a new job," Karen tells her Monday night. "So the hours will be a little crazy for a while." She sits on the couch in América's room, looks around to see if she has made any changes.

"No worry, I take care everything."

Karen hands her a sheet of paper. América studies the colored blocks with the children's names and the place and phone number of where they're supposed to be at various times.

"This is the schedule for Meghan this week. Tomorrow she has a play date with Lauren Rippley."

América looks up. "Excuse?"

"Meghan." Karen enunciates slowly, her eyes intent on América's.

"Yes, Meghan. She has . . . I no understand." Her entire body burns with embarrassment.

"Oh." Karen smiles. "A play date. That means she's going over to her friend's house to play."

"Ah, yes. How you call? Plé det?"

"Play date," Karen enunciates again. "Play date."

América nods. Plé det, she repeats under her breath. Plé det.

"The Rippleys' housekeeper will pick them both up at school and bring Meghan back around three." She hands América Kyle's schedule.

"Then they have their swimming lesson. Do you remember how to get to the health club?"

"Yes." On her drive yesterday, América made sure she could get to all the places Karen expects her to know about, like the children's school, the health club, the supermarket, the karate and gymnastics studios where the kids take classes.

"I'll be home around 7:00 P.M." Karen looks down at another sheet of paper with phone numbers for her and Charlie, the children's doctors, the pharmacy, the two sets of grandparents in Florida, a close neighbor. "I taped one of these by the kitchen phone, but I thought you'd like to have one by your phone."

América puts it on her bedside table without looking at it.

"And this," Karen says, handing her a booklet, "is a school directory, where you can find the names and numbers for the children's friends. I've highlighted Kyle's friends in yellow and Meghan's friends in orange."

"You so organized," América says admiringly.

"If I weren't, life around here would be chaotic."

Maybe that was my problem in Vieques, América considers, I wasn't organized enough.

"It would probably be best if you fed the children early, around five-thirty, so they don't have to wait for us."

"Okéi."

"And you know how to reach me, in case of an emergency."

"I have all your numbers."

"Kyle knows how to dial nine-one-one."

"Excuse?"

"You know, the emergency number . . ."

"Oh, okéi." Karen is so thorough, América can't think of anything to ask that she hasn't already mentioned.

As she walks out of the room, Karen looks at the thermostat on the wall. "You like it warm in here."

"Is cold outside."

Karen smiles. "Good night, then," and closes the door behind her.

The thermostat is set to the highest temperature possible, four notches over the gold number 80. She's not turned it down since she arrived. It is the only room in the house that's warm enough, and América now wonders if Karen Leverett is criticizing her for having the temperature up so high. After all, they're paying for it. She turns it down a couple of notches, then gets ready for bed, putting on an extra pair of socks in case she gets cold overnight.

The Rippleys' baby-sitter is a bouncy young girl with long blond hair and eyes so clear they appear colorless. She jogs to the front door with Meghan on her hip. América has been waiting for them, worried that she'll be late to pick up Kyle if they don't come in the next five minutes.

"Hi," the baby-sitter chirps, passing Meghan to América. "She had a snack. We made Rice Krispie treats."

"Oh," América responds.

"Okay, bye." The baby-sitter bounces down the front steps and jogs to the waiting car, where an equally pale little girl waves languidly.

"What you say?" América encourages Meghan.

"Thank you," she calls out as the baby-sitter pulls out of the driveway.

"You have good time?" América asks, and Meghan nods. "Okéi, we get Kyle now for to swim." She locks the front door behind her and walks around the house holding Meghan by the hand.

"I have to pee," the little girl says as they reach the car.

"Now?" América asks, with a hint of exasperation. Meghan nods, and América picks her up and runs her to the house. "We no have time," she says as she opens the door. "You make peepee fast." She runs Meghan to the hall bathroom, helps her pull off her jacket so that she can get to the overalls underneath. She unhooks the overalls, is about to pull down Meghan's panties when the little girl screeches.

"I do it myself!"

"Okéi, okéi." América backs off, stands at the open door waiting for her. Meghan sits down.

"Close the door."

"Okéi." América closes the door, stands outside listening to make sure Meghan flushes. These American kids are so independent! She remembers wiping Rosalinda's bottom until she was four. "Hurry, we late," she calls.

"I'm done." Meghan comes out of the bathroom struggling with her overalls.

"I help," América offers, but Meghan turns from her and manages to hook one side. "Here your jacket," América says, but Meghan is still fiddling with the second fastener. "Plis, Meghan, we have to go." She hates herself for pleading with a three-year-old. She waits a few seconds, but Meghan is unable to hook the fastener.

"I do," she says, turning Meghan around to face her. She pins up the overalls, stuffs Meghan's arms into the jacket. Meghan resists her, crying that she can do it herself. "We have to go," América explains, ducking Meghan's little hands as they try to push her away. "We no have time you do yourself." Meghan wails her frustration, but América is determined. She hoists her up onto her hip and runs out the door, Meghan pushing away from her with surprising strength, screaming, "Let me go, let me go, let me go." She forces her into the car, straps her in the car seat with difficulty because Meghan is struggling to get out of it, kicking and screaming to leave her alone.

América is nearly in tears herself. She hates having to use her strength against the little girl. As she fastens the safety belt around Meghan, the child scratches her face, and América slaps her hand before she realizes what she has done. Meghan screeches even harder. América closes the car door and leans against it, her hands over her face. "Ay, Dios mío," she mutters, "I hit Meghan. Ay, Señor." She composes herself, enters the driver's side with a sidelong look at Meghan, who is still crying and struggling to get out of the car seat. América starts the car, her head buzzing with the knowledge that, should Meghan tell her mother that América hit her, América would be out of the Leveretts' house without a second chance.

"Meghan." She turns around to face the girl. "Plis stop crying. I sorry. I so sorry." América reaches for Meghan's hand, but she pulls it away. "Plis, baby, América very sorry. You pardon América, yes?" Meghan's crying becomes softer. América reaches for her hand again, and Meghan lets her hold it. "I no do again. I promise, baby." She's aware of the sound of her voice, the soft pleading tone Correa uses when he's trying to pacify her. "I love you very much," she tells Meghan, ashamed at having to borrow from Correa the one thing she always resented most. His use of the word *love* as blackmail.

With Karen and Charlie gone all day and the children in school, she has the house to herself most mornings and is able to tidy the rooms, load the dish and clothes washers, iron the children's and Karen's and Charlie's casual clothes.

The Leveretts spend most of their time at home in the kitchen, their bedrooms, the family room, and den, so that the other rooms don't get as messy and don't require deep cleaning as frequently. By the middle of the second week, América has settled into a routine. The children start school at eight-thirty, and most days Karen drops them off on her way to work. Meghan is dismissed earlier than Kyle and often has a play date, either at home or at a friend's house.

América gets in the car at eleven-fifty in the morning and spends most of the afternoon driving Meghan to or from a play date, picking up Kyle from school, driving them to swimming lessons at the health club, Meghan to gymnastics, Kyle to karate.

They don't usually return home until 5:00 P.M., at which time América prepares and serves dinner for the three of them and lets them watch a half hour of television before Karen arrives, which signals the end of América's workday.

The first time she goes to the supermarket by herself, she finds the Goya section. When Karen comes home, a whole shelf in the cupboard is filled with products that weren't there before.

"What is this?"

"Adobo, sazón, achiote, I don't know how to say in English. I need for to cook Puerto Rican."

Karen examines the labels. Her lips are pursed into a critical pout as she squints at the small print. "Hmmm . . . "

"You like food in Vieques?"

"We ate a lot of fried food," she says regretfully.

"Tourist food not good. Puerto Rican food healthy. Rice and beans. You see, I make for you." As she speaks, she realizes why salespeople have to smile foolishly as they talk and why the words tumble from their mouths so fast. They can't give customers a chance to think until the sale is made.

"We don't eat a lot of meat . . . "

"I cook without." Ester, if she heard this, would roll her eyes. Her rice is sautéed in sizzling salt pork before she pours in boiling water, her beans are generously seasoned with diced smoked ham.

"But what if the kids don't like it?"

"Don't worry, they like."

"I don't know," Karen says tentatively, still reading labels.

"If they no like, I make American food."

"You're planning to cook two meals at once?"

"No. If they no like Puerto Rican food, I make something else. But I think they like. In Vieques they eat tostones."

Karen returns the jar of achiote to the shelf. "What else do you eat besides rice and beans?"

"I surprise you tomorrow, okéi? I make something good."

"Just don't get insulted if we don't like it."

"You like it, no worry."

*   *   *

The next day she makes a thick chicken asopao, taking care to remove the skins so as to cut down on the fat.

"What is this?" Kyle asks when she sets it in front of him.

"Chicken rice potato soup."

"It doesn't look like soup."

"You eat. Is good, make you strong."

"There's a leaf in mine!" Meghan whines.

"Is laurel leaf. Give taste. I take out."

The children stare at the asopao suspiciously.

"You eat everything, I give surprise."

"What surprise?"

"In my room I have surprise if you eat everything."

"I want my surprise now!"

"No, Meghan, surprise in my room after if you eat asopao."

"Come on, Meghan, it's not so bad," Kyle says, spooning a bit into his mouth. "Uhmm, it's good." At first he's pretending, but after the third spoonful, he means it.

Meghan dips her spoon in and tastes the broth that sticks to it. She makes a face. "I don't like it." She sets her spoon down, crosses her arms on the table, and begins to cry. "I want the surprise."

"You're such a baby," Kyle taunts her.

"I'm not a baby!" she screeches.

"You stop molest little sister," she warns Kyle. "Come on, baby, don't cry." América tries to pick her up, but Meghan pushes her away.

"I'm not a baby!"

América strokes her hair. "No, I sorry, you not baby. You my baby."

As usual when they're confused by what she means, both children look at her as if she's lost her mind. Meghan's blue eyes get bigger, and Kyle stares as if trying to get into her brain. "Meghan América baby, sí?" she repeats, and the little girl falls into her arms, burying her nose into América's bosom as if seeking a long-lost fragrance. "You eat asopao América make for you?"

"It tastes funny," Meghan insists but with less conviction.

"If you eat five spoon, I give surprise."

"Five spoons?" Kyle gasps.

"Five spoons with soup inside," she corrects herself, and Kyle giggles.

"How many spoons do I eat?" he asks, and América doesn't understand that he's laughing at her until he cracks up. Then she realizes her mistake and laughs with him. Meghan spoons up some asopao.

"I ate one spoon." She giggles, and Kyle announces that he's on his seventh, and counting spoons, they finish their asopao to the last kernel of rice.

"Tomorrow," América says, "you eat forks." And the children's laughter is like music to her, the empty bowls the happiest sight since she left Vieques.

The promise of a surprise after dinner works. They eat her asopao, or rice with beans over it, or spaghetti Puerto Rican–style, garlicky and not as slimy as Karen's. Every night after dinner, they go up to her room and she pretends to search all over for a surprise and finally comes up with a handful of M&M's, or a couple of Hershey's Kisses, which they eat sitting in front of the TV in her room. Afterward she makes them brush their teeth, so their mother won't see chocolate stains when she comes home.

Later that week, she's hungry around 10:00 P.M. and goes down to get a snack. She thought everyone was asleep, but when she reaches the bottom step, Karen scuffs out of the den in her bear-paw slippers and sweatsuit.

"Oh, it's you."

"Sorry. I scare you?"

"No, it's all right . . . I just . . . it was so quiet here. Good night." She scuffs back to the den and sits in the corner of the couch, where, to judge from all the papers and books scattered around, she's been working.

América takes an apple up to her room. Charlie was not home for dinner tonight, nor the night before. In the ten days she's been working here, he has only been home for dinner three times. The other days, she's heard the garage door under her room rise and drop after midnight, but the next morning, when he comes down, he looks as fresh and ready as if he'd had ten hours' sleep.

Karen, too, works hard. She's up late most nights, reading on the couch, even though she has an office on the third floor and another at the hospital where she works. Most mornings she comes downstairs with the portable phone to her ear, scribbling notes as she sips the first of three cups of coffee before she drives the kids to school.

Do they ever have fun? Two of the nights she's been here, Karen has told her that she's meeting Charlie for dinner in the city. They arrive late at night, and the next morning the bed linens are rumpled more than usual and there are faint stains in the middle, where neither of them sleeps. She wonders if Karen, who is so organized, schedules their lovemaking the way she schedules the kids' play dates, then chides herself for being disrespectful.

She hasn't had sex in over two weeks. The last time she saw Correa he came to the house after an evening of dominoes and drinking with his buddies. She was awakened from a deep sleep by his hot breath on her neck and his hands crawling under her nightgown. "Baby," he whispered, "baby."

Her breasts feel overfull, like when she first nursed Rosalinda and made more milk than the baby could drink. Correa drained her breasts then, and on those days when he didn't come to her, she had to pull them up to suck them herself or they would hurt. She closes her eyes now and imagines a lover touching her as she's touching herself, her nipples hard and erect, a pillow between her legs. A lover who whispers "baby, baby" in her ear. A lover who looks, feels, and touches her the way Correa does when he's not angry, when he's tender and loving.

She has only had one lover, but he has been like two: the rough, violent man who batters her, and the sweet, gentle lover who swears he adores her. Tonight she holds on to the latter image as if the other didn't exist, as if his violence were a thing of the past, an aberration, a fault of judgment, a part of his nature that he can't control. Tonight the beatings are forgotten as she remembers his large hands on her breasts, the weight of his hips against hers, his fleshy lips on hers. In those few seconds when her body snakes against the mattress, when she has no control over her thoughts, she forms his name as if he were a deity. But then it passes, and in the half sleep before dreams, her hands, which for a moment felt like his, form into fists and she drifts into darkness cursing his name.

He Likes You

On Sunday América wakes up early, packs a change of clothes into a shopping bag, and drives to the station. She's never been on a train, and her image of one has been formed by the iron black locomotives in westerns, the kind that chugs into the station whistling a mournful "choo-choo." She's disappointed when a steel gray, squarish car dragging other cars like it whishes into the station, its horn bleating like a hoarse goat. Inside, the train is clean, its red-and-blue seats padded, the windows large and clear. She holds a ticket Karen bought her for the round trip to the Fordham station, and when the conductor comes through, he punches it smartly and nods at her as if he agrees with her destination.

The countryside whistles by like a movie in fast forward. Her eyes capture fleeting images, and before she interprets them, they catch another, until she has a sense of the whole that bears no resemblance to the way things really are. When they go over a bridge, she remembers that she's never been on a bridge on a train, and for the first time in two weeks she realizes how she's already taking this new life for granted, as if it has always been and always will be this way.

I am América Gonzalez, she tells herself, the same woman who fifteen days ago folded her maid's uniform and put it on the bottom of an empty dresser, in case she needs it again. Just because I'm driving around in an almost new Volvo and I live in a big house and I can take a train into the city . . . she's smiling. She catches her reflection in the window and sees a big, self-satisfied grin on her face. She chides herself for forgetting that her life now is the same life she brought with her. But it's different, she argues with herself, it's different. For the first time I can remember I'm in control. I couldn't say that two weeks ago.

Leopoldo meets her at the station. He takes her shopping bag, insists on carrying it to a battered Subaru, opens the door for her with old-fashioned gallantry. He's older and more deliberate than she remembers.

"How long has it been?" he asks, "since we saw you?"

"About five years."

"That long?" He sighs regretfully. He's a quiet man, a few inches taller than she is, with a solemn manner that suits him better now that he's in his fifties than when he was younger. In the family photographs he's always in the background, hovering behind his wife, a content smile on his lips. "It's hard to believe we haven't been to Puerto Rico in so many years."

She doesn't know how to respond. Leopoldo has always seemed to her like a man whose mind is never where his body is. It's not that he's absentminded. He is, in fact, the most solicitous, deliberate person she's ever met. But talking to him reminds her of the only time she ever went to confession. The priest sat behind a screen, and she could only see his silhouette. As she began to talk, she had the feeling that the priest was totting up the take from the previous week's collection. She didn't know why she had that feeling, but she did. She stopped midsentence and left, never to return to church. Leopoldo's absent manner gives her much the same feeling that the faceless priest did. He appears to be paying so much attention to her that she suspects he must be faking it.

They drive along a broad avenue between rows of three- and four-story buildings, the bottoms of which are storefronts: a bodega, a botánica, a check-cashing service. It's Sunday. Most of the stores are barricaded with corrugated steel garage doors tagged with elaborate graffiti. Even at this early hour, people are out on the street. Women push strollers with children bundled up inside them. A group of teenage girls with torn jeans, combat boots, and perfectly coifed hair dances down the street to implied music. An old woman is guided by a boy into a van. Men loiter in front of a coffee shop.

"So this is New York," she says softly.

"Haven't you been here before?" Leopoldo asks, then answers his own question. "No, that's right. You almost came, but you couldn't."

Correa wouldn't let me, she tells herself, and feels heat rise to her face.

A loud thumping comes from behind. At first she thinks something's wrong with the car, but then a Camaro pulls up alongside them, the radio blasting salsa rap. Two young men are in front, and both windows and the sunroof are open, the better to share the deafening sound coming from speakers that take up the entire backseat.

Leopoldo frowns in their direction. "¡Desordenados!" he mutters, and for a moment she sees the anger he keeps so well hidden most of the time. The car races ahead of them the minute the light changes, and the music fades, leaving behind a rhythmic thump-thump-thump that dissipates as the car turns under elevated train tracks.

"It's different here from where I live."

"Oh, sure, you're up in the country. We took a trip up there one summer. Our church had a picnic at a lake near where you live."

"I didn't know New York was so big."

"Oh, it's enormous. From here, we can drive north for seven hours and still be in New York."

"Wow! In Vieques, you can go across the whole island in twenty minutes."

"Sí, claro, it's a small island. But you don't have people blasting their radios in your face on Sunday morning."

"Saturday nights are lively."

"People in Puerto Rico still know about respect," Leopoldo

continues as if he hasn't heard her. "They're still considerate of others. Here"—he waves his hand at the avenue in front of them—"it's all gone downhill. This area used to be quiet."

They turn into a neighborhood of two- and three-story homes behind hurricane-fenced cement yards. The street is narrow, lined with parked cars on either side. A few tortured trees seem to defy the cement sidewalks, which their roots have cracked and broken into ruts. At the corner there is a taller building, pale green with olive window casements. With considerable maneuvering, Leopoldo parks his car in a space América wouldn't even think of trying. Next to the green building there is another small house, and beyond it, on the corner, a gas station on another broad avenue.

"Here they are!" Paulina's voice comes from above, and when América gets out of the car, she looks up to the top story of the green building, where her aunt is leaning out the window, waving happily.

"Hola, Tía," she calls, and waves back.

Leopoldo carries her shopping bag into a hall with a locked door beyond it. A buzz opens it, and they go up three flights of steep stairs to a door where Paulina waits exuding childlike excitement.

"Ay, mi'ja, it's been so long!" Stroking her hair, "You look beautiful as a blonde," wrapping her arm around América's waist to lead her in, "and you're nice and plump." Her enthusiasm is contagious, and América finds herself smiling, remarking how long it's been, hugging her aunt back with a warmth that she doesn't remember sharing with anyone else.

A petite young woman comes out of one of the rooms and hugs and kisses her on the cheek. It is her cousin Elena, Leopoldo and Paulina's youngest daughter. She has thick, chestnut hair down to her waist, which she wears in a single braid down her back. She smells like roses.

"It's so nice to see everyone," América says, suddenly overcome with tears. Paulina hugs her close, leads her to a large stuffed chair by the window.

"It's all right, mi'ja, you're with family."

Elena fetches a tissue.

"I'm so sorry," América sniffles. Paulina and Elena hover around her, rub her shoulders, murmur comfort. Leopoldo brings her a glass of water. "Thank you." She sips, keeps her eyes down, ashamed to meet their concerned expressions. She's mortified that she hasn't been with her relatives five minutes and already they have to worry about her. She can't explain, even to herself, what happened, why Paulina's embrace and welcoming manner broke open a wave of sadness that she didn't know was there.

"Ay," she sighs, composing herself with a deep breath, "it's so nice to be speaking Spanish!"

Paulina, Leopoldo, and Elena smile with relief, accept this explanation for América's tears, willingly and without question. Of course she misses Spanish! She's been living among Yanquis for two weeks, poor thing. But América can't convince herself so easily. It's a relief not to have to translate her thoughts, but the relief it brings is the same as slipping into a comfortable shoe; after a while you forget the initial pleasure.

They ask about Ester and Rosalinda and Vieques, and she answers, even though it's not new information to them. They don't ask about Correa, they know she's here running from him, but she wishes they would, if only to tell them that she doesn't care what he's up to.

"Come keep me company while I cook." Paulina leads her through a dining room to a cramped kitchen at the rear of the apartment. Elena and her father excuse themselves and disappear into different rooms.

"How lovely Elena is," América tells Paulina. "The pictures don't do her justice."

"Ay, mi'ja, what good is being beautiful when your head is full of straw?" Paulina takes a blender out of a cabinet.

"What do you mean?"

"That child, I should say woman, she's twenty years old already, takes after her father. Dreamers, both of them, only Leopoldo has a serious side to him, you know. He's responsible and has been a good provider." From a drawer, she pulls out onions and a large head of garlic. "Elena is a dreamer, but without ambition. She works as a receptionist in a clinic down the street. I'm hoping she'll meet a nice young doctor and get married soon."

"Let me help you with the sofrito," América offers, and Paulina hands her a paring knife and the garlic. América removes the crackly skin from each clove as Paulina peels and quarters onions. It's the first time she's heard Paulina complain about her children. On their infrequent, brief visits to Vieques, Carmen, Orlando, and Elena always seemed much too well behaved to be real. Ester claimed that her sister and brother-in-law drugged their children so that they wouldn't behave with the wild abandon of normal kids. They were affectionate with their parents, with Ester, América, and Rosalinda, who was nine the last time they visited as a family. América knows that Ester has a soft spot in her heart for Orlando, her only nephew and, as far as América knows, the only boy to have been born in her family in several generations.

"And how is Orlando?"

"He's good, mi'ja, he'll be here soon with his wife and daughter. That child is the sweetest thing you'd ever want to meet."

"Such an unusual name, Eden."

"Ah, imagine, her mother is a yoga teacher. Kind of strange for a Puerto Rican, you know, so Americanized she can barely speak Spanish. But I'm teaching Eden some words here and there. She's a delight, wait till you meet her." She doesn't wait for América to ask about her eldest daughter. "Carmen is a teacher. The only one of my children to have a real profession. Orlando is a salsa singer. He always had a lovely voice, you remember. So he's decided to be a singer, and I don't know how he can support his family as he waits for his big chance, you know how hard a business that is, and his wife a yoga teacher. Can you imagine, a Puerto Rican yoga teacher! Ay, Dios mío."

She scoops up the peeled garlic and quartered onions and dumps them into the blender. "Where's the green pepper? Didn't I get one out of the refrigerator?"

"I didn't see it."

"Ay, Dios mío, I'm really losing it these days." She opens the refrigerator door, exasperated, searches around until she comes up with a firm pepper and a bunch of dark green, fragrant leaves.

"Is that recao?" América asks, incredulous.

"Sí, I get it at the bodega down the street. It was owned by a Puerto Rican, but now it's owned by a Dominicano. Everything that used to be owned by Puerto Ricans is now owned by Dominicanos."

América washes a few leaves of the recao, lingering on their prickly feel. "There's a lot of Dominicanos in Puerto Rico, too. Not so many in Vieques, but on the big island." She dries them one at a time, each leaf a childhood memory of Ester in her garden, delicately choosing fresh recao, oregano, and achiote for that day's meal.

"Those poor people!" Paulina dumps the recao in the blender, throws in a few peppercorns, punches the button that whirs the blade violently around the garlic, onions, pepper, recao, chopping everything into her pungent sofrito, much greener, América thinks, than Ester's. "Their country is as backward as Puerto Rico was thirty years ago. They come here just like we did, full of dreams, expecting the streets to be paved with gold."

Paulina's chatter is comforting the way a radio is comforting. Everything she says is as familiar as if América had heard it yesterday, yet it's all new, and she muses on the difference between her mother and her aunt, daughters of the same mother, one of them an alcoholic, the other sober, with a long-standing marriage and children who, despite her complaints, are still loving of their parents and respectful of their expectations. Ester never had Paulina's spirit. Her life, circumscribed by her garden, her soap operas, her occasional couplings with Don Irving, is all she seems to want. Maybe, if Mami had been more like Paulina, my life would be different. She flushes, ashamed of such thoughts as soon as she's conscious of them.

While the cooking progresses, the apartment fills with people. First comes Carmen, Paulina's eldest, taller than her mother, with fuller lips, wider eyes, thicker hair, but with the same sunny smile and giggle, as if they had practiced until they sounded alike. Then Orlando, holding by the hand Eden, his six-year-old girl, followed by her mother, the Puerto Rican yoga teacher Teresa. Both mother and child are wiry, alert, with a savage look as if they have emerged from some ancient cave and are still learning to be with people. Orlando is as handsome a man as América has ever seen, tall and slender, with the assurance of the good-looking but with none of the swagger. They all greet her with such enthusiasm that she again comes close to tears.

When the cousins have all asked and she has answered about life in Puerto Rico, including el problema con Rosalinda and her own surreptitious departure from the home she was born in and has lived in for most of her twenty-nine years, another group of people come in, the downstairs neighbors Lourdes and Rufo and their son, Darío, with his two children, the twins Janey and Johnny.

After introductions, discreet questions, and evasive answers to the nonrelatives, Paulina announces that dinner is ready. The women go into the kitchen and the four men into the living room, and the children play somewhere in between until all the food is put out on the crowded table with mismatched chairs. The children are set up at the end of the table, and the men take their place while the older women serve. América keeps offering to help, but she's not allowed. She's seated next to Elena, who asks her questions about her life in Bedford and manages to keep her entertained until everyone is seated and Leopoldo asks God to bless the food and all present.

América can't remember the last time she sat at table with people who pray. Likely, it was the last time Paulina and Leopoldo came to Vieques. Likely too, Ester grunted through the whole prayer, and Correa was there, eyes cast down, hoping the encounter with religious people would serve him well when he appears at Saint Peter's Gates. Because, while Correa is not a religious man, he is faithful to God. He indulges in the sins of debauchery, adultery, and lechery but observes Ash Wednesday and Lent with a vehemence América has pointed out more than once is hypocritical.

Across from her Darío stares mournfully in her direction. She pretends to ignore him, to look past him at his mother sitting to his left, or out the window at the tops of other buildings and beyond them at a bridge, perhaps the same bridge she crossed on the snowy night she landed in New York.

I want nothing to do with men, she tells herself. I especially want nothing to do with men who look at me with those tearful eyes of his. I've never seen anyone look so sad and lonely, even in the midst of all these people.

"... and you should come too, América." Orlando's clear voice reaches her as if he had touched her on the shoulder.

"Yes, do, América," Elena begs.

"Where?"

"Another dreamer in the family," Paulina mutters, her girl-like giggle softening what América imagines is an insult.

"I'm sorry, I was just looking at that bridge over there." As if they'd never seen it, everyone at the table follows her gaze, and Leopoldo actually goes to the window to get a better look at a bridge he must see every time he passes this way.

"Oh, the Whitestone," as if it has been missing and has reappeared in the middle of dinner. He sits down again.

"Anyway," Orlando continues, "it's not a fancy club, but the bassist plays with Rubén Blades's orchestra and the pianist played with Celia Cruz."

Elena leans closer to América. "My brother is making his debut singing with a famous salsa orchestra. He wants us all to come."

América smiles at her gratefully. Like at the Leveretts', meals are used in this family to catch up on one another's business. The willingness with which they share their lives makes her uncomfortable.

Carmen announces she has a new boyfriend, "who shall remain nameless for now."

"Why didn't you bring him to dinner, nena?" asks Paulina.

"He's not ready for a Puerto Rican family," Carmen says coyly.

"Ah, another Americano, then?" asks Lourdes with a twinkle.

"Who knows?" murmurs Paulina.

"As a matter of fact," Carmen says, "he's Asian."

There's a gasp, as if the idea of an Asian were so foreign, so unexpected, that it scares them all. Leopoldo is the first to recover.

"There's a very nice Chinese man in my office. He's kind of quiet, though, doesn't mix with the rest of us."

"He's not Chinese, Papi, he's Korean."

"My father fought in Korea," announces Rufo, "and my older brother was stationed there for three years."

Elena leans over to América. "My sister has never dated a Puerto Rican in her life."

"Nor do I intend to," Carmen says. "Puerto Rican men are machista."

"Watch it, nena," Paulina warns, "your father, brother, and neighbors are Puerto Rican men."

"I wasn't talking about them," she says quickly, like a guilty child, even though she's two months younger than América.

"Ah, then, if you weren't talking about us," her brother says with a grin, "go ahead, insult the rest of them."

"I think you have some residual machismo," says Teresa from her corner of the table, where she is wedged between Rufo and Elena.

"You be quiet, woman," says Orlando in a play gruff voice, and everyone laughs except Teresa.

"That's not funny, you know."

"Come on, Teresa, don't take it so seriously," says Rufo, "he's just playing."

"Don't you defend him," says Lourdes, leaning across Darío, pointing a fork at her husband.

"Señoras, señores, we have company," says Leopoldo, and everyone laughs and looks at América.

"She'd better get used to our little arguments," laughs Paulina.

"Don't worry," América tells them, "before long I'll be starting some of my own." They all laugh at this, generously, she thinks, for even as she said it, it sounded like a threat more than a joke.

After dinner Teresa sits with the children in front of the television, where they are all equally enthralled by a movie about a lost dog. The men set up a game of dominoes in the dining room. Elena and Carmen take América by the hand and away from the kitchen, to prevent her from helping Paulina and Lourdes with the dishes.

"You do enough during the week," Carmen says, pushing América into Elena's room.

"This is so beautiful," América takes in the fragrant room with drapes on the two windows, the matching bedspread with a lace canopy, the fluffy pink wall-to-wall carpet.

"My sister adores Martha Stewart," Carmen explains.

"Who's that?" América asks, and the sisters laugh.

"She's a decorator." Elena shows América a magazine with a glamorous blond woman on the cover, her arms laden with cut flowers. "That's her," she says in English.

América leafs through the pages rich with photographs of interiors, advertisements for china and flatware, step-by-step instructions for making wreaths and centerpieces. "This is nice," she says, to be polite. The truth is that the rooms look claustrophobic to her, with their profusion of furnishings and pillows, pouffy drapes, patterned walls.

Carmen laughs. "Martha Stewart is not for everyone." In English she says, "She's the WASP queen of the universe."

"What's that?" América asks, and Elena and Carmen laugh again.

"WASP," Elena explains, "means White Anglo-Saxon Protestant." She switches to Spanish. "It's not a very nice word," she says, glaring at her sister.

"I think the people I work with are Protestant," América says thoughtfully. "I haven't seen any crosses or statues of saints around."

"They could be Jewish," Carmen offers. "What's their name again?"

"Leverett."

"That's not a Jewish name," Elena says with conviction.

"How would you know?" Carmen challenges.

"It doesn't sound Jewish, that's all."

América wonders what a Jewish name sounds like but doesn't want to ask because it seems that these sisters like to argue and she doesn't want to get them going.

Carmen stretches full-length on Elena's bed, where the three have been sitting. The other two adjust to give her room.

"Darío likes you," she says in Spanish, looking at América, who shifts uncomfortably. "Don't look so scared! He's a nice guy," she adds in English, sitting up, then flops back down again. "Since he stopped taking drugs," she says under her breath.

"What?"

"Darío had a drug problem," Elena explains. "He and his wife were addicts."

"But then she caught AIDS," says Carmen, "and died."

"Ay, Carmen, you make it sound so ugly."

"There's nothing pretty about AIDS," Carmen says seriously.

"Of course not," answers Elena, "but what he did was really wonderful."

América has been looking from one to the other, trying to follow the conversation, which has been in English. "He has AIDS?" she asks.

"No, his wife had AIDS." Elena's face is suddenly solemn, "When she came down with it, he took care of her. She died in his arms," she says, moist-eyed.

"My sister," Carmen says, "thinks life is a telenovela. No matter how bad things are, she manages to put a romantic spin on it."

"My mother is like that," América says, remembering Ester sitting before the television set night after night, watching the tortured lives of soap opera characters.

"That's where you get it, Elena," Carmen says, throwing a ruffled cushion at her sister, "from Tía Ester."

The door opens and Teresa steps in. "What are you girls up to?" Her big black eyes scan the room, as if someone else were hiding in it. "Did I miss anything?"

"We were just telling América the sad tale of Darío Perez Vivó."

"Ay, we'll be here for days," Teresa laughs. She flops on a stuffed chair, pulls her feet up, and curls them into a yoga position.

"How do you do that?" América asks, admiring the ease with which Teresa pulls her feet through the V formed by her thighs.

"It's called the lotus posture," Teresa says, "it's easy once you know what to do."

"I tried to do it once and thought my knees would never recover." Carmen chuckles.

"You forced yourself into it, I saw you," Teresa reprimands.

"My sister is very determined," Elena says to América, as if this comment makes up for Carmen's earlier statement about her.

"So where were we in the story?" Teresa asks, pulling her long black braid around to the front of her body.

"The dramatic death of Rita in the arms of Darío."

"Ay, Carmen, stop teasing your sister," Teresa says, laughing. "I think he likes you," she says to América.

"I smell coffee," América responds, and flees from the room, followed by the others' giggles.

How can they be so flip about a sad life, she asks herself. It's not his fault his wife died of AIDS. She catches a glimpse of him bending over the dominoes, the skin on his face so tight it's easy to imagine the skull beneath. He looks like a drug addict, she concludes. At least, he has the same look as Pedro Goya, a Viequense who returned from New York to the island an emaciated skeleton that no one could recognize. He died too, in his mother's arms, when a horse felled him on the pavement of the beach road.

"You can't help," Paulina chides her. "We're all done here."

"I think she smelled the coffee." Lourdes laughs, pointing a finger at América, who smiles and grabs a cup from the stack on the kitchen table.

"Have those girls been filling your head with stories?" Paulina asks with a glint in her eye, and América nods and hides her smile behind the steam coming from her cup.

"These are our Sundays," Paulina tells her later. "Every week they can, the kids come. And almost always Rufo and Lourdes and Darío, and of course, the twins."

"Every week?"

"Every week, mi'ja. Sometimes other relatives come, or other neighbors. But I always have a full house on Sundays."

Elena has gone to the movies with Carmen. Leopoldo is slumped in front of the television watching a documentary about penguins. Paulina and América sit at the kitchen table, their voices subdued.

"You seem to have such a nice relationship with your kids, Tía," América says with such sincerity that Paulina beams with pride.

"Yes, I do. Leopoldo and I try not to get in their way too much. We let them make mistakes."

"I tried to do that with Rosalinda, but it didn't work."

"Giving them the freedom to make mistakes doesn't mean they won't make them, América."

She considers that a minute, and the familiar tightness in her chest returns, a sorrow so deep she can't name it, can't push it aside. Tears slide down her cheeks.

"You've taken it so personally," Paulina says with real wonder, as if it had never occurred to her that her children's mistakes would reflect on her.

"Wouldn't you, Tía?" she says resentfully. "What if Elena had run off with her boyfriend when she was fourteen. Wouldn't you have taken it personally?"

"Nena, you have no idea what suffering my children have caused me." Paulina brings her hands to her chest.

América looks up as if seeing her for the first time. "They

have?" It doesn't fit with her image of the smiling faces in the Christmas pictures on Ester's wall of memories.

"If I were to count the hours I spent sitting at this very table waiting for Orlando to come home from these dangerous streets, or the battles I had with Carmen over her friends . . . Ay, no, nena, you don't want to know." Paulina stares at her hands, which are wrinkled, spotted, with short, blunt fingernails and thick cuticles.

"What I don't understand," América says, "is what a mother has to do to keep her children from repeating her mistakes. How do you teach them that your life is not their model?"

"You can't teach them that, nena, they have to figure it out on their own."

"I can't agree with you, Tía. Why are we mothers if not to teach them?"

"You can't teach them," Paulina insists, "you can only listen and guide them. And then, only if they ask for guidance." She touches América gently on the forearm. "You heard Carmen talking this afternoon about her boyfriend?" América nods. "Every Sunday she comes with another story of another boyfriend, to taunt me. Like she wants to punish me for all those years I wouldn't let her date. Every time she comes to dinner, it's a different boyfriend, from a different country, as if she's looking to see which one is going to set me off screaming and yelling for her to stop." Her voice is choked with tears. "I'm a religious woman, nena. I've devoted my life to being a good Christian. You can imagine what it feels like to have my daughter, almost thirty, come home every weekend to tell me about another boyfriend from another country. And to know that she's sleeping with fulano de tal from who knows where." She blows her nose on a napkin from the plastic holder in the middle of the table. "I tried to bring up my kids as best I could, as best we could, because Poldo was always there for them. He's always been there." She sighs deeply.

"I think Rosalinda ran away with Taino to punish me for something. I don't know what, though. I can't figure out what I did that would make her do this."

"Maybe she wasn't thinking about you at all, when she did it," Paulina suggests.

"If she'd been thinking about me, she wouldn't have done it. She knows what I expect from her." She looks at her aunt's tired eyes. "But if she hadn't done it, I probably wouldn't be here tonight talking to you about it." It is a cinder, a tiny little spark that glimmers briefly. Maybe Rosalinda was trying to force me to face my own situation. She shakes her head to erase the thought. Rosalinda is neither that sophisticated nor that willing to sacrifice herself for someone else's sake. She went with Taino because she didn't want to lose him. It's that simple. At fourteen, all you care about is whether you get what you want. And she wanted Taino, and there was only one way to get him. América had forgotten how hard it is to lose when you're fourteen.

"Rosalinda will be all right," Paulina reassures her. "From what you said earlier, it sounds like she's going to school, trying to be a normal teenager."

"I shouldn't have left her," América blurts out as if she's been holding it in for a while. "I should have brought her with me."

"How could you have managed that, nena? If she were here, Correa could accuse you of kidnapping. Did you ever think of that?"

She eyes Paulina with astonishment. "No."

"You are in a situation . . . forgive me, I don't want to offend, but . . . you've let your situation drag on much longer than it should have. It was about time you did something about it." She says it with finality, as if she's been waiting for the opportunity.

América is stunned. It's not that she's surprised that her aunt knows about Correa's abuse. It is common knowledge in Vieques, and Ester has surely confided in her sister. But it embarrasses her that her "situation," as Paulina puts it, should have occupied any space in her distant aunt's mind.

"There are places here," Paulina continues, confidentially, "where you can get counseling."

"Counseling?"

"This sort of thing," Paulina is tentative, searching for the right words, "it's important to talk about it with someone."

"A psychiatrist, you mean?"

"No, not exactly. There are groups of women . . . women like you . . . in your situation. Places where you can go and talk about it," she repeats.

"Why would I want to talk about it? I've run away from him, what more should I do?"

"It's not about doing more, América. It's . . . this sort of thing . . . the violence . . . I'm sorry, I've offended you. Believe me, nena, from the bottom of my heart, I'm trying to help you."

Does she think I'm crazy? Why would I go to a psychiatrist? I didn't do anything. He's the crazy one. He's the one who needs help.

"I appreciate your concern, Tía," América says icily, "but I can take care of myself."

"Ay, you're insulted. Please forgive me, nena, I didn't mean to."

"I'm kind of tired . . . "

"Of course, let's open the sofa bed. I'm sorry, mi'ja. I didn't mean to offend you."

"Don't worry about it, Tía." But she's distant, formal, wrapped in a hard, impenetrable layer that makes her back stiff and her speech clipped. She thinks it's my fault, she tells herself; she's blaming me.

From the sofa bed in the living room, América hears the murmur of Paulina and Leopoldo's voices in their room. In the apartment below, Janey and Johnny screech at each other for what seems like hours before a man's voice quiets them and sends them crying into another part of the apartment. Sirens wail, trucks rumble by close enough that they seem to be just under the window, one truck after another all night long. It's not quiet in the Bronx the way it is in Bedford, the way it is in Vieques. She's never been quite so aware of life around her as she is now. She's distracted from sleep by the neighbors calling to each other, the television downstairs, Paulina and Leopoldo's voices, a radio somewhere, horns, sirens, footsteps on the sidewalk three stories below. The sofa bed is lumpy in places, and she tosses and turns trying to find a comfortable spot. Somewhere, a clock tick tocks, and she focuses on its sound until the steady, predictable clicks put her to sleep.

Sometime in the middle of the night, Elena tiptoes in, leaving in her wake the scent of roses.

Homesick

'm so glad you're here!" Karen says the minute América walks
in on Monday. "The baby-sitter never came." The kitchen is a
mess, and Meghan is on her mother's lap, crying. Karen looks
frazzled and tired. "I had to leave work early to get the kids from
school. I had no way to reach you." There is the tiniest hint of
reproach in her voice.

"Where Kyle?"

"Kyle is isolated in his room," Karen says, tight-lipped. At
mention of her brother, Meghan wails.

"I help. One minute." América drags in two large bags.

"Have you been shopping?"

"My aunt gave. Warm clothes." Paulina, still apologizing for
offending, insisted América take the best she had in her closet.
Wool sweaters and pants, a pair of leather boots, several pair of
jeans, a couple of jackets, all hardly worn by Carmen and Elena,
to whom they belonged. "I have surprise for kids too." América
singsongs toward Meghan, who looks up, tear-stained and hopeful. "You come América room?"

Meghan looks up at her mother, who smiles encouragement,
and reluctantly leaves her lap to follow América up the stairs to
her room over the garage.

"He hit me," Meghan explains when they go past Kyle's

door, through which they can hear him plaintively calling out, "I'm sorry, Mom, I'm sorry."

In her room, América searches the bottom of one of the shopping bags and pulls out a cellophane pack of Cien en Boca.

"What are these?"

"Cookies. They good." She takes out a few fingernail-size cookies and eats them. "Mmmm."

She sets Meghan in front of her television set to munch on the treats, then runs downstairs. Karen is on the phone.

"Just a minute . . . Yes, América?"

"Kyle can come out?"

Karen looks at her watch. "Yes, he can, it's been ten minutes."

"Okéi." She runs up. When she knocks on Kyle's door, he opens it, scrunches his face in disappointment to see her rather than his mother. "Mami say you come out."

"No!" He slams the door.

She swallows a breath to squelch the anger that has risen up and tightened every muscle in her body. She knocks on the door again. "Kyle, plis open door. I no angry with you. Plis open."

"It's not *plis*," he says, opening the door, "it's *please*. You're not saying it right."

"Plees."

"Please, please." He stomps his foot.

"Plees. I no can say better." It's preposterous. She's standing in a hallway being given pronunciation instructions by a tear-stained seven-year-old. "I come in your room?"

"Can you come in? No."

"You come out? I need say you something." She stands in the hallway. The door to her room opens, and Meghan peeks out. "You wait for me, baby. I come soon." Meghan closes the door.

"She's not a baby."

"I like call her baby because she little girl. You big boy. You no baby."

"She's a brat!"

"What means brat?"

"It means she's stupid and spoiled and dumb."

"Not nice call people names. Not respect."

"She always gets me in trouble."

"Is no good hit little sister."

"She hit me first."

"Is no good. You stronger, bigger."

"She's a brat."

"You no hit no more, promise?"

"I hate her."

"Promise you hit little sister no more." She holds his shoulders, seeks his eyes. "Promise to América you no hit sister. Promise you never hit girls. Promise." Her eyes are wild, insistent, scary.

"Okay, I promise." He shakes loose from her, frightened but pretending not to be. "Jeez!" He presses his back against the wall. "It was just a little push."

"Never, okéi?" She's still looking at him with that wild look, those wild eyes.

"Okay, okay."

"Good boy. Come, I give surprise in my room."

After the children have been put to bed she takes out all the clothes from the shopping bag, trying to determine which sweater goes with which pair of pants. There's a knock on the door.

"I need to speak with you," Karen says.

"One minute, plis." América clears the couch for Karen. "Is mess here."

"Nice things," Karen remarks absently, not really looking. She plops on the couch, exasperated. "This is just not working."

América's heart drops. "I do best I can."

Karen shakes her head, brings her hands up as if to appease América. "Oh, no, I'm sorry, I didn't mean you. I meant the arrangement."

"Arenge-ment?" She feels stupid. Two days of speaking Spanish, and it seems she has forgotten what English she knew.

"Let me start over." Karen presses her hands on her knees,

takes a deep breath. América sits on the chair opposite, waits for Karen to collect her thoughts, wonders how Karen can be so successful in her work when she's this tentative in her personal life. "Okay. The problem is that Monday is a very busy day at the hospital, and I can't afford to have the same thing happen next week that happened today."

"What happen?"

"Johanna has the flu. She was sick all weekend but didn't call me until just before I expected her here. I didn't have any way to reach you . . ." This time it is said with reproach.

"I give my aunt phone." América moves to the bedside table, her back to Karen, so that she won't see her resentful face. It's my day off, she thinks, I can go where I please without having to check with you.

"You don't need to do that now."

"I have." América writes the numbers on a pad that was put in the drawer, doubtless, by Karen, who thinks of everything.

"Thank you," Karen says, studying it as if to check that the handwriting is neat. "Anyway, I wanted to talk to you about changing the days you work. Instead of Tuesday to Saturday, could you work Monday to Friday? I'll have Johanna cover on weekends."

"Okéi."

"Oh, good!" Karen seems surprised, as if she expected an argument. "So let's start this weekend?" Tentative again, prepared for América to change her mind.

"Okéi, no problem."

"Great!" She pushes off the couch with finality, glances at the clothes scattered on the floor, the bed. "Those are really nice," she repeats, and América again has the feeling that she's not really looking at them, that she just needs to say something. "Well, good night," Karen says, moving to the door. She looks at the thermostat, smiles, and shuts the door behind her.

América doesn't remember when she got up to follow Karen, but she's holding on to the doorknob with great force. She studies the clothes scattered on the bed and floor, the tops and bottoms lined up one next to the other in stiff-armed, stiff-legged attitudes.

Just the way she feels, rigid and stiff and peculiarly cold, even though the thermostat is back up to its highest setting.

"I tried calling, but the line was busy."

Rosalinda mumbles something at the other end, and even though América doesn't catch it, she decides not to pursue it.

"Are you feeling better now?"

"I wasn't sick."

"You were mad at me."

"Yeah." It's both a statement and a challenge.

"Are you still mad?"

"Yeah." Positive.

"Can you get over it?"

"Yeah." Unsure, quivering with held-back tears.

"I'm not doing this to hurt you, Rosalinda."

"I know." Small-voiced, childlike.

"If I thought I was hurting you, I'd come back."

"You would?"

"I would."

There's an intake of breath, a gasp without surprise. "How come last week you said you wouldn't?"

"Last week you were asking me to come back for your father's sake."

"Oh." Rosalinda considers this. América can almost see her biting her lower lip, her eyes cast down in the attitude she takes when she's thinking very hard about something. "Are you happy there?"

Now it's América's turn to bite her lower lip, to finger the pattern on the comforter. "I'm not as nervous about things."

"What's it like?"

América pushes the pillows behind her back, gets in a comfortable position, and tells her daughter about snow, about icicles shimmering in cold sunlight, about trees that look dead but that everyone says will have leaves in another month or so. She tells Rosalinda about the Leveretts' enormous house with its swimming pool, summer cottage, sloping lawns.

"Are you near a town?" Rosalinda asks, and América tells her about the beige statue of Christopher Columbus and the brown one of the Indian looking in the other direction, about Spanish-speaking Chinese women and rutted dirt roads lined with mansions. She tells about going to the Bronx to see her aunt and cousins, the clothes Paulina gave her, and how some of them don't quite fit so she will send them to Rosalinda because they're more her style.

They laugh about how serious Leopoldo is, and about how Paulina thinks it's strange that her daughter-in-law is a yoga teacher. She describes riding on a train. "It goes so fast," she says, "you can hear the wind whistling." It is the longest conversation she's had with her daughter in months, one in which Rosalinda learns something and seems grateful for it.

When she hangs up, after over an hour, América hugs herself, rocks back and forth on the bed in the large room with the sloped ceiling and many windows, rocking and laughing and crying at the same time, astonished that Rosalinda listened and seemed happy for her and didn't ask her to come back.

Charlie is like a visitor in his own home. If she didn't wash his clothes and clean his bathroom, she'd never know he lived there. Over the weekend, she finds his casual clothes in the basket, wrinkled, sweaty, man-smelling. During the week, his cotton shirts, each identical to the other except for color, seem not so much wrinkled as stroked. As if the body in them moves so seldom that it leaves no impression, even in the clothes he wears. She wonders what he does in his office in the city. It has something to do with hospitals, like Karen, although neither of them is a doctor.

In his third-floor office there are pictures of Karen and the children, of an older couple, whom she assumes are his parents, of Charlie atop a snowy peak, ropes dangling from his waist. In another picture, he's suspended by what seems to América a very thin rope over a rocky chasm, a distant flat horizon way below him. One of the closets in the basement is filled with ropes, long straps, boots, colorful metal hooks and rings. Another contains camping equipment.

"That's Charlie's stuff," Karen pointed out. "You don't need to go in there."

But América loves looking at the bundled sleeping bags, the tents, the elaborate backpacks with sturdy frames and loops and straps and mesh pockets. She admires the craftsmanship of tight seams, the cleverness of Velcro fasteners. She loves the colors, deep purple and forest green, burgundy, fuchsia.

His job is probably boring, she tells herself; he needs some excitement in his life. She imagines him climbing mountains spiderlike, attached by a thin rope that someone else must have tied at the top, but then she can't figure out how that someone got up there to tie the rope in the first place. It's crazy, she concludes, the things people do for excitement.

His collection of knives still frightens her. She supposes he needs them to cut the ropes when he goes climbing. But why would he want to cut ropes? If anything, América reasons, he would want the ropes holding him up to be as long as possible. When she dusts the case, she avoids looking at the knives. Even though they're locked behind glass, she can't help but think of them as a threat.

América wonders how Karen and Charlie were ever able to conceive two children. The sheets on the master bed are seldom rumpled from lovemaking. Karen's diaphragm stays in its little case inside the drawer of her bedside table night after night after night, forgotten, unused.

Some nights their muffled voices wake her up, not because they're loud, but because the silence until then has been so complete. They argue briefly, and then Karen cries and it's over. The next morning Charlie appears downstairs as chipper and cheerful as ever, and Karen comes down in her usual hurry, made up and ready for work. On the days after a fight, he comes home early enough to have dinner with Karen and read the children a bedtime story, but then he either works out in their home gym or holes up in his upstairs office while Karen spreads her papers on the leather couch in the den.

I wonder if he hits her, América asks herself. The first time she heard them arguing, she pressed her ear to the door, her

hand on the knob as if ready to run out. She couldn't understand their words, only the high notes of their raised voices,
hers accusatory, his defensive, and then the roles reversed and
he sounded wounded and she hard. But there were no screams,
no sounds of struggle, no choked gasps of pain. They argue, and
one of them leaves the bedroom to sleep in one of the guest
rooms. Sometimes it's Charlie, other times Karen. She can tell by
the hair on the pillow.

On those mornings when she knows they were arguing the
night before, she can't look them in the eye. Charlie comes
down, ready for work, and she trembles so hard she has to hide
her hands in her pockets, or run water and pretend to be rinsing
the bottom of the sink. He doesn't seem to notice. He fetches his
coat from the closet, tugs his tie left and right, grabs his suitcase
and gloves from the corner of the table, and leaves.

Karen, too, behaves as if nothing has happened. She sits
with the children and waits for América to serve one of the
elaborate breakfasts she has decided the family ought to have.
Fluffy omelets with onions and cheese, blueberry pancakes,
cream of wheat flavored with cloves and cinnamon, crunchy
french toast topped with strawberry preserves. It's as if what
happens behind the closed doors of their bedroom stays there,
doesn't spill into the rest of the large house, doesn't affect the
rest of their lives.

How can they do that? América wonders as she dusts the
shelves, vacuums the rugs, wipes down the counters. How can
they fight and then the next day neither of them is angry? Her
own fights with Correa lasted for days. The rage, the resentment,
the revenge fantasies, stayed with her long after she had forgotten why they fought in the first place.

Not that the why mattered. Their fights had no logic to
them, no clear pattern. The only thing certain about them was
that Correa would hit her. He hit her if she paid attention to
another man, and he hit her if she didn't, because ignoring the
other man meant she was pretending she didn't know him and
therefore hiding her true feelings of lust. He hit her if she didn't
look pretty and well groomed, but if she looked too well turned

out, he hit her because she was drawing too much attention to herself. He hit her if he'd been drinking. He hit her if he was sober. He hit her if he lost at dominoes, and if he won, he hit her because she didn't congratulate him enough.

She doesn't remember having an argument with Correa in which she hasn't come out bruised, so that even on those instances when he's sweet and contrite, she doesn't trust him. He kisses her, brings her gifts, strokes her flank gently and tells her she's beautiful. And she listens and sometimes believes him, but she's still wary.

It's hard for her to believe that Charlie, with his ropes and knives and brusque manner, isn't violent when he's angry. She wonders whether Karen and Charlie's fights have been so polite because they know she's there, at the end of the hall.

But she dismisses the thought. The forced closeness of living with the Leveretts, she thinks, affects her more than it affects them. It is their house. They can be themselves in it. She's the one who has to watch every step and be always on the alert. She's the one who must always be conscious of how they perceive her because she's dependent on them. But they depend on me too, she contradicts herself, at least Karen does. She presses hard on the pillowcase she's been ironing. How stupid can I be, she chides herself; rich people don't depend on anyone. I can be replaced with a phone call.

"I'm getting used to it," América tells Ester when she reaches her at home after days of trying. "The hours are long, though. I'm exhausted by the time I go to bed."

"Do they pay you extra for working late?"

"It's just for a little while, until Karen settles into her new job."

"You didn't work as hard here."

"I didn't work as long, but I worked as hard."

There's a long, slow inhalation as Ester drags on her cigarette. "I got your money order," she says. "I used it to pay the electric and water."

"Another one is coming this week."

América doesn't want to ask about Correa, doesn't want Ester to know she's curious as to whether he's still looking for her. "I saw Paulina and the family last Sunday."

She tells Ester the same things she described to Rosalinda, only it's forced, not as interesting even to herself. "Elena is gorgeous, bien delicadita." She talks about the visit, describes the view of a bridge from Paulina's window, what she served for dinner, the clothes she gave América, but in the back of her mind is the gnawing question of Correa. She wants to give Ester the impression that she's moving on with her life, enjoying New York. But has he forgotten me already, she wants to know, does he still look for me?

Ester doesn't mention Correa. América stretches the conversation as long as she can, until there's no more to tell, until she's asked for news of everyone she can think of but not Correa, not him. Ester doesn't summon Correa's name, and América is ashamed to come right out and ask. She hangs up, frustrated, angry with herself. Why should she care what he's doing and where he is? She's left him for good, doesn't ever want to see him again. It doesn't matter what he's up to. It's over between us. It's over. It's over.

"Speak the Spanish?" The voice is hesitant, quiet, heavily accented. The woman is short and plump, nut brown with straight black hair, black eyes, full lips that a movie star would envy.

"Sí, hablo español." América has been pushing Meghan on a swing. She and the woman have been looking at each other for the past ten minutes while the children they brought to the playground run, jump, and swing from metal rings suspended from the play structure.

"My name is Adela."

América introduces herself. She's shivering. The damp March air, which Karen says means spring is just around the corner, feels no warmer to her than the air in February did. Meghan wants to play in the wooden tunnels, so Adela and América follow her, chatting and getting to know each other.

"I work interna," Adela tells her, and points to the two little girls she cares for. She's from Guatemala, where she worked as a nurse in a private clinic. "But here, as you know, we have to do what's necessary." Her husband lives in another town, where he does odd jobs and landscaping. "It's hard to find work for a couple," she says, "and when you do, they don't want to pay as much."

"But when do you see him?"

"He picks me up every Saturday night. He doesn't work on Sundays, so we spend the day together. We rent a room in a house with three other couples."

Adela's Spanish is so musical that América keeps asking questions, fascinated by the sound of Adela's voice, the rhythm of her words.

"How long have you worked around here?"

"In May it will be three years, but I wasn't, uhm, married when I first came."

Adela asks América about herself, but América is not so willing to talk about her life and gives as little information as she can without being rude.

Meghan runs up, her hands between her legs. "I have to go peepee."

"Okéi, we go home." América scoops her up and calls Kyle from the slide.

"I don't want to go yet!"

"We have to. Meghan needs toilet."

"You go and come back then!"

"Home too far. You come now." She walks toward the car. He pretends to ignore her, but when he sees she's not looking back, he reluctantly follows.

Adela runs up. "I live right up the street. You're welcome to use the bathroom there."

"Oh, no, thank you. It's time we went home anyway."

Meghan bounces on América's hip. "I have to go bad!"

"The little girl might have an accident," Adela points out.

América looks at Meghan, whose face is scrunched into a grimace. "Okéi," she says, "but we can't stay long."

She straps Meghan into her car seat. Kyle pulls his Game Boy from the backseat pocket, and before they're out of the parking lot, he's grunting at creatures hopping around the small screen.

She's so friendly, América thinks as she follows Adela's Caravan out of the playground lot. América doesn't consider Adela's friendliness a good thing. She thinks Adela is too open, that asking a woman she just met to come inside the house of the people she works for, not even her own house, is taking liberties that signal disrespect for her employers.

She follows the van into a long driveway leading to a house that looks to América like the dwellings of murderers and ghosts that she's seen in the movies. It's painted dark brown. It has turrets on the second floor, a wraparound porch on the first, elaborately carved decorations that give the impression of lace around the eaves and along the porch.

"It looks like the Addams Family house!" Kyle squeals.

"Who Adam's family?" América asks.

Kyle hums a tune and snaps his fingers.

"Okéi, Meghan, let's go. You stay in car, Kyle. We come out soon."

Carrying Meghan on her hip, América follows Adela and the two girls into the house. A huge, elaborately carved door opens onto a dark, wood-paneled foyer.

"The bathroom is here." Adela leads them to the back of the house. Meghan runs in and closes the door before América has a chance to come in with her.

"Would you like a drink or something?"

"No, thank you," América responds, "I have to go home and make dinner."

"Oh, you cook too?"

"Yes. Don't you?"

"No. I'm just a baby-sitter. La señora cooks."

"I cook for the kids," América lies, defensive all of a sudden.

"All done." Meghan comes out of the bathroom struggling to snap her jeans herself.

"Big girl!" Adela compliments her, and América takes the little girl's hand and starts down the hall.

"Thank you."

"Maybe we can get together sometime," Adela suggests. "Here, let me write my number down. You call me."

América takes the scrap of paper, torn off a magazine, and dashes down the porch stairs.

"See you," she calls out.

Adela is the first Spanish-speaking housekeeper she's met since she came here, and she's both excited and apprehensive about getting to know her. She's so . . . América struggles to find the right word. Familiar. That's it. Even though they addressed each other formally, using usted, América still feels as if Adela assumes they can be friends just because they're both maids. But friendships, she tells herself, depend on much more than a common occupation. She shakes her head, mutters. What am I talking about? I have no friends.

She pulls into the driveway of the Leverett house, walks to the back entrance and unlocks the door.

"You forgot Meghan!" Kyle screeches as América leads him into the house.

The little girl is weeping quietly and refuses to look América in the eye when América tenderly lifts her out of the car seat, hugs her tightly to her bosom, and carries her in.

She goes to the Bronx for the weekend because she doesn't know where else to go. It's a damp, windy Saturday morning when she climbs the steps up from the Fordham station. There's no one to meet her. She stands under a store awning, shivering, wondering how long she should wait before calling Paulina. Across the street, a car pulls up with a piercing screech of brakes. When she turns toward it, Darío waves from the open window. She waves back and watches in horror as he does a U-turn from the right-hand lane, causing cars in both directions to swerve and brake in order to avoid him. He double-parks in front of her, ignoring the beeps and curses from other drivers.

"I'll take you," he says, coming around to open the door for her. "Doña Paulina sent me because Don Leo is not home." He's wet from head to toe, and his pale, bony figure reminds her of a chicken after its feathers have been plucked out. América hides her smile as she slides into the passenger seat.

"I'm sorry you had to wait," Darío apologizes as he gets into the car. "Doña Paulina called me at the last minute."

He pulls into traffic without signaling, steps on the accelerator with his left foot on the brake. América searches for a seat belt but can't find one. She grips the armrest, presses her right foot onto the floor until it seems she'll go through it.

"It's not far from here," Darío says, taking his eyes off the road to address her.

"Oh, good," she says, afraid that conversation will distract him and endanger her life further. He runs two stop signs without slowing down, making liberal use of his horn as he approaches the intersection. When she spies the tall green building at the end of the block, América breathes a sigh of relief. The street is crowded with parked vehicles. América is afraid Darío will want to drive around the block looking for a space, but he stops in front of the building to let her off.

"No sense in you getting wet," he explains, coming around to open the passenger door.

América runs into the foyer, leans against the door to catch her breath and send a little prayer of thanks up to heaven. He's a nut, she tells herself, buzzing Paulina's apartment.

"Ay, mi'ja, he wouldn't have been my first choice to pick you up," Paulina tells her later. "But I didn't want you to wait in the rain."

"He was probably trying to impress you," adds Elena.

"By trying to kill me?"

"He's a taxi driver," Paulina explains. "They all drive like that."

"You're going to scare América into walking everywhere, Mami," Elena says with a smile.

They have spent the day finishing new curtains; ruffled white eyelet in the living room, green voile in the kitchen, fruit patterns in the dining room. Standing on one of the sturdy kitchen chairs, Elena has hung the curtains and drapes, and the three women now walk from room to room admiring their work and arranging furniture in new configurations.

"That's the thing about dressing the windows with new curtains," Paulina sighs; "everything else looks old and shabby."

"Maybe we should paint," Elena suggests, hands on hips, squinting critically at the pale blue walls.

"Ay, nena, please! I couldn't stand the mess."

"Just the living room. We could finish it in one afternoon."

América slinks into the background, afraid Elena is including her in the "we."

"It would look nice with a deeper blue on the ceilings," she hears Elena say as she ducks into the kitchen and serves herself some juice. Outside, the rain continues in a steady, sheetlike torrent that reminds her of the tormentas that strike Vieques from time to time and wash the soil from the hills into the ocean. When she was a child, América followed one of the gullies from the hills of Puerto Real all the way to the beach, where the rainwater flowed into the sea, carrying leaves, twigs, and dead animals with it as if returning them from whence they came. It occurred to her then that if it continued to rain hard, the whole island of Vieques might wash out to sea. For weeks afterward she had nightmares that she was drowning. Rainstorms still leave her with a terror of imminent danger, with the sense that the ground beneath her is not solid and she might slip and fall at any time.

That can't happen here, she tells herself, looking out the window and seeing nothing but roofs. There's no earth to wash away. It's all hard cement, not a patch of soil. She's filled with sadness, with a longing she can't quite identify because it's so new. She sips her orange juice and watches the rain pelt the dark roofs of buildings and wonders what this new sadness means. It takes her a while to realize she's homesick for the familiar vistas of Vieques, the green hills and yellow light of the warm sun, the salty ocean breezes, the flat-roofed houses. She turns from the window as if to erase this new world so hard and gray, so cold, devoid of memories.

Darío stares at her throughout the Sunday dinner. His gaze is steady, lizardlike, fixed on her every move. But every time she looks in his direction he lowers his eyes and a faint blush tints his pale complexion.

"He's shy," Elena tells América when the young women are gathered in her room after dinner.

"The poor guy is afraid of you," Carmen suggests.

"You haven't given him any encouragement," adds Teresa.

"I don't want to encourage him."

"Good men with steady jobs are hard to find," warns Carmen.

"I'm not looking for a man."

"But it's good to have one on hold in case you change your mind," says Teresa, and the girls laugh and high-five one another.

"Here's what you do," Carmen says. "Be nice to him. Smile every once in a while. Let him take you out for dinner, or to the movies or someplace where you don't have to talk to him if you don't want to."

"Ay, Carmen, that's terrible." Elena pouts. "You're telling her to use him."

"Why not? Men use women all the time!"

"But that wouldn't be good for América," Teresa pipes in. "She's still recovering from a bad relationship."

At this the other two women avoid looking at América, whose face has turned a bright red. "Excuse me," she says, and leaves the room.

"What did I say?" Teresa asks the others in a plaintive tone.

América locks herself in the bathroom. The mirror over the sink reflects her reddened face, eyes shadowed by a deep frown. She'd like to wash the shame with cool, fresh water, but that would mess her makeup. She turns her back on the reflection.

A bad relationship, she said. Fifteen years of my life summed up in three words. As if "a bad relationship" were a disease, like cancer or the flu. Something to recover from.

There's a scratching at the door, followed by a soft "Can I come in?"

"I'll be right out," América calls, flushing the toilet. As she opens the door, Teresa enters without letting América come out.

"I'm really sorry if I offended you," she says breathlessly. "I didn't mean to—"

"It's all right." América avoids looking at Teresa's wide and lively eyes.

"It's not all right. You're insulted and hurt and wish I would leave you alone. Don't protest, I know it's true." Teresa leans against the door, her skinny arms crossed in front of her nearly flat chest.

"I'm a little sensitive about it, that's all," she apologizes.

"You have every right to be, and to tell people like me to mind their own business."

Then mind your own business, América thinks but doesn't say.

"Look at me," Teresa says. "It bothers me that you won't look me in the eye when we talk."

América is startled. Does Teresa read minds? She lifts her eyes to Teresa's. They're kind eyes, large and round, as if they see more than other people's.

"I'm sorry," América says.

"You apologize too much."

"I'm sorr . . ." América laughs.

"You should laugh more."

"You have a lot of opinions."

"My mother is psychic," Teresa says nonchalantly, as if everyone's mother were. "She doesn't speak. She makes pronouncements. I guess that's where I got it."

"Are you psychic?"

"No way! I couldn't tell you what I'm doing in the next five seconds." She looks at América. "But I can tell you something about yourself that you may not know."

"What?"

"Everyone here is your friend and wants to help you make a fresh start."

"Thank you—"

"I won't pretend I haven't heard all the stories about that man you lived with . . ."

"Correa . . ."

"And I can tell you no one here blames you for leaving him. So you should stop feeling guilty about it."

"I don't feel guil—"

"It wasn't your fault that he beat you. Men like that don't need an excuse to hit women. And just because he's like that doesn't mean all men are the same." Teresa unlocks the bathroom door. "That's all I wanted to say." She reaches behind América and flushes the toilet. "See you later," she says with a grin and leaves.

Now it's América's turn to be breathless. As Teresa spoke, América felt herself grow faint with rage. Who does she think she is, lecturing me as if I were a child? She turns to her reflection again, only this time the reddened face looks fierce, the eyes sparkle with fury. She scares herself.

Ay, Dios mío, she murmurs as she brings her hands up to her face. This is the face Rosalinda sees when I'm angry. She rubs her hands across her warm cheeks, presses her lips, tightens her eyes, as if all this effort were necessary to reclaim the untroubled face she thinks she presents to the world. When she opens her eyes again, there's the familiar América with the lined lids and rouged cheeks. She swallows hard several times, as if the lump formed in her throat by frustrated rage were solid as food and fed a part of her buried deep, deep, deep in her entrails.

Las Empleadas

Karen Leverett wears expensive underwear. The first time América tidies Karen's dresser she finds five pairs of panties and three bras with the price tags still on. Each panty was fifteen dollars, each bra thirty. There are fifteen other panties with the same brand name, and twelve other bras. In underwear alone, América calculates, Karen Leverett spent $750, not including tax. How much, she wonders, does Karen Leverett pay for the clothes people can see?

One of Karen's three closets is filled with tailored business suits in muted colors and fabrics. There are ten silk shirts and four cotton ones, twelve dresses, three pantsuits, twenty-three pairs of shoes, six pairs of boots. In another closet she keeps her dressier clothes, with their own beaded shoes, tiny handbags, two cashmere wraps, and two fur coats, one short, one long. Then there are the casual clothes, which she keeps in the third closet of her dressing room. A stack of jeans, sweaters, turtlenecks, thick woolen socks, four pairs of sneakers, three pairs of flat shoes, black, brown, olive green.

"I love clothes," Karen told her as she showed her around, and América, who loves clothes too, wonders what it's like to wear fifteen-dollar panties and thirty-dollar bras. They can't feel that different, she muses as she fingers the delicate lace, the tiny bows, the miniature pearls stitched between the bra cups. She folds and arranges them in rows by color, so that the whole drawer is a rainbow of shimmering silk and satin.

Seven hundred and fifty dollars, she mutters, in underwear. It would take me two and a half weeks to earn enough to hold up my breasts and cover my culo. Karen Leverett must make a lot of money at that hospital.

She examines the shoe boxes in the closet: $260 for a pair of suede slip-ons, $159.99 for sneakers, $429 for a pair of boots. América turns these items over in her hands, strokes the inside where Karen's toes have pressed against soft leather, creating gentle bumps and valleys. They feel different from my twenty-dollar shoes, she concludes, but not that different. She dusts and vacuums around the three closets, rubbing up against the rustling silks, the warm woolens, the soft prickly furs. If you add it all up, she figures, the clothes in this closet alone probably cost as much as a house in Vieques, maybe more. She stops to wipe the sweat off her brow. One week of my work puts her out the price of a pair of shoes. She pulls the vacuum out of the lighted closet, presses the door shut with her rear. It doesn't seem right, she concludes. When my three-month trial period is up, she determines, I'm asking for a raise.

"Why would you work interna if you're Americana?" Adela asks one day while they're watching the children at the playground.

"But I'm not Americana," América protests, "I'm Viequense, Puerto Rican I mean. It's just that Puerto Ricans have citizenship."

"But doesn't that mean you're Americana?"

"No, I'm Puerto Rican, but I'm a citizen. It means we don't need permission to live and work here."

Adela doesn't understand the distinction, and until Adela started asking her questions about her legal status, América hadn't given it much thought.

"So your social is real?"

"Yes, I got it when I was born." A legal social security card, which she has taken for granted, turns out to be as coveted as a green card, which she's heard about but has never seen.

"If I were Americana like you, I'd be able to practice my trade as a nurse. I told you I was a nurse in Guatemala, didn't I?"

América nods. Almost every time they talk, Adela mentions how the work she's doing is beneath her because in her country she worked as a nurse.

Because on her first meeting with Adela she didn't get a good impression, América resisted calling her for a few days. But finally, out of loneliness and curiosity, she relented and agreed to meet Adela at the park. Through her, América has met other women who work in the mansions and large homes tucked at the end of long driveways that light as you drive up. Liana, from El Salvador, was a bank teller. Frida, from Paraguay, was a schoolteacher. Mercedes, from the Dominican Republic, was a telephone operator. They see one another at the playground, or when they drop off and pick up their charges at one another's homes. They all have one thing in common. They've entered the United States illegally, and they're amazed that she, an American citizen, would work as a maid.

"I don't mind the work I do," América tells them, and they seem horrified, as if her American citizenship entitles her to aspire to greater things. "I like taking care of a house, and I like children."

"But you can be a schoolteacher," Frida suggests.

"I don't like being cooped up all day long," she protests, "having someone watching my every move."

"I wouldn't mind taking care of my own house," says Liana. "But doing it for someone else is different."

"It's a job like any other," América says. "There's no shame in it."

"I didn't say I was ashamed," huffs Adela.

"But it's true," says Frida. "All work is valuable in the eyes of God."

"But some work is more valued than others," Adela insists. "Maybe it's different in this country, but where I come from a nurse is more important than an empleada."

She doesn't use the word *maid;* none of them do. They call

themselves employees, or say they work in houses, or call themselves baby-sitters or nannies even though housework is as big a part of their job as watching children.

"You have a point," says Frida. "It's the same all over."

"We don't have a choice when we come here," Adela persists. "We have to take whatever work we can find. But you, an American citizen. And you speak good English—"

"My English is not that good."

"Still . . . you can go to school, learn a trade. You don't have to do this kind of work the rest of your life."

Maybe, América thinks the next day as she vacuums the downstairs rugs, Adela is right. I'm not ambitious enough. All those women, living in fear of being sent back to their countries, have big dreams for themselves. I don't. Did I have dreams as a child? Did I ever want anything more than what I had? I wanted my own home, but every woman wants that. I wanted a husband and children, nice furniture, a car. That didn't work out. I wanted to be taken care of. The whine of the vacuum cleaner is like a lament. That's all I ever wanted, to be taken care of.

"Do you know what you might like to be when you grow up?" She asks Rosalinda when she next calls.

"What kind of a question is that?"

"A normal question. The kind of question a mother should ask her daughter."

"It's the kind of thing you ask a little kid."

"Have I never asked you before?"

"I don't know." The sullenness in her voice says no.

"Well? Do you have any ideas?" She wants to sound playful, to make it seem as if she's making conversation. But Rosalinda's suspicious nature doesn't buy it.

"Why do you ask all of a sudden?"

"I was wondering, that's all." In spite of herself, it sounds like an apology.

There's silence at the other end, as if Rosalinda were going through a list of possibilities before answering. "You can't laugh."

"Why would I laugh?" she giggles.

"I want to be a vedette."

"A what?" She laughs out loud, delighted with Rosalinda's sense of humor.

"I knew I shouldn't have told you."

She's serious. Oh, my God, this isn't a joke. "No, nena, no, don't get me wrong. It's just such . . . a surprise." Images of scantily clad women shaking their buttocks at a television camera, and above the rhinestone-studded nipples, her daughter's face, darkly made up, hair teased into a mane threaded with feathers. "Tell me more," she says, hoping she misunderstood.

"I'm in a play, and the teacher says I'm a good dancer. And Dina says I have the look."

"Who's Dina?"

"You don't know her, she's my friend's mother."

"And she told you you look like a chorus girl?"

"She's a choreographer. She's worked for MTV and for Iris Chacón."

The words are out of América's mouth before she can stop them. "But those women are little more than prostitutes. How can you even consider—"

"How can you say that? You don't even know her."

"But I know what a vedette is, I wasn't born yesterday."

"You don't know anything!" Rosalinda slams the phone down.

This can't go on. She shouldn't hang up on me every time she doesn't like what I say. A vedette! She wants to be . . . A rumble of laughter begins deep inside and erupts in carcajadas. This is what you get for asking a question like that. Your fourteen-year-old daughter aspires to be a chorus girl. She laughs, alone in her room, deep, satisfying laughter that brings tears to her eyes. This is my life. I start out with such good intentions, and this is what happens. She's laughing so hard her stomach hurts. I fall in love with a man, he beats me up. I try to take care of my mother, she drinks herself to sleep. I work like a dog cleaning up after other people, and they pay me less than they spend on underwear. And my daughter wants to be a vedette when she grows up. It's too funny. Now I know what God was thinking when he made me. My life is supposed to be a joke. It's not meant to be taken seriously. That has been my mistake all along. I take everything seriously. This beats all. A vedette. I wonder what Correa will say when he hears. His precious daughter a vedette for every man to ogle! It's too ironic. He probably won't even get it. He might even be proud of her.

She turns over on her bed, and the laughter subsides, replaced by the image of Correa's smiling face.

One morning she looks out the window and the dead trees have come to life. They are covered with an intense green fuzz that, on closer look, is budding leaves. A yard two houses down is a sea of daffodils. Birds chase one another in and out of trees. Deer emerge from the foliage to munch on budding tulips. Shopkeepers, the school crossing guard, the fuel delivery man, all seem to have a smile on their faces. América, too, finds herself smiling at nothing.

"Spring fever," Karen remarks one morning when they all giggle at nothing in particular as she's serving breakfast.

Karen shows up with bunches of flowers one evening, and they fill vases and put stems in the family room and den, in the master bedroom, children's rooms, and even in América's room. They have no scent, which América finds unusual. These beautiful flowers, which last for days, give off no fragrance.

Charlie doesn't like spring as much. "Allergies," he explains when he comes down one morning, his eyes puffy, his voice nasal.

It's difficult to keep Kyle and Meghan at home. Even though there is a play structure in the backyard, they prefer the playground, where there are other children to chase, to argue with over who can climb higher, to push and be pushed by in the swings.

On any given day, América is likely to meet Adela, Mercedes, Liana, or Frida, and sometimes all of them. She likes some of them more than others. Adela, she still thinks, is too free to reveal confidences, and América is careful when she's around not to say anything she doesn't want to hear repeated. Mercedes is young, with a raunchy sense of humor and fun that América admires even as she wonders how someone can be so free-spirited. Liana is somber and serious, and whenever she's around her, América gets depressed. Frida is the oldest, in her late forties, with a take-it-as-it-comes attitude that América finds comforting. All of them have left behind children to come to the United States, where they care for other people's children.

"In another month I'll be able to send for them," Liana tells Mercedes and América. "My father has already arranged it with the coyote. They'll come in through México."

"But what are you going to do once they get here?" Mercedes asks. "Where will they live?"

"An apartment in White Plains. My sister Genia will take care of them while I work."

Liana has not seen her two boys since they were toddlers. Now eight and nine, the boys know their mother from photographs. Every other week she calls a telephone center in a town ten miles from their village and talks to her children, tells them she loves them and that she will send for them. Until two months ago, she also talked to her mother, who watched the boys. She died of a blood infection, and Liana's father insists that she either come back to care for her children or send for them.

"Will their father help you?" asks América.

Liana came with her husband, properly married, she explains. The only work she could find was as a live-in maid. He worked for a landscape company. Like Adela and her husband, they saw each other on weekends, until Liana found out he lived with another woman weekdays. "I don't even know where he is," she says. The three fall silent, recalling perhaps, their own men's intractability.

"It's going to be so nice for you to have them near." América brings the subject back to the boys.

"Mrs. Friedland is giving me two weeks paid vacation," Liana adds, and everyone murmurs about Mrs. Friedland's generosity. "Only, I have to arrange it during spring vacation, when they'll all be in Disney World."

Then the murmurs are about how difficult that's going to be, given that Liana's elderly father and two children have to travel by land from El Salvador through Guatemala to Mexico and who knows how long they'll have to wait to be walked into the United States. The air around them is heavy again.

"Hola, mujeres," says Frida, walking up. In another minute Adela, too, joins them. The two girls she watches chase each other to the slide.

"I have to find another job," Adela says without greeting them. "I can't take it anymore."

"What happened?"

"Ignacio lost his job." This is not the first time this has happened. Ignacio gets fired almost as often as he works. With uncharacteristic reticence, Adela never says why, but América suspects he's a drunk. "I asked for a raise, and they said no. I've worked there three years, you'd think they'd be more considerate!" She's fuming. Her dark eyes are hidden by a deep frown, and her mouth is tight across her face, as if she were biting back what she doesn't want to say.

"But didn't you get a raise last Christmas?" asks Frida. They all know what the others make. When they first come to one another's houses, they look at the size, the number of children, whether there are animals, whether they cook or not, in order to assess their situation against one another's. América excepted, they all clean other houses on their days off from the live-in work. Even the ones with men have to supplement their income with part-time jobs.

"I've been with them three years," Adela repeats, "but I make less than any of you." Adela's employers, whom she refers to as Ella y Él, so that none of them have ever heard her say their names, don't live in a mansion. Their house, while large, is in town, without the broad lawns and protective woods around them, and is not considered, by the maids, the home of rich folks, the way the Leveretts' is, or Liana's Friedlands'.

"Did you quit?" Mercedes asks, worried.

"I'm desperate but not crazy," snaps Adela. If a maid wants

to leave her employers, she notifies the other maids first, in case they know of a better situation.

"I haven't heard of anyone looking," says Frida, whose network extends to three states, since her sister and daughter work as maids in Connecticut and New Jersey.

"What I'd like to find is a situation for a couple. That would solve all our problems."

"We'll keep our ears open," says Liana, whose sister Genia works only day jobs but occasionally hears of a house that needs a live-in.

The truth is, none of them would recommend Adela, who, they have noticed, is not a particularly thorough housekeeper. Then there is the problem of her "husband," whom none have met but whose frequent run-ins with employers does not bode well. Adela describes him as proud, which probably means that, like her, he thinks he's too good for the kind of work he does.

"Did you hear about Nati?" Mercedes asks, and they all turn to her, grateful for the change in topic. "They had to send her back."

"Oh, dear Lord, why?" Liana's gasp is like a sob.

"She went crazy."

"Who's Nati?" América asks.

"She was an empleada from Peru. A young girl," Frida explains, "what was she, twenty-one, twenty-two?" The others nod in agreement to both figures. "She worked for two brothers who live together. Two old men, alone in this big house. She was worried at first that they might try something, you know." They all know.

"Maybe if they had, she wouldn't have gone crazy," Mercedes jokes to lame laughter.

"They left while it was still dark and didn't come home until eight, nine o'clock. She had to clean the house, take care of their clothes, and make them dinner, that's all."

"And they didn't make that much of a mess, since they were never there," Liana adds.

"So Nati was alone all day in this big house. She spoke no

English. She didn't drive." They all shake their heads. "Stuck in that house alone day after day, with no one to talk to."

"She went crazy," Mercedes repeats. "In six months she was like an old woman. She didn't take care of herself, since there was no one to appreciate it. She talked to herself. The viejitos couldn't understand what she was saying, but they thought it was Spanish."

"Didn't she try to kill herself?" Adela asks, her face still furrowed. She turns to América. "The viejitos found her one night on the kitchen floor. She took aspirin or something that made her throw up but didn't kill her."

"So they sent her back," Mercedes concludes.

"Didn't anyone try to help her?" América wonders.

"What could anyone do?" Frida asks. She focuses on removing a pebble caught in the sole of her sneaker.

"I called her a couple of times," says Liana, "but she was kind of aloof."

"She was probably crazy when she came here," reasons Adela.

"Poor thing." América murmurs, and the empleadas allow how sad it is, and how this kind of thing happens, and how you have to live with it.

The gloom is broken by a scream from the swings. As one, the women run toward a little girl crumpled on the ground. Her mother, who had been sitting in the sun reading a magazine, reaches her at the same time as Mercedes, who kneels down to console her.

"Don't touch her," the mother screams, and Mercedes freezes in place. The woman scoops up the little girl and takes her away, soothing her. "It's all right. It's just a boo-boo. Let's get a Band-Aid, okay?"

América, Adela, Frida, and Liana gather the children they watch, check them for bruises on arms and legs, even though none of them cried. Mercedes finds the twins she cares for, inspects them, sends them off.

"We're leaving soon," she warns as the children resume their play.

The women return to their places on the edge of the playground. They stand close together, like five birds on a line, protecting one another.

"What was wrong with that woman?" Mercedes pouts. "I was just trying to help."

"You're not supposed to move a person that's fallen until you check them," Adela says with authority, "in case they broke a bone."

"I didn't move her."

"You know how these gringas are," explains Frida. "They panic at any little thing."

They fall silent again, thinking about the same thing. The woman panicked not at her daughter's fall but at the sight of a dark-skinned stranger bending over her.

"'Don't touch her,'" she said, like I'm contagious or something."

"You're reading too much into it." Frida pats Mercedes's shoulder. "Don't make yourself crazy."

They saw the mistrust in the woman's eyes, the resentment, the "why don't you go back where you came from" look. It's a look that follows the empleadas everywhere they go. In stores clerks hover over them, expecting them to steal whatever they touch. On buses and trains people won't sit next to them, as if sharing a seat were too intimate an association. On the street, people avoid looking at them, as if not seeing them will make them disappear.

"It's like they need us," Mercedes continues after a while, "but they don't want us."

"She didn't mean anything," Adela protests. "You know how scared of strangers these gringas are." But none of them are so willing to dismiss the woman's scornful look, the deliberate turning of her back on them.

Later, as América drives Kyle and Meghan to their swim lessons, she tries to remember if she's seen this look directed at her. In Vieques she saw something similar. The tourists couldn't say, "Go back to where you come from," because they were the guests. But she thought they saw her as a different species of creature from themselves. She felt like part of the tropical land-scape they came to experience, something to be stared at with curiosity and forgotten the moment they returned home.

But here, she says to herself, they can't forget us. We're everywhere, and they resent us for it. It's incomprehensible. If it weren't for us, none of these women would be able to work. And their husbands wouldn't have it so easy, either. If we weren't here, who would clear the tables at their restaurants? Who would mow their lawns and build the stone fences around their properties? Who would clean their offices, restock store shelves, disinfect hospital rooms, make their beds, wash their laundry, cook their meals?

"América, can we go to McDonald's?" Kyle asks as they drive past it.

"No, we dinner home after swim."

"But I'm hungry now," he whines, and Meghan adds her lit-tle voice so that América feels guilty until she turns the car around and drives up to the take-out window, where a young man with a pronounced accent serves them.

"You no make mess in car," América warns, and the chil-dren, used to her rules, quietly munch their Chicken McNuggets and salty french fries, dutifully using their napkins rather than the cuffs of their jackets to wipe away the grease from their faces.

Isn't it strange, she smiles to herself as she pulls into traffic. They're learning so much from me. Karen and Charlie hardly ever see them, between their jobs and the kids' weekend play dates. Frida, Mercedes, Liana, and Adela are teaching the chil-dren they watch. All these Americanitos are learning about life from us. We're from a different country, we speak a different lan-guage, but we're the ones there when they're hungry, or when they take their first step, or when they swim across the shallow end of the pool on their own.

At the health club she joins other women walking briskly with their children, equally as many mothers as empleadas. She can always pick out the mothers, because they're expensively dressed. They open the door to the club with a sense of entitlement, while the empleadas seem to be apologizing for taking up room where they don't belong. The brown and black ones, anyway. The white-skinned ones behave like the mothers, with the same confidence and unapologetic decisiveness.

Adela claims the white empleadas are paid more than the Latina and black housekeepers, and they work less. As housekeeper/nannies, América and her friends are in charge of both the house and the children. The European au pairs and white nannies usually do little or no housework. That's why Frida and Mercedes, Liana and Adela have day jobs cleaning the homes of people who have help. Most of the time the help is white, like the householders, and they look down on the "cleaning lady," who does the work they refuse to do.

"Well, that didn't last long," she says to Ester, surprised at her anger.

"Irving is a good man, but I'm too set in my ways and so is he." By the sound of Ester's voice, América can tell she's had a few drinks. That's what she means by she's too set in her ways. "Besides, someone needs to take care of this place. The garden is beginning to look like a jungle."

América imagines Ester's unruly garden, the rosebushes that attack anyone who dares enter the gate, the profusion of herbs planted in crooked rows in back of the house, the lemon and grapefruit trees, their thorns sharper and harder than any she's ever seen. If that garden can look worse than it did when she lived there, it's worth whatever it takes to get Ester back to tend it.

"Did you have a fight?"

"No," Ester says, "we have an understanding. We just can't live together anymore." She probably gave up drinking while she lived with Don Irving and has now chosen beer over him. That's the understanding.

América sighs deeply. "Well, you know best. It's your life."

"Yes," Ester says with no hint of bitterness. "It's my life." América hears the metallic clack of a can on a table. "Correa came to see me the other day."

The effect on América is sudden, familiar. A chill, a thud at the pit of her stomach. In two months of phone calls, Ester has mentioned Correa only once, when she described how she chased him out of her house with a machete.

"What did he want?" She wants to sound nonchalant, unafraid.

"He said to tell you he's sorry."

"For what?" After the fear, anger, solid and red.

"Just that he's sorry. I'm sure he figured I knew what he was talking about." She drags on her cigarette. A gulp. Metal touching wood. "I told him you wanted nothing to do with him. He said he didn't blame you. He said he deserves your desprecio. He said you were too good for him and he should have appreciated you when he had you."

"He was drunk, wasn't he?"

"I wouldn't say he was walking straight, but he sounded all right." Like Ester would know the difference.

"You said he came over? I thought you threatened—"

"He just wanted to talk, wanted me to tell you he's sorry, that's all."

"And you believed him?"

"I listened, and then he went away. Didn't even come into the house."

"I should hope not."

"He apologized, said that, after all, we have Rosalinda to consider."

"Have you talked to her?"

"I called her yesterday. She's in a school play."

"Yes, I heard about that."

"Did you have a fight with her?"

"Almost every time I call she hangs up on me. I can't do or say anything right."

"She's going through a rebellious phase, that's all. She'll get over it."

"I'm not going to call her for a while."

"Mmm." It sounds as if Ester is falling asleep.

"I'll call you next week."

América leans back against her pillows, hugs her stuffed

white cat. They all seem so far away. Ester with her drinking, Correa in a conciliatory mode, Rosalinda rehearsing her life as a vedette. They seem like characters in a story, not like people who until a couple of months ago dominated her thoughts and actions. How many times did Rosalinda slam the door on her face? How many cases of beer has Ester consumed in the past year alone? How many times did Correa beat her?

She's surprised that this is what she remembers about them. Rosalinda's sullenness and rebellion, Ester's drinking, Correa's beatings. Is that all they are to me? Not people but problems?

I want nothing to do with them, América tells the cat. I'm going to worry about myself from now on, about what I want and what I need. I can't count on any of them. On anyone. I'm alone, and it's my life, and I'm not going to let them spoil it anymore.

A Night Out

aulina calls América every night of the week before Orlando's debut at the nightclub.

"I'm so nervous, mi'ja. It's worse than if it were me up there."

"But hasn't he been singing at your church for years?"

"Oh, he's been singing all over the place, but this is his first time at a nightclub."

América doesn't understand what the fuss is about. At the Sunday dinners Orlando hasn't seemed at all nervous about his upcoming debut.

On Saturday she catches an early train. The plan is for her to accompany Paulina to the hairdresser. "I don't know why, but I hate to go anywhere alone," Paulina explains as they walk down to the shopping area near the apartment.

It's the warmest day América has experienced since she arrived in New York. The street is teeming with shoppers, kids on Rollerblades, teenagers hanging out in small groups. It's as if the whole neighborhood has come out to celebrate the changing of the seasons.

"This used to be a quiet neighborhood," Paulina grumbles as they near a group of boys clustered around a lamppost. They're not doing anything that América would consider loud. They seem to be doing nothing at all, but their nonchalant attitude is threatening. The teenagers eye América and Paulina as they pass, but they say nothing, as if their silence itself were an insult. Paulina quickens her pace, and América, who's wearing high heels, has to catch up. Paulina giggles. "You'll have to learn to walk New York–style," she says. "Here we can't afford to stroll like you do in Vieques."

Most of the stores have opened their doors, and some display their merchandise on tables on the sidewalk. Outside the bodega where Paulina gets her spices, the piles of ñame, malanga, yautía, batata, and fresh bunches of recao remind América how long it's been since she ate viandas with eggplant, which Ester prepared for her almost every Friday. She sighs sadly. The homesickness that seemed a new experience a few weeks ago has become as familiar as her own face in the mirror.

"Here we are." Paulina stops in front of Rosy's Salon, which is wedged between a pizza shop and a pawnbroker. It is a long, narrow storefront. White lace curtains cover the window that faces the street. When América and Paulina walk in, the women already in the salon fall silent and evaluate them. Once they've looked América and Paulina over, the hairdressers and clients go back to their chatter.

Everything in the salon is either gray or pink. The hairdressers' stations are along the left wall, each with a gray Formica table facing a pink chair. The pink dryers with their gray chairs underneath are along the right wall, facing the hairdressers. The walls are covered floor to ceiling with mirrors, so that when she seeks her reflection, América is dizzy with the image of herself repeated to infinity.

"And who do we have here?" asks the owner after she embraces Paulina warmly.

"My niece, América."

"Welcome. I'm Rosy." She's a big woman, tall, full-busted with wide hips, but one would never call her fat. She's solid, curvy, and accentuates her proportions with tight-fitting jeans and a low-cut leotard top from which her bosoms seem about to burst out. Her hair is a shade América knows as "Spring Honey," which is what her own hair was supposed to be.

"Who did this to you?" Rosy asks, fingering América's curls. "Never mind, we'll fix it." She leads América to the sinks at the back of the salon.

"I don't really need—"

"I'll just trim and even it out. It's all lopsided. We can't do anything about the color now, you just did it, right?"

América blushes. "Last night."

Rosy washes América's hair while keeping an ear on and commenting upon several of the conversations taking place around them. Most of the talk is in Puerto Rican Spanish, and América closes her eyes and listens to the familiar sounds with gratitude, relaxing in a way she's not able to do around the Leveretts or even the other maids with their varied accents.

Rosy wraps a towel around América's head and leads her to a chair. She pumps a pedal under the seat a couple of times to bring América up to the right height. América looks in the mirror at the room behind her and catches the eye of the manicurist, who works from a wheelchair. She looks familiar to América, but she can't quite place where she knows her from. The woman smiles, and América returns the greeting.

"He looked just like a woman, with tetas and everything," one of the customers tells her hairdresser.

"Maybe he already had the operation," the hairdresser offers.

"No, you could tell he was a man because even with a ton of makeup you could still see the stubble on his face."

América and Paulina, who is on the next chair, exchange an amused smile in the mirror.

"I feel sorry for them," a customer offers from her spot under the drying lamps. "They try so hard to be women, and they never can be."

"They can, if they have the operation," pipes in the hairdresser.

"No, they can't. Just because you exchange a prick for a cunt doesn't make you a woman." Everyone turns around to look at the speaker. "Don't you think?" she adds in a plaintive voice.

"I think they know more about being a woman than most women do," says the customer who started the whole thing. "They know how to dress, how to put on makeup, false nails—"

"What you mean," interrupts Rosy as she rolls América's hair, "is that they know how to *look* like a woman. The only way to know what it's like to be a woman is to be one, and no matter how many operations they have, and how many hormones they take, they can never be female."

"Who'd want to be a woman, anyway?" asks the customer whose fingernails are being painted by the manicurist, and everyone laughs.

After a while, the conversation shifts in a different direction, but América remains thoughtful, asking herself what she would do if she had a choice. Would she be a woman, or would she rather be a man? She has barely enough time to ask herself when the manicurist rolls her wheelchair up to where América sits.

"You don't remember me, do you?" she asks, looking at América intently, as if by presenting her face so openly, América's memory will be jolted.

"You look familiar . . . "

"Nereida Santos," the woman says, smiling, "and you're América Gonzalez, aren't you?"

"Ay, Nereida, yes, I remember you!" The women hold hands warmly. "I didn't know you lived in New York," América says. "Last I heard—" she stops herself, and Nereida lowers her eyes and blushes.

"Okay," Rosy says, "we're all done here. Let's go to the dryer."

Oh, my God, América thinks, as she lets Rosy adjust the height and temperature of the hair dryer, this woman is from Esperanza. Now everyone in Vieques will know where I am. América glances toward Paulina, who has observed the encounter with a concerned expression.

Nereida pulls her manicure table and places it in front of América. América had planned to do her own nails later but doesn't want to offend Nereida by refusing the manicure. She dips her trembling fingers in the warm sudsy water Nereida puts before her.

Nereida asks about Ester and Rosalinda, and América answers in as few words as possible. To change the subject, she asks about Nereida's family, and similarly evasive answers are given.

"Mamá mentioned you had left Vieques," Nereida says as she wipes América's nails with a cotton ball dipped in polish remover. "But she wasn't sure where you had gone." América doesn't respond. "I don't blame you for running away," Nereida says conspiratorially. América doesn't know what to say to this, so again she remains silent. "I had to do the same thing."

This time América stares at Nereida with surprise, and the latter curls her lip in what might be a smile if there weren't such bitterness in the gesture. "I guess the story didn't reach Esperanza," she says softly as she clips América's cuticles.

"I heard you had an accident—"

"The hijo de la gran puta ran me over with his car," Nereida says with immeasurable anger. América pulls her hand away. "I'm sorry, did I cut you?" She wipes and disinfects the pinprick of blood on América's finger.

The last time she saw Nereida, América was standing in the Santos's yard, urging on the single girls vying for Nereida's bouquet after her wedding. América remembers vividly that she wore a lilac dress with a bow at the hip, and that Rosalinda was six years old and had been the flower girl. América also remembers that the Yanqui sailor Nereida married had befriended Correa and asked him to be one of his groomsmen.

"What color?" Nereida asks, and América answers "Lilac" before she realizes she's supposed to choose from a trayful of nail polish. She feels like crying, as if the memory of Nereida's wedding day were as bitter to her as it might be to the manicurist. She points to a bright red bottle, and Nereida sets it aside.

"How did you . . . you said he . . ." Unused to prying into other people's lives, América can't bring herself to come right out and ask Nereida about her "accident." In Vieques, the story was that Nereida slipped on an ice patch and fell behind her husband's car while he was backing out of their driveway.

"My own mother won't accept the fact that Gene tried to kill me," Nereida says. "He still sends her Christmas presents." Again that crooked smile, but this time América detects the hurt, the betrayal. Nereida paints América's left pinky in two strokes. "He started beating me on our wedding night." Left ring finger, middle finger, index. "When I told Mamá, she said men do that to see if you still love them." Left thumb, right thumb, right index. "She said if I was a good wife, he wouldn't have to hit me." Right middle finger, right ring, right pinky. "I was a good wife," she says, using her thumbnail to wipe streaks of polish from the edge of América's nails. "And look where it got me."

América coughs to relieve the tightness in her chest. But for the hum of the dryers, the salon is quiet. Nereida applies a second coat of polish on América's nails without seeming aware that every eye in the room is on her, every word she has uttered has been heard and one woman is weeping quietly.

"Perro!" Rosy spits out, as if by calling Gene a dog she will clear the air in her shop of the sadness that has descended on it. "Why is it," she asks, "that the minute we talk about men we all get depressed?"

A few women chuckle, others don't get the joke. Paulina and América again exchange a look, but this time América sees pity on her face and doesn't know to whom it is directed.

The nightclub is on a dark street lined with warehouses between empty, burned-out lots. The only lit doorway, in the middle of the block, is guarded by a large bald man in a tuxedo, who consults a clipboard as gaily dressed people give their names. He checks the Ortiz party off the list. "Table one," he says, and waves them in.

Another large man is at the foot of steep stairs. He stamps their hands with a smiley face and points up. Leopoldo leads the way. The stairs are lit by a yellow overhead bulb on the landing and Christmas lights along the banisters. At the top there is yet another muscular man in a tuxedo, who opens a heavy black door that admits the partygoers into a loft.

The room is an enormous square with brick walls on two of

its sides and blacked-out windows on the others. Colored Christmas lights twinkle from the high ceiling and around steel beams. In the center a shiny dance floor stretches before a low stage with musical instruments already set up. On either side of the stage two massive speakers blare music selected by a disc jockey in a glassed enclosure off to one side. Long tables with folding chairs are set up around the dance floor. At the back of the room, opposite the stage, there is a bar, almost invisible behind a crowd of men.

The tables are numbered, and Leopoldo finds theirs to the left of the stage, directly in front of one of the speakers. As they're yelling and signaling to one another trying to determine who sits where, Teresa appears from behind the stage and hugs and kisses everyone.

"I've already ordered," she mouths, and points to the table, at either end of which there are bottles of champagne on ice, two bottles of rum, several Cokes, a cup full of sliced limes, a stack of plastic cups, and a filled ice bucket.

América sits between Elena and Carmen, facing the stage. Several couples are already dancing. Leopoldo, Rufo, and Lourdes prepare drinks for everyone, without asking what they want, since they can't be heard above the music. Darío, who sits across from América, hands her a Cuba Libre, and América feels Carmen step on her toes and Elena poke her in the ribs. As they were getting dressed at Paulina's, the two sisters teased América that she shouldn't worry about finding a dance partner at the club. Darío, they claimed, had been practicing merengues for weeks in preparation for this night.

The disc jockey puts on a bolero, and the dance floor clears, then fills again with a different group of dancers. Some women wrap their arms around their men, flatten their hips into their partners', whose palms press them closer by squeezing their buttocks. América feels a familiar warmth between her legs, heat rising from her belly, intensifying the fragrance of the perfume she liberally sprayed on. She blushes and avoids looking at the dancers, at Darío, who as usual has his eyes fixed on her, at Lourdes, whose hand has strayed to Rufo's thigh.

The musicians take their place onstage as the last strains of the bolero fade. They open with a blare of horns and the throbbing of congas. The audience applauds, and the orchestra leader, a dark, wrinkled man with an enormous nose and a small hat perched precariously on his balding head, raises his hand, waits for the applause to stop, and launches into a furious solo on his conga drums that infects even the most stalwart nondancers. Hips shimmy on chairs, feet tap the floor, fingers rap the tabletops, heads bob above shaking shoulders. The loft vibrates with the pounding rhythm of the congas, which rises and falls in pulsating waves primal as a heartbeat. When he stops, suddenly, as if he had grown tired of beating the drums, the whole place explodes in applause, which the orchestra leader acknowledges by lifting his hat. He walks over to the microphone in the middle of the stage.

"Damas y caballeros," he says, wiping his brow with the back of his hand, "tonight we have the pleasure of introducing a wonderful new talent." Paulina and Teresa applaud, and everyone else at the table follows. "I see he brought his fan club," the orchestra leader says with a grin. "Ladies and gentlemen, Orlando Ortiz!"

Everyone at table 1 cheers and applauds. Orlando smiles and waves at them, and launches into a salsa tune about being in love and not knowing why. He sings in a clear tenor filled with emotion. The audience applauds after the first verse, and those who want to dance make their way to the floor. Teresa and Paulina are annoyed that people aren't listening, but Orlando signals that they should dance.

Leopoldo extends his hand to Paulina, who smiles coquettishly and follows him. Rufo squeezes Lourdes's shoulder, and they too stand up and join the dancers. Darío is left on his side of the table facing Elena, América, Carmen, and Teresa. Carmen again steps on América's toes, and América kicks her back playfully. América feels Darío struggling with what he should do. If he asks her to dance, he would be leaving three young women unattended at the table. He decides to wait with them, and pours each another helping of rum and Coke. This time América feels Elena's foot on her toes.

After two numbers, Leopoldo and Rufo return their wives to the table. Leopoldo offers his hand to América and Rufo to Carmen. Darío asks Elena, and the three married women are left alone at the table. As she follows Leopoldo, América sees a man approach Teresa, who refuses him by pointing at the ring on her finger and at the stage.

Leopoldo is a competent dancer who moves in tight circles but always in the same direction. His hands are warm and fleshy, small-fingered, heavier than she expected. América is about the same height, but they studiously avoid looking at each other as they dance. It is a peculiar feeling for her, not to look at her partner's face, not to feel his eyes on hers. She again feels the warmth of desire, but this time it has a name, and she tries to wipe it away by observing the other dancers.

Every so often she notes the inviting glances of men whose partners have their back to her, and even though this gives her a thrill of pleasure, she looks away and concentrates on a spot just below Leopoldo's ear. They exchange partners for the next song without leaving the floor: Leopoldo with Carmen, Rufo with América, Darío returns Elena to the table and brings his mother out. As Elena sits down, the man refused by Teresa asks her, and she jumps up and follows him to the dance floor. The couples twirl complex circles around each other, exchanging happy smiles, their bodies bumping against those of strangers.

When Rufo returns her to the table, América sips from her drink, but no sooner has she caught her breath than hands appear in front of her, and she's again up and dancing with a stranger who smells like vanilla, and after him, a short, rotund man with hair parted in the middle, and then a tall, skinny man whose many gold chains jingle as he moves.

When the orchestra takes a break and the disc jockey takes over, Orlando joins them. He is congratulated and kissed by all the women and by some from neighboring tables, while Teresa hangs on to him with that possessive air América knows so well. They pop open the champagne and toast Orlando's success. In between, there is more dancing.

América doesn't sit a single number out. Every time she's

returned to the table to quench her thirst, another hand appears in front of her. She follows these men to the dance floor remarking how different each feels from the other, how varied their styles of dress and grooming, the way they touch or avoid touching her, the vague whiffs of cigarette smoke or cologne that emanate from their bodies. Each one she measures against the only standard she knows, the imposing, muscular frame of Pantaleón Amador Correa. And she's not surprised that none of these men are as handsome as he, as good a dancer, as comfortable in their skin as Correa is in his. But even though they are so different from him, they make her happy. América is breathless with excitement, with a joy she can't describe or explain. Her head buzzing from too much rum and freedom, she's as radiant as a jewel, her lips parted in a smile that holds no secrets, no pain, no fear.

When the taped music stops and the dancers return to the tables, Teresa impulsively reaches her skinny arms around América, hugs her warmly, and kisses her on the cheek. Surprised at this, América kisses her back, believing that Teresa is so thrilled with Orlando's performance that she's kissing the first person she touches. She sits for a minute intending to rest a while and listen to Orlando sing. She's hot and light-headed, so she gulps her drink down, munches on the ice left at the bottom of the cup. A man offers his hand, but she refuses him, waving her fingers in front of her like a fan to let him know she's too hot to dance.

She's alone at the table with Teresa and Darío, who hasn't danced with her because every time he tries she's already up and following someone else. He smiles, hands her a napkin so she can wipe her brow. He pours her and Teresa another drink. When he's not singing, Orlando dances from one side of the stage to the other, so that América thinks people are missing a pretty good show by not watching the singer. At the change, everyone comes back to the table, but within seconds they're all up again, in different combinations. Darío's trembling hand appears in front of América, and she accepts it and follows him, to the amusement of Carmen, who's dancing with the man with many gold chains.

It is a bolero. Orlando's voice sounds heartbroken as he describes his beloved's raven hair and apple-red lips. Darío looks lovingly at América. He maintains a respectful distance between them, even as other couples press against them and each other. His right hand resolutely planted on her upper back, he guides her by firm pressure on his fingertips. He's slightly taller than América, but with heels on she can look him straight in the eye if she wants to, which she doesn't.

"Those eyes, I told myself, are my destiny," Orlando sings, "and those brown arms are my home."

As they dance, América and Darío relax the stiff formality that characterizes their encounters, and América finds herself leaning closer until they're cheek to cheek.

I'm drunk, she tells herself, nestling her head on his shoulder. She lets it rest there as Darío gently draws her closer and wraps his arms around her. He's so skinny, she tells herself, I can feel his bones. His breath comes in shallow, mint-scented drafts. Orlando reaches for a high note and sustains it breathlessly. Darío pulls América closer, and she presses against him. He clears the bangs from her forehead and kisses it. The bolero is over. América pulls herself away.

"Excuse me," she says, and heads toward the ladies' room. Carmen, who has seen everything, leaves her partner in the middle of the floor and follows América. There's a line outside the bathroom, but América pushes her way in and bangs on a stall until the woman inside it comes out. She has barely enough time to kneel in front of the toilet and vomit.

Carmen finds her in the stall and holds her head and rubs between her shoulders until América is done. Elena also appears with moist paper towels to wipe América's mouth and chin. Next thing she knows, América is being half carried down the stairs, crashing against people coming up. Once outside, she has to run to the curb to throw up between two parked cars. Paulina holds her by the waist, and Elena again appears with moist towels. Then she's inside a car, speeding somewhere, her head resting on Paulina's bosom.

A Walk to the Park

The clock on the bedside table says 5:22. "Morning," América mumbles, and raises herself on her elbows with the intention of getting up, but a blinding headache forces her to lie down again. She closes her eyes, and then it's 8:54 by the bedside clock. She's in Elena's room. Against the far wall, Elena is fast asleep on what América always thought was a couch, but with cushions removed, it's another small bed.

América moves slowly, both because she doesn't want to wake Elena and because her head still throbs with every motion she makes. She's wearing a T-shirt with sequins on it that doesn't belong to her. She opens the door and looks to her right, toward the living room, and there she sees Carmen asleep on the sofa bed. She tiptoes into the bathroom.

The mirror facing the door greets her with a reflection she would rather not have seen. Her eyeliner, mascara, and shadow have all settled into black circles around her eyes. The rest of her face is mottled with makeup combined with sweat and who knows what else. Her hair, which Rosy had arranged in cascading curls from her crown to her shoulders, is a hive of tangles and hairpins sticking out every which way.

She finds Pond's cold cream inside the medicine chest and slathers it on her face, then wipes the makeup off with toilet paper. Each swipe of the tissue reveals her natural, unmade-up features. Without pencil, her eyebrows are a thin line of single hairs over slanted chocolate eyes, which are bloodshot. She examines the sides of her long, well-shaped nose for blackheads and finds none. Her lips, which she usually lines to make them look fuller, are dry.

She rinses her face and stares into her sly eyes. How am I ever going to face Darío again, she asks the reflection. I practically threw myself at him. She smiles. I think I scared him. She giggles. I think I'm still drunk.

She takes off the sequined T-shirt and steps into the shower. Once the water hits her, she remembers she hasn't taken the pins out of her hair, so she comes out again, dripping on the rug. Rosy must have put a ton of hair spray on, because the pins are welded to the curls. She gives up trying to remove them and climbs into the shower again, letting the hot water wash away the hair fixer, the smell of stale perfume, the strange feeling that last night she crossed a threshold she'd never crossed before.

"Ay, Tía, that was so embarrassing," América tells Paulina later, as they sit at the kitchen table chopping vegetables and skinning chicken parts for soup.

"Don't worry about it, mi'ja. We all had too much to drink last night."

"I spoiled it for Orlando."

"No, you didn't. He didn't even realize we were gone until the end."

"You sure made an impression on Darío, though," Carmen says, shuffling in from the bathroom.

"Ay!" América drops her head with a blush. The three of them laugh.

"What's so funny?" Elena comes out of her room in her nightgown. Even newly awake she's as fresh as dawn.

"I was about to describe how Darío carried her out of the ladies' room and down the stairs of the club."

"He didn't!"

"Ay, Carmen, you're always exaggerating," Elena chides her

sister. "We carried you out of the ladies' room. He only carried you down the stairs."

"Oh, mi Dios." América covers her face with her hands.

"I've never seen him drive so fast," Carmen adds, and Elena signals her to stop. "I mean, he was so worried about you." She looks at her sister with a "What did I say?" look.

"He must think I do this all the time."

"I wouldn't worry about him." Carmen stands behind her and massages her shoulders. "Believe me, he's seen worse." Again, Elena gives her a look, and Carmen once more doesn't know what she's done wrong.

"Enough," Paulina interrupts. "Go get dressed so you can help me here." Elena and Carmen turn to their mother, who, with a look, lets them know they'd better leave América alone.

"Grown women, and they still behave like teenagers," Paulina grumbles after them.

América's head throbs, even after three aspirins and two cups of coffee. She's only half awake, she thinks. Her reflexes are slow, and she's conscious of a general malaise like when she had the flu three years ago.

I wonder, she asks herself, if this is the way Mami feels every day after drinking all night. This is probably the way Correa feels too, those days when I make him caldos de gallina to help his hangover.

She shakes her head, as if to erase the image of a drunk Correa. The motion makes her dizzy. If Correa had seen her last night, she wouldn't be sitting here today. All those men, one after the other, their hands all over her. A couple of them whispered things in her ear that she couldn't hear, but she got the gist of it just the same. They were propositioning me, she tells herself with an amazed smile. She looks up at Paulina, whose back is to her, as if about to share this news with her aunt. But another thought interrupts her intentions. They propositioned me because I was alone and unprotected. It chills her to think of herself as prey.

"Let's go for a walk, it will clear your head," Carmen offers when she returns. The last thing América wants to do is move, but Carmen grabs her hand and pulls her up. "See you later, Ma," Carmen calls out, followed by América, whose knees shake as she descends the stairs.

"Where are we going?"

"Just around the block. It's so stuffy in the apartment."

They head away from the avenue and turn right onto a tree-lined street with two- and three-story houses divided by driveways.

"This is nice," América comments.

"Most people think of the Bronx as rundown and poor, but a few of these old neighborhoods are thriving." Carmen walks fast. América has trouble keeping up and, after the first block, is out of breath. Carmen stops in front of a row of brick houses. "These homes were built in the thirties," she says, "and those over there are later, the forties, maybe."

"How do you know?" América asks.

"I can tell by the style of construction, by the details on the windows and along the roof." She starts walking again. "I wanted to be an architect when I was younger."

"What happened?"

"Oh, I just lost interest, I don't know." They turn the corner. "Actually I messed up by falling in love with the wrong guy."

América looks at her, expecting more, but Carmen just bites her lip. She looks at América from the corner of her eye and laughs. "Don't look so worried! What happened was, I had an affair with one of my professors and flunked out. I've always had a weakness for Germans."

She laughs merrily, and América can't quite figure out why. A love affair, she thinks, is nothing to laugh about. But if, like Paulina says, Carmen has many lovers, maybe affairs have a different meaning, although she can't imagine what makes them funny.

At the end of the block there is a playground and basketball court. A game is in full swing, the fences surrounding the court are crowded with people cheering the players. The playground is filled with children and their parents. América is sure these adults are parents because they look like the children, not like in the playgrounds she frequents, filled with white children watched over by Latina and Caribbean empleadas.

"Hi, Carmen! Hi, América!" Janey and Johnny are atop the slide. Near them, Darío is sitting on a bench reading a newspaper. América groans. He jumps up when he sees them.

"I swear I didn't plan this," Carmen says in a low voice, then, louder, "Hi, everyone!" She bounds over to the bottom of the slide to catch Janey when she comes down, leaving América stranded in the middle of the playground with Darío rapidly advancing toward her.

"How do you feel?" he asks softly, and she wishes she were wearing makeup to hide the blush she knows is coloring her cheeks.

"Okéi."

"There's no need to be embarrassed," he says. "That sort of thing happens."

América is not sure what she was expecting, but it certainly wasn't this preemptive forgiveness that leaves her feeling like she owes him something. "Thank you," she says.

She's happy to see Carmen and the children running toward them so she doesn't have to think of something more to say.

"Papi, can we have an ice cream cone?" Janey asks, and her brother seconds her.

"My treat," Carmen adds.

"Sure." Darío turns to América. "Would you like one too?"

América has been making faces at Carmen to indicate that they should go, but when Darío turns toward her, she says, "No, thank you." Carmen gives her a mischievous smile. "I'll just take the kids then," she says, grabbing each twin by the hand, and off they go.

"Well," says Darío, "we can walk back to the apartment."

"Okéi."

One good thing about Darío, he walks slowly. One bad thing about Darío's slow step is that América takes mental count of how many blocks they have to go and can't imagine what they will say to each other until they reach the tall green building.

"I'm glad we have a few minutes alone together," Darío confides after a while, and América's heart flutters with fear because she thinks he's going to ask her out. He clears his throat. "It's so hard to talk with everyone around."

"Yes." They pass an old man sitting on a stoop. He gives them a dirty look and mutters something under his breath. América and Darío quicken their pace until they're past him.

At the next corner, Darío stops and faces her. "You must know I like you . . ."

Three kids go by on Rollerblades, and América uses the distraction to collect herself. "You stare at me," she says as they cross the street.

"You're so beautiful," he counters, unfazed.

She pretends not to have heard. "And you drive like a maniac." •

"Occupational hazard."

She smiles. When did he become charming?

"I'd like to know you better," he says seriously, "and for you to know me." When she doesn't say anything, he continues. "I'm aware that you're recently separated . . ."

It sounds so official, "separated." It sounds surgical. Like when they separated those twins from the Dominican Republic who were born connected at the head.

"I don't think—" she starts. They turn the corner.

"We can just talk on the phone. We don't even have to go out if you're not comfortable."

They're in front of the green building. He looks at her earnestly, as if every second she vacillates is torture for him. "I'll give you my number," she says after a while.

The smile on his face is so happy, so hopeful, that it makes her laugh. He opens the door for her, follows her up the stairs to Paulina's apartment without stopping at his own. When they walk in, Elena and Paulina exchange a look. América finds a scrap of paper by the phone, rummages around for a pen, and finally has to fetch one from her purse. She writes her number down, thinking that she must still be drunk and will probably regret this in the morning.

On the train to Bedford, she can't stop thinking about this new development in her life. Other than with Correa, she's never been on a date, has not been alone with a man in fifteen years. Just to talk, Darío said. Do men do that? It doesn't seem possible. There's too much sexual tension. But maybe that's me. I'm oversensitive because of Correa. Because he's so suspicious of other men, I've become that way too. Maybe it's possible to be friends, although I've never seen it. Mami doesn't have any male friends. She doesn't have any female friends either. Rosalinda had some boys who were friends. But look what happened. No, it's not possible.

Besides, what could she and Darío talk about? He's so quiet, so timid. Although the few minutes they were alone together he seemed a different man, charming and open. Maybe when we're with family he's respectful, like his father and Tío Poldo, who let the women do all the talking and planning. That must be it. He doesn't want to seem too forward in front of my relatives.

The Leverett house is dark. She goes into her room and prepares for bed, her mind preoccupied with Darío.

Just to talk? I could tell him how many beds I made and how many toilets I scrubbed. She laughs. I wonder what it's like to be a taxi driver. Well, that's something to talk about. How many people did you run over today, she asks the stuffed cat on her pillow.

By giving him my number, I'm encouraging him. I'll tell him right off that I just want to be friends. That way, he won't get any ideas. ¡Qué presumida! Just because a man wants to talk, I think he has other plans. But that's how it was with Correa. He started talking, and next thing I knew, I was running away with him. Maybe that's what happened to Rosalinda. You talk to a man, and when you run out of conversation you have to do something to spice it up. A kiss here, a hug there, and before you know it, you're not talking anymore. You're listening to him yell at you. No, forget it, I don't want to talk to any men right now. When he calls I'll tell him straight out that he shouldn't call again. Put an end to it right away.

firm but fair

⧜⧜⧜⧜⧜⧜⧜⧜⧜⧜⧜⧜⧜⧜⧜⧜⧜⧜⧜⧜⧜⧜⧜⧜⧜⧜⧜⧜

Every morning the corner of Green and South Moger streets in Mount Kisco is crowded with men waiting to be picked up for work. They're dressed in jeans and work boots, many of them wear western-style hats, and some carry a thermos. Pickup trucks drive past slowly, and the drivers study the laborers, who turn their eyes hopefully in their direction. The drivers don't get out of the trucks. They lean over to the passenger side, make their deals, and wave the lucky few selected for that day into the truck bed. In the evening the same trucks drop off the men at the corner, and they drag themselves home to the rundown houses on the periphery of the village, or to the high-rise apartment building at the edge of the commuter train tracks.

"They make even less money than we do," complains Mercedes, who has fallen in love with an Ecuadoran man who, she says, was an accountant in Quito. "You should see his hands at the end of the day. They're all cut from the rocks." Reinaldo has helped build many of the stone walls that border the mansions in the Bedford area.

"The same thing happened to Ignacio," says Adela, "until I bought him a pair of gloves."

They're at Mercedes's house, which has an indoor swimming

pool. The six children they care for are happily splashing in the water, while the empleadas sit at the periphery, watching them and warning them to stay on the shallow end. The only empleada who knows how to swim is América, who is sitting with her feet on the steps of the pool.

"Did Liana hear from her kids?" América asks.

"Last she heard they were in Mexico. The coyote took the money and left them stranded."

"They're not traveling alone?"

"Her father is escorting them. But he's an old man. He got sick, and she had to send them money for a doctor." Adela adjusts the button on her blouse, which has popped open. "If you ask me, she's crazy to bring those kids here."

Since no one has asked her, no one responds. Adela has no children, so it's difficult for her to understand how desperate Liana is to have hers near. Desperate enough to risk their lives by hiring a coyote to sneak them into the United States.

"Frida and I went to church on Sunday," Mercedes announces. "We lit a bunch of candles for those kids."

"They're going to need all the help they can get," Adela says somberly.

Kyle is a good swimmer. The younger kids wear floaties on their arms to help them stay above water. One of the little girls Adela watches is drifting away. "You stay on the shallow end, Annie, don't go deeper than that." The little girl drifts back.

"How's your daughter?" Mercedes asks América.

"She's in a school play," América responds, and the other two nod. She has told the empleadas she has a daughter but hasn't gone into any details they don't need to hear about. She sees no sense in telling them that Rosalinda ran away with her boyfriend, or that her life's ambition is to be a vedette. If some-one told her that story about their child, América would criticize the mother for allowing her child to run wild.

It's different when it happens to you, she thinks, so she has withheld most details of her life. She has told them she's divorced, without mentioning Correa beat her. Nor has she revealed that her mother is an alcoholic. She has told them

Rosalinda is a student at a parochial school, which América pays for by working as a maid. The women know about sacrificing their lives for the sake of their children, and respectful in front of her, they don't press her. América wonders, however, what they say about her when she's not there. They all talk about one another when the others are not around.

Often América feels guilty around the other empleadas. Their lives back home sound so bleak. Two of them come from rural areas where there is no electricity or running water. Their first encounters with American homes were shocking. The excess, the way Americans live apart from their families, are a constant source of discussion among the empleadas, all of whom describe lives tied to the fates of large extended families dependent on them.

"Americans don't like their parents," they've concluded, since not one of them has ever seen their employers' parents at the house. "They send them to Florida to get rid of them," is the consensus.

They all make less money than she does, even after Karen Leverett deducts taxes from her salary. They get paid in cash and are nervous about being robbed because all their savings are kept in boxes under their beds or in their closets.

"If I open a bank account," Mercedes once said, "la migra will find me and send me back."

They dispatch most of their salary home via courier services set up for that purpose. And they pay rent for a room for weekends, since they don't feel comfortable or welcome when they're not working in the houses where they live during the week.

"If I stay there," Adela complains, "I end up working on my days off."

América has a bank account, into which she deposits a fourth of her salary. She sends money orders to Rosalinda and to Ester every week and keeps a small amount for personal expenses, which are few, since she gets room and board at the Leveretts'. Her dream is to have a credit card, so she can charge whatever she needs without having to carry cash.

"You're so lucky," the empleadas tell her, "to be an American citizen."

They describe how, in the places they come from, everyone dreams of coming to the United States. When she tells them that where she comes from people are fighting to win independence from the United States, they seem amazed. "But you have it so good!" they assure her.

It confuses her sometimes, to talk about these things. The empleadas describe wars and guerrilla killings, corrupt priests and the burning of villages in the night. The governments in their countries are repressive and brutal, and anyone who complains ends up dead.

Back home, protests against the United States presence in Vieques are commonplace. Every so often a sea turtle is blown to bits by the shelling offshore and the residents complain to the U.S. Navy. Or the fishermen's cooperative blockades the target beach by circling their boats where the Navy maneuvers will take place. The men and women involved in that kind of thing are viewed as heroes by their supporters, and América respects them for their commitment and passion for their cause. Just before she met Correa, she was involved with a group of students planning to demonstrate at the gates of the Navy base. But Correa put an end to that. "Women," he told her, "should stay out of politics."

So many things I didn't do because he said not to, she tells herself as she drives back to the Leveretts'. It didn't occur to me to challenge any of his opinions, his rules. And our daughter is the same way. We close our brains when he speaks. We've been docile as faithful dogs. Of course he'd take advantage of that. Who wouldn't?

She hasn't talked to Rosalinda in over a month. Every time she's picked up the phone to call her number, she changes her mind, believing she needs to punish her daughter for her rudeness. It occurs to her that she didn't warn Rosalinda that this would be the consequence for her behavior, so she decides to write and let her know, so that her daughter doesn't feel like América forgot her.

Dear Rosalinda:

Here is your money order. I haven't called you the last
few weeks because I'm sick of having the phone
slammed every time you don't agree with what I say. If
you want me to call you again, you have to promise
not to do that anymore. I talk to Mami every week, so
call her and tell her if you agree with this condition.

Love,
Your mother

P.S. I have a lot to tell you.

She posts the letter, feeling proud of herself. She's being firm
but fair, she thinks. She got the idea for this letter from a radio
psychologist who answers questions over the air. América is in
the car, driving to or from school with Kyle and Meghan, when
the psychologist is on, and so she has a chance to listen to fifteen or twenty minutes of advice every day. Being firm but fair is
one of the things the psychologist recommends when her listen-
ers complain about their kids.

América has decided that one of her problems is that she
hasn't been firm enough. For example, the first time Darío
called she had every intention of telling him never to call again,
but all she could muster was, "I'm sort of busy now," and he said
good-bye and hung up without waiting to hear what she was
doing. The second time he called she didn't want to be rude, so
they talked for about forty minutes. She told him how many
beds she makes in a day, and he told her how frightening it is to
be a taxi driver in New York City. "Every passenger you pick up,"
he said, "can be the last person you see." The idea of facing
death every night was so fascinating that she asked him many
questions, and he told her stories of the close calls he'd had. He
called again the next night, and they talked for twenty minutes.
She didn't tell him never to call again, and now she thinks it
may be too late.

She has to be firm with Karen. All of last week, and most of
this one, Karen has worked late at the hospital. Charlie has been

out of town, so América has put in fifteen-hour days. She thinks she should get paid extra for working more than the eight hours Karen Leverett told her she would be working. The truth is that América is on duty by seven in the morning and doesn't get to her room until after eight every night. That's more than eight hours. América hopes that Karen will agree with her. After all, a woman who spends fifteen dollars for a pair of panties should be able to afford a couple of extra dollars for the woman who cares for her kids.

After the children have been put to bed and Karen has settled on the couch with her papers, América tiptoes downstairs. She's never had to ask for a raise, so she's not sure how one approaches these things. She figures if she's firm but fair, Karen will go along with it.

"Excuse, Karen?"

"Yes, América?" Karen removes her glasses, which she wears when she takes off her contact lenses.

"I need tell you something."

Karen nods, doesn't ask her to sit down. América stands on the other side of the sharp-edged granite table, her hands in her pockets so Karen won't see them shaking. She takes a deep breath. "I work hard longer than eight hours every day."

Karen tenses, the corners of her lips press against her teeth.

"I think . . ." Be firm but fair, América tells herself. "I need raise."

Karen unfolds her legs from under her, folds them in the opposite direction. "You've only worked with us for three months. You get a raise after a year, as we agreed." She settles her papers on the other side of the couch.

"I know, but you say I work eight hours. I work more than eight hours."

"How can that be? The children are in school most of the day."

"I clean house when kids in school."

"For six hours? Really, América . . ." Karen shakes her head, chuckles to herself.

"Is big house."

"But we're not here all day. We haven't entertained in weeks. It's really mostly the kitchen and the bedrooms that you have to clean. That can't take you six hours every day."

Have you ever cleaned a house? América wants to ask but knows that would be rude. Of course Karen Leverett has never cleaned her own house. That's what maids are for.

"I careful. Many delicate things. I clean under beds, in back furniture. It takes long time."

"I still can't believe it takes you six hours every day to clean this house, come on." She fiddles with her glasses, apparently eager to get back to her paperwork. "I tell you what, you should take some time off in the mornings, when the kids are not here, okay?"

She's not being fair, América tells herself. "But if house not clean?"

"I'm sure you can work this out, América. You just need to be more efficient, so you can have the time. I know you can do it, okay?"

"Okéi," América says, not because she agrees but because she's angry and doesn't know what to do with her anger. She starts out of the room, and Karen Leverett calls out "Good night!" in a cheery voice that grates on América's nerves. She doesn't wish Karen Leverett a good night. She wishes, in fact, that Karen Leverett will have the worst night of her life. She closes the door to her room and locks it.

I should have told her that it's not six hours, she fumes, it's four. I have to pick up Meghan from school by twelve. And I should have told her I do the laundry and iron most of their clothes. And I have to cook. I didn't remind her of that.

She gets ready for bed but knows she won't get much sleep tonight. She's too upset. If she had given me twenty dollars more a week I would have been happy. She didn't need to double my salary. Just twenty dollars more a week. That's less than she pays for a bra.

"I asked Doña Paulina if I could pick you up," Darío says when he meets her at the station.

"I want to get there in one piece," she says. She's still annoyed from last night's meeting with Karen and is not happy to see Darío's hopeful smile.

"I'll drive as carefully as a little old lady," he jokes, strapping himself in. "There's a seat belt over there."

"This wasn't here last time, was it?"

"I put it in to impress you." He smiles at her, taking his eyes off the road. "Oops!" he says, facing forward.

In spite of herself, América smiles. He must be on drugs, she thinks. How else to explain this change in his personality when they're alone?

"I'm working tonight," Darío says, "but tomorrow I'm taking the kids to the circus. Have you ever been to one?"

"No, they don't bring them to Vieques."

"Would you like to come with us?"

She thinks a minute before answering, not because she's not certain, but because she doesn't want him to think she's too eager. "Yes, thank you."

"Great! We're going to the early show, so we have to leave here around nine in the morning."

"Okéi."

He lets her into the apartment building, and in the confines of the foyer between the street and hall doors, she senses how close they are, almost as close as when they danced. He seems to feel it too, and gets close enough to kiss her but at the last minute changes his mind, sticks the key in the inside door, and steps back to let her by.

"See you later," he says, the familiar mournful expression darkening his face.

"Aren't you coming up?"

"I have to go to work." He nods in her direction and disappears behind the street door.

América stands in the hall for a minute. Even though she really doesn't want anything to do with men, this man is not so bad as the others. As the other, she reminds herself as she starts up the stairs. They're not all like Correa.

*   *   *

Janey and Johnny are so excited that Darío has to keep telling them to stop bouncing on the backseat of the car or they'll turn back and forget the circus. The children quiet down for a few minutes and then begin again, unable to sit still.

América is equally excited. She has never been into Manhattan, and when she told Darío this, he said they would take the scenic route. They drove down by the side of a broad river, then into the center of the city.

"This is Times Square." Darío drove slowly down the broad avenue lined with tall buildings and lit billboards. Behind them, cars honked their horns and taxi drivers gave them dirty looks.

"On top of that hotel," Darío pointed, "is a restaurant that goes around, so you can see the whole city."

América can't imagine how a room turns around and is still trying to figure it out when they arrive at Madison Square Garden. They line up with thousands of people waiting to get in. Vendors offer balloons, shaved ice, cotton candy, hot pretzels, plastic swords that light up, stuffed animals. Everything they see, Janey and Johnny want, and Darío stops at almost every kiosk to buy it for them.

"I know I spoil them," he apologizes to América, who hasn't said a word.

Their arms laden with every conceivable souvenir, they finally make it to their seats and have to hand everything to Darío and América because there's no place to keep it. They have a row of four seats fairly close to the middle ring.

América, no less than Janey and Johnny, is fascinated with everything she sees. Madison Square Garden is the biggest place she's ever been in. Music comes from somewhere up above, drowning out the sounds of children squealing with delight at the antics of a few clowns running around the three rings.

No sooner have they taken their seats than the place darkens and a man announces the beginning of the circus. Spotlights fix on the garage-size openings at one end, and a parade of animals, acrobats, and clowns circles the three rings. There are elephants and tigers in cages. Tiny horses. Camels with golden bridles.

Clowns that run up and down the aisles making funny faces at children. One of the clowns sits on a woman's lap. Another kisses a man. A third gives a little boy a handkerchief, and when he walks away there are a hundred more tied one to the other stretching from his pocket.

After the parade, three women do tricks high up on a rope suspended from América doesn't know what. A muscular man holds a whole family of acrobats on his shoulders. Two boys perform tricks on bicycles. Trapeze artists swing each other across, then jump onto a net. It is the most wonderful thing América has ever seen. When the lights go on and she stands up to go, Darío tells her it's only the intermission and there's more.

She takes Janey to the bathroom, where they have to wait on a long line. Then they all buy hot dogs and popcorn and ice cream. When they return to their seats, there are more clowns, a man who makes tigers jump through hoops lit on fire, a woman who makes horses dance, a man who folds himself into impossible positions. Twelve elephants lift their massive front legs on top of each other until there's a long line of elephants on two legs. There's a man who eats fire, stiltwalkers, a woman who twirls from a rope that she grabs with her teeth.

"Did you like it?" Darío asks as they follow the throng to the street.

"It was wonderful!" América says in the same wonder-filled voice as Janey and Johnny. "Wasn't it great?" She turns to the children, embarrassed that she feels like a kid who's never seen anything, has never been anywhere, and didn't know there were such marvels in the world.

On Monday when she's cleaning Kyle and Meghan's rooms, she finds souvenirs from the circus and wonders if the Leveretts were there at the same time as she was.

"We went Saturday," Kyle informs her when she asks, "and I got to see the elephants up close."

"Me too," América says.

"But we got to touch them," says Meghan.

"Really?"

"After the circus Daddy took us to where they keep the elephants, and the tigers," Kyle adds.

"But we couldn't pet the tigers," Meghan says seriously.

"No, they too scary," América says as she serves Meghan a helping of potatoes mashed with plantains.

"Daddy knows the head clown," Kyle says, "that's why we could go where they get ready and stuff." He looks down at his plate. "What is this?"

"Puerto Rican potatoes," América answers. She's learned not to tell them too much about what's in the food she cooks. Mention of anything other than salt makes them refuse to eat.

"I like them," says Meghan.

"The clowns?"

"No, the portican potatoes." Meghan giggles with delight. "América is so funny."

"Maybe I be clown in circus," she says, making a silly face. The children laugh and make faces at each other and at her. "Me too, me too. I'm a clown in the circus," they sing.

"Okéi," América says. "No more play. Eat now. You finish everything, I give you surprise."

She can count on Darío to call sometime between nine and eleven every night, depending on his shift. She's annoyed with herself that she actually looks forward to his calls. Of all the people she talks to on the phone, he's the only one who she thinks listens to her without giving her advice or slamming the phone.

"It was different working at La Casa," she tells him, "I worked fewer hours, for one."

"Do you have enough privacy?"

"I have my own room and bathroom, but if I get hungry in the middle of the night, I feel funny going downstairs to get something to eat."

"Why?"

"I don't know. It just feels . . . like it's not my house. One time I came out of my room after they'd gone to bed and the minute I stepped into the hall Charlie was out of the bedroom asking who was out there." She laughs, "I almost fainted from fright."

"I bet you scared him too."

"Probably." There are silences in their conversations, moments in which she knows he's wondering what to say next and she's going over her day to see if anything interesting happened.

"Janey got a hundred on a spelling test."

"She's intelligent."

"Johnny is too, but he didn't have a test this week."

"Kyle, the little boy I take care of, got his orange belt in karate."

She's never asked about his late wife, and he's never asked about Correa. She's never asked about his drug use, and he's never mentioned el problema con Rosalinda. It's as if there's a gate into the other's life that neither wants to open just yet.

Happy Bird Day 2 Ju

W e'll take you out to dinner tonight, so don't cook," Karen tells her the next morning on her way out the door. "I'll be home around six, and then we'll go."

"Is Daddy coming too?" asks Kyle.

"Daddy has to work." Karen avoids looking at Kyle. "It will just be the four of us, okay?"

"We don't have to," América says.

"Nonsense, it's your birthday, and we should celebrate." They troop out, and América is left alone in the house, embarrassed that she mentioned today was her birthday. Now Karen feels like she should do something for her.

She does her morning chores. The Leverett house, once so formidable, now feels small compared to the other homes she's been in. Liana works in a much bigger house; so does Mercedes. They don't have to cook, though.

Even though she tried, América hasn't been able to find the extra hours Karen claims she can get if she's just more efficient. Efficiency, to América, means doing things well in as short a time as possible. And she finds that the more efficient she becomes in one area, such as ironing, the more time she has for things she thinks ought to be done around the house, such as scraping old dirt from the narrow space between the baseboard molding and the wall-to-wall carpeting.

In the three months she's been with them, Karen and Charlie have not entertained at home. They've had dinners out, and once some friends came over on a Friday night after dinner and they all went downstairs and watched videos in the sports den.

América feels tension between them, even though they try to hide it from her and the children. It's like a tide, sometimes strong, other times barely perceptible. But it's always there.

For the past few days, Charlie has been sleeping in the guest room. He comes in late and goes right up to his office and sleeps up there. Once she heard them arguing in their bedroom, but the next morning he hadn't slept with her and her diaphragm had not been used.

When she washes Charlie's shirts, América looks for signs of another woman's lipstick or makeup. But his shirts are as unmarked as always, so América concludes that he's not sleeping around, or if he is, he's very good at hiding it. Charlie doesn't strike her as the type of man who would have mistresses anyway. Men who have a roving eye direct it at everything that moves. She's never felt like he's looking at her as anything but another person in his household.

Maybe I'm not his type, she tells herself, wondering if any of the other empleadas have ever been bothered by the men they work for. It's a subject that comes up in their chats every so often. They all feel vulnerable to the unwanted advances of their employers, but none has ever admitted to anything like that happening to them.

While she's picking up in Kyle's room, she hears the phone ring in her room. By the time she gets to it, it has stopped, and she stands near it for a few moments, hoping whoever it was will call again. It could be Paulina or one of the empleadas, to find out if she'll be at the playground later. When the caller doesn't try again, she goes back to her work. Several times that morning the same thing happens. But no matter how long she stays in her room to wait for the next call, it doesn't come until she's too far away to get to the phone on time. She dials

Paulina's number, but there's no answer. She finally gives up, fig-
uring it's one of the empleadas.

When she picks up Meghan from school, the little girl is
holding a creation made with macaroni, ribbons, and glitter
stuck to a paper plate.

"For you," Meghan says.

"Is beautiful, thank you." On the lower edge of the paper
plate, Meghan has pressed her handprints in bright red paint.
América touches the scratchy surface with her pinkie, as if making sure it won't rub off. "I love."

"I made it all by myself," Meghan announces, "but Mrs.
Morris helped with the ribbons."

"Is very beautiful," América repeats, and hugs the child.

After lunch, Meghan's friend is dropped off. América moni-
tors their play and again is bothered by the insistent telephone.
It's as if the caller can see her coming and hangs up just as she
enters the room. When it's time to pick up Kyle, América drops
off Meghan's friend first, then drives the Leverett kids to the
playground. Frida and Mercedes are there.

"I called you earlier, but there was no answer," says
Mercedes.

"I was wondering who was calling so many times."

"I only called once," Mercedes says, insulted at the implica-
tion that she has nothing better to do than call América.

"My phone has been ringing like crazy, and the minute I go
to answer it, they hang up."

"I hate it when that happens," says Frida, "and then I
remember that eighteen months ago I didn't even have a
phone."

Mercedes and América laugh.

"Adela found a job," says Mercedes.

"Already?"

"That woman is so lucky," Mercedes adds. "A couple they
share their apartment with is going back to Guatemala, so they
recommended her and Ignacio. It's in Larchmont, near the water
and everything."

"I hope he doesn't ruin it for her," mumbles Frida.

"It's what they've been hoping for all along," says América.

"Yes, but he's used to his freedom," argues Frida.

"It's different for the men to work interno," adds Mercedes. "They live in a house that's not theirs, and it's usually the lady of the house that's telling them what to do. Our men like to wear the pants in the family."

"In this country you can't be too proud," declares Frida, "you have to do what it takes. There's no place for that kind of machismo." Mercedes and América both turn to Frida with a startled look. Frida smiles sheepishly. "Mrs. Finn gave me a book. It's by a Latina, and she talks about what we mujeres should do to get ahead in this country."

"You sound like a feminist," Mercedes says coyly. "You'd better watch it."

"I'm not a feminist, but this book makes sense. I'll lend it to you, if you like. It's in Spanish."

"No thanks, I hate to read," Mercedes says airily. "I'd better get the kids home." She walks toward the tire swing, where the twins are being given a ride by Kyle. "Hasta mañana."

"It's funny," América says softly.

"What is?"

"What you just said, about machismo and pride." Frida looks at América as if surprised that anyone was listening. "I never thought about it that way."

"What way?"

"Latinos invented machismo, and I always thought of it like . . . only as the way they treat women, possessiveness and jealousy and all that." She searches for the right words. "But it's really about pride. I never thought of it that way." She smiles apologetically, as if Frida knows the answer to a crucial question and she's just guessing.

"Hmmm," says Frida, watching a bird alight on a fence post.

"Anyway," says América, "I'd better take the kids home." She doesn't know why she feels embarrassed, as if she has just revealed a great secret that will be all over town by tomorrow. Then she realizes why. She's not used to talking to people about ideas, has never tried to enter a discussion where an important

question with no possible answer is thrown out and you're supposed to come up with possibilities.

Men do that all the time. Correa, Feto, and Tomás sometimes sat under the mango tree in the backyard of La Casa del
Francés and discussed politics and newspaper stories. They had
an opinion about everything, it seemed, and she looked down
on it because most of the time it sounded like three men who
didn't know what they were talking about pretending they did
so as not to lose face. Every once in a while, however, they'd get
into subjects that were interesting. Like when they discussed the
fate of Vieques if the Navy were ever to leave the island. They
brought forth arguments based on historical events, and quoted
figures and projections and people she'd never heard about to
support their arguments. She loved to hear them talk then,
when they were serious and passionate about their beliefs, when
the discussions were more than three peacocks trying to scare
one another with false eyes.

They gather the children, who, as usual, don't want to leave.
América wishes she'd asked Frida for the book. She'd like to
learn something new, to look at life from a different perspective.
I missed so much by not staying in school, she laments. That's
what I kept telling Rosalinda. That's where she could do things
differently from me. I could have made something of myself,
learned a profession. But I never thought that far ahead. I never
had dreams of being a schoolteacher like Frida, or a nurse like
Adela, or a bank teller or telephone operator. Maybe that's been
the problem. I've never had any dreams of my own, so Mami
and Correa and even Rosalinda walk all over me. They try to,
anyway. They have no respect for me. She shakes her head. I've
had no respect for myself.

The restaurant is a huge diner in the center of Mount Kisco.
She's passed it many times but has never been inside. They're
seated at a booth, Karen next to Kyle and América next to
Meghan. The waiters and busboys are all Latinos. They speak to
one another in Spanish, then turn around with an obsequious
smile and ask the customers for their orders in English. She's

now become adept at guessing where they're from by their accent. The woman who waits on them looks and sounds Guatemalan, like Adela.

América doesn't know what to order. She's hungry and it's her birthday, and she'd love to eat a lobster like the one she saw the waitress carry past a minute ago. But she doesn't want to order the most expensive thing on the menu so that Karen will think she's taking advantage of her. The menu is large enough that she can hide behind it as she eyes what other diners have in front of them or what the waiters carry past their booth to other tables. The portions are enormous, each one enough for two or three people, she thinks, and perhaps Karen expects her to order one platter and share it with the children. But Karen is talking to the children about what they might like and seems to have already made up her mind as to what she will have.

"Does anything look good to you?" she asks América.

"Oh, yes, everything look good," she responds enthusiastically so that Karen knows she's happy with the place.

"What do you think you'd like?"

"I don't know, is so many things." She knows there are various chicken dishes, and she saw lasagna and spaghetti and a whole section on burgers. But her English is not good enough to understand everything that's on the menu.

"The prime rib is good here," Karen says, "if you like that sort of thing."

Obviously, thinks América, Karen doesn't. The waiter goes by with shrimps covered with a garlicky sauce. América wonders how much that is and scans the menu for the word *shrimp,* but there are several listed and she doesn't know which is the one that just went by. They're all expensive too.

"Maybe you would like some chicken?" asks Karen, and América scans the prices following the word *chicken.* They're lower than the ones next to shrimp.

"Okéi," she says, emerging from behind the menu, "chicken."

The waiter passes with another platter of lobster, this one with shrimps on the side.

"Maybe you'd prefer lobster?" asks Karen, following her gaze.

América blushes deeply. "No, no. Chicken okéi."

"But it's your birthday, you should have something special," Karen insists with an encouraging smile.

"Yeah, América," pipes in Kyle, "ju it lobster," imitating her accent. They laugh, and Meghan decides she too can imitate América.

"You eat lobster," she says, not as good a mimic as her brother.

"It's settled, then," Karen says. "Lobster." And they all laugh and América is relieved not to have to argue, since that's what she wants and they did insist.

"A glass of wine with your dinner?" Karen asks.

"Oh, no, thank you, I no drink."

"Never?"

"No, never," she says, her face hot.

Once the orders are out of the way, the children chatter about their day in school and at the playground. Karen tries to include her in the conversation, but the children are intent on having their mother's attention to themselves, and so the meal progresses much as if América were not there, except for the times she reaches over to help Meghan cut up her hamburger, or when Kyle spills his drink and she has to get up and find the waiter and a rag to wipe the table.

For dessert, Karen orders chocolate cake, and América's comes with a sparkler on it. They sing happy birthday, and people at other tables join in, which América finds mortifying, because everyone turns around to look at her and she feels foolish when she tries to blow the sparkler out and it stays lit until it wears down.

They return home and she helps get the children ready for bed. When Karen takes them to her room to read them a story, she retreats to her own room, feeling giddy, as if she had accepted the glass of wine after all. The phone is ringing, but when she gets to it, it stops. She stamps her foot in frustration. She undresses and runs a hot bath, then pulls the phone cord as far as it goes, short of the bathroom door. She can't relax in the bath, however, expecting the phone to ring, and when it doesn't, she curses softly, angry with herself when she should be mad at whoever is calling. There's a knock and a lot of giggling outside her room. She throws on a robe and opens the door.

"We forgot to give you this." Karen and the children, in their night clothes, hold a large box. They troop in mock ceremoniously, the children giggling, holding the corners of the box as if it contains something fragile.

"I helped wrap it," says Meghan as they set it down on the couch.

"Is so nice, I so surprised," she blubbers, embarrassed and pleased, not knowing from their expressions if it's a real present or a joke.

"Open it," says Karen with an expectant smile. They watch her undo the tight bow and struggle with the many pieces of tape holding the edges of the wrapping paper. The phone rings.

"I'll get it." Before América can stop him, Kyle picks up the phone.

"Leverett residence," he says as he's been instructed to do. He waits. "There's no one there," he says, annoyed, and sets the receiver down.

"Maybe they thought they had the wrong number because it wasn't América's voice," Karen suggests.

"I don't know," says América, puzzled that whoever it was should have hung up so rudely.

"Open the present! Open the present!" Meghan chants, and América tears the wrapping off and finds a box, brightly decorated with the children's handprints and "Happy birthday" scrawled in Kyle's handwriting.

"Open it!" the children squeal, and she does to find another box, not as elaborate, and inside it another box. Kyle and Meghan laugh happily. América laughs with them, although she doesn't think it's very funny at all. Karen watches her with a bemused smile.

She opens the fourth box to find a lot of tissue around a sweatshirt decorated with two cats playing with a ball of yarn.

"We know you like cats," Karen says, looking at the white one on her bed.

"Is very nice," América says, pulling it out and holding it up to her shoulders.

"There are pants, too," says Meghan, rummaging through the tissue. "Here they are."

The jeans that match have kittens on the back pockets. "Is beautiful!" América says with more enthusiasm.

"If it doesn't fit, we can get another size," says Karen.

"No, it fits," América says. "Is perfect."

"Great! Okay, guys, it's past your bedtime." Karen seems in a hurry to leave the room.

"Thank you very much." América kisses the children warmly, walks them to the door. She feels awkward in front of Karen, as if thanking her is not enough and more is expected.

"Happy birthday," Karen says, and América again thanks her, not knowing what else to say, shamefaced, humbled.

When she's alone in the room, she tries on the outfit, which fits perfectly. It feels like good fabric, and the tag identifies it as coming from Lord & Taylor, which she knows to be an expensive store. It's something she knows Karen would never wear, and it touches her to think that she chose it with such care that even the size is right.

"I'm calling because it's my birthday, and you can't call me. I thought you might like to congratulate me."

"Feliz cumpleaños," Ester allows.

"They took me out for lobster, and they gave me a present."

"That was nice."

"Have you talked to Rosalinda?"

"She called asking for your number. I told her I didn't have it, but she didn't believe me."

"How do you know?"

"She hung up on me."

"I can't believe the phone is in one piece with Rosalinda banging it down all the time."

"Are you going to call her?"

"Maybe."

"She's your daughter. You shouldn't hold grudges." Ester is very good at giving advice she doesn't follow.

"I'll call her. And if she hangs up on me again, that's the end of it."

"She sounded upset."

"I'll call her."

"All right. Happy birthday, then."

She's had a nice day so far, and the thought of calling Rosalinda and getting into another fight is not appealing. Paulina called to wish her a happy birthday and promised they would celebrate this weekend. Then Darío called, and they talked for a half hour. She didn't tell him it was her birthday, because she didn't want him to think she expects a present. She turns off all the lights in her room, except for the lamp on the bedside table. She wants to be comfortable when she calls Rosalinda; she wants to be calm. She promises herself she will listen, will not say anything she hasn't thought over for a few seconds at least. The phone rings.

"Happy bird day 2 ju."

She freezes.

"Happy bird day 2 ju."

He sings softly, as if there were someone else in the room whom he doesn't wish to disturb.

"Happy bird day, dir América—"

She hangs up as if the receiver were burning her fingers, covers her face with her hands as if not wanting to face the room with the many windows, the slanted ceilings, the pale green stars above the bed. "Oh, my God. He knows where I am." She murmurs over and over again. "He knows where I am."

How Correa Knows

⚬⚭⚬⚭⚬⚭⚬⚭⚬⚭⚬⚭⚬⚭⚬⚭⚬⚭⚬⚭⚬⚭⚬⚭⚬⚭⚬⚭⚬⚭⚬⚭⚬⚭⚬⚭

A re you all right?" Karen asks the next morning. "You look like you didn't sleep well."

"Is okéi," she responds. "Time of month."

"There's Motrin in the medicine chest if you need it."

"Is okéi, thank you."

She manages to make breakfast for everyone, to get them off to school and work, to clear the dishes and clean the kitchen and pick up in the den and family room, to make the beds and bring the soiled clothes to the basement. She does her job automatically, with less efficiency, perhaps, than when she's paying attention. But everything gets done, and after a morning, the house is sparkling and she's still in a fog.

He knows where I am. It's like the verse of a song, repeating in her brain over and over again. He knows where I am doesn't leave room for any other thought, for reason to enter and begin gnawing at fear. He knows where I am punctuates her breathing, her walking, makes her jump when the gardener drives up with his lawn mower and rakes. He knows where I am follows her to school, where she picks up Meghan, to Liana's house, where the children watch Power Rangers. He knows where I am plays in her brain as the women talk, complain, joke, and tell stories.

She returns home, makes dinner, feeds the children,

although she barely touches her own food. It's Friday, and both Karen and Charlie come home early because they're taking the children to a party at a friend's house. She'll be alone tonight, and she talks herself into not being afraid. *He knows where I am, but he's in Vieques. He's not here.*

She draws the shades, locks her door. Because she's home, the Leveretts did not set the alarm when they left, as they would if the house were unattended. *But I shouldn't be afraid. He's in Vieques, and I'm here.* Every time she passes the phone, she expects it to ring. But it's silent.

Rosalinda picks up as if she too has been waiting for the phone to ring.

"Oh, Mami, hi." Wary, mistrustful.

"How are you?" She will remain composed, will think before she speaks. Will not let on that she's nervous, afraid, or worried.

"I'm fine. I got your letter. I'm sorry I hung up on you." An insincere apology, meant to appease her.

"Is everything all right?"

"Yeah." Uncertain.

"Have you seen your father lately?"

A gasp, short but perceptible. "He was here this week."

"Where is he now?"

"I don't know." Defensive.

América takes a deep breath. "Does he know where I am?"

"I . . . don't think so." Doubtful, lying. "I mean, I think he knows you're not in Puerto Rico."

"Where does he think I am?"

"I guess he thinks you're in New York." She's a poor liar. Her voice shakes, and she speaks too fast.

"Did you tell him that's where I am?"

"No." Her voice quivers, on the verge of tears.

"Did you?"

She breaks. "He saw the envelope . . . when you sent a money order and that letter."

América breathes, long even breaths. She will remain calm. "I didn't put the address on the envelope."

Rosalinda's voice rises. "It was in the postmark."

A cry escapes her. América bites her lips so that she will not be taken by surprise again.

"The name of the town was printed right in the postmark."

"Did you . . ." América falters in her efforts to remain calm, stops herself, tries again. "Did he find it, or did you show it to him?"

Silence. For a moment it seems to América that Rosalinda has again hung up on her. But she hears her breathing on the other end, quick, sharp breaths.

"I'm sorry, Mami." Rosalinda whimpers. "I was so mad at you, at your letter. And then he came over and found me crying." América lets her cry. This time Rosalinda's tears don't affect her the same way. She listens to her, doesn't question her, doesn't interrupt the sobs. Rosalinda continues, as if her mother's silence were an inducement. "He wrote down the name of the town, and then he checked the sheets from the guardhouse. He looked for names from the same place."

"So he has my address, too."

The resignation in her mother's voice startles Rosalinda.

"I was so mad at you." As if that excuses everything. "You shouldn't have written that letter." She's so self-righteous, so unwilling to take responsibility. "You always yell at me and criticize everything I do." Am I really that bad? Have I been such a terrible mother that she owes me no loyalty? "I tried to call and warn you, but I don't have your number. You should have given me your number."

América bites her lips, doesn't say anything.

"He . . . ju-ju-just w-w-w-wants . . . he jjjjust . . . he just wants to talk to you." Now she's angry, frustrated.

"All right, nena, take it easy. If you see him, tell him I'll talk to him." She will remain calm at all costs, will not let on that she's afraid.

"You will?" Rosalinda sounds unnerved, as if she has been found in a game of hide-and-seek.

"Tell him I'll talk to him."

"I will, Mami."

"Is he there now?"

"No, he went out."

"Okéi, mi'ja."

"You're not mad, Mami?"

"Don't worry."

"I'm sorry, Mami."

"I'll call you next week."

She sets the phone down gently, delicately. She's exhausted. Her arms feel tense and tight, as if she's been lifting weights. She sits propped up by pillows, her white stuffed cat on her lap. There's nothing to do now but wait. Correa will call, she will talk to him. She doesn't want to think about what will happen after that.

Margarita Guerra

He doesn't call. She stays up watching television, not really seeing it, show after show in which white Yanquis talk incessantly to one another and the audience laughs. All the humor seems based on misunderstandings. After the comedies, an information program. They show high-tension electric wires and confirm Ester's theory that electricity gives you cancer. Then the news, all bad. Sports. Weather. Then more funny shows she doesn't laugh at. And he doesn't call.

When a car drives up, she tenses. The garage door opens, slams down. Interior doors open and shut, Karen and Charlie come up the stairs, shush the children, who are whining from exhaustion. They settle and then everything's quiet again. After a while, voices, distant moans. Karen and Charlie make love for the first time in a week. And quiet returns, and she still waits for Correa to call. But he doesn't.

It's Viernes Social in Puerto Rico, Social Friday. He's probably out with his friends, drinking and having a good time. Has probably forgotten all about me. Maybe he's out with his wife. Maybe, as I wait here, he's entangled in her arms. The thought makes her furious. She turns off the television, prepares for bed, lies down with her eyes open until the stars above have faded. And then it's morning, and he hasn't called.

*   *   *

"I'm sorry, Tía. I was planning to come, but I'm needed here." She hates lying to Paulina, hopes she will accept the excuse and not drag her into explanations that will increase the lie.

"We hoped to celebrate your birthday," Paulina says regretfully. "Next weekend, maybe."

"Yes, next weekend."

"Bueno, we'll talk during the week."

She stays in bed, wrapped in the comforter, face down, a pillow under her belly. She has menstrual cramps, which she thinks were brought on by all the tension of waiting for Correa's call. The birth control pills used to give her short, light periods, with no pain. But she didn't bring her pills, she wouldn't need them, she thought, doesn't want their depressing side effects. Maybe, she considers now, the blue days were the fault not of the pills but of my life.

The family putters down the hall. She'll wait until they leave, then she'll go down and make some chamomile tea. Saturday mornings Meghan goes to gymnastics and Kyle goes to karate. If Karen takes them, Charlie will probably be in his office or down in the exercise room, so she will have the house to herself for an hour or so.

The phone rings. She crawls up to reach it.

"América?"

"Oh, hi, Darío." She can't help sounding disappointed.

"Paulina said you're not coming this weekend?"

"I have to stay here." That's not a lie.

"You aren't mad at me for something, are you?"

"No, why would I be mad? No, how could you think that?" She falters. "I have to stay here to receive a phone call, and I don't really know when it's coming, so I thought it was better if I stayed." Why am I giving him all these explanations?

"A phone call from whom? Never mind, it's none of my business."

"I'll be there next weekend, okéi?" Now she sounds like Karen Leverett appeasing one of the children.

"All right. I guess I'd better get off the phone."

"Oh?"

"In case your caller is trying to get through."

"Oh, yes, right, okéi."

He hasn't believed her. He thinks she's made up this excuse to avoid seeing him. Ay, Dios mío. She turns over on her belly again. I have the worst luck with men.

She comes downstairs after she's heard two cars drive away and the house sounds quiet. The kitchen is a mess of dirty cups and bowls, dishes on the counter, on the table, in the sink. In the toaster oven two pieces of toast are so crispy they crumble when she removes them. She's tempted to clean the mess but remembers there's a woman who comes on weekends, and she thinks it's the woman's job to clean up, not hers.

Someone is fumbling with the front-door lock. She freezes in place, listening, trying to decide whether to run upstairs to her room or to check and see who it can be. The door opens before she has time to decide.

"Hey, hi!" Charlie jogs in, his shorts and T-shirt soaked with sweat. "Beautiful day, isn't it," he asks, not expecting an answer. He opens a bottle of water and swills it down in a few gulps, his right hand on his hip, his eyes closed as if he can't drink and see at the same time. "Ah! That's great!" He throws the bottle into the recycling bin. "So," he says, and leans his hands on the counter, facing her across it as if about to interrogate her. "How are things going?"

"Okéi," she says with a dim smile.

"How do you like Bedford?"

"Is very nice."

"Well, we're glad to have you here," he says, pushing away from the counter. "See you later." He disappears down the stairs.

She shakes her head. I wonder what he would have said if I told him how things are really going. My mother is an alcoholic, she mouths silently, and my fourteen-year-old daughter sleeps around and wants to be a chorus girl when she grows up. But that's not all, Mr. Leverett. My marido, who is not my husband, is a jealous, possessive woman beater whom I ran away from to come work for you. He now knows where to find me because my daughter, the vedette, who hates me, showed him an envelope with a postmark. And he's so resourceful that he found your address, Mr. Leverett, in those stupid sheets the tourism office keeps to help you tourists feel safe on the beach in Vieques. And now, Mr. Leverett, I'm afraid to leave your house because I'm waiting for my marido, who is not my husband, to call and insult me on the phone so that I can know, at least, that he's in Puerto Rico and not in your neighborhood looking for me. And how are things going for you?

She takes her tea and toast up to her room, closes the door, and sits on the couch. She's fuming. This is what he wants. Even from Puerto Rico he's controlling me, keeping me locked in my room waiting for him.

She sips the tea, munches toast, takes her time because there's nothing else she can do. She sits, stares out the window at the dark green leaves of a tree in the front yard. There are no butterflies here, it occurs to her. Back home, if I looked out a window, I'd always see butterflies. But I haven't seen a single butterfly since I arrived. Maybe it's too cold for them. Everything dies here in the winter—birds, butterflies . . . The phone rings.

"América." He whispers her name, the way he does when he's making love to her.

"Correa." And she names him under her breath, as if to do so out loud would conjure him.

"You taught me a lesson, baby." There's a smile in his voice.

"Rosalinda said you wanted to talk." She will be strong, she will not cry, will not let on that she's afraid.

"We're talking, aren't we? We're talking, baby. We should have talked long ago."

She will ignore his patronizing tone, will pretend they're having a normal conversation. "How are you?"

"I'm fine, fine. Real fine! And you?"

"I thought you would call me last night. I told Rosalinda to tell you to call me." The resentment bubbles through in spite of her efforts to squelch it.

"I was busy last night, baby. But I'm here now. I miss you

like crazy, you know you're my woman." He's playing with her. She can't tell if he's being sarcastic or not.

"Are you in Fajardo, or in Vieques?"

"Do you miss me? Do you?"

He wasn't being sarcastic. "Yes, I miss you." She is.

"You shouldn't have run away from me like that, América. It made me crazy. But you taught me a lesson. I promise to change, baby. I'm getting a divorce, and you and me will get married. In a church and everything. I miss you so much, baby, you're the only one for me. You know that, don't you?"

"Yes." She will play along with him, anything to keep him talking like this, like a lover. To keep him from swearing at her and calling her ugly names and making threats. Anything to keep him from getting angry, from finding ways, at this great distance, to hurt her.

"Forgive me. I swear I'll never raise my hand to you, I make you a solemn promise on my mother's grave, I swear it."

"All right."

"I'll fix up the house, and we'll live there. In my house, not Ester's house. I'll fix up a room for Rosalinda too. She wants us to be a family again. She's such a sensitive girl. This whole thing has been real hard on her. I'm not blaming you. I blame myself too. I just love you so much, América, I can't stand the thought of ever losing you. Do you understand that, baby? Do you hear what I'm saying to you?"

"Yes."

"You won't have to work anymore, either. I want you home being my wife, and taking care of our daughter, and maybe, have a couple of more kids. You'd like that, wouldn't you, baby? We'll try for a boy this time."

"All right."

"Yes, baby, all right. You're talking to a new man, baby. A new man. You've taught me a lesson I'll never forget. I miss you baby. Do you miss me? Do you?"

"Yes." Is he deaf? Doesn't he hear the flatness in her voice, the automatic responses? She's telling him what he wants to hear. She's playing with him.

"We're going to be happy, you just wait. We'll grow old together, you and me. We'll be the best looking viejitos in Vieques, okay, baby? Okay?"

"Okéi."

"All right. I'll call the airlines, and I'll get you a ticket for tomorrow. You pack your bags, baby, and I'll come get you at the airport in San Juan. And tomorrow, you'll see a new man waiting for you."

The image of Correa waiting for her at the other end of a flight wakes her from the semitrance in which she has been listening to him. "Tomorrow . . . Correa, tomorrow is too soon."

"What do you mean, too soon?" The beginning of a snarl, the beginning of anger.

"I mean, well, I have my period . . . and it wouldn't . . . "

He chuckles, a low, patronizing chuckle. "I see what you mean, yeah. But we won't do anything, even though it's been months. I can control myself until—"

"I'd like to be . . . nice and fresh for you . . . and, I'd like to buy some presents for Rosalinda, and for Estrella who has been so good . . ." She hates herself, the tone of her voice, the girlish sound meant to seduce, the innuendoes. But it works.

"You're right, baby, you're right. I'm being selfish. It's just that I want you here so much."

"The people I work for have young children. I should give them time to find someone."

"You tell them in a couple of days you're gone. You're going home to your man. You tell them that." As if a couple of days were a huge concession. "I'll call the airlines and get your ticket. You don't worry about a thing."

"A week, Correa. Can I come home next Monday?" To herself she sounds as if she were begging. "They need time to find someone."

He hesitates. "A week?" She holds her breath, then relaxes when he relents. "All right, one week. I'll call later to let you know about your flight. You wait for me to call."

"Okéi."

"I love you, baby."

She waits for him to hang up, sets the receiver down gently, and sits staring out the window. There are no butterflies here. They all die.

Between the money she brought with her from Puerto Rico and what she has saved after sending Ester and Rosalinda money every week she's worked, she has $397.22 to her name. She can't get very far on $397.22.

"Hi, Frida. Do you have a minute?"

"Sure, Mrs. Finn took the kids to the movies. I've been ironing all day. I hate to iron."

"I was wondering if your sister or daughter might know of a situation."

"For you? Hold on." She can hear Frida set the iron down, pull out a chair, and get ready for a nice long chat. "I thought you liked the Leveretts."

"I need to move, but not around here."

"What's the matter? You sound upset."

"I'm sorry, I didn't mean to." She wipes her nose on the back of her hand. "I have a problem, and I need to find another place to live."

América envisions Frida leaning into the phone, waiting for details. She doesn't give any.

"Bueno," Frida says, unwilling to seem like a busybody by asking more than América is ready to tell. "I can call to see."

"I'd appreciate it."

"Sure."

"Thank you, Frida."

"Sure, no problem."

It's taken all her energy to make that one call, to admit to someone that she needs help. América imagines that by the time she walks across the room, Frida will have called Mercedes, who will call Liana, who will call Adela, until they all know she's looking for another job. They will speculate about the reason and cite conversations that might hint at why she's leaving the Leveretts after a few months. They will wonder whether the Leveretts will now need someone else and whether they might get more money from them than their current employers pay them. But they won't commit to the Leveretts until they know why she's leaving.

As for me, I have one week to figure things out. One week to disappear to God knows where. And once I do, I will not tell anyone. Not Mami. Not Rosalinda. Not even Tía Paulina. None of them. I'll go someplace where no one knows me. A place with no Puerto Ricans, so that there's no chance I'll see anyone I know. I might even change my name. But I'm not going back. Not for him. Not for her. Not for anybody.

She's hungry but doesn't want to use the Leverett kitchen. It was such a mess when she came down earlier, and now the kids are home, and so are Karen and Charlie. She doesn't feel like talking to them, to pretend everything's fine. She will drive to Mount Kisco for Chinese food. She could use some fresh air.

"América is here," Meghan announces when she comes down. The family is at the table, having an early dinner or late lunch, she doesn't know which.

"I go out. Is okéi I take Volvo?"

"Yes, of course," says Charlie.

"Can I come?"

"No, you guys stay with us. This is América's day off, and she has things to do, okay?" Karen tries to look stern, but it's not in her nature. She smiles too much.

A large woman comes out of the bathroom. She has long, straight hair caught in a ponytail, with girlish bangs over blue eyes. Only she's not a girl, nor is she a mature woman. Her unlined face is fleshy, high-cheekboned, with the kind of pretty features people usually remark on followed by "too bad she's so heavy."

"This is Johanna," Karen says, not getting up from the table. "Johanna, this is América."

"Hi," Johanna says, friendly, open.

"Hello." She'd like to seem happier to meet her, but she's not. This is the woman who baby-sits the children on weekends, who leaves the kitchen a mess, who doesn't straighten the rooms all weekend long, so that when América comes back she spends the better part of her morning putting toys away and picking up clothes from every corner of the kids' rooms. "Nice to meet you," she lies.

Johanna sits between Kyle and Meghan, like part of the family. América takes the keys to the Volvo from the drawer. "I see you later."

"Adiós, América," the children sing.

"Have a good time," Charlie calls out.

She'll have to tell them she's leaving. Next week she'll walk out of this house, away from these people, and never see them again. She'll tell Karen when they're alone. She doesn't look forward to the questions, the hurt looks, the knowledge that Karen will feel betrayed. She should tell her tonight, give her time to find someone else. Maybe Johanna can fill in.

She's about to climb into the car when Karen runs out. "Uh, América, before you leave."

"Yes?"

"I was wondering if you could work next weekend." She stuffs her hands in her back pockets, which makes her look young and vulnerable. "Charlie and I would like to go away for the weekend, just the two of us." She blushes.

"Johanna can't?"

Karen seems surprised that América doesn't jump at the chance. "We'd rather you stay. It would be less disruptive for the children."

"I don't know." How to tell her next weekend she might not even be here?

"Of course, we'd pay you extra." As if she were doing her a favor.

América feels the heat rise to her face. If she were to say anything now, it would not be polite. So she nods. "Okéi." Quiet, humble, no problem.

"Oh! Great! Well,"—Karen backs away, hands still in pockets—"we can talk about it when you come back, okay?" She vanishes into the house.

América sits at the wheel for a minute before starting the car. This is the second time that Karen Leverett has wanted to change América's schedule for her convenience. She thinks I have no life other than the one that solves her problems. It's not enough that I work fifteen hours a day, that I'm bringing up her children, that I pick up after them and cook for them and maintain their home so that it's clean and comfortable when they get back from work. I'm also expected to suspend my life, to be available on my days off to make it easier for her to have her life. As if her life were more important than mine.

Is it? she asks herself. Is Karen Leverett's life, with its important job, its meetings and early-morning phone calls, its ton of papers strewn all over the den, more important than mine? She's afraid to answer the question.

I should never have come here. I was stupid to think this could work. Of course Correa would find me. And the longer it took him, the worse for me.

She backs out of the driveway, into the dirt road.

I was lucky to have the last three months. Three months away from my real life. The life with the embittered mother and the resentful daughter and the man who says he loves me as he beats me up. Three months, two longer than I spent away from my life then, when I was just a girl and he was a man like no other man I knew.

She turns right onto the paved country road, curving this way and that, bordered by stone fences with electronic gates.

Both times I've left Vieques, I've been so full of hope, and I come back disillusioned.

She drives past the village common with its subdued antique shops, real estate offices, fragrant gourmet stores where a pound of coffee costs eleven dollars.

It's destiny, I suppose, that my life should have turned out this way. One home, one man, one child, three months of freedom. She sighs.

The road curves downhill, past the sprawling high school with playing fields, a track, a pond, its own theater. Beyond it, the highway, south to the city, north to she doesn't know where. She's never been on it, but she turns onto it now, heading away from the city, toward where she's never been. She looks down at the gas gauge. Full. She wonders how far the road extends, what's at the other end, and whether it's any different from what she has seen in the only places she's ever been: Vieques, Fajardo, the Bronx, Madison Square Garden, Mount Kisco, Bedford, Westchester County, New York.

She drives for about three hours, on a wide, clean highway that rolls endlessly up and down a countryside broken now and then by small towns. I won't stop until I run out of gas, she promises herself, but when she passes the city of Hartford, the stretches in between towns seem longer and lonelier and she's spooked by the darkness along the side of the road. She gets off at the next exit, follows the arrows pointing to Food Gas Lodging. She drives through a Burger King and munches her Whopper as she enters the highway heading south again, in the direction from which she just came.

I can't run away. Where would I go? Besides, if I did run away, I'd get arrested for stealing the Leveretts' car. She laughs out loud. This is the farthest I've ever gone for a hamburger.

By the time she gets to Bedford, it's past eleven o'clock. The Leverett house is dark, except for the faint glow of the night-lights in the children's rooms. She has a key to the back door, and as she steps behind the garage, a light goes on by itself, brightening the rear yard. She fumbles with the key before inserting it in the lock. As she enters the dark kitchen, a shape looms toward her from the back stairs landing. She screams, drops her purse, falls back against the door.

"América!"

The light goes on. Charlie, wearing nothing but rumpled boxer shorts, stands in the landing, Karen behind him.

América sobs hysterically, propped against the door, her handbag at her feet. Karen comes over, puts her arm around her.

"We're sorry, we didn't expect to see you. We've had all these hang-up phone calls. We thought you were gone for the night, like the other times. We're sorry."

She leads América to a chair. Charlie disappears and returns with a robe on. América can't stop shaking, sobbing as if all the tension of the past two days reached its climax when she saw the dark shape move toward her.

Karen and Charlie exchange a look. "Do you have a Valium?" he asks, and Karen nods. He disappears again.

"I'm so sorry, América. Please stop crying, we didn't mean to scare you. Here's a glass of water, here's a pill. It will help you feel better."

"No, no. I okéi. No pills plis." She pushes their hands away, stands up, searches for her purse. "I okéi now. I go my room. Is okéi." She picks up her handbag and runs up the stairs. Karen and Charlie are left holding the glass of water and the Valium.

The room is dark, stifling hot. She closes and locks the door behind her, stumbles in the dark toward the bed, throws herself into it, hides her face in the prickly fur of her stuffed white cat with the blue eyes. The drive to the Burger King was soothing to her nerves. She listened to the radio most of the way there and back, kept her mind occupied by the scenery whizzing by, thinking how nice it would be to live up here, in the woods, where no one knows her. She would change her name to Margarita, in honor of her great-great-great grandmother. Her last name would be Guerra, for war. Margarita Guerra. She practiced saying the name out loud as she drove down the highway toward Bedford. Margarita Guerra. Margie, maybe, if she were to Americanize it, but changed her mind because it didn't have enough syllables. Margarita. She likes the name because it's also the name of a flower. My name is Margarita Guerra, she said in different voices. Margarita Guerra is my name. I am Margarita Guerra. She said the name so many times that, when she entered the house and heard the loud "América," it was as if she'd been found out. As if all the planning she'd done, all the fantasies of a new life, incognita in the woods of Connecticut, had been discovered. The dark shape looming toward her, the name América yelled in a man's voice, broke through the dream of safety she'd formed in the long drive to and from a Burger King in another state. I am América. América Gonzalez. And everyone knows it.

*   *   *

"I called you earlier and there was no answer," Correa says in the middle of the night.

She's groggy, half asleep, half awake from a dream in which she was being chased by butterflies through a field of daisies. "What?"

"Are you alone?" he asks. He's drunk, she can hear it in his voice, the slurred speech, the stumbling over simple words.

"I was asleep. You woke me up from a dream."

"Were you dreaming about me?" He laughs lasciviously, wetly.

"I don't remember," she says, forgetting that it's a game, that she should play with him.

"Where were you?" Angry now, his voice a threat. "I've been calling all night. I called all their numbers."

She shakes her head, tries to clear it of daisies and butterflies and his voice. "What numbers?"

"Char-less Leverett. Karen Leverett. They have a lot of numbers." He's exasperated, as if Information were out to thwart him.

"You've been calling them?" Panicked, her voice sounds like a screech.

"I was looking for you."

"What did you say to them?" Calm down. Don't let him know you're afraid.

He takes a breath. Liquor slows his reflexes, and while he can hear the fear in her voice, it's taking him longer to process it. "Nothing. I hung up, like the other night when the gringito answered." He's confused. They've never had a fight on the phone. He prefers to fight her in person, where he can't be contradicted.

América sits up, clearheaded now. "This is my number. The other numbers are for the house."

"You didn't wait for my call." He's recovered, remembers why he's calling at one-thirty in the morning.

"I was hungry. I went out to eat." Keep your answers simple and straightforward. Don't add fuel to his fire. Change the subject. "Are you with Rosalinda?"

"You shouldn't be out alone at night. You know I don't like that."

"It's very safe and quiet around here. I didn't go far."

He's tired. He speaks at the speed of a slow record. "I got you a ticket. For Monday. You come home Monday. I'll be waiting for you." A threat.

"Okéi."

"Are you bringing me a present?" Lewd, suggestive, she can almost see where his hand is as he speaks.

And she plays with him, her voice low and syrupy. "Yes, of course. Something very special."

"Oh, baby!"

"Something you like very, very much," she whispers, and his breath quickens. As she tells him what he wants to hear, she listens, alert to any variation in the sound of his breath, in the growled professions of his love. "Over and over again," she promises. Anything to keep him seduced to the image of his lover América, not América the woman who left him. She pacifies him with words and listens for sounds that will give her a clue to where he is. For a radio on a Spanish station, or familiar voices, or better yet, the distant, soothing sound of a coquí.

Sunday morning she sleeps so late that she wonders once she's up if she did take the pill the Leveretts offered her the night before. But she doesn't feel groggy so much as exhausted. She drags herself to the bathroom, runs a cool shower, and still that feeling of exhaustion, as if she were towing a great weight with each step.

Johanna and the children are at the play structure in the back of the house, and they too seem languid and slow, not really committed to what they're doing. She dresses and prepares to have breakfast out, so as not to interfere with anything the family might be doing. When she comes down, the kitchen is cleared and Karen is cooking.

"Good morning," Karen says warily. "Are you feeling better?"

"Yes, sorry I was so scared."

"Oh, I don't blame you. I would have fainted, if it had been me." Karen throws some vegetables in the Cuisinart. Over the din of the motor she explains, "We have friends coming."

"Is okéi I go?"

"Yes, of course. Johanna is with the children. We'll be fine."

"I see you tonight." She leaves quickly, waves at the children when they see her.

Karen is like a new woman, bright, cheerful. She and Charlie have made up again. All last week he slept in the guest room, but the last two nights they were together. They wear the assured glow of lovers. Ten years of marriage and they don't have to pretend to love each other. They can fight and make up and fight again and make up, and stay in love.

When did I fall out of love with Correa? Was I ever *in* love? At fourteen it can't be love. I was impressed with him, and he was so handsome! He conquered me with his beautiful green eyes and manly voice. And the promises. I can't even remember them. Does Charlie make Karen promises? If he does, she believes them still.

She drives to Mount Kisco, parks near the Christopher Columbus statue. The couples that three months ago induced such loneliness now seem girdled by a dark cloud. The women whose looks were like a challenge seem pathetic. As she passes, they eye her a warning, hold on to their men as if they were a prize of conquest, instead of its price. América stares them down. There's a reason, she wants to yell at them, men call a successful courtship la conquista.

She spends the afternoon at the movies, watching what she thinks are the two most stupid-looking men she's ever seen act even more stupid than they look. The theater is full of parents and children. The empleadas, América muses, are off, so even though it's a nice day out, the local movie theater is full of parents whose idea of spending time with their children is sitting in a movie theater eating popcorn and watching obnoxious men do fart jokes.

When she gets back, there are four cars in the driveway. It's dusk, but Kyle and three children América has never seen are

chasing one another around a tree, while Johanna pushes
Meghan on the swing. She'd like to slip into the house unseen,
but there are people in the family room. When she enters they
look at her curiously, then avert their eyes, the way the tourists
do in Vieques. She walks through to the back stairs quickly,
wishing she were invisible. As she's going up, Karen peeks
around the corner, as if someone has alerted her that there is a
stranger in the house, and she waves and says to no one in particular, "Oh, it's just América."

She locks herself in her room, changes clothes, and gets
ready to call Ester and Rosalinda. When she's done, she gives
herself a clay-mask facial and sits watching an old Argentinian
movie on the Spanish television station. Tomorrow there will be
a lot to do in the house. The children have tracked in mud from
the yard, and she noticed that the adults in the kitchen and den
seem to have a problem keeping their dip on their potato chips.

Everybody Has Problems

Monday morning dawns dank and cold. She would like to stay in bed, curled up inside the warm comforter, but she has to get up and cook breakfast.

Being in this country has made me lazy, she reflects; I never had such trouble getting up in the morning.

She showers, dresses, slips downstairs in the dark to the kitchen. She brews coffee, toasts two slices of Wonder bread, which she likes better than the gritty stuff Karen and Charlie eat. She keeps her loaf of Wonder bread in the downstairs freezer, where Karen rarely ventures.

¡Ay! She moans out loud as she comes up the basement stairs. Every bone in my body hurts, like an old woman's. Four days past my thirtieth birthday and I'm already falling apart.

She sits with her toast and coffee and waits for Charlie to bound down the stairs. When he does, with his usual, "Hi, how you doing?" which requires no response, she washes her dishes and, as soon as he leaves, goes upstairs to get the kids ready for school. They're cranky, overtired from yesterday's party, which lasted until after ten.

Karen, as usual, comes down at the last minute, hair freshly blow-dried, eyes sparkling. They must have made love again last night, América guesses.

Then they're all gone and she has the house to herself, and she has to clean, to wipe, vacuum, and scrub this house that is not hers. To change bed linens and pick up dirty underwear from the floor and gouge dried swirls of spilled toothpaste from the sinks. She works slowly, methodically, feels herself moving in slow motion to the lyrics of her favorite danza, which repeat over and over in her brain.

> *Siento en el alma pesares*
> *que jamás podré olvidar*
> *tormentos a millares*
> *que hoy me vienen a mortificar.*

The family-room floor tiles are crusted with crab dip, and she has to get down on her hands and knees to scrub it with a plastic sponge. Bread crumbs pulverized into the pile of the dining room rug have to be vacuumed with the upholstery attachment. Used wine and beer glasses on the tables and mantelpieces must be retrieved, washed and dried by hand. The granite tabletop in the den is gritty from dried spilled wine, the surface dull like the original rock from which it was quarried.

She has worked clockwise starting in the kitchen and is now back by the stove, not even halfway done. In another twenty minutes she has to pick up Meghan, but first she must answer the phone. Mercedes invites her to bring the children over.

"It's such a dreary day," she says, "I baked a torta." She giggles. Once the empleadas had a great laugh over the meaning of the word in their respective countries.

"I have too much to do here," América explains. "They had a party yesterday."

"You poor thing! Another time, then."

América wouldn't have gone anyway. Frida has probably told Mercedes about her call yesterday. She doesn't want to talk about it, to reveal her life to anyone, not even these women who consider her a friend.

I have no friends. I only have Correa.

> *Cesaron para mí*
> *el placer, la ilusión,*

¡Ay de mí,
que me mata esta fuerte pasión!
y tú ángel querido,
no has comprendido
lo que es amor.

Somehow she gets through the day, drags herself from chore to chore, the same song playing in her head whenever she's not attending to Meghan or Kyle. When Karen Leverett comes home, the house is clean, the children have been picked up from school, driven to their swimming lesson, fed and bathed and readied for bed so that all she has to do is read them a story and tuck them in, kiss them perhaps, on the forehead before curling up on the leather couch in the den, her papers strewn all over the brightly polished granite coffee table.

She has forgotten there's another man in her life, but Darío calls her just as she's drifting off to sleep.

"Did you get your call?"

"Call?"

"You said you couldn't come this weekend—"

"Oh, right. My call. Yes, I did."

The silence that follows is not like those of a few days ago. Those silences were filled with expectation. This one is empty, nothing but a low electric hum.

"Are you all right?" Darío is tentative again. She can almost see his hurt puppy expression. She wants to reassure him, but she resents this feeling that she has to take care of him.

"Darío, I'm really tired—"

"Okay, I see." Another awkward silence in which she imagines he's trying to understand what she really means. "Do you want me to call you tomorrow?"

"Yes. Tomorrow. Call me earlier, okéi? I'm just really tired now."

"Good night, then. Get some rest."

She falls asleep almost the minute she hangs up the phone.

Correa calls at two in the morning, professing his love but really checking up on her. He's in Vieques. Rosalinda told her that's where he went when he left Estrella's house yesterday morning. Rosalinda, her daughter, who she now thinks of as Correa's alcahueta. She had once asked herself whose side Rosalinda was on, and now she knows.

And they say, América broods, that a daughter never leaves you. It's not true. They leave as soon as they can get away with it, as soon as they're weaned. They leave you physically, but first they leave you spiritually. They pry the child in themselves from your grip the minute they realize they'll never have you the way they did when they suckled at your breast. Then they want to get away from you as fast as they can, to find another to cleave to—a man, always a man.

And it's Tuesday. She didn't sleep well after Correa's call.

"Did you get a present for me?" he asked, and she didn't know what he was talking about. But then she remembered. He wanted her to talk to him the way she did a few nights ago. She didn't want to, but he kept asking if she loved him, if she was bringing him sweet honey, and hot with shame, she had to say yes.

"Are you all right?" Karen asks when América drops and breaks a mug.

"I'm okéi," América says, smiling, and Karen doesn't press her.

Her head feels wrapped in gauze. "Can I have my toast now?" Kyle asks, and she sets it down, not remembering how long she held it over the plate.

"You look tired," Karen suggests, and América smiles and says she's a bit tired, but she's okéi. No worry.

They leave, and she's alone in the house again. This house that's not hers that she takes care of as if it were. Better.

Seven days left. Correa will be waiting for me at the airport.

She picks up Meghan from school and takes her to the playground, but it's damp again today, and there are no other children. Meghan stands in front of her, forlorn.

"But there's nothing to do, América," she complains.

"Go slide." América points toward the plastic orange tunnel leaning against a wooden platform.

"But there's nobody here." Meghan looks around as if to make sure. "See?"

"You want go home?"

"Yes. It's cold." She presses herself into América's arms.

"Okéi, baby, we go home." América holds her tight, so tight Meghan cries out.

"You're squeezing me!"

"You América baby, yes?"

Meghan doesn't answer, and América doesn't ask again. They drive home in the drizzle, listening to a tape of children's songs. "Willoughby wallabee woo, an elephant sat on you."

Frida calls that evening.

"I talked to my sister and my daughter. They'll ask around about a situation."

"Okéi."

"Are you all right, América? You sound sad."

"I'm a little tired, that's all."

"Hopefully we can take the kids to the playground tomorrow, if it's nice out."

"Yes."

"Maybe we'll see you there?"

"Maybe."

They will all be there. Frida and Mercedes, Liana and Adela, waiting for her, curious to know why she would leave the Leveretts after only three months. But she will not be there. She will not tell them the truth, and she will not tell them a lie. So she will not be at the playground tomorrow, even if it's a nice day.

He calls at nine-thirty. To make sure she's there, she knows, but he says it's to give her information on her flight. "I paid for the ticket," he says. "All you have to do is identify yourself at the American Airlines desk."

"Okéi."

"Do you have a ride to the airport?"

"I'll get one."

"Who? The man of the house?" He chortles.

"My aunt."

This phone call is like their old conversations. He's no longer the sweet lover. He's telling her what to do. Every once in a while he calls her baby. But now that he knows where she is, and that she's willing to come back to him, he's the man he's always been.

Darío calls at ten.

"Is this a good time?" he asks.

"I'm sorry about last night. I didn't mean to be rude."

"I thought maybe I said something—"

"It wasn't you, Darío. You didn't do anything." She'd like to tell him what's going on, but why get him involved in something that has nothing to do with him? "I have some . . . family problems."

"Is there anything I can do to help?"

"I don't think so, but thank you."

He makes a sound, a hum, the beginning of a song, maybe. But nothing comes after it.

"You know how to reach me at my parents', if there's anything I can do," he finally says.

It's the concern in his voice that breaks her resolve to keep it all to herself, to not involve him. "I had a call from . . . from the man I lived with . . . in Vieques."

"What did he want?"

To rape me, to beat me, to show me who's boss. "He wants me back." Her voice quavers, and she presses her fingers against her lips to keep them from trembling.

"Are you going?"

"I don't want to . . ."

"Don't go then. Your life is here now."

"Some life," she mutters, but he doesn't hear her.

"It's not easy to make a fresh start, believe me, I know . . ." Is that a sob she hears? No, it isn't. It's his voice, crackly, nervous. "Doña Paulina might have mentioned . . . or your cousins . . . I had some problems—"

"Everybody has problems." América cuts him off, hoping he'll stop.

"I . . . I was just a kid, you know, and got involved with the wrong people . . ."

He takes a deep breath, and América covers her eyes. She can sense the beginning of a confession, and she doesn't want to hear it, she just doesn't want to hear it right now.

His voice drops to a near whisper. "I had a drug habit. It almost killed my parents. It killed my wife . . ." He breathes a sigh of relief.

On her end, América is tensed into knots. How does one respond to such an admission? What does he expect me to say? "I thought she died of AIDS."

"Yes, she did."

"You said the drugs killed her."

"She got AIDS from an infected needle."

He sounds testy, and América realizes this is not what the confession is about.

"Do you forgive me?"

"For what?"

"I just told you something . . . were you listening?" He's upset, she can hear it in the way his voice cracks.

"You told me you were a drug user and your wife died of AIDS. What's there to forgive in that?" And then it occurs to her, maybe he killed her.

"You don't care that I used drugs?"

"Are you still using them?"

"No. I've been clean for four years. Did you notice I didn't drink at the nightclub?"

"I don't care what you did years ago. It has nothing to do with me." And, she wants to say, I have my own problems, today, right now, that have nothing to do with you. Why am I lying here listening to your life story?

"You're mad at me."

"I'm not mad at you, Darío. Why would I be mad?"

"You're not being very kind."

América is offended by this. "I have to go," she says. "It's late."

"Good night."

He's the one who's angry now, she thinks. But what did he expect? I tell him I have a problem, and next thing that happens is he's telling me his. Like mine don't matter. Like I'm supposed to forget about mine and worry about his. Who does he think he is?

She's so agitated that she can't get comfortable. What's wrong with me? Why can't I meet normal men? Why do I have to be involved in one place with an abuser and come all the way across an ocean to get involved with a victim? She punches the pillows into shape. Well, I'm not really involved with Darío. Just a few phone calls, a trip to the circus. That's nothing.

It's something. I've been beat for less than that. Correa has punched me in the stomach for just walking on the same side of the street as another man. For just looking in his direction. If Correa knew half the encounters I've had with Darío, he'd kill me.

She covers her head with the pillow, as if warding off a blow. Oh, my God, whatever made me think I could get away with this?

In six days Correa will be waiting for me at the airport, she thinks on Wednesday morning.

She's picking up in Kyle's room. She lines up the Mighty Morphin Power Rangers next to one another on the shelf and under them, Lord Zed and his minions. On another shelf she stores the Game Boy next to a stack of games. On the floor, Kyle has left a half-completed puzzle. It's a map of the United States, with Hawaii floating on the left lower corner and Alaska floating on the left upper. And nothing else. No Canada, no Mexico, no Caribbean. The fifty colorful puzzle pieces are all labeled with the names of the states. Tennessee. Oregon. Nebraska.

What I'll do, América tells herself, is cash the ticket in and buy one to somewhere else. Arizona, maybe. She doesn't know where the puzzle piece for Arizona fits, but it doesn't matter. If she doesn't know where it is, maybe neither does Correa.

Paulina calls that evening. "Ay, mi'ja, call your mother." Paulina is poised on the edge of an attack of los nervios. "Ester called. She wanted to talk to you but didn't want me to give her your number. She said she can't be trusted with it. What is this all about? Your own mother doesn't know how to reach you?"

"She thought it might slip out when she's . . . like that."

"Like what? What do you mean? She's your mother."

"She's not reliable if she's had a few beers."

"Oh, dear Lord!"

When América calls her, Ester is as agitated as Paulina.

"I came home from work," she says as soon as she recognizes América's voice. No preamble, no how are you. "And most of the stuff was gone. He's been taking things out of here all day."

She's not sure, at first, who Ester is talking about.

"The first thing I noticed was that the rocker was gone from the porch. Then the couch in the living room. I thought we were robbed. I went to my room, but nothing there was gone, thank God. But your room was empty. Your bed and dressers, all the stuff you left. He took the coffeemaker and the vajilla, too."

"Slow down, Mami, take it easy."

Ester stops, takes a breath. "He cleaned out Rosalinda's room. He even took the television." Querulous, as if that were the greater tragedy.

"Is he coming back?"

"How would I know if he's coming back or not? That sinvergüenza! He waited until I wasn't home."

"Well, don't let him in if he does."

"What would he come for? There's nothing left that belongs to him."

"Just in case, Mami."

"That sinvergüenza," she repeats.

"Maybe you should go over to Don Irving's."

"Nah, I won't bother him. He's no good at this stuff." Like she is. "I just thought you should know."

"Well, thank you," she says dryly.

"He's up to something," Ester speculates. "He's probably found himself another woman and wants to make you jealous."

I wish, thinks América. "He won't bother you anymore."

"I have my machete, just in case." She laughs halfheartedly.

On Thursday evening, Karen gives her details of the trip she and Charlie are taking.

"We're driving to Montauk," she says. "We'll leave early to avoid the rush."

They're in the family room. The children are in bed. América came down to get a cup of tea, and Karen walked out of the den with a list in her hand.

"This is the number of the hotel where we're staying, but you can also page us." In case América doesn't already have her and Charlie's beeper numbers in twenty different places, she's written them down on this list too. "But we'll also call every night."

"Okéi." She will not tell Karen she's quitting, won't spoil her weekend. But on Monday, when they come down for breakfast, she will be gone.

"Here's the money for this week," Karen says, handing her an envelope, "and some grocery and incidental money. In case you want to take the kids to the movies or something."

She will take the car to the station early in the morning, will leave a note on the counter, in as much English as she can remember, saying she's sorry, but she had to go.

"We'll be home early on Sunday," says Karen.

"Okéi." América nods. "I take care everything. You no worry."

When she returns to her room, she's glad she went down, because if Karen had come up to talk to her, she would have seen the clothes stacked in neat piles on the couch and chairs. One pile is clothes she will take. One pile she will leave in the closet for the next empleada. Another pile she will drop off at the Community Center box where Karen donates the children's outgrown clothing.

"So you can't come this weekend either?" Paulina asks.

"I'm sorry, Tía, the Leveretts are going away, and I have to take care of the kids."

"You're working too hard, mi'ja. Two weekends with no days off."

América's face reddens. Paulina has been kind to her, has tried to help her.

"I'm sorry, Tía," she repeats.

"Is everything all right with your mother? Did you call her?"

"Yes, everything's okéi."

"She's an alcoholic, then?" Paulina says as if this were a personal disappointment.

"She's been drinking more and more the last few years."

Paulina sighs. "What are you going to do?" she asks, and at first América thinks she's asking her for a real plan, then realizes it's just an expression.

"Así son las cosas," she agrees.

"Well, I guess we'll see you next Saturday, then? Orlando is singing at the club again."

"That sounds wonderful," América says. "You have been so kind to me, Tía," she adds. "I've really appreciated it."

"Ay, mi'ja, we're family. Don't embarrass me by thanking me." But América can tell she's beaming. "We'll see you next week."

She will not be able to say good-bye to them. To Carmen with the foreign boyfriends that no one has ever met, to earnest Leopoldo, to Orlando whose voice can wake the dead, to Teresa, the Puerto Rican yoga teacher. I will miss the scent of roses whenever Elena goes by, she thinks as she stuffs the give-away clothes in a plastic bag. I'll even miss Darío.

She wonders if she should call him. But what would she say to him? She doesn't think she should apologize. But then why does she feel so guilty?

She continues with her packing, folding all but the necessities in the suitcase she brought from Puerto Rico. There's the photo album with the pictures of Rosalinda. The first picture in it is of América, pregnant, standing on the porch of Ester's house. She looks so young! Her belly looks false, as if she had stuck a pillow under her dress to pretend pregnancy. She tries to remember what it felt like to be fourteen and pregnant, but the only image that surfaces is of a guanábana. She craved guanábanas, and Correa had to go to Puerto Rico to find her some, because there were none to be had in Vieques.

A few pages later there's a photo of América, Correa, and an infant Rosalinda at her baptism. América is sitting on Correa's lap, Rosalinda on hers. He has his right arm around her waist, his left hand, almost as big as the baby, on her knee. She still looks like a little girl, and it occurs to her that Correa was a pervert. No, she shakes her head. He's stayed with me even after I've become a woman. But she wonders if there have been other little girls she doesn't know about, and the thought chills her. Could he have touched Rosalinda? No, it doesn't seem possible. She thinks she would have noticed. No. Correa is cruel and violent. But he's not a pervert. She can't bear the thought.

She puts the photo album on the bottom of the suitcase, wrapped in a pair of jeans. When the phone rings, she's deep in her own sadness, as if running away from Correa again were a leaving of herself. When his unmistakable, seductive voice whispers her name, she shivers, rubs her arms to calm the goose bumps.

"I'm coming to see you, baby."

"Yes, I know. I'll be there."

"No, baby. I can't wait. I'm coming to New York."

She gasps. "Why?"

"Don't you want me to come?"

And she must recover, must not allow him to suspect her real plans. "No, yes, I mean, of course."

"I've come into some money," he says with a snort, "and I thought to myself, I'm taking my baby on vacation. You'd like that, baby, wouldn't you?"

"Wh . . . where? A vacation where?"

"Nayágara Fols," he says. "We'll go on an advance honey-moon." Is it triumph in his voice?

"But Correa—"

"We're going." A command, and then he remembers this is a new albeit old conquista. "I rented a car." Smooth, seductive. "It's only a couple of hours away from where you are." A promise.

"Where are you, Correa?"

"You get ready, baby, I'm coming for you."

"Where are you?"

But he's hung up.

And it's Friday. She hasn't slept all night. She called Rosalinda, but she hasn't seen Correa since last Sunday, when he left for Vieques.

"Are you all right, Mami?" she asked, and América was tempted to confide in her but didn't. "See you next week, then," Rosalinda added brightly, as if they were girlfriends planning a shopping trip.

"He sold all our stuff," Ester said when she called her. But no, she hasn't seen "that sinvergüenza. If he dares show his face around here . . ." The threat dies in a fit of coughs and sighs.

América prepares her coffee and toast. Two small leather suit-cases lean against the door to the garage. Karen is so organized, América marvels again. She leaves nothing to chance. She plans her life, every moment fitting into the next like links on a chain. Why is it that, when I try to do the same, the links are all different sizes, don't fit together, or break?

At the time Charlie usually comes down, he appears, dressed casually, shirt open at the collar under a daffodil-yellow V-neck sweater that brings out the gold in his hair. Karen follows him, in a soft yellow pantsuit, as if to dress alike underscores their attachment to each other. They look radiant, and América is so jealous it hurts to look at them.

"I'll take the bags out to the car," says Charlie, and Karen smiles at him lovingly.

"Uhm, coffee." She pours herself a cup.

"Karen, I need say you something," América begins, so softly that Karen doesn't catch the end of it before Kyle appears at the top of the stairs, rubbing his eyes and crying.

"I thought you were gone." He throws himself into his mother's arms.

"I wouldn't leave without saying good-bye, honey." She holds him, caresses his tousled hair, kisses him. As Charlie comes in from the garage, Karen looks up. "He thought we were gone," she explains, but it sounds like an apology.

Charlie takes his son from his mother's arms. "Come here, buddy."

And then Meghan comes down, wailing. "Don't go, Mommy! I don't want you to go!"

"I told you," Charlie says under his breath, "we should have left earlier."

Karen sends him a dirty look over Meghan's head, and Charlie's face hardens. They have forgotten América, who stands against the counter, reluctant to come near the children clinging to their mother and father while the two adults glare at each other.

"All right, guys." Charlie puts Kyle on the ground. "Mommy and Daddy have to go now."

Kyle leans against his mother as Meghan sobs in her arms, and Karen looks as if she's about to cry herself. América stands by, unable or, perhaps, unwilling to intercede.

"Meghan, sweetie, you go with América, okay?" Karen tries to disentangle Meghan's octopus grip in a replay of the scene in Vieques. "Mommy and Daddy will be back the day after tomorrow, okay? We talked about this, remember?"

It takes them fifteen minutes to calm the children with the promise of presents and the wonderful things that will happen when Mommy and Daddy return. As they drive off, América wishes she had added her voice to that of the children begging Karen and Charlie to stay home and not leave them alone this weekend.

No Coquís

Once their parents are gone, the children sniffle and whimper as América gets them ready for school. She makes them a warm breakfast. They eat in depressed silence, enhanced by América's gloomy presence. After she drives them to school, she performs her usual chores, her thoughts on Correa.

If he called from Vieques, the soonest he could leave the island would be seven this morning. Then he'd have to get over to the airport in San Juan. She imagines that, even if he were to arrive in New York late this afternoon, it would take him at least an hour to find his way out of the airport, and who knows how long to find Westchester County, a place he's never been. She begins to relax. Chances are he'll be driving around in circles for days before he figures out the numbered curvy routes that lead to the unlit dirt roads of Bedford. But then she remembers that Vieques, too, has a system of curvy dark routes and rutted dirt roads leading to mansions. She tenses again.

Fridays Kyle has a half day of school so that he's out at the same time as Meghan. América has barely enough time to finish the housework before she has to pick them up. They don't have play dates today, so she takes them out for pizza.

"Can we go to the playground?" Kyle wants to know.

"No, we go home."

"But it's boring there!" he complains.

"You have million toys to play."

"I don't want to go home," pipes in Meghan.

Exasperated, she takes them to a different park, so as not to run into the empleadas. The children play dispiritedly, as gloomy as she is, and after a while they ask to go home.

Once there, she locks all the doors and checks the windows to make sure they too are locked. Meghan is tired but will only take a nap if América lies down with her. Kyle goes into his room to build a Lego city, and América and Meghan curl up together in Meghan's narrow bed.

When Meghan drifts into a dream, América carefully gets up. As her chest and abdomen separate from Meghan's warmth, she feels a cold emptiness encroach, an agonizing pain like the memory of childbirth, of pushing forth a creature that no longer belongs to her, that in this case never did. She kisses Meghan's head, and the child holds her bunny closer, and América strokes her hair and kisses her again and wonders how Meghan will betray her mother, and when.

Dinner is asopao, because the children like it and it's so easy to cook that América doesn't have to concentrate much. It's six of clock, the hour she has decided is the earliest that Correa will arrive in New York if he wasn't playing with her when he said he was coming.

It's possible, she has told herself often today, that he was just testing me, to see how I would respond. It's possible that today, Viernes Social in Puerto Rico, he's out carousing with his buddies and the putas who flatter him.

They eat, and afterward she plays Barbies with Meghan while Kyle adds height to his Lego city, which now sprawls horizontally in one long line from one end of his room to the other.

Her phone rings, but by the time she gets to it, the caller has hung up, and she waits by it for a few minutes, as she did several nights ago, waiting for Correa to dial again, if it is him calling. But he doesn't.

They go downstairs to watch the same stupid situation comedies she watched last week, with the same white Yanquis embroiled in similar misunderstandings with the same results. The shades are down in every window of the house, and it feels as if they're all inside a huge warm cocoon from which she doesn't want to emerge.

Karen calls, as promised, and Meghan and Kyle talk to her and Charlie, crying, begging them to please come home soon. More gifts are pledged, more hours of fun, and then Karen asks América how things are going, and she says, "Everything okéi. You have good time."

The children don't argue when she shoos them to bed. They seem shell-shocked after the conversation with their parents. Like América they're suspended in time, which for them doesn't move fast enough. But for her every breath feels as if she were being sucked into an unseen black hole. She leaves the door to her room open, in case the children should wake up in the middle of the night. Then she goes to bed, hoping the phone will ring and it will be Correa, drunk in Puerto Rico, asking her once again if she's his baby.

But he doesn't call.

It's morning, wet and blustery. Kyle and Meghan wake up and seem surprised their parents aren't home. When reminded it's only one more day until their return, they seem confused, not sure whether to mourn their absence or celebrate their impending arrival. She feeds them, gets them ready for their karate and gymnastics lessons.

She can only wait. Correa will either show up at the Leveretts' door or will call and make a joke about Nayágara Fols. If he finds Bedford, she thinks, he will probably not do anything stupid. He's intimidated by wealth. She will calm him down if he's excited and tell him she can't leave until the Leveretts arrive. Then, when they do, she will tell them she's leaving with her husband and take him away from there as fast as she can. Whatever he does to her, she hopes, he'll do in Nayágara Fols, or wherever he takes her. Not in front of the Leveretts. Not in front of the children.

Driving the kids to their classes, she can't help looking at every driver in every car that passes. Especially the few American cars. Correa's unpredictability is one thing, but his habits are another. He loves American cars, and even in a jealous rage she believes he will show up at the Hertz counter and ask for a Buick. The drivers of the Land Rovers, Mercedes Benzes, BMW's, and Toyota Land Cruisers that pass her are not used to being scrutinized by an empleada in a Volvo. They return her stares with cautious belligerence and that look of entitlement she has come to recognize so well.

On one side of the American Gymnastics building Meghan learns to tumble, while on the other, Kyle delivers futile punches and kicks, fantasizing perhaps, about the damage he'll do when he grows a couple of feet and gains a hundred pounds.

Maybe if I knew karate, the first time Correa hit me would have been the last. She imagines herself hurtling through space, one leg aimed at Correa's crotch, her fists tight, ready to punch if she misses the kick. It's a satisfying image, pummeling Correa with her fists the way Kyle is now doing to a foam pad held by his teacher. Punching him and kicking him until his virile face is pulpy, like those boxers on television, their features swollen beyond recognition.

"América?"

She's startled out of her fantasy by Kyle, no longer punching a pad, but standing in front of her, ready to go.

"¡Ay! Let's go get Meghan," she says, scrambling up.

"You had a scary face," Kyle says as they walk to the other end of the building.

"I think something ugly," she explains, and he giggles.

"Can we go to McDonald's?" the children ask the minute they get in the car. She doesn't argue. It will give them something to do, and she won't have to make lunch when she gets back.

The restaurant is crowded with children and their parents. The servers and kitchen workers are all from Guatemala or El Salvador. The three cashiers take the orders in English, punch them into the register, and translate them into Spanish to the people preparing and wrapping the food. América orders in Spanish.

"Dos Happy Míls con chísberguers sin pickols, dos Coca-Cola y un McChicken con papitas y una Sprite."

"Those people are staring at you," Kyle announces when they sit at a booth by the window. América freezes, is afraid to look, and when she does, Adela waves at her from inside a car that has just picked up an order from the drive-through. At the wheel is a man with straight black hair cut as if he'd placed a bowl over his head, then trimmed around it. He nods in her direction. América waves at them, smiles politely, and hands the children their Happy Meals.

"Not respectful point the fingers," she says, helping Meghan open her cheeseburger.

"Not polite to stare," Kyle responds, mimicking her accent.

"You too smart for me," she says, smiling.

When they leave the restaurant, the children want to go to the movies. It's still dreary out. A fine mist that's not quite rain surrounds them as they walk to the car.

"Movies too crowd today. We get videos better."

Blockbuster Video reminds her of a supermarket. It's enormous, the last store in a strip mall that would probably go out of business if Blockbuster decided to relocate. It's bustling with children and their escorts looking for videos that will while away the rainy afternoon.

América helps Meghan and Kyle look for something they like. They find a couple of Disney movies for Meghan, but Kyle decides to get Nintendo games instead of videos. In the foreign section, América finds *Como Agua para Chocolate*, which by the looks of the box seems like a romantic story. When Correa went to the video store in Isabel Segunda, he always came back with and made her watch movies about airplanes crashing, cars blowing up, or muscular bare-chested men shooting men in suits. It's a new experience to have the choice of something she might like.

They return home, and it isn't until they pull into the driveway that América feels the familiar sense of dread at Correa's possible arrival.

Once the children are settled in front of the televisions,

Meghan in the upstairs den and Kyle in the sports den, she does her rounds of the house, making beds, picking up dirty clothes, lightly dusting dressers and shelves, alert to the sound of her phone, which doesn't ring.

Every so often Meghan or Kyle come looking for her, and she plays with one or the other, building bridges in Kyle's Lego city or taking Princess Jasmine and Aladdin on yet another flying-carpet ride. She feels split in two, the body going through the motions of playing with the children, giving them a cup of cocoa, changing the video for Meghan or watching Kyle kill green monsters on the computer screen. But her mind is elsewhere, mentally seeking Correa driving around the country roads of Westchester County or lying drunk and happy on some puta's bed in San Juan. The latter image is the one she hopes for.

She cooks dinner, serves it, eats with the children, whose eyes are glazed from too much television. She would like to interrogate them, the way Karen does, about what they did today, but she knows what they did. So she lets them chatter about she doesn't know what, and when the chatter turns into fighting, as it usually does, she puts a stop to it with the threat that she will tell Mommy and Daddy not to come back to children who can't get along.

Karen calls again, and the children relate the trip to McDonald's and the video store, leaving out the fights. When Karen asks to speak to her, América repeats yesterday's instructions. "You have good time. I take care everything," and Karen seems satisfied.

Later, she runs from Kyle's to Meghan's bathrooms as they play with toys in the tub, afraid the minute she leaves one the other will drown in the bath water. Kyle does not want to be helped into his pajamas by América, so she leaves him in his room while she dresses Meghan, who loves to be powdered, combed, dressed in any of the pretty nightgowns with Princess Jasmine or Belle or the Little Mermaid in front.

Kyle comes into Meghan's room, very proud of himself, wearing his green Power Ranger pajamas, his hair combed flat against his skull. América resists the smile creeping onto her lips.

"Can you read us a story?" Meghan asks.

"I no can read inglis, baby."

"It's too early for bed," Kyle complains.

"You come América room we make drawing," she suggests, and they troop after her. They reach her room as the phone rings. She dives for it, surprising the children.

"¿Haló?"

"Baby."

"Correa, where are you?"

"You sound upset, baby. What's the matter?"

"Where are you?"

"I'm coming to get you, baby."

"Don't do this to me. I told you I was coming back. Why are you doing this?" Kyle and Meghan stand by the bed, watching América tremble, speak her foreign language into the phone as if she's going to bite the person at the other end.

"I told you, we're going on vacation. We've never taken a vacation together." Oh, he's so smooth. Even when he's drunk, his voice is like a radio announcer's, low and modulated.

"América, can you hang up now?" Meghan asks. She looks frightened, and Kyle too stares at her as if she had suddenly turned into one of the humanoid characters from his video games.

"Correa, I have two kids here. I have to put them to bed. Don't hang up. We need to talk." She's trying to get the honey back in her voice, the syrup of seduction. But her jaw is clenched tight, her tongue feels swollen, and it's an effort to speak at all, because her whole attention is on listening to him, to the whish of cars driving by somewhere outdoors, somewhere where there are no coquís.

She props the phone on her pillow without waiting for his answer.

"You go bed now. América talk on phone," she tells the children as she nudges them out.

"But I don't want to go to bed now," argues Kyle, staring at the silent phone.

"You go your room, wait for América."

Reluctantly, the children shuffle away. She waits until they're far enough down the hall that they won't hear her, then closes her door and runs back to the phone.

"Correa?" The phone is dead. She hangs it up, her hands shaking. "Oh, my God, oh, my God." She tries to collect herself, to stop the pounding in her heart, the trembling that makes it hard to walk the short distance from her bed to her door.

Both children sit cross-legged on Kyle's bed, looking through a picture book. The minute she walks in, they look up, search her eyes, and see the fear in them.

"You go bed now, kids. Is late."

They don't argue. She carries Meghan to her room, tucks her into bed, props her bunny on her pillow. "Good night, baby." She kisses her forehead, and the little girl reaches up and hugs her and wishes her good night.

Kyle has tucked himself in. She wraps the comforter tighter, pulls his teddy bear up so that its nose is outside the covers, as Kyle likes it. "I'm not tired yet," he complains but makes no effort to move, as if he understands that it's important to her that he cooperate. She leaves both children's doors open, as she did last night, and goes into her room, to wait for the phone to ring.

Dingdong

The doorbell. Two tones, dingdong, just like in commercials. In the three months she's been there, no one has rung the doorbell. She's been sitting motionless on the edge of her bed next to the phone for so long that she has to think about moving before she can. And then she runs, down the hall, down the back stairs, to peek out the shaded windows of the den at the front door and see who rings the doorbell at ten on a Saturday night. Knowing who it is but wishing it's someone with car trouble needing to use the phone, or a neighbor seeking a lost cat.

Dingdong. It's a leisurely sound, a friendly reminder that company has arrived.

Correa is on the gracious semicircular steps framed by columns. He stands as if he's visited here many times, neither skulking in the shadows suspiciously nor looking around to acquaint himself with the place.

The door does not have a chain stop. If she opens it, there's nothing between them. She stands with her back against it, trembling, not knowing what to do. Dingdong. Maybe, if she doesn't answer, he'll think there's no one home and go away. Dingdong dingdong.

"Mommy!" Meghan is at the top of the front stairs.

América runs up on tiptoe. He mustn't hear. He must think

there's no one home. "Shh, baby, shh. No make noise. América coming."

Dingdong dingdong dingdong.

"Who's ringing the doorbell?" Kyle stands in the hall, rubbing sleep from his eyes.

"Is nobody, go back your room." She scoops up Meghan, carries her to her bed. Kyle follows her.

"Somebody is at the door," he says louder, as if she didn't hear him the first time. He's about to turn on the light.

"No! Kyle. No lights." Kyle stops. Meghan, who has been half asleep, whimpers. "No make noise," América says, drawing Kyle close. They all sit on Meghan's bed, both children now aware that something is wrong.

Dingdong dingdong dingdong. Thump.

"Is it a burglar?" Kyle asks.

What do I do now, she's asking herself. He's trying to break down the door, what do I do? Charlie's knives. I must get one of the knives, so I can defend myself.

"Is it a burglar?" Kyle repeats.

"Berglar? I don't know berglar." She stands, wraps both children with Meghan's comforter. "You stay," she warns. "No come out. Comprend? No come out." She closes Meghan's hall door, drags a chest in front of it.

"I'm scared," cries Meghan.

"You take care little sister," she charges Kyle, who looks just as frightened but hasn't expressed it. "No come out." She tiptoes to the back of Meghan's room, toward her playroom.

"Shouldn't we call the police?" Kyle asks.

"Police?" She stops with her hand on the doorknob as if this were a new concept. "Police," she says, "Yes, police. I call."

There's a crash, the sound of breaking glass. "You no come out," she orders in a cracked voice, as filled with fear as the children. She tiptoes through Meghan's playroom, steps quietly across the hall into Kyle's playroom, through his bathroom into the bedroom. The door is open, and she peeks into the dim hall. She can run across it into the Leveretts' bedroom and call, or she can run down the hall into her own room. But then she'd have to go past the back stairs, and she hears shuffling down there. And she'd be too far from the children in her room. She presses against the wall, whimpering. Her hands are formed into tight fists, the fingernails digging ridges into her palms.

I should have opened the door for him. I should have let him in, made some excuse for not going tonight. Oh God, help me.

All is quiet downstairs. It might have been her imagination before. Maybe, she hopes, he broke a window and is content with that. Maybe he knows he's in trouble if he damages other people's property. Maybe he thinks he came to the wrong house and is now driving away, lost. Maybe. Maybe. Maybe. She steps into the hall, runs into the Leveretts' bedroom.

When she picks up the phone, a bright green light goes on, enough for her to see the dial pad. Nine-one-one. Karen has a label stuck on every phone. Emergency 911. She must translate it into Spanish. Nueve once. A woman answers the phone, and América whispers.

"Emergencia, por favor, ayudénme, por favor, emergencia." Crying quietly now, whispering over and over, "Emergencia, por favor, policia, emergencia."

The woman on the other end responds in English. When América switches to English, "Plis," a hand covers her mouth and yanks her away from the phone, and she smells his scent, Brut, and liquor, and his sweat, and he's pulling her away, away from the chattering phone, which is now speaking Spanish.

"You think you're so smart," he whispers. "You think you're really something." He hangs up the phone.

"Ooph!" she says when he slams her against the wall. "Ooph!" when she falls, out of breath with a blow to her belly. "Ooph," when he kicks her.

"You cunt! You bitch."

She crawls away from him, half drags herself toward the open bedroom door. He kicks her ass, sends her sprawling at Kyle's feet. Kyle is there, in front of her, silhouetted on a rectangle of light. And Meghan is behind him. Kyle steps back, and

América can see the expression on his face, the terror, pure and innocent.

"Run, Kyle, run, Meghan, run!" she yells. Meghan screeches, and both children run screaming down the hall.

She turns over on her back as Correa lurches toward her. He must have seen the children, but he's not interested in them. He grabs her hair, pulls her up to her full height, and then she sees a flash, the gleaming flash of a blade arcing toward her. Her first thought is that he got to Charlie's knives before she did. But no. It's a kitchen knife, the one she uses to cut plantains into tostones.

She ducks as the blade comes down, and it burns into her left shoulder. There's warmth where the blade plunged, no pain, just a burning when he pulls it out and raises it again. He's going to kill me. He wants to kill me. She forgets she's shorter than he is, lighter by fifty pounds at least, weaker. All she knows now is that Correa, the man who claims to love her, is trying to kill her. And somewhere in the house, Meghan and Kyle are screeching. She pushes against Correa with all her strength, is as surprised as he is when he stumbles back and drops the knife. In that split second, she's able to run out of the room, yelling at the top of her lungs.

"Run outside, run, Kyle, Meghan, run outside! Run! Run!"

She hears the children scrambling down the back stairs, so she heads down the front, because Correa is chasing her and she doesn't want him to come near the kids. Not with a knife in his hand. Not with the intention of killing. I won't let him. He won't kill me. He won't.

She's at the front door, but her hands are wet, wet with something slippery, wet with blood, her blood, and she doesn't know where it's coming from. There's blood on the white wall and on the carpet, on the shiny wood floor where the runners stop.

Correa is behind her. There are cars outside. Meghan and Kyle are screaming outside, safe. He plunges the knife into her back, and she falls against the door. The knife flashes silver and red, and in the split second it takes him to lift it, she dodges under his arm, but with the other hand he grabs her hair and pushes her hard against the wall of the den. He comes around to face her, and she can't recognize him. No, this can't be him, this can't be, his green eyes so dark, so savage. There's no love there. It's hate that she sees, hate that she feels as she uses her last bit of strength to kick him hard in the one place she knows she can hurt him, between his hairy legs. He doubles over with a groan, and she kicks him again, connects against his lowered face this time, and he turns and falls. There's a crack, like a twig breaking, as Correa's head bounces against the angled edge of the granite coffee table. She watches him fall, then lie there, still. Oh, he's so still. Her back against the wall, she slides down down down down, and there are voices, Meghan and Kyle crying and a man shouting "Police!" and Correa is so still, so quiet. Her chest burns and she can't breathe. Correa is so still, and the house is full of people, men in heavy shoes and I can't breathe I can't breathe I can't breathe.

What Happened?

When she comes to, she smells roses. Elena is sitting nearby, reading.

"Mami!" Rosalinda's voice comes from her left side. When América turns toward it, Rosalinda throws herself at her mother, sobbing into her bosom.

"It's all right," América murmurs, not sure if it really is. "It's all right."

Elena stands by her now, caresses her cheek. "I'll go get the others," and then she's gone. Rosalinda still sobs, and América doesn't know how to make her stop. So she cries too.

The others come. Leopoldo, Paulina, Carmen. Ester. What's Ester doing here? A woman in a pink jacket tells them they can't all be in the room at the same time, but no one moves. América can't stop crying, neither can Rosalinda. Paulina is crying too. But Ester is smiling.

"What happened?" she asks, but even though their mouths move, none of what they say makes sense. She closes her eyes, and when she opens them again, she's alone. I dreamed it, she thinks, and closes her eyes, and then Lourdes is sitting in the chair where Elena was, and Rosalinda is standing by a window. Was there a window there before? It's daylight and then it's night and everyone is gone again. No there's no window. My arm hurts. I have a tube up my nose. And then it's daylight and Rosalinda is sitting in the chair and Ester is sitting next to her.

"What happened?"

Ester and Rosalinda look at each other.

"How do you feel?" Ester asks.

"I'm alive," she says, and Rosalinda and Ester exchange a look again. "Are the kids okéi?"

"They're fine. The lady was here. She left these." Ester points to a flower arrangement.

"Where are we?"

"I'm not sure," Ester says. "They drive me here and back, so I don't know."

"Are you okay, Mami? Do you feel okay?" Rosalinda caresses América's hand, the one with no I.V. needles.

"What happened?" América asks again.

"Don't you remember?" Rosalinda seems incredulous. "She doesn't remember," she tells Ester, who's across the bed.

"Don't worry about it now. You just get better."

"I want to know." América looks from her mother to her daughter. They're hiding something from her. "Tell me."

"Correa," Ester says, "won't be bothering you anymore."

No, of course not, she thinks. He's in Puerto Rico. And we are . . . where are we? In New York. Rosalinda sobs again and once more seeks her mother's bosom. Ester looks older than the last time América saw her. When was that? It's too hard to focus. She closes her eyes again and sleeps.

América's Dream

⌇⌇⌇⌇⌇⌇⌇⌇⌇⌇⌇⌇⌇⌇⌇⌇⌇⌇⌇⌇⌇⌇⌇⌇⌇⌇⌇⌇⌇⌇

S he gets up early, sets the coffee to brew and two slices of
Wonder bread to crisp before she goes in to shower. When
she comes out, the toast is just as she likes it. She smears grape
jelly on it, takes the plate with the toast and her mug of coffee
into her bedroom, sips and chews as she brushes her hair,
applies makeup, and puts on her uniform. The apron she stuffs
in her pocket.

The apartment is small, two tiny bedrooms, a kitchen/din-
ing/living room. It's in the Puerto Rican part of the Bronx, not
the quiet neighborhood with the tall green building. Paulina
advised her against living here, but América didn't follow her
advice. She reasons that the more peace and quiet a person
seeks, the less she's likely to get it. So she lives on the Grand
Concourse, above a bodega, close to the subway station that
takes her into Manhattan five days a week.

She likes working in a big hotel. The guests never stay more
than a day or two. She hardly ever sees them. Mostly businessmen, they arrive at the hotel late and leave early. The hardest
part of the job is having to wait for the supervisor to reconcile
the minibar before she cleans the room. It's a stupid rule. She
could be in and out of rooms faster if she didn't have to wait for
him.

It's also hard to be cooped up inside all day. The hotel has big windows that don't open, so she gets to see the sun but not feel it. The interior halls of the hotel are elegantly dim, the carpets thick and luxurious. It's so quiet a guest can sneak up on you before you know they're there. But they don't. Guests don't sneak up on maids. They mostly ignore her. They don't even see her half the time. She finds the indentations of their bodies on the bed, discarded scraps of paper with mysterious notes written on them, crumpled name tags. Sometimes they leave a dollar in the envelope with her name on it. But not as often as she'd like.

Even so, she makes more money and works less hours than when she was an empleada. She gets overtime, too, and health insurance.

She could have used health insurance to pay for the two weeks she spent at the hospital where Karen Leverett works. It would also have helped pay for the physical therapy necessary to get her punctured lung working again and to gain movement in her left arm where a couple of muscles were severed with the kitchen knife.

While she was at the hospital, the other empleadas came to see her, Frida toting a newspaper with the headline HOUSEKEEPER KILLS INTRUDER.

"Is he dead, then?" América asked, and Frida looked at Mercedes and they both looked at Ester, who was sitting by the window. "Is he dead?" They all looked so scared.

Ester stepped to the bedside, held her hand. "It was self-defense," she said. "He would have killed you."

América closed her eyes and tried to conjure up an image of Correa, but it wouldn't come. The empleadas said something about the painkillers affecting her and left. Not so the police-woman who showed up to interrogate her. If América closed her eyes and pretended to sleep so she wouldn't have to answer the policewoman's questions, she just waited. She sat there, it seemed to América, a whole day, asking how long she'd known Correa, how often he hit her, whether he'd visited her at the Leveretts' house.

Karen Leverett came down to see her a couple of times, but

then there was another newspaper headline, INTRUDER WAS MAID'S
LOVER. América wondered why she was a housekeeper the first
time and a maid the second.

The day América was to leave the hospital, Karen came to
see her again.

"How kids?" was the first thing América asked.

"They're fine." Karen fidgeted with an envelope, didn't meet
América's eyes. "They send their love."

América's eyes teared. "I so sorry, Karen."

"You should have told me. We would have helped you." She
seemed on the verge of tears herself.

"It was mistake to run away." Karen looked at her uncomprehendingly. "From Puerto Rico." América amended. "Not possible
run away from problems."

Karen seemed about to say something but changed her
mind. She handed América an envelope. "Your salary."

It was a white envelope. In the center of it, Karen had
printed "America Gonzalez."

"Under the circumstances, you understand," Karen continued, "I've hired someone else."

América nodded, stared at those neat block letters, at her
name spelled without an accent. "Okéi," she said. "I understand."

Karen hugged her and said good-bye. América didn't take
her eyes off her name in the center of the white envelope until
it was too blurry to make out, until tears splotched onto the letters, one two three.

América wishes that "the circumstances" hadn't been discussed in the newspapers and talk radio. She received letters at
the hospital from women who said they'd been battered themselves and she had given them courage to act. Are they all going
to kill their men, she wondered. There was a stream of people
who wanted to talk to her, lawyers, a psychologist, a counselor
from a battered women's shelter, a woman who wanted to write
her life story. People, she was sure, she had passed on the street
and had never so much as looked in her direction. They all
wanted something from her, and it was a relief when, on the day

Paulina came to pick her up, she didn't have to talk to or see any of them anymore.

Every once in a while she still gets a call from people who haven't forgotten. Last week it was a producer from the Geraldo Rivera show.

"You should do it, Mami," Rosalinda insisted. "They say your story might help some women in the same situation."

"How would it help? I didn't do anything. I kicked him too hard and he fell and broke his neck. How's that going to help anyone?"

"You fought him, Mami. You won."

"I wouldn't consider making my daughter an orphan a victory," she told Rosalinda, and that shut her up. Whenever that night comes up, Rosalinda tries to make América feel good about what happened, as if to make up for her betrayal. She rarely mentions her father, doesn't like to talk about their life in Puerto Rico, has forgotten all about being a vedette when she grows up.

It amazes her that Rosalinda seems so well adjusted. She's in school, is learning English faster than América would have predicted, and seems to like living in the Bronx, although América frowns at some of the friends she's made. Girls with lots of makeup and bored expressions, boys with pants that are too big, so low on their hips that América can see the crack of their culos through their shorts.

Ester says América should let Rosalinda make her own decisions about who her friends are. But América doesn't listen to Ester's advice. Since she appeared on Cristina Saralegüi's show to talk about how domestic violence affects the lives of all members of the family, Ester has become an expert on human behavior and a celebrity in Vieques. She's more opinionated than ever.

When América wipes down the mirrors in the hotel, she can't avoid looking at her face. There's a scar running across her nose. It wasn't there before Correa attacked her with Karen Leverett's kitchen knife, and América doesn't remember being cut. Darío says it's invisible, that no one else can see it but her. He once ran his finger across it, tracing a line from under her right eye to just beyond her left. That was the first time she allowed him to kiss her on the lips.

To her, the scar is not invisible. It irritates her when people pretend it's not there. It's a reminder of who she is now, and who she was then. Correa's woman was unscarred, but América Gonzalez wears the scars he left behind the way a navy lieutenant wears his stripes. They're there to remind her that she fought for her life, and that, no matter how others may interpret it, she has a right to live that life as she chooses. It is, after all, her life, and she's the one in the middle of it.